ST. MARTIN'S

MINOTAUR

MYSTERIES

PRAISE FOR S. J. ROZAN AND *CONCOURSE*

"A fine successor to S. J. Rozan's wonderful debut novel, *China Trade*. Bill Smith and Lydia Chin have a chemistry between them that is as exciting and as electric as any I've ever read. Combine that with S. J. Rozan's sharply drawn portrait of the dark underbelly of New York and you've got a book you won't put down. What a voice!"
> —Steven Womack, Edgar Award-winning author of *Way Past Dead*

"Rozan writes knowingly of the place where politics, big money and medical care for the elderly intersect odoriferously."
> —*New York Newsday*

"Richly and rewardingly plotted."
> —*Kirkus Reviews*

"Rozan nails down the promise of *China Trade,* her debut and the introduction of memorable New York City PIs Bill Smith and Lydia Chin."
> —*Publishers Weekly*

"S. J. Rozan's plotting is first-rate."
> —Les Roberts, author of *Lemon Chicken Jones*

"A top-flight series . . . A distinctive voice [and] talent."
> —*Booklist*

"Rozan manages to create original characters while recreating on paper an exotic city within an exotic city."
> —*Purloined Letter*

ST. MARTIN'S PAPERBACKS TITLES
BY S. J. ROZAN

China Trade
Concourse
Mandarin Plaid
No Colder Place
A Bitter Feast
Stone Quarry
Reflecting the Sky

CONCOURSE

S. J. ROZAN

St. Martin's Paperbacks

Excerpt from "Epigrams and Epitaphs" in *Poems* by C. S. Lewis copyright © 1964 by the Executors of the Estate of C. S. Lewis Ptc. Ltd., reprinted by permission of Harcourt Brace & Company.

CONCOURSE

Copyright © 1995 by S. J. Rozan.

Excerpt from *Mandarin Plaid* copyright © 1996 by S. J. Rozan.

Cover photograph courtesy of the Bettman Archive.

Library of Congress Catalog Card Number: 95-34741

ISBN: 0-312-95944-3

Printed in the United States of America

St. Martin's Press hardcover edition/October 1995
St. Martin's Paperbacks edition/September 1996

10 9 8 7 6 5

For Deborah Norden
(1954–1994)

Here lies one kind of speech
That in the unerring hour when each
Idle syllable must be
Weighed upon the balance, she,
Though puzzled and ashamed, I think,
To watch the scales of thousands sink,
Will see with her old woodland air
(That startled, yet unflinching stare,
Half elf, half squirrel, all surprise)
Hers quiver and demurely rise.

—C. S. Lewis,
  Epigrams and Epitaphs No. 13

AUTHOR'S NOTE

To protect people who probably don't deserve it I have played fast and loose with the geography of the Bronx. I know the area north of the courthouse is not in the 41st Precinct. There is no Chester Avenue. The timeless Ehring's has been closed, sold, renamed, and reopened—substantially the same—since this book was written. As for the rest, if you can find the flaws, you're a Bronx scholar. Don't call me, call Dr. Tieck.

ACKNOWLEDGMENTS

Thank you to:

My agent, Steve Axelrod
My editor, Keith Kahla
perfect gentlemen

Michelle Slung and Kate Stine
and they know why

David Dubal, for music
Terry Blackwell, for scams
Steve Landau, for expeditions
The group, for Tuesdays
Deb Peters, for years

Steve, Hillary, Julia, and Max (it's alphabetical, guys)
toujours en famille

and
Nancy and Helen
the without whomest

ONE

At Mike Downey's wake the coffin was closed.

In the large front room at Boyle's Funeral Home dark-dressed women kissed each other's cheeks, murmured gentle words. The older men stood together in small groups, looked uncomfortable in out-of-date suits; the younger ones, Mike's friends, passed a surreptitious flask, and told each other stories about Mike they'd all heard a hundred times, and laughed too loudly at the stories.

Bobby Moran nodded to me across the flower-choked room. He spoke parting words to the men around him and headed over. His limp was worse than I'd seen it, giving him a halting, rolling gait.

"Kid," he said. "Thanks for coming." His face, usually ruddy, was gray, the slackness on the left side pronounced. His blue eyes were pale, washed-out. Twenty-five years ago, when I'd met him, Bobby Moran's eyes had been sharp and clear as a January morning.

"I'd have come anyway," I told him. "Even if you hadn't called."

"I was afraid you'd be out of town. Upstate."

Bobby knew me well enough to know that about me: that I try, if I can, to spend some time at my cabin this time of year. I was born in the South, raised on Army bases in Europe and Asia, and though I've lived in New York since I was fifteen, the extravagance of an eastern hillside in autumn still amazes me.

"I was going," I told Bobby. "I put it off."

"Thanks." He looked away. "Seen Sheila yet?"

"Just now." Mike's widow, to whom I'd said clumsy words, sat by the coffin. She was quiet, but she seemed to be trembling inside, like a teardrop.

Bobby and I stood in silence for a moment, surrounded by voices and soft light. The air was sweet with white roses, camellias, lilies. Bobby said, "I need you, kid."

"I owe you, Bobby. You know that."

He scowled. "No, to hell with that. I'll hire you. I'll pay you. Pay you better than the dumb fucks who work for me now. Pay you better than I used to."

I shook my head no. He nodded his yes.

"It's just—I'd do it myself," he said, his voice tight with targetless anger, "but I can't. I've got no one else to ask, kid. I've got no investigators anymore. I gave that up, because of this. . . ." He trailed off, gestured at his left side, where the arm hung slack and the leg limped. "This" was Bobby's stroke. "But the guard business, I thought I could keep that up. Take dumb fucks, train 'em and pay 'em, how hard could that be? How goddamn hard?" He didn't meet my eyes.

"Come with me," I said.

We worked our way through the crowded room, Bobby's eyes fixed savagely ahead, acknowledging no one's words of comfort or greeting.

We crossed a deeply carpeted hall to a small, plain chapel where a crucifix hung. Beside it a stained-glass St. Patrick, staff raised and halo glowing, drove the snakes out of Ireland. The panel shone from behind, lit by fluorescent lights. Bobby gave me a shaky grin.

"Ah, piety," he said.

From my jacket pocket I took my own surreptitious flask, handed it to him.

"I'm not supposed to," he told me.

"Who is?"

He eased onto an upholstered folding chair. The chairs were set in rows; I swung one around to face him. He pulled on the flask, handed it back.

"It wasn't your fault," I told him, words no one who needs them ever believes.

"Yeah," he said. "My sister's son. The dumb fuck." He looked at St. Patrick, or maybe at the snakes. He said to me, "How soon can you start?"

I drank from the flask. I'd filled it with Bushmill's, Bobby's drink, thinner than my bourbon, and smoother. "Just tell me what you want me to do."

Bobby turned away from St. Patrick, to me. "Do? Do what I goddamn taught you to do, kid. Do your job." He looked around the chapel as though searching for something to help him say the words. "Find out who killed Mike."

TWO

We sat in the St. Patrick chapel for a while, as Bobby sketched for me the place I'd be going and the people I'd meet there. It was like the old days, Bobby giving me a job, sending me out; but it wasn't like that at all.

"You can trust Al Dayton," Bobby said, running down his mental list, but absently, as though his thoughts were elsewhere. "Been with me seven, eight years. Been job super out at the Bronx Home since I took it on three years ago."

"Who had it before you?" I tried to ask normal questions, things I'd need to know, as though this were just a normal case.

"Nobody, they did it themselves. Their maintenance guys doubled for security, like in a lot of places. But the neighborhood got worse. You know." He shrugged. "Arab shopkeeper on the next block was shot in the back by some local punks. That was the last straw for the organization that runs the place. Helping Hands, they're called. Their offices are in the Home building."

"They're a charity?" I passed him the flask.

"Yeah. And listen, watch out for the lady who runs it."

"The Home?"

"No, that's Dr. Reynolds. Nice guy. No, I mean Mrs. Wyckoff. Eats guys your size for breakfast. Only thing she cares about is Helping Hands' reputation. Just don't make the place look bad, you'll be okay."

I sipped whiskey. Bobby said, "Listen, kid, you want me to tell Dayton why you're there? He's a good man. Ex-Navy man, like you." He tried a smile, but it didn't get far.

"Not a recommendation," I said.

He grunted. "Could help, having someone who knows the place working with you."

"No. I'll go in alone. But I'll want someone working with me, on the outside."

"Doing what?"

"I'm not sure. Poking around."

I expected more discussion, maybe even an argument, but Bobby just shrugged and said, "Okay, kid. Play it however you want. Let me know, whatever you need."

I let my eyes wander the chapel: the soft cream walls, the altar where candles waited to be lit, St. Patrick glowering down on us the way Bobby used to glower when I screwed up, in the early years. I wanted to say something that would erase the pain and helplessness from Bobby's eyes, but I didn't know what that was, what could do that. So I drank some whiskey, and I said, "I'll need to talk to the police, whoever's handling the case. Can you set it up? Is it someone you knew?"

He shook his head. "I've been off the job a long time, kid. There's almost no one left I knew. But I set it up already. Hank Lindfors, at the four-one."

I had to smile at that. Bobby knew my moves; but then, he'd taught me most of them. "Did you speak to him?"

The old fire flashed in Bobby's eyes, just for a second. "For Chrissakes, I'm a cripple but I'm not senile! Sure I spoke to him. Asshole," he added.

"Me or Lindfors?"

He looked as if he were making up his mind; then he said, "Lindfors."

"What did he say?"

"He said, I've been off the job twenty years and I don't know what it's like out there anymore. He said, he doubted if I liked it when civilians crapped up my cases then, and he doesn't like it any better now. He said, there's an ongoing police investigation and if my private talent screws it up, he's going to throw you and me, and everyone we ever met, in the can, just to make his quota."

"Big quota."

Bobby looked away. "He told me to go back home and wait, not to call him again. He said he'd call me if anything broke.'' Anger and shame darkened his face. ''Like an old man, kid. Like what you'd say to an old man.''

''Asshole,'' I said. ''Lindfors,'' I added.

Bobby shook his head. The color receded, left him gray and tired, like before.

''Will Lindfors see me?'' I asked.

Bobby took the flask from me, drank. ''Yes.''

''Why?''

''Christ, kid, I don't know. Maybe because he doesn't know you.''

''Oh, thanks.''

He looked at me swiftly, then gave a short laugh. ''Well, he's all yours.''

I started to take out a cigarette, but St. Patrick glared. I shoved it back in the pack. ''Does Lindfors have any leads?''

Bobby waited before he answered. ''It's his opinion—'' he emphasized each syllable in 'opinion'—''that Mike surprised a gang of kids who came over the wall. He faced them down and he lost.''

''But you don't buy it.''

He didn't answer. I asked another question: ''And why shouldn't I go in straight? Why undercover?''

Looking at the stained-glass saint, he said, ''Kid, I'll tell you something. I was twenty years on the job, private another twenty. Something about this stinks.''

''Meaning what?''

''I don't know.'' Still not looking at me, he said, ''Someone took an awful lot of trouble with Mike. You didn't see him, how it was. I don't know,'' he repeated, talking now as though to himself. ''Seems to me you come to steal, someone interrupts you, you shoot him or cut him or hit him with something. Beating the shit out of a guy so he don't even look human when you're done—you only do that for a reason, kid. Only for a reason.''

Bobby fell silent, watched the flask he was holding. I waited.

''And there's another thing,'' he finally said. ''Mike.''

''What about him?''

''Something. Something about him.'' He met my eyes, but he didn't hold them. ''I moved him to that shift six weeks ago. Before that we weren't running the third man up there.''

"Why'd you start?''

"A trucker got beat up making a delivery to that place one night. They got spooked up there, so we added a man to the night shift, no fixed post, a troubleshooter. I moved Mike there, with Howe and Morales.'' He paused. "Mike liked that shift. He could be home with Peg, when Sheila was at work. . . .'' He pressed his eyes shut. I looked away, gave him time.

Bobby went on: "But Mike—something happened with Mike. I don't know . . . had you seen him much lately?''

"No. I think the last time was when he helped me with some repairs in Shorty's basement, a few months ago.''

"Yeah, I remember he told me. Said you blew up at him a couple times.''

"I guess I did. He was good, but he never shut up. He wanted to know everything about everything, why we were doing it this way, why you didn't do it the other way. He wanted to know why gypboard screws are black when all the other screws in the world are chrome. He drove me nuts.'' I added, "I should have been more patient.''

Bobby smiled again, a soft smile that this time was echoed in his eyes. "I knew another kid like that once,'' he said. "Had to know everything, couldn't let anything go. Good kid, but Jesus, he was annoying. Finally he started to keep his mouth shut and just watch and listen. Then he started to learn.''

My half-embarrassed smile answered Bobby's. "Mike would have figured that out, too, Bobby. Sooner than I did.''

"Yeah,'' Bobby said. "He would have. He could learn fast, always, from when he was a kid. But the last couple weeks, there was something he stopped being able to do.''

"What, Bobby?''

"He stopped being able to look me in the eye.''

From home, after I'd poured a drink but before I'd started to drink it, I sat down by the phone and called a number I could dial in my sleep. Sometimes, in my dreams, I did.

"Chin Investigative Services. Lydia Chin speaking,'' a woman's voice answered, a little out of breath. Before I could say anything she said it again, in Chinese.

"Hi," I said. "What are you doing that you're breathing so hard?"

"Bill!" she said. "Hi! I was just coming in the building as the phone was ringing. I ran up the stairs." I could hear her gulping water between sentences. "I have a race on Saturday. I was down at Battery Park working out."

"On roller blades? Does that mean you're in the black spandex thing with the green stripes down the sides?"

"Uh-huh. And I'm soaking wet and I smell like sweat socks."

"Eau de Locker Room. I love it. I'll give you a quart for Christmas. Listen, do you have anything on?"

"The spandex."

"On your *calendar*. This is a legitimate call."

"Oh, whoops, didn't recognize it." She gulped some more water. "Actually, I haven't worked in a week. Why? You have something for me?"

"Yeah, I do." I told her then about Mike Downey, and Bobby.

She was silent for a few moments, after I'd finished. "Oh, Bill, I'm sorry," she said gently. "Is Mr. Moran all right?"

"It's eating him up," I said. "He blames himself. He wants to charge in and do something, but he doesn't know what and he doesn't think he can. So he called me."

"What are you going to do?"

"Investigate. That's what I do. And I want you with me."

"With you how?"

"I want you to check that place out. The Home. Helping Hands, the people who run it. I'm not sure what else, but it's a beginning. I'm starting there in the morning, as a guard. I'm going to poke around, and when I get a better idea what I want, I'll tell you. Can you do it?"

"Yes, sure."

"Great. Thanks. I'll call you tomorrow."

"Just to check around, that's what you want? Nothing more specific than that?"

"Well, one thing."

"What?"

"Would you rub the phone all over the spandex before you hang up?"

She said, "I don't think so," and hung up.

THREE

It was still beautiful here. The sky was a perfect morning blue, the air chill and clear. In the park by the Bronx County Courthouse the trees were turning, to brown-red, scarlet, rust. Some were as thickly yellow as the sunlight that lay like a benediction on them and on the graffiti-trapped, decaying buildings along the Grand Concourse.

I drove the unmarked Moran Security car farther north than I needed to, drawn by the ghosts behind the boarded-up windows and the roll-down store shutters that hadn't been rolled up in years. On the façades I made out names, "Kat" and "Lifer" and "PTA", in the garish colors and fluid strokes of spray paint. Where the buildings were brick, the painted names had a textured look, something almost innocent, like an old woman's needlework. On the side of one building, in a place where the painter must have hung from a rope to reach, "Snake" was written in huge silver letters outlined in gold. The paint glittered in the sun as I drove by.

I cruised past travel agents and layaway furniture stores, fast food takeouts and storefront clinics. The Concourse flowed through the Bronx like a river between high banks of stone and brick. Well-made and once-proud, the apartment buildings on either side stood together like elderly cousins lined up for the last family photograph. At Fordham Road I swung south again, toward the Bronx Home, to take the dead man's place.

I parked on the street, lit a cigarette. In the tape deck I had Richard Goode playing a Schubert sonata, the B-flat Major. I was learning it, had worked on it last night after I'd burst from a four A.M. dream, heart pounding, face drenched in sweat. I know those dreams. I can't sleep after them, but usually I can play. Last night, though, I couldn't do anything right.

* * *

The dream had been about Annie. She was nine, wearing the clothes I'd last seen her in, seven years ago: a chestnut jumper, a scarlet blouse. In the dreams I see every detail of her clothes, though if you'd asked me as I drove away from my ex-wife's house that day how my daughter had been dressed, I don't think I'd have been sure. When Annie was with me, I mostly only saw her smile.

In the dream she was searching for me through a shadowy house being built or demolished—I couldn't tell which—and though I tried to call to her, I had no voice and she didn't hear. I was desperate to see her, talk to her, even though I knew, the way you know in those dreams, that it would be the last time, that after this she would be gone forever. But she didn't hear me, never found me. I watched her leave the house, knew she was skipping down a flight of steps I couldn't see, and the panic that rocks those dreams woke me before the squeal of brakes, the screech of metal on metal, the irrevocable crash of broken glass could reach me from the accident I had not been there for, had not even known about until it was far too late.

Now, in the Bronx, in the bright early sunlight, fear, fury, acceptance, and desperation alternated in the music, washed over me like water. I closed my eyes, felt the notes in my fingers. For a moment I let myself wish I were home, at the piano, with a strong cup of coffee and the phone turned off. Then I left the car, threw away the cigarette, creaked open the gate in the wisteria-draped wall.

I stood for a moment, taking in a sight I wasn't prepared for, although I'd been told. Across the sunken garden, resplendent in the morning sun, The Bronx Home for the Aged spread its three-story limestone wings to meet the garden walls. The sun sparkled in the tall windows of the central pavilion, gleamed off the tiled roof. A broad stone porch curved over the garden. The garden itself, seven steps below street level, took up fully half the block. From the street the crowns of the tall trees, sweetgum and oak, had been visible, moving in the gusting wind. Now I saw the others: evergreens, dogwoods, cherries. There were splashes of gold and white chysanthemums in round beds, and a few pink roses still clung to bushes bordering the walk.

That's where Mike Downey had been found, beaten to death beside that walk, his blood splattering the pink roses.

As I walked down into the garden Mike's cocky laugh echoed in my head. The earth smelled damp and rich, but the garden, close up, had the melancholy look of gardens in autumn. Even the chrysanthemums were past their prime; the wind was tugging at the roses. Fallen leaves whispered underfoot. The lawn and path were dotted with sweetgum burrs, round and brittle. I started up the porch steps, thinking I was alone.

A loud whisper startled me: "Wait, you'll scare them!" I stopped still, looked around. In a corner of the porch a tiny woman knelt, her hand out to me like a traffic cop's. In front of her, a black cat crouched on the stone railing. A black-and-white splotched kitten and a tiger one prowled the floor near a plastic bowl full of glop.

With difficulty and determination, the woman rose and backed stiffly away, watching the cats. I waited; finally she waved me on. As I joined her she dropped an empty can into a paper bag, folded the top twice. Her hands were small and spotted; her hair was a short halo of white silk threads.

"You're the new man." Her voice held an edge, as if she wasn't sure that the new man was a good thing for me to be. She read the nameplate on my jacket. " 'W. Smith'." Her chin thrust upward. "What's the W for?"

"William," I told her. "Bill." I held out my hand.

We shook. "Ida Goldstein," she said. I'd once had a sparrow perch on my finger. Her touch reminded me of that. "We're not supposed to feed them," she said.

"Why not?"

We watched as the cat and kittens tore hungrily through the glop.

"Because they're dirty. Because they're wild and have diseases. Of course they do! Nobody takes care of them. Do you like cats?"

"Yes."

"That's good. Did you know the other boy? The one who's dead?"

The question threw me. "Mike Downey? Yes, I did."

"He liked them. He smuggled me the cat food. It got him in trouble with the Boss Lady, because when she caught him with it, he wouldn't tell her who it was for.''

She looked back at the cat and the kittens. The tiger was perfectly still; then, suddenly, it pounced on a leaf rolling across the stone.

''They're right,'' Ida Goldstein said, as suddenly. ''I shouldn't feed them. What's the point? Something bigger will only kill them. Or they'll grow into big, savage things themselves and kill something else.'' She gave me a narrowed stare. ''I don't think I want to get to know you.''

She turned abruptly, took stiff steps toward the iron-and-glass front door. She poked her finger onto a button on the jamb. The door swung open. Ida Goldstein, leaning on the button, looked back at me. ''You be careful,'' she said, and hobbled in.

FOUR

I stood on the porch at the Bronx Home in the sharp early sunlight. I watched Ida Goldstein disappear; then I went in also.

The iron-and-glass door gave into a wide short hallway with a framed landscape on either wall. At the hallway's other end was an intersecting corridor. From somewhere came the clink of dishes, and a breakfast smell of coffee and toast.

In the intersection, a man in a uniform like mine sat at a desk. His nameplate read ''A. Dayton, Supervisor.'' Another man in uniform lounged in another chair, filling out forms on a clipboard.

I gave A. Dayton my name, offered my hand. He shook it solemnly. He was a dark-skinned black man, younger than Bobby, older than I. His close-cut hair was graying, his mustache gray already.

''Mr. Moran called me about you.'' Dayton had a deep voice and a slow way of speaking, the air of a man using exactly the words he wanted to use. He nodded toward the other man. ''This is Henry Howe. He's supervisor on the graveyard shift.'' I shook hands with Howe, a redheaded, potbellied fellow whose eyes were sharp and alert behind deceptively heavy lids.

"Mr. Moran says you're experienced," Dayton said. The eyes with which he looked me over were deep and unreadable.

"I've been on my own for a while," I said. "But I started in Bobby Moran's shop, close to twenty years ago."

"Well, I'm glad to have you. Did Mr. Moran explain how things work here?"

"Three shifts," I answered. "Three men on each shift. One man at each door, one on the grounds. That's me, right?"

"Correct. You don't patrol the building, just to go through from the front to the back. Inside isn't where the trouble is. And normally we don't have the third man but at night. Now . . ." Dayton shrugged.

An old man, mouth half opened, emerged in a wheelchair from a door down the hall. He worked the chair across to another door not with his hands but by digging his heels into the carpet, hauling himself along. Dayton turned his eyes to the man and chair; when they'd disappeared, he turned back to me. "If you're ready to start, you can clock in. There are lockers in the basement, next to the boiler room, if you need to put anything away."

"Why ain't he on my shift?" Howe spoke suddenly, words addressed to Dayton but his eyes on me.

"You get one of the day men. Turner." Dayton gave Howe a sharp glance.

"Permanent? He replaces Downey permanent?"

"Yes." Dayton nodded, a slow, considered movement. "Mr. Moran didn't like to start a new man on the graveyard shift. Especially now."

That was only half the answer. I had wanted to start out with days. Talking to people would be the best way to learn things, if there was anything to learn. Later, if there was any point to it, I could work Mike's shift.

"Downey wasn't new. Fat lot of good it done him," Howe snorted. He looked at his watch, swung his bulk up out of the chair. "I'm done. See you tomorrow, Alvin. Smith, you enjoy yourself. It's a beautiful day." He clattered the clipboard onto the desk, punched the time clock, wandered out whistling "Zipadee-doo-da."

Dayton looked after him silently. Then he turned his eyes to me again.

"Mr. Moran sets great store by you."

"He told you that?"

"He told me he was sending me the best."

All morning the sun was strong and the wind blew wildly. Heavy clouds flew across the bright sky, pulling brief, dark shadows behind them. The dappling light splashed through leaves in constant motion, giving the garden an unreal, underwater quality.

I covered the garden, checked the wall, the single gate, getting to know the place. I had a smoke outside the gate, looking over the Concourse, letting the street see me. It had been a long time since I'd worked a straight security gig, but some things I remembered.

I went back in through the building, exchanged nods with Dayton, went down the stairs. The block sloped so sharply west from the Concourse that the back entrance was a floor below the front one. On my first pass through I introduced myself to the back-door guard.

"Hey, man," he said, shaking my hand. "So you the shotgun, gonna save us from all the wild Indians?"

"Is that the problem?" I asked. "Indians?"

He shook his head and grinned. His name was Fuentes; he was a small, quick man with a thin black mustache and a thick Puerto Rican accent. "No, man. The problem here is slime. You know what I mean? They hatch under rocks thinkin' the world owes them a livin', you know? Then they crawl out to collect."

The parking lot, the side doors, back through the building to the garden. The garden, the ground-level windows on that side, back through the building to the lot. The morning went like that. I did my job, patrolled, looked big and reassuring. I smiled at residents if their stares weren't vacant, if they looked up from their private dreams or away from the television in the dayroom, but I didn't stop to talk with anyone.

Dayroom; that's what they called it in prison. Maybe here it was called something else.

I did the back door on Fuentes's break, the front door on Dayton's. On my own break I went out to get the car, bring it into the lot. I took a spin around the block. The area was mostly brick apartment buildings, mostly occupied, poverty displayed in humble ways: bedsheet curtains; glaring fluorescent-lit lobbies; bent and dented frames on glass-and-aluminum doors. Some buildings were abandoned, windows vacant or thick with concrete block. I saw some construction, and that seemed hopeful, though each project wore a blue-and-orange sign marking it as sponsored by one agency or another of the City of New York.

On Chester Avenue, behind the Home, a retaining wall rose like a concrete cliff, compensating for the relentless slope of the land away from the ridge of the Concourse. Nothing of the Home was visible from down here but the tops of the birch trees in the parking lot. Surrounded by a wall, sitting on a plinth, the Bronx Home for the Aged floated in this sinking neighborhood like wood in a whirlpool.

I noticed a set of doors, big wooden ones like old-fashioned stable doors, in the center of the retaining wall. They were peeling and grimy and shut. I wondered about them, about whether in its early days the Home had kept horses and carriages back here, and what back here had been like then.

Then something else grabbed my attention.

Across the street at the end of the block a knot of people strained toward each other. Tension pulsed from them like radio signals. I could hear voices raised, though I couldn't make out words. Heavy gold jewelry flashed in the sun.

I drove nearer. Five men—some of them young, boys really—in sweats, Nike Airs, elaborate fade haircuts, made a jeering semicircle around a man in blue coveralls. The coveralled man, ignoring them, spat words at a skinny guy who towered above the rest. Six-seven, I judged, or six-eight, wearing a leather jacket patterned in red, black, and green, with black-and-white eight balls on the elbows and back.

"I ain't saying this again," the coveralled man shouted.

"You don't come near her, Snake. Ain't no more discussion, that how it be."

The tall guy smiled slowly. "Let's show the brother," he said to the group around them, "the way it be."

The fight that had been simmering boiled over. The skinny guy grabbed the coveralled man, slammed him against the wall. The man started to come back, but a fat kid tripped him. Suddenly there were four guys on top of him. Only the skinny guy stood aside, watching.

None of your business, Smith, don't be an idiot.

That thought came and went as I stomped on the gas, screeched the car onto the sidewalk, threw my door open. It caught two of them; I exploded out and caught a third myself, the fat one. I hauled him off the guy in blue and pounded my fist into his soft gut. While he was thinking about that I hooked my foot around his ankle, swept it forward, shoved his shoulders back. He hit the pavement hard.

A moment later so did I. Someone had blindsided me, knocked me on my back. He was on top of me now. My head rang, breath was hard to get; I threw a fist out wildly. It connected with something. I forced my eyes to focus, found the face of the tall, skinny guy. His dark eyes glinted with excitement, and something else.

I twisted, trying to dislodge him. His fist slammed my face. Through the exploding colors I grabbed for his throat, but his arms were so long he was a mile away up there. I heard gold chains jingle on his chest; I couldn't get near him.

His groin was closer. I jabbed at that, stiff-fingered, then clamped on his balls and yanked. He yelped, lifted half into the air. I twisted again, shoved him off, started to stand; but someone else grabbed my left arm from behind, pulled me off balance as the skinny guy rolled to his feet. Skinny kicked me in the chest.

That was enough of this shit. Before the next kick I fumbled into my jacket, swept out my .38.

"Freeze!"

His eyes met mine for the briefest second; I went cold when I saw what was in them. Then he grinned and whispered, "Oh, later for you, my man." He stepped back, yelled, "Yo! Yo, Cobras! Chill!"

Suddenly no one was holding me. I lurched forward from

the release. There was the percussion of feet on pavement, then silence.

In the silence someone was breathing heavily, besides me. I looked around. The guy in the blue coveralls groaned, stirred, pulled himself into a half-sit.

I slipped the gun back in my shoulder rig as he fixed dark eyes on me. "You crazy," he pointed out in a rasp.

I breathed a little, until breathing seemed like a natural thing anybody could do. "Uh-huh," I said. I added, "Bill Smith."

He shook his head, rose to his feet carefully, helped me to mine. He said, "Martin Carter." He eyed my uniform. "You work at the Home?"

"Yeah. Started today."

"I work there too," Carter said. "Maintenance." I saw, then, the red stitching on his coveralls that said "Bronx Home for the Aged."

"What was this about?" I asked, wiping sweat from my face.

Carter shrugged. "Business."

"Sounded to me," I pushed, "like two guys fighting over a girl."

"Well," Carter said deliberately, "then that what it sound like to you."

We looked at each other for a few moments, sizing each other up, filing things away. He was young, dark-skinned, a few inches shorter than I, handsome.

I was aging, beat-up, and unmistakably white.

"But thanks," he suddenly said. "You save my ass, no question. You okay?"

"Yeah, I think so. You?"

He rubbed his jaw and nodded. "Will be." He cocked his head at me. "But you gonna have a shiner. Coming up already."

"I can feel it. And you're not going to tell me why?"

Carter looked at me, looked away, shrugged again.

"All right. I've got to get back to work. Nice meeting you." I walked the few steps to the car, which was angled on the sidewalk, driver's door wide open. I got in, slammed the door, lit a cigarette, turned the key. To hell with him.

There was a pounding on the other door. It was Carter, grinning. I leaned over, let him in.

"Can I get a lift?" he asked, the grin growing as he settled himself on the seat.

I said nothing, backed the car off the sidewalk, headed it along the street. From here we'd have to circle the block to get back to the lot gate.

"You do this often?" Carter asked. "Bust up fights, guys you don't even know?"

"If I feel like it."

"You been a cop?"

"No, never. What made you ask that?"

"Cop might do that. Plus, it look like a cop gun, that piece you waving around."

"It was," I said. "My uncle left it to me."

"Left it?"

I said nothing.

"Oh," Carter said. "Hey, sorry, man. None of my business." He was silent for a minute. Then he said, "This wasn't nothing. Just a fool talking to a ignorant man."

"Which are you?"

He laughed ruefully. "Both, most likely."

"And that tall guy? He's both too?"

"Snake?" He just shook his head.

"He's good with his hands. Fast," I said, feeling my eye, remembering.

"Yeah, well, that the book on him. He the one made that chill with the Cobras."

"Made what chill? And who are the Cobras?"

"Man, you come round here, you don't know shit?"

"Enlighten me."

"Those guys was Cobras. They run these blocks. And they got your number now."

"I'll change my number. Made what chill?"

He made a wordless, impatient sound. "Most of the crews round here, they pack all different shit. Cobras strapped too, but don't use nothing but hands and feet unless they have to. It a thing with them, show they tough." He gave me a strange look, said, "You want to be looking out for them, now."

I shrugged. Except for Snake and the fat one, I wouldn't recognize any of them anyway.

Carter was reading my mind. "Snake, he run the crew. Skeletor coming up. And don't go thinking he soft cause he fat. Nothing soft about that mother." He looked over at me. "Each Cobra wear a tattoo. Here, dig?" I glanced over. He traced a line on the sleeve covering the inside of his right forearm. "They put a snake there. Cobra, see?"

"Even the ones as dark as you?"

"Black ink," he said shortly.

We'd reached the entrance to the Home parking lot.

"You got the key, I get the gate for you," Carter offered. I dug the Moran keys out of my pocket. When I'd driven inside he leaned in the window, gave me back the keys. "Say your name Smith?"

"Uh-huh."

He grinned. "I got cousins name Smith. You suppose we related?"

"You better hope not. All my relatives are as ugly as I am."

"No shit," Carter said. He appeared to be thinking deeply. "Well," he finally announced, "sad as that be, I'm declaring you my relation. What you need, if I got it, you got it." He stuck his hand in the window.

We shook. I said, "Thanks, cousin." He grinned again, straightened up, wandered back into the Home. I parked the car and did the same.

FIVE

You're late." Dayton scowled as I went to clock back in.

"I'm sorry. I ran into trouble."

"I don't want—" He broke off, staring. "What happened?"

I give him the Reader's Digest version.

He shook his head. "This isn't good, Smith. The Home doesn't need enemies in this community. Especially Cobras."

"Right," I said. "I should have left him there."

He didn't answer that. Instead, he asked, "Does Mr. Moran know you're armed?"

"Yes."

"It's not the usual thing here."

"It is for me."

"Smith—" He didn't finish that thought either. "Go downstairs and see the doctor."

"I'm all right."

"And you're on my crew." Dayton picked up the desk phone, punched in two digits, asked for the doctor's office. A wait; then a brief discussion about whether the doctor was in. He was and would be available shortly, it seemed. Dayton hung up. "Dr. Madsen's office is on the north end of the hall. Come back here when you're finished. I'm going to call Mr. Moran. He may want to pull you."

I hadn't thought of that, but Dayton was right. If the Cobras decided I was worth targeting, I'd be a magnet for trouble, not a shield from it.

I crossed to the stairs past three elderly ladies, one with a walker, waiting for the elevator. Two were arguing crossly; the third, in a blank, deliberate way, picked invisible lint from a shawl she carried. None of them looked at me.

Finding the doctor's office wasn't hard. The basement was all offices, storage rooms, and maintenance areas. On the east side, where the Home nestled against the garden, the rooms had light wells and windows high in the wall; on the west, Dr. Madsen's side, the windows were large and barred and looked out over the parking lot.

Madsen's nurse was a middle-aged Hispanic woman with smiling crimson lips. She told me the doctor would be right with me and in fact he was; I hadn't sat down before the door to the inner office opened and a bony man, about my age, with active eyes and thinning hair, ushered a bent old man out past the nurse's desk and to the door of the suite. "You'll be fine until tomorrow, Mr. Domenico. I'll see you then." His words came out fast. The old man didn't look convinced but the doctor shut the door behind him.

The doctor shook his head, mumbled something I didn't catch; then he spun around and looked me up and down. "Who're you?" His face was lined, his complexion sallow, like a man who worries and doesn't get out in the sun.

"Smith," I said. "Mr. Dayton sent me down. I had some trouble on the street; he wants you to look me over."

"Trouble on the street," he repeated after a short pause. His words were still fast, as though to make up for the pause. "All right. Come on." He turned on his heel and walked through the inner door. I followed him past a cramped-looking office into an examining room.

"What happened?"

I told him briefly.

"Strip to the waist. Sit there." He pointed at the exam table; I stripped and sat. The room smelled of rubbing alcohol and iodine.

Madsen had nothing to say when I unstrapped the gun, but when I took my shirt off he grinned. "Christ!"

"What?"

He gestured at my left arm with the surgical cotton in his hand. "Hippie or Navy?"

I glanced down involuntarily, saw the blue snake that wraps my arm from the elbow to the shoulder. "Navy."

"Do the Cobras know about this?"

"No."

He snickered. "They'd kill you from jealousy. They pay a lot for their tacks, but they can't match this. Where'd you get it?"

"Singapore. I was eighteen, in the Navy, on a three-day pass. We started to drink the minute we hit shore and I don't remember anything else about it." He gave me a sardonic smile. I asked, "Have you seen a lot of Cobra tattoos?"

"Some. You will too. You can't help it around here. Anybody bite you?"

"What?"

"The Cobras. In the fight. Did any of them bite you?"

"No. Do they do that?"

He shrugged. "Guys do that in fights all the time. You can get some nasty diseases that way. Hepatitis, bacterial infections. Some of those punks would do that on purpose."

He looked at my eye, at the back of my head where I'd hit the pavement, at my chest. His hands were gentle for such an abrupt man, almost as though they operated independently of him.

"Headache?" he asked, moving the cold stethoscope

around on my back. "Blurred vision? Nausea? Dizziness?"

"Yes, no, no, no."

He pulled the stethoscope down around his neck. "Get dressed. You're all right. Take a few days off, rest. I'll tell Dayton."

"I'd rather not."

"Why? You love your work so much?"

"I'm new here. If I'm out now they'll replace me."

"Could be your lucky day, being out of a job in this shit-hole. All right. Take something for the headache. Aspirin? Advil? You want something stronger?"

"No, aspirin." As I put my shirt back on I said, "This doesn't seem like such a bad place to me."

"Really? Good for you."

"What's wrong with it?" I persisted.

"Oh, it's a great place. Half these people don't know which way is up and the rest don't even know there is an up." He pulled a physician's sample card with two aspirin on it out of a drawer, tossed it to me. There were paper cups by the sink. As I swallowed the pills he said, "In a decent world they'd all have died years ago. But not in this world. You know why?"

"No. Why?"

He smiled the same sardonic smile. "They're a growth industry. Look at all the people making a living here. You, me, a hundred other people. All the people who supply the crap we buy, all the bureaucrats who process the paperwork we do, and all the inspectors who come to inspect. State, city, federal. Medicare, Medicaid, Building Department, Social Services, Health Department. Now *there* are the people who love this place. Why not? It's clean and well-run and it's indoor work." He ripped the paper off the table where I'd been sitting, smashed it into the trash can. "You think anybody gives two shits about these people? Sits with them or listens to their stories? Ha. We just can't afford to do without them. This—" he spread his arms— "this isn't for them, it's for us."

He turned, washed his hands. I finished dressing in silence.

As I was leaving he had a thought. "Who did you say the other guy was?"

''Martin Carter. He's in Maintenance.''

''Ha. That explains why he hasn't been in to see me.''

''Why?''

''You work for Al Dayton. He's a nice guy. Carter works for Pete Portelli. He's a shit. Carter's black, Pete must be already looking for a reason to fire him.'' He shook his head. ''But I guess I'd better get him in here.''

I zipped the Moran Security jacket over the .38.

''Are all you security guys armed?'' he asked me.

''I don't know.''

He fixed his intense eyes on me, then turned and opened the outer office door. ''Good-bye. Elena, call Pete Portelli. Find out where Martin Carter is. I want to see him.''

He spun around, was back in his office before she said, ''Yes, Doctor.''

SIX

Mr. Moran doesn't want to pull you, but he doesn't want you showing yourself on the street, either,'' Dayton told me when I came back upstairs. ''I'll get your lunch for you today when I go out. From tomorrow, bring it with you. What did the doctor say?''

''I'm fine.''

''Mr. Moran is prepared to send someone else to finish the day.''

''No, thanks. I'll stay.''

Dayton nodded. ''Smith, I'm sorry if I was harsh with you. You saved Martin Carter from a lot of pain.''

''I just can't resist a good fight.''

He said sharply, ''I hope that isn't true.''

''Don't worry,'' I said. ''I'll try to control myself.''

''See that you do. I have a hundred fifty old folks here, scared to death by what happened to Mike. You're here to reassure them as well as protect them. They're in need of both.''

I looked at him, at his deep eyes and guarded expression. ''You like working here, don't you, Dayton?''

''This is my job.''

"I mean beyond that. Here rather than somewhere else. You like these people, don't you?"

He looked at me unwaveringly for an extra beat. "Yes, I do."

I was glad to hear that.

As the morning wore on and the sun warmed the day, the residents of the Home began to appear on the wide porch, wrapped in shawls and blankets. They were brought out and settled by small, solid-looking Latina women, whose white uniforms glowed against the red tile floor and the yellow limestone of the building front. One of these women, with a long nose and a wide, laughing mouth, greeted me in English as I came up the stairs. Then, fastening the sweater of an un-responding old man, she gave a giggling Spanish commentary to the women nearby about my height, my bruise, and my general level of appeal. I suppressed the urge to answer her in Spanish, just walked on with a wink and a grin.

The residents wore blank looks or trembling smiles, mostly, though here and there small groups of two or three leaned together in conversation, as though on a park bench or at a bus stop, back in the world. Others sat alone, angular and motionless as lizards.

I went in and out, doing my job, wondering how Mike had organized the route, wondering how the garden smelled at night, what sounds there were at four A.M., what sounds there had been on the night he died.

Coming up the stairs on one of my circuits I heard music, muffled by a half-closed door. It was the Chopin Ballade in F, played with great feeling on a piano not worthy of the music, or the pianist. I crossed the thick carpet, stood in the doorway. In a high-ceilinged room with carpets and curtains a man in a wheelchair smiled softly while Ida Goldstein played Chopin.

I watched her move with the music against the brightness of the windows; and suddenly I was gripped by a memory unexpected but so sharp and complete that it displaced the scene before me.

Another old woman sat at another piano in a curtained, carpeted room, smaller than this but with the same autumn

brightness. A nine-year-old boy stood in the doorway, unable to speak, unable to say the good-bye he had come to
say. The music then was Chopin, too, a nocturne, and the old
woman was lost in it, her back straight, her small hands low
over the keys. The boy's hands were already bigger than
hers, and she marveled at them when he played, as though he
had done something clever, to grow such big hands.

The boy felt his eyes sting, his throat begin to ache. He
stood and listened for the last time, his hands curling and
uncurling, as the black walnut tree in the yard scattered leaf
shadows across the window and music filled the room in the
old, familiar house.

"Well, come in and sit down. You make me nervous, standing there like that. And what on earth happened to your
eye?"

My heart jumped; for a second I was disoriented. Then I
realized Ida Goldstein had finished playing and was speaking to me.

The bluntness of her tone was welcome, helped to bring
what was in front of me into focus again. I swallowed to ease
my throat, walked farther into the room. "I had an accident."

"That's not very reassuring in a security guard."

"I'm sorry."

"You play, don't you?"

For the second time that day a question from her threw me
off balance. "How did you know that?"

"The way you were watching me. There's a look you
only see in musicians hearing music. I used to see it sometimes in a student. The one in a hundred with real talent."

"You taught piano?"

"For forty-five years. Who taught you?"

"My grandmother started me." The notes of the Chopin
nocturne still echoed in my mind. "After I was nine we
moved around a lot. I didn't play much again until I was out
of college."

"You didn't have a piano?"

"Most of that time, no."

She seemed to be waiting, as though she knew there was
more. There was: the piano my increasingly desperate

mother bought for me in Amsterdam when I was fourteen, trying to give me something that would keep me out of the kind of trouble I went looking for, wherever we were. My father sold that piano without a word while I was in a Brooklyn hospital at fifteen. From the hospital I moved straight in with my uncle Dave; not a lot of cops had pianos. Then the Navy, college, my brief, fiery marriage, and it wasn't until I was divorced and living above Shorty's at twenty-five that I touched a piano again.

Lost, lost years.

Ida Goldstein must have gotten tired of waiting for a story I didn't seem about to tell. She swiveled on the piano bench to face the old man in his wheelchair. "Eddie, this is Mr. Smith. He's here because of Mike. Mr. Smith, this is Eddie Shawn."

"Bill," I said. I offered the old man my hand. "Pleased to meet you." He inclined his head, smiled, said nothing. His thick glasses made his watery brown eyes look enormous. The hand he offered me, his left, was all bone, trembled as we shook.

"Eddie's had a stroke," Ida Goldstein told me, looking at Eddie. "He doesn't speak anymore."

I didn't know what to say to that, nor to whom. Eddie Shawn made it easier by winking at me, as if his not speaking was a problem for no one, except possibly Ida Goldstein.

"Eddie," said Ida suddenly, "why aren't you wearing a sweater?" She looked at him as if seeing him for the first time that day. "For heaven's sake, you'd think those women would know better, with you right out of the hospital." Eddie Shawn shook his head, dismissing her annoyance, while she rearranged the crocheted blanket around his knees. "Not that he belonged in the hospital, either," she went on, to me. "That doctor's an idiot."

"Dr. Madsen?"

Her blue eyes gave me a sharp look. "No, of course not. He's just bad-tempered and unpleasant. That's probably why they threw him out of Wisconsin."

"They did what?"

"He can't practice medicine there anymore. That's why he came here."

"How do you know that?"

Her tone became casual. "Oh, he was complaining about corn-fed self-righteous hypocrites to a nurse one day in the common room. He must not have seen me over on the sofa."

Eddie Shawn snorted in disgust.

"I was not eavesdropping," Ida protested. "Besides, it's their own fault for thinking we're all deaf and stupid. Anyway, that's all I heard, so that's all I know."

She looked at me defensively, daring me to say anything more on the subject.

I didn't take her up on it. "What doctor did you mean was an idiot?" I asked.

"Dr. Reynolds," she said. "The other one. He's sweet and patient and he smiles and sends you to the hospital for a hangnail. He's sent Eddie three times this year already. I hide when I see him in the hall." Eddie Shawn, in his wheelchair, pulled away from her fussing hands. She sighed, straightened up stiffly. "I used to look after him, until they moved my room. Now he's never put together right."

"Why did they move your room?"

"Because I complained about the noise in the middle of the night. Now, they didn't believe me, because I'm never right. When you get old, you see, you automatically get stupid. But they gave me a room on the garden side to shut me up."

I looked at her with a grin. "I'll bet it didn't work."

Eddie Shawn in his wheelchair started to shake, to emit wordless noises. I was alarmed until I realized he was laughing.

Ida Goldstein tilted her chin up, the way she had when we'd met that morning. "Aren't you afraid of offending me? I'm an old lady—excuse me, a senior citizen. You're not supposed to joke with me. I might not get it. You're supposed to talk to me the way you would to a three-year-old."

"I'm not supposed to talk to you at all. I'm supposed to be out patrolling."

"Well, here." She slipped her hand into the pocket of her dress, pulled out something folded small. "Here's ten dollars. That's almost three weeks' worth, but don't bring it all at once, because I can't hide so much."

I waited for enlightenment, but it didn't come. "Sorry?" I finally said.

"The cat food," she said to me patiently, the way you would to a three-year-old.

"I don't—" I began, but I didn't have to finish.

"Ida," a voice interrupted, a silky voice with ice in it, "what are you doing?"

We all three jumped, Eddie Shawn in his chair, Ida and I standing beside him. I turned toward the voice, which came from the doorway, where a tall woman made taller by the blond coils piled on top of her head approached us, walking as deliberately as an army on the march.

"Oh, Mrs. Wyckoff," sighed Ida, in the voice of a teacher dealing with a particularly tiresome parent. "Bill, this is Mrs. Wyckoff. Mrs. Wyckoff, this is Mr. Smith. He's the new security man—"

"Yes, I can see that." Mrs. Wyckoff, with an air of distaste, looked me up and down.

"Mrs. Wyckoff," Ida Goldstein told me, "runs the organization that runs us."

"I'm the Executive Director of Helping Hands," the tall blond woman informed me. "And I would appreciate it, Mr. Smith, if you wouldn't socialize with the residents. I'm sure Dr. Reynolds would agree. You're large and uniformed and you could easily frighten these people."

"Oh, for heaven's sake," said Ida.

"Ida, please." The blond woman smiled a closed-lipped smile. She wasn't an unhandsome woman, but she somehow made me wish I were in Florida.

"I'm sorry," I said. "I thought the opposite. I was trying to put them at ease."

"I suggest you stick to guard patrols and let us look after the residents."

"Yes, ma'am."

"But before you go about your business I'd like you to give back the money you took from Ida."

"He didn't take it. I gave it to him."

"And why would you do that, Ida?" Mrs. Wyckoff asked.

Ida's eyes caught mine for a second, then flicked back to Mrs. Wyckoff. "He's helping me out," she said blandly. "He's buying a present for one of my great-nephews. The one who flies planes."

"Don't be foolish, Ida. A man you've barely met? If you

need that sort of help, one of the social workers will be glad to provide it. That's what we have them for.''

Mrs. Wyckoff turned to inspect me. Behind her back, Ida Goldstein twisted her face into a mask of demented idiocy, including a tight-lipped smile, then was instantly demure and attentive as Mrs. Wyckoff looked back to her. I bit the inside of my lip to keep from cracking up.

Mrs. Wyckoff surveyed us all. "No, I think something else is going on here." The tight smile grew by a millimeter or so. I wondered if her lips cramped up by the end of the day.

"I think we should tell the truth, Mrs. Goldstein," I said. Ida started to say something. I addressed Mrs. Wyckoff over her words. "It was my fault. When I met Mrs. Goldstein this morning, we made a bet. She lost; she insisted I collect. I'm sorry. I should have known better." I pressed the folded bill into Ida's tiny hand, closed her fingers around it.

"Is that so?" Mrs. Wyckoff tipped her head, looked from me to Ida. "What was this bet about, if I may ask?"

"But now I'm not so sure I lost," Ida said. "Except on a technicality."

"And what was the bet about?" Mrs. Wyckoff repeated.

"I bet him," Ida told her, "that he'd be in trouble with you before lunch."

Mrs. Wyckoff's eyes flared, and she flushed a color which was not becoming with her shade of hair. She threw a poisonous glance at me; then she turned on her heel and stalked away.

In his chair, Eddie Shawn was jiggling and squeezing his knee in wordless laughter.

SEVEN

The parking lot, like the garden and the building itself, was a rectangle running the length of the block, built up over the retaining wall. I walked the lot in the moving shadows of paper birches planted along the fence and in the small turnaround. Their leaning trunks and weeping branches gave them an old-fashioned, Victorian look. The turnaround had a stone bench on it, between two trees; I wondered how long it had been since anyone sat there, waiting for a car or a carriage or a visitor dropping by during a Sunday stroll.

I walked to the edge, looked over the wall at Chester Avenue thirty feet below. Two young women wandered along, pushing carriages. A man worked on a car to the urgent rap beat of its radio. There was no sign that there'd been a fight down there earlier. There was no sign of the Cobras.

I checked the side door on the south, found it well locked. I ambled back through the lot, tried the north side door. Locked, too. I went in, perched on Fuentes's desk, took out a cigarette.

"Hey, you better not," he grinned at me. "Can't smoke in here, man. Nowhere in the buildin'. An' you better not get caught sittin' around, too. La Gringa see you, she gonna get on you ass. She won't care what kinda hero you are." I had told him the story, minus the part about the gun, when I'd first gotten back to work. "Then she gonna call Mr. Moran an' *he* gonna get on you ass."

"La Gringa?" I stood up off the desk, tucked the cigarette back in the pack.

"Lady runs the place. Mrs. Wyckoff. She got hair sorta like this." He made round gestures at the top of his head.

"I thought Dr. Reynolds ran the Home."

"Well, yeah, Dr. Reynolds, he's the boss, but she's his boss. You look out for her, man. She think everyone born was born to cheat her. You know?"

"Thanks." I checked my watch. "I'll be back in half an hour, relieve you for lunch."

He grinned again. "That's good, 'cause by then I'm gonna have to pee real bad."

I turned to go, turned back. "Fuentes—"

"Pablo," he said. "You call me Fuentes, I think I'm my *papi*."

"Pablo," I acknowledged. "How long have you been working here?"

"Maybe about a year."

"Ever had any trouble before the other night?"

"Never had the kinda trouble you just had."

"Have you had any, at all?"

He smoothed the ends of his mustache. "Not me. I mean,

there's trouble round here all the time, but usually it don't make no difference here. Even all that equipment stuff, that don't happen here.''

''What do you mean, equipment stuff?''

''Oh, man, you don't know about that? Big problem over here,'' he said, but he was grinning. ''They steal equipment you got outside your buildin'. Air-conditionin' stuff, and ducts, and you got copper pipin' from your roof, they steal that too. Sometimes they go right in your basement. Like in the summertime, they stole the burner out from a boiler they got down the street. Super didn't know nothing about it until he goes to turn it on in the winter, give the people some heat.''

''He never checked before that?''

''Hey, you go down in the cellar every week, make sure your boiler still got a burner in it?''

I had to admit I didn't.

''An' those faces,'' he went on. ''Like they got on churches?''

''Gargoyles, you mean?''

''*Gargola, sí.* Monster faces on the roof. Some of the fancy buildins around here, they got them.''

''They steal those?''

''Man,'' he grinned, ''they steal them faces right off the buildins. They steal them faces right from under you nose.''

I grinned back, rubbed my nose. ''But no one tries that here?'' I asked. ''Because there are guards?''

He shook his head. ''I don't think just that. It's like we got a 'Off Limits' sign. That guy who was beat up, that was about the only thing. Until, you know, Mike.''

''The guy who was beat up. You mean the trucker?''

''*Sí.* Makin' a night delivery. You heard about it? Got the shit kicked outta him. Right down here.'' He gestured to the lot, the wall, Chester Avenue below. ''Still in the hospital. Been six weeks. Over at Samaritan.''

''He didn't work for the Home, did he?''

''No, man. Just some trucker deliverin' here. What I'm sayin', usually no one here gets trouble. Like there's some kinda truce. We keep outta the neighborhood, you know, just come and go from here, and nobody bothers nobody. Like it's a island, you know? Like a different world.''

* * *

I did the doors again, while Fuentes and then Dayton had lunch. Dayton brought me a roast pork sandwich from the bodega on the corner. I badly wanted a beer, too, but I'd given Dayton enough to worry about for a while.

"You can eat downstairs. There's a room the maintenance staff uses," he told me. I went on down, found the place he meant. It was on the east side, the buried side. Green-and-gray linoleum tiles, fluorescent lights, vinyl-covered chairs taped where the stuffing had tried to escape. I sat in one of them, ate, drank thick Latin coffee. I listened to the lights buzz and tried to pretend I didn't ache.

When I was done I went and found the lockers, in an alcove near the boiler room. There were two dozen of them, dented, green, and old. None of them had names; about half of them had locks.

"There are empties," Dayton had said. "Ask Pete Portelli."

"Who's he?"

"Building superintendent."

I went looking for Pete Portelli.

I found him in an office off the boiler room. The plastic sign on the half-open door read, "Stationary Engineer." The office was small, windowless, and smelled of cigarette smoke and beer, both stale. I knew the man behind the battered wooden desk was Pete because it said so in red stitching on his coveralls. The desk was piled with invoices, bills, notes scrawled in thick pencil on torn scraps of paper. Over the file cabinet was a girlie calendar from Aberg Tool Works.

When I knocked he looked up and grunted.

"I'm Smith," I told him. "I'm the new guy on days for Moran."

"Swell. What're you doing here?"

"Supervisor said to talk to you about a locker."

He leaned back in his chair, surveyed me. I stood in the doorway and did the same to him. He was stocky, gray-haired, sloppily shaven. His hands were square, the nails dirty.

One side of his mouth tugged upward. "Where'd you get the mouse?"

"Interrupted something that was none of my business."

His smile widened; he seemed to think that was funny. "Smith, huh? That for real?"

"Uh-huh."

He shrugged. "If you say so." He stuck out his hand. "Pete Portelli, that's me."

"Pleasure," I said.

"It's a crappy job."

"Mine or yours?"

"Ahhh, both. But I get to sit down sometimes, and guys work for me."

"And I get to stroll around and I have no worries."

"Oh, yeah. Except some punks climbing over the wall and beating your brains out."

"You mean like happened to Mike Downey?"

He snorted in agreement. "Bunch of moulies playing Knockout. Fucking animals. They'll break your head for no reason, no reason at all."

"Knockout?"

"Yeah." He picked something out of his teeth. "It's a game the moulies play up here."

I must have looked mystified; he grinned in satisfaction. "Knockout, way you play is, kid jumps a guy, tries to knock him out. Some stranger, y'know, a man, not another kid. Longer it takes, worse his score is. You didn't hear of that?"

"No," I said. "I hadn't."

"Well, think about it. Big guy like you's probably worth double. Except you're messed up already, so maybe not."

"You think that's what happened to Mike Downey?"

"Well, no one stole nothing that night, car radio, nothing." He spread his palms. "Ask me, they were out hunting. Jungle hunting." He smiled some more; he must have thought this was funny, too.

"Maybe they got scared off."

"By who? Some basket case from upstairs? Not that asshole Howe. He didn't hear a fucking thing."

"I thought he found the body."

"Yeah, when he finally caught on Downey wasn't doing his route and went looking." He shook a Camel from a crumpled pack, held the pack toward me.

"I have my own," I said. "But I thought you couldn't smoke in the building."

"Why, Wyckoff might getcha?" He lit his cigarette, dropped the match in an overflowing ashtray. "Funny, I wouldn't've figured you for a guy afraid of women."

"Some women," I answered.

"Mistake." He shook his head. "You gotta show them who's boss early, then you don't get no more trouble. Me, I got Wyckoff under control."

"Really? How'd you manage that?"

"Broads scare easy." He grinned a brown-toothed grin. "Like my wife. You married? Kids?"

"No."

"Lucky you. Single guy, you get variety, huh? Spice of life." A wink went with that. " 'Course, being married don't slow *me* down, you know? Carter!" he suddenly yelled past me. I half turned, moved out of the doorway and into the room. My new cousin stood behind me in the hall. He nodded vaguely to me; I took the cue and did the same. "Carter, where the fuck you been? I been looking for you half an hour!"

"I been upstairs rehangin' the door to Miz Weeks' room," Carter said.

"Oh, yeah? And just who the hell told you to do that?"

"No one told me. Miz Weeks ask me yesterday, say she can't close her door."

"Her mouth, you mean! That old bat could talk the ear off a fucking fish." To me, Portelli said, "Him and her was probably sitting around exchanging stories about the good old plantation days. Carter, you work for *me!* You don't scratch your ass unless I tell you to. You understand that, or you want I should use smaller words?"

Carter's spine stiffened, but all he said was, "I understand."

"Swell. Now get the fuck back to work. Ahh, shit, wait." He sighed, a man weary with the burdens life thrust upon him. "Doctor Feelgood's looking for you. I told him he had ten minutes, then I want you back here. See him first."

Carter turned and left, without a look at me.

Pete looked at me, though. "Damn moulies stick together, don't they? You suppose he'd've spent ten minutes hanging a door for some one of those kikes up there?'' I didn't answer. He smashed out his cigarette. ''So, you got nothing to do? What're you hanging around here for?''

''A locker,'' I reminded him.

''Oh, shit, yeah, okay.'' He rummaged through a desk drawer, came out with a file folder with a couple of pieces of ruled paper in it. He looked through them. ''Eighteen,'' he said. He scrawled my name next to the number, with the note ''Moran'' next to my name. ''Bring your own lock. G'bye.''

The garden was a welcome relief after Pete Portelli's office, and my own company a welcome relief after his.

EIGHT

I ran into my new cousin toward the end of my shift, invited him to join me for a quick beer after work.

''Can't do it.'' He shook his head. ''Got somewhere to be. Rain check?''

''Sure.''

''Look forward to it. Hey, thanks for staying cool with Pete before.''

''Well, I don't know what I was staying cool about, but you obviously didn't want to know me.''

''Not exactly that. Pete find out I been messing with the Cobras, he'll fire my ass.''

''What about Dr. Madsen? Didn't he tell Pete why he wanted you?''

''Naw. He tell Pete he need a quick look at me, have to do with my health insurance.''

My respect for the cynical Dr. Madsen rose an abrupt notch.

''That Pete's a real peach, isn't he?'' I said as we fell into step along the corridor. ''Is he always like that?''

''Nope. Sometime he in a bad mood. Unless you Italian. You Italian?''

''Uh-uh. Half Irish, half cracker.''

''Cracker from where?''

''Kentucky. Louisville.''

''Don't sound it.''

"Didn't live there long. Listen, I'm on break and I'd just about kill for a cup of coffee. Is there a coffee machine or something around here?"

He hesitated. "No machine. But if you really desperate, they got coffee in the staff room. We not suppose to go in there, and probably you not either, but seeing as you new, maybe it be all right."

"I'll take my chances. Point me toward it."

I thought about that cup of coffee a lot, later. If I'd focused less on finding some caffeine, more on why I was there, I might have remembered what I'd already forgotten. A simple question, a simple answer, and I might have cleared up what I was there to clear up and left a lot of other things untouched. As it was, before I saw the answer floating on the surface I was in so deep that I was turning up the mud at the bottom, exposing things that couldn't stand the light.

The staff room was bright and neat, three square tables with chairs around them, two sofas, a small kitchenette with a stainless-steel counter. Rectangles of late-day sunlight striped the floor in front of the barred windows. It was quiet and empty and smelled of coffee.

A full Mr. Coffee on the counter was waiting patiently just for me. I poured a cup, clinked a quarter into a can with a slotted top, and took the cup to the windows, to lean and drink and watch.

Golden sunlight outlined each leaf on the parking-lot birches. I thought of the maples on the hillside above my cabin, wondered if they'd turned yet. I felt the coffee warm my chest, caught the gentle jolt in my brain as it kicked in.

A flash of sunlight bounced across the parking lot as the back door opened. Dr. Madsen, medical bag in hand, strode briskly through the lot and down the hill. That was curious, I thought. The subway was the other way; if he drove to work, his car would be in the lot. Maybe he was picking up a sandwich at the bodega, but then why take his bag?

These were interesting questions, but my musing on them was interrupted by a silken, angry voice.

"Mr. Smith!" Mrs. Wyckoff stood rigid in the doorway. "You're paid to patrol these grounds, not to hide from your work in rooms where you don't belong!"

"Union gives me a fifteen-minute break twice a day." I finished my coffee. "To take care of bodily functions. My body needs caffeine to function."

"This room is for professional staff only." She wouldn't be mollified. "Possibly you didn't know that, but you know it now."

"Mrs. Wyckoff," I said, rinsing my cup, setting it on the counter, "we seem to have started off badly. If it was my fault I'm sorry. I'm only trying to do my job—"

"Then I suggest you get back to it." She interrupted my apology, held the door open for me. It was too bad. I'd been about to say something nice about Helping Hands' good name; she might have liked that.

At four, when my shift ended, I left my tie and uniform jacket in my locker, changed into a windbreaker of my own. I took the car and headed north and west across the Bronx to Kingsbridge, to meet Hank Lindfors at a place of his choosing, the way Bobby had set it up.

I drove the full length of the Concourse this time, curving with it as the apartment buildings gave way to short bursts of bustle at Fordham and again at Kingsbridge Road. I waited for a stoplight beside Poe Park, where the trees blazed red and gold in the long low sunlight.

Where the Concourse ended I swung west, worked my way down to Broadway. A block over I found the place I was looking for: Ehring's Tavern, a corner bar. I circled for a place to park. The neighborhood was small apartment buildings, one-story stores, a library, a couple of churches. Paper pumpkins and black cats hung in the window of the candy store where I stopped for cigarettes; the granite bank had a show of third graders' artwork in the lobby.

North of here lay the vastness of Van Cortlandt Park, and then Yonkers, Westchester, and the rest of the world; south was Manhattan. East, where I'd come from, the Bronx faded through tired and shabby to desolate and desperate. And to the west, up the hill, was Riverdale, the high ground where the money in the Bronx had retreated so it wouldn't get its feet dirty.

Across the street from Ehring's I found a phone in one of those perforated metal enclosures that pass for phone booths now. I punched in Bobby's number, lit a cigarette while I listened to the ring. I waited longer than I usually have the patience for, but sometimes it took Bobby time to get to the phone.

The seventh ring was cut off by a sharp growl. "Moran!"

"Smith," I countered.

"Ah, Jesus!" Bobby growled some more. "Where the hell are you? Are you all right?"

"Never felt better."

"Al Dayton says you're a mess."

"He exaggerates."

"Al Dayton," Bobby said pointedly, "had to give up fishing because he couldn't lie. He's a regular George Washington. You, on the other hand—"

"I'm at a pay phone. If you're going to critique my character I'll have to get more change."

"Forget it. You can't afford it. What happened?"

I told him about the fight.

"You made some enemies," he said, when I was through.

"And a friend. Listen, Bobby, there are a few things I want to ask you about, now that I've spent some time at that place. Can you meet me for dinner at Shorty's?"

"Yeah, sure. When?"

I looked at the clock in the bakery window. It was four-thirty. I might be an hour at Ehring's, another half hour getting home. "Eight?" I asked. That would give me two hours at home, and I wanted that.

"Okay," Bobby said. Then, "Kid? You sure you're all right?"

"I'm fine, Bobby. I'll see you later."

We hung up. I gave the phone another quarter, punched in Lydia's number. It was answered on the second ring, but it was answered by a machine.

"You have reached the offices of Chin Investigative Services," it told me. "There's no one available to take your call right now, but if you leave a message we'll get back to you as soon as we can." Then it told me again, in Chinese.

"It's me," I said, after the beep. "Are you there?" I waited a few seconds but she didn't pick up. "Okay, listen. I'm having dinner with Bobby Moran at Shorty's at eight. Can you meet us there?" I was out of things to say, so I just said, "See you later," and hung up. Feeling slightly cheated, I crossed the street to Ehring's.

There weren't many people in Ehring's, but it was the kind of place that could never look empty. The heavy, paneled door brought me into the end of a long, narrow room, where the bar ran down the left side, leaving no space for tables on the right. Beyond the bar was a room where booths lined both walls and an aisle ran between; to the left of that was a dining room.

The walls were dark-paneled wood, and every inch was hung with framed photographs, ancient fraternal banners, and menus from testimonial dinners given in 1923. There were shelves of decorated beer steins and oversized pilsners, hunting horns on pegs, and a string of Christmas lights above the bar. The whole place was watched over by trophy heads: three deer, a moose, a wolf, a civet cat. One of the deer had Christmas lights for eyes.

I sat at the bar under the suspicious eyes of the trophies and the regulars. The bar stool was leather, worn soft with the years. Down at the far end, the red-cheeked, round-shouldered bartender was talking to two men who looked like they were spending their retirement here. In time he wandered over, dropped a coaster on the bar, asked affably, "What can I get you?"

"Beer," I said. "Bud."

As he pulled the handle and my beer foamed into the mug, he asked, "How about some ice for that eye?"

That was my opening to tell my story, draw the regulars into talk, buy a round and get bought one, begin not to be a stranger here. But I was tired, and I was here for a different reason.

"Too late for that." I dropped four bucks on the bar, didn't pick up the change when he brought it back. "I'm meeting a guy here. I don't know him, but he said to ask at the bar. Hank Lindfors."

"Why didn't you say so? He's here." He jerked his thumb over his shoulder, toward the back room. "You're Smith? You're early. He said to look for you around five."

"Thanks." I took my beer and headed down the narrow room to the booths in the back.

Only three were occupied, only one by an obvious cop. He had the lined cop face and the walrus cop mustache and the hard, guarded cop eyes. He was a big man, broad, his age hard to tell. He could have been younger than I was, not much over thirty; or older than I, pushing fifty. His weathered face and thick dark hair would swear to either story. He sat facing the door, one arm flung along the low back of the booth. His expression didn't change as he watched me walk toward him, and his big hands were still, but I knew that deceptive cop quiet, too. I knew that if he thought he had to, he could drop me fast.

"Lindfors?" I said, standing above him. "I'm Smith."

He nodded; he knew some things, too. He gestured with his glass at the green leather bench across from him. "Sit down."

As I slid in, he said, "You're early."

"So are you." And probably for the same reason, I thought. For the edge.

He took a drink—he was drinking something brown, with ice—and said, "Look, I told Moran and I'll tell you. I don't like P.I.'s." He looked at me out of eyes like glass, glittering and dark. "Cowboys and shakedown artists. I don't want you screwing up this case and I don't want to be sitting here talking to you."

"Why are you?"

He drank some more, emptied his glass. "You're Dave Maguire's boy, aren't you?"

I felt myself stiffen a little, as though my skin were hardening protectively. "Dave was my uncle."

Lindfors signaled the bartender. "Maguire talked about you a lot. I don't know if you knew that." He didn't look as if he cared if I knew it, either. "He was a fucking good cop, Captain Maguire. I had him at the Academy. Served under him at the Third Precinct. I felt it when he got taken out, Smith. I felt it." His hard eyes searched mine. He said, "You were there."

It wasn't a question, but I answered it. "I was there."

"You were hurt bad. You took out one of the trigger men before you went down."

This wasn't a question either, and I didn't say anything.

"I was on the task force," he said. "To find the other hit

man and the fucker who ordered it. We weren't fast enough. Someone else smoked the hit man, and fucking Malaguez went back to Colombia and got whacked in a coke turf war. You know all that.''

I did, but I waited.

"So I guess what I think is, they got what was coming to them, but it wasn't justice.'' He spat that word, as though he'd long ago lost his taste for it. "I guess what I think is, I owe Captain Maguire one.''

A waitress in a dirndl skirt appeared then, with a fresh drink for Lindfors. She made a gesture toward my beer and I shook my head.

Lindfors tried the new drink. "So I'm talking to you.''

I lit a cigarette, shook the match into a ceramic ashtray that said "Ehring's" at the bottom. "Bobby Moran was a friend of Dave's. You were pretty rough on him.''

"Moran's all busted up because the vic was his nephew. And worked for him. Screws hell out of your guard business if you can't keep your guards alive.'' Under his mustache his upper lip curled. Maybe it was a smile; I didn't know. "He's got this asshole idea that the killing was more than it was.''

"What was it?''

"Random,'' he said, looking at me, emphasizing the word. "Oh, maybe not quite. Maybe because the kid was in uniform, that's why it was him and not three other guys. But it had nothing to do with the kid, any more than you gave a shit in Nam who you were shooting at. Anyone in those fucking pajamas was the fucking enemy. Were you in Nam?''

I shook my head. He narrowed his eyes with the unasked question.

"I was in the Navy,'' I said. "I didn't see any action.''

"Well, you should've. It would've prepared you for this.''

"For what?''

"For fucking war, asshole. What the hell you think is going on out there? Why the hell you think that kid was killed? He was the enemy. White kid in uniform over there, what did he expect?''

Lindfors looked down into his glass again. It was still al-most full, but he emptied it in a sudden fierce gulp, slammed it on the table. The young couple in the next booth jumped.

Lindfors spoke without looking at me. ''They got armies over there. They got fucking kid armies and they got no reason in hell not to kill you. They'll kill you for cash so they can buy crack and sneakers and they'll kill you for fun. They'll kill you to be tougher than some other kid that never killed anyone. They'll kill you to see if their gun works. There's nothing in control over there, Smith. There's no one in charge. You don't know who's shooting at you and if you did you couldn't stop him. Just like Nam. Fucking kid armies!''

He stopped, looked at his empty glass, looked up at me. He smiled a bitter smile. ''That's what happened to your vic, Smith. He got killed in the war.''

I took my cigarette from my mouth. ''Who killed him?''

He stared at me; then he made a sound like a laugh. He signaled the waitress, motioned for new drinks for us both. I looked around the small room, at the menus and newspaper clippings and photos of another time, of the time before the war.

''Hey,'' Lindfors said, ''that's what they got juries for. This is America, Smith, haven't you heard? We got the greatest legal system in the world.''

I put my cigarette out, finished my beer.

''No, see, I'm just a cop,'' Lindfors went on. The couple in the next booth stood up, collected themselves. Lindfors ran his eyes over the girl, followed her swaying rear as she ambled out of the room. ''I just bring 'em in. I bring in shitloads of evidence, I Mirandize 'em, I'm real, real, careful not to touch a hair of their precious heads. And it don't matter a fucking damn, because they're back out again before you got time to jerk off.''

The waitress brought the drinks. Lindfors sipped at his, put it down with exaggerated care exactly in the ring the one before it had made on the tabletop. He gave me a casual shrug. ''But, hey, Smith, this Downey kid? Well, yeah. Yeah, I do know who killed him.''

NINE

Ehring's had started to fill up around us. Tired middle-aged executives stopped for a quick one on the way home, sat at the bar next to young guys who drove trucks or worked at gas stations and had their whole lives ahead of them. The rhythm of voices got faster and the pitch got louder. The vinegar aroma of bratwurst and sauerkraut was added to the warm beery smell. The waitress came by again, left us a bowl of pretzels and a sweet smile.

I tasted my new beer, waited for Lindfors to go on.

Low, not looking at me, he said, ''There are a lot of motherfuckers out there, Smith. A lot of guys, if I could lock them up for this, I would, and I wouldn't give a shit whether they done it or not.'' He sipped his drink. ''But I can't lock up anybody. Not fucking anybody.''

''Lindfors—''

''Yeah, yeah.'' He drank again. ''You heard of a street gang over there, the Cobra Crew?''

I was surprised. I wondered if it showed. ''The Cobras? Real tall skinny guy named Snake? And a fat kid, Skeletor? They wear tattoos?''

Lindfors stared, unmoving. ''Yeah. Friends of yours?''

''Go to hell, Lindfors.''

His face suddenly reddened. He half rose from his seat. My whole body tensed in answer, because I recognized what was in his eyes. I knew that anger, that volcanic rage that claws a man apart inside unless he finds a way to let it erupt; and so he searches, in a bottle, in a stranger's unthinking words or a friend's meaningless joke, for an excuse, a trigger, a reason to explode. I knew that too well not to recognize it in another man.

But Lindfors must have seen something in my eyes, too. Slowly, he settled against the bench again. He drank, lifting his glass with care. He smiled a cold smile, directed inward, not at me.

''That tall guy, Snake LeMoyne,'' he said. ''He's a bad

son of a bitch. If he didn't do your boy personally, one of his
posse did.''

I wanted another cigarette. It went with the beer and the
anger; but I held off.

"That's what they do," Lindfors said. "The Cobras." He
snapped off a piece of pretzel, stuck it in his mouth, licked
the salt off his fingers. "When LeMoyne was a kid, he used
to come around a PAL program they had over there. That
was in the days when you thought, maybe . . ." He didn't
finish. He swirled his drink around in his glass. "He learned
karate there. He was good, long legs, long arms. Skinny runt,
but he made up for it. Had what they used to call heart, in a
fighter. You shoulda seen his eyes, pounding another kid.
Ten years old, already mad enough to kill. A couple of bouts,
he had to be pulled off the other guy. You shoulda seen it.''

I drank my beer and thought of the eyes of the kid who'd
held me down that morning.

The waitress went by and Lindfors watched her pass.
Then he went on. "When he got the height—that's when he
started to call himself 'Snake'; his name's Anthony—he
went out for basketball. Good, but nothing special. Never
had the moves. An average kid. But average don't make it
over there. Special don't make it. Genius maybe. Genius
could get you to an NCAA school even if you can't fucking
read, and then maybe a kid would have a chance. The rest of
them, the average kids . . ." Lindfors gave me the curled-lip
smile again. "The rest of them get drafted.''

"That what happened to LeMoyne?''

Lindfors nodded. "Six, eight years ago, the City closed
the community center the PAL program was in. Sold the
building. Reopened the center a few months later, across the
Concourse, but by then Snake was hanging with a gang
called the Icemen. The new place wasn't on Icemen turf.''
He shrugged, drank. He rubbed a corner of his mustache absently, his eyes far away.

"Snake came up through the Icemen. Started on the street
corner as a lookout, worked his way to enforcer. Had his
own special style, Snake did.'' Suddenly he gulped down
what was left in his glass. "Where the hell's that waitress?
Annette!'' he bellowed. "C'mon over here, sweetie.'' He
asked me, "You want another? No? Your loss. Annette,

baby, get Daddy another drink.'' The waitress smiled again, took his glass.

Lindfors fell silent, stared broodingly at the table. I was trying to think how to prod him on without coming across as belligerent. He was at that stage of drunk where he could head off in a dozen different directions, and I didn't have the patience for it. But he jump-started himself.

''They're better armed than the fucking Marines, those gangs.'' He seemed to be talking only half to me now. ''They got Uzis and TEC's, AK-47's, every other cocksucking piece you could name. But Snake, he was proud of his hands. He was quick and quiet and he liked the personal touch. Enjoyed his work. It got so you could tell a LeMoyne job, you know how?''

''No,'' I said. ''How?''

''You'd find the vic beaten to a blob on the sidewalk. Something you couldn't even recognize anymore. After you scraped him up, you'd find he'd been shot through the foot, once, with his own piece. After he was dead.'' Lindfors's eyes moved around, found mine again. ''We found a twelve-year-old like that once. A kid named Laurence Brown. He was a runner for the Icemen. His friends said he'd been skimming a few bucks off each payment he delivered.''

I pulled out the cigarette I'd intended not to have. ''And you found Mike Downey like that?''

''Yeah,'' Lindfors said. ''Like that.''

I needed to say something else, not to let the silence start. ''What happened to the Icemen?''

''What happens to those guys? They do time, or they die, or they die doing time. Snake and another kid, the Rev, they took over the territory. Then the Rev got busted, and the fat kid, Skeletor, took up with Snake.'' He poked his finger through the bowl of pretzels. ''We thought Snake might have trouble with Skeletor. He's one smart, ambitious bastard. But there's no trouble. Skeletor's just waiting. Someday Snake'll go down, and the whole thing'll be his. See, it's endless over there. Fucking endless. Save one kid, wouldn't matter anyway.''

Annette came over with Lindfors's fourth drink, or at least the fourth I'd seen.

''What are you drinking?'' I asked.

"I'm drinking fucking Dewar's and what's it to you?"

"I just wondered. In case I ever need to buy you a drink."

"You won't ever need to buy me a drink, because you're not going to be drinking with me anymore. This is a one-time-only, Smith. For the Captain. I pay this debt, you and me are history."

"How will you know when it's paid?"

He stared at me over his glass. "Fuck you," he said, and drank.

"Did you bring LeMoyne in?"

"Of course I fucking brought him in. Then I let him go. He has three eyewitnesses where he was all night. All *I* got is an M.O. that everybody in the Bronx knows, and, as Snake's very clever motherfucking lawyer pointed out, anyone could imitate."

"Lindfors," I said, "why would the Cobras have done that to Mike?"

"Ah, shit. You don't get it, do you? They didn't do it for a reason. They don't gotta have a fucking reason. Maybe they were high. Maybe they were graduating a new Cobra. That's one of the exams you got to pass, to make it to the top of the crew."

"Random murder?"

His eyes, when they lifted to mine, were sad, old, and tired beyond belief. "Yeah," he said.

There wasn't much more. He hadn't brought the M.E.'s report and he told me what I could do with my request to see a copy of it. He told me what was in it, though. "No blunt instruments. No wood splinters or rust or stone chips in the wounds. Hands and feet, Smith. Leather gloves and leather shoes, that's how you do that. Gloves and shoes. Shit."

I stayed a little longer, asked a little more, but it was no use. Lindfors had said everything he'd decided he was going to say. His speech was distinct, his movements controlled and careful; but a deep, angry drunkenness looked out of his eyes.

In the end I gave up. When he was looking somewhere else I folded two twenties, slipped them under my beer mug. That would take care of where Lindfors had already been and help him along if he were looking to go farther. I stood to leave.

"See you, Lindfors," I told him.

"Not if I can fucking help it," were his parting words to me.

TEN

Traffic was bad all the way downtown and I didn't get home until close to six-thirty. That left me with less time than I'd wanted but I spent some of it showering, anyway. I stood in the pounding heat, washing away the soreness, the sweat, the old people with vacant eyes, the young ones with empty futures, what I'd seen, what I'd heard, the Bronx.

Dry, I pulled on fresh jeans, T-shirt, sneakers. I set the timer so I wouldn't have to think about the time, poured an inch of Maker's Mark and went to the piano. Sipping the bourbon, I tried to clear my mind.

I started with exercises, to warm up. When I was ready, I breathed controlled and slow; then I moved into the Schubert B-flat Major, which I'd been hearing in my head all day. I hadn't been playing it through very long, only a week or so, and that was all I wanted to do tonight: put it together, make the connections. That's when I really start to learn a piece: after I hear what I've got, what I'm able to do that I didn't know about, what I can't do that I'd hoped I could.

The piano demanded, as it always does, total focus, absolute single-minded concentration. It was the piano that saved me, when Annie died; and after Dave was killed, caught in an ambush that put me in the hospital for a month, the worst hell was the weeks, even after I came out, that I couldn't play. Time will bring with it the ability to go on—but only if you can somehow live through those first days and weeks. There are only two ways I know to do that. One is the bottle, and the other is music.

I finished before the timer went off, though my speed was not good, especially at the end. I'd have to work on that, I thought as I wiped my face with a towel; but overall I was pleased. I was playing much better than I had the night before, playing close to the core of the piece. Soon I'd know it well enough to go to working as a watchmaker would on the smallest elements of it, adjusting, refining, until what the music brought to me and what I brought to it had merged under my hands.

More than anything I wanted to play it again; I wanted to do nothing but play it for the next few days, until what was about to happen had happened. A piece can slip away from you at this point, and if it does sometimes you can't get it back. It had taken me years to feel ready for this sonata, and I didn't want to lose it.

But it was eight, and I was meeting Bobby. And Lydia.

I switched the T-shirt for a sweatshirt; I wasn't in the mood for comments on the tattoo, even the regular ones from the regulars. I closed the piano, switched on the alarm. Then I clattered down the two flights from my place, went out the street door, twelve steps east, and through the beveled-glass, gilt-lettered door to Shorty's Bar.

The smell was liquor, cigarette smoke, grilling burgers. The conversation was low and the faces familiar. I crossed the tiled floor to the L-shaped bar in the back, exchanging greetings and wise-ass remarks with the people I passed. On the side of the bar I preferred, the short leg of the L, there were no empty stools, but that was all right. At Shorty's I didn't mind sitting with my back to the door.

Shorty O'Donnell, behind the bar, looked over as I sat down, started a smile that fizzled when he saw my eye. He tried to keep his doubts from showing on his face, but they were there.

"Hey, kid," he said, in the hoarse voice that has never been clear in all the years I've known him. The greeting was more tentative than I liked, but I had no one to blame but myself.

"It's okay, Shorty," I told him. "I was helping out a friend and I got in the way."

Shorty's face relaxed then, probably less because of what I'd said than what he'd heard in the way I'd said it. His bristling eyebrows, almost as white as his hair, smoothed out, and he stretched for the square Maker's Mark bottle. He poured me a shot over ice. "You want to tell me about it?"

"It's no big deal," I said, but I described the fight briefly so he wouldn't feel like I was holding out on him. The only change I made was to make it sound as though I'd known Carter already, as though I'd been coming to the aid of a friend, not a stranger. This was because I'd been thinking a lot about how really stupid you have to be to do what I really did.

Shorty took in what I had to say without comment. That meant it was okay with him and I wouldn't hear any more about it. "You want something to eat?" he asked me.

"Later. I'm meeting Bobby and Lydia; I'll wait for them."

"Oh, shit, kid. She called."

"Lydia?"

"Yeah. She said she can't make dinner, but she can get here around ten, if you want. She said she left a message with your service but she wasn't sure you'd call in for it."

Of course she was right; I hadn't called in. "What am I supposed to do? Call her?"

"Only to tell her not to come. Otherwise she'll be here later. Hey, cheer up, kid. It's only two hours."

I didn't answer that. "If Bobby comes in, tell him I'm here." I slipped off the bar stool, took my drink to the phone by the rest rooms.

I called my service, to see if anyone besides Lydia had anything to say to me. No one did, and Lydia had said just what Shorty had said she'd said.

When I got back to the bar Shorty was standing over a booth, talking to Bobby. Bobby had trouble with the bar stools since the stroke, and he didn't come in as often as before, but he was still a regular. And it seemed to me, though I couldn't be sure, that when he wasn't here there was always a booth or a table empty, waiting, even on those rare nights when Shorty had a crowd.

I slid into the booth opposite Bobby. Shorty's benches and tables were wood, old and scarred with names and cigarette burns. I lit a cigarette of my own. Bobby put down his beer, looked closely at me. Before he could say anything I said, "It's okay. It just looks bad."

"Yeah, well, it does that," Bobby said. "What are you drinking?"

"Bourbon. I'm set."

"You hungry?"

"Uh-huh."

"This Rosie's day?" Bobby asked Shorty.

"No, José's. He made this chicken thing. With sausage. He says his grandma used to cook it when he was a *muchacho.*"

Bobby looked at me. "Sounds like something you'd eat. I'll have a burger."

I ordered the chicken thing. When Shorty was gone Bobby said to me, "Shorty says you asked your girlfriend to come down. Business or pleasure?"

"Business. I told you I wanted someone on the outside; Lydia's it. And lay off the girlfriend stuff when she gets here, okay?"

Bobby made a sympathetic noise. "Still no action?"

"Bobby—"

"Hey, no problem." The hand he could lift he lifted innocently. "What's she been doing?"

"For now, just backgrounds. Poking around. I'm working blind, Bobby."

"Did you talk to Hank Lindfors?"

"Christ, yes." I sipped my bourbon. "Whatever he's carrying around inside him, I don't want to be in the room when it blows."

"Yeah, me either. What'd he say?"

I rolled the tip of my cigarette in the ashtray, said casually, "The gang I had the run-in with today, the Cobras? They're the ones Lindfors has pegged for doing Mike."

Bobby stared. Then his face flushed with the anger I'd been expecting. "Oh, great! And now they'll be coming after you? Forget it, kid. You're off this. If he's right—"

"Bobby, cool down. You're forgetting why you put me on it."

"What the hell do you mean?"

"It didn't sound right to you before. It suddenly does now that the suspects have names?"

"If they have names Lindfors must have a reason."

I shook my head. "Not much of one. Just that he recognized the M.O. And even if he's right, he hasn't been able to find anything that would put them away for it. Maybe I can. Bobby, tell me something: was Mike armed?"

Bobby stopped short, reining in the anger. When he answered his voice was calmer. "No." He drank some beer. "Armed guards, it's a whole other thing, different insurance, all kinds of shit. I get a call for armed guards, I use ex-cops and moonlighters. No one else carries when they work for me." He added, "Except you."

"In the old days I didn't."

"No, for the same reason I wouldn't let Mike. You weren't trained as a cop and you were a goddamn hothead." He paused. "Why? You think if Mike'd been armed he could've—"

"Oh, Christ, Bobby, no. No. But Mike was shot, after he was dead. Did you know that?"

Bobby didn't really move, but his chest seemed to deflate a little. Seeing the look on his face made my hand clench tight around my glass. In a small voice he said, "No, they didn't tell me that."

I said, "It's what makes Lindfors think it's the Cobras that did it. It's a sort of a trademark with them. But they usually shoot a guy with his own gun."

"So what? Mike didn't have one, so they used theirs."

"Why? Shooting a guy after he's dead with his own gun makes a sick kind of sense. Shooting him with yours is just wasting a slug."

Bobby was quiet, didn't answer that. He said, "Tell me about Lindfors."

I replayed my conversation with Lindfors, easing up a little on the description of what a LeMoyne hit looked like. I don't know why; Bobby had seen Mike's body.

Bobby listened through my report the way he used to, saving all his questions until the end. By the end our dinner had come. Kay, the waitress who brought it, kissed Bobby's cheek and told him how sorry she was about Mike. When she left Bobby stared at the burger he'd ordered. "Ah, shit. I'm not hungry."

"Eat it, Bobby. It's bad for you. It'll do you good."

Bobby gave me an unsure look, then doctored the burger with onions and ketchup and relish and salt.

My bowl of thick chicken stew was giving off clouds of garlic. I speared my fork into some hot Spanish sausage.

"What did you think of that place, kid?" Bobby asked. "The Home."

I thought before I answered. "The isolation," I said. "It's not normal; or maybe it is, but it isn't right." I swallowed some spicy broth. "The neighborhood's going to hell in a handbasket and that place has fruit trees and a big high wall. It's weird, and I'm not sure it's what they'd want, if you asked them."

"The old folks?"

"Uh-huh. They're cut off. It's like an island. They're stuck for the rest of their lives with nobody but each other and they don't have anything in common except being old. Christ, Bobby, I don't know. It's like doing time, except that it's beautiful."

Bobby said, "You remember that place I was in?"

"The rehab place? Yeah, I do."

"That's what I was afraid of," he said. "Being stuck there forever. Just that damn yellow room, all those damn people in those other damn yellow rooms wetting their beds and drooling. I was scared to death."

He looked at me when he said this, and I met his eyes, but it was hard. I'd visited Bobby almost daily through the four months he was in the rehab hospital, but I'd never wanted to go, and that still shamed me. At first it was Bobby, helpless to control his body or any part of his world. Later, as Bobby got better, got ready to leave, it was the other people, the ones who weren't going to get better, would never leave. I'd done six months behind county bars once, in another state. I used to look at the guards and visitors, people who could come and go when I couldn't, the same way the people at the hospital looked at me.

"Kid, do you think I'm crazy?"

"Crazy how?"

"About this whole thing. Maybe Lindfors is right. I'm just a crazy old man. Maybe because I can't do anything about what happened, I'm trying to make it into something I can do something about."

"You never operated like that. If your gut says there's something else going on here I'll buy it."

"And you wouldn't just be humoring a crazy old man?" His eyes didn't waver but his voice did, a little.

There were a dozen comebacks to that, cracks that would have broken the mood, but what I said was, "I would never do that, Bobby. Not to you." I hoped it was true.

As I was polishing off the chicken stew the door opened, and I looked up toward it for the twentieth time since I'd sat down. A compact figure, her hands in the pockets of her unzipped leather jacket, stood for a moment in the doorway. She looked around, registering everything. When she spotted me she smiled; I felt a warmth that didn't come from Latin spices, or from bourbon.

She moved through the room, waved to Shorty behind the bar. When she reached our booth I rose. Bobby half stood also, then sank back. Lydia kissed my cheek, slipped in beside me on the bench. I moved over to make room, but not so far that I couldn't feel the warmth of her thigh, an inch from mine, or smell the freesia in her hair.

"Hi," I said.

"Hi." Lydia flashed me the smile again, then turned to Bobby. Her face softened. "Hi, Mr. Moran. Bill told me about your nephew. I'm really sorry." She squeezed Bobby's hand.

"Thanks," Bobby said. There was a short silence; then Lydia lifted her hand to my eye. Her touch was soft and cool. "Was it fun, the fight where you got this?"

"Five on a one-to-ten," I said. "But I'm getting a lot of mileage out of it. Are you hungry?"

"Oh, no, thanks. My brother Andrew came for dinner with a friend, and my mother put on a show. Steamed pork buns, watercress soup, and a thing that translates as 'peculiar chicken.' I don't think I'll eat for a week."

"Was it peculiar?" Bobby asked.

"It was wonderful. I wish I could cook like my mother."

"You just don't get enough practice, that's all," I said. "You could practice on me. I could buy all kinds of strange ingredients and you could cook them and teach me their Chinese names. I promise I'd eat anything you fed me."

"As long as I swallowed anything you fed me?"

"Me?" I asked innocently.

Bobby said, "If you two want to do this in private—"

"No, Mr. Moran, it's okay. This isn't what I came for."

I sighed. "It never is. Okay. Let's get to work."

Kay came over to take away the plates and see if Lydia wanted a drink. Lydia ordered club soda with a splash of orange juice, Bobby got another beer, and I got coffee. When the table was clear, I lit a cigarette, said to Lydia, "Did you find anything?"

"Well, I have what you wanted."

"True."

She shot me a look as she pulled a file folder from her black leather shoulder bag. "Anyway," she said pointedly, and read from the file: "The Bronx Home for the Aged is owned and run by a not-for-profit called Helping Hands, Inc. They're very highly regarded in the industry."

"The not-for-profit 'industry'? They call it that?" My mind went back to the caustic Dr. Madsen.

"That's right," Lydia said.

"Okay. Go on."

"Helping Hands owns a bunch of other institutions in the Bronx. Two other nursing homes, three drug rehab centers, a group home for multiply handicapped people, another for juveniles, and a halfway house for ex-cons. Their administrative offices are at the Bronx Home. They were established eight years ago. I have a list of the administrative staff, if you want that, and the Board of Directors."

"Is there anyone interesting on them?"

"I'm sure they're all fascinating people. Do you want me to check them out?"

"Yes." I picked up the list of the Board of Directors. None of the names were familiar, with one exception.

"Hey," I said.

Lydia leaned close to read over my shoulder. There were blue glints in her short, asymmetrically cut hair. "What do you see?"

"Arthur Chaiken. Chairman of the Board."

"You know him?"

"I worked for him a few times. He's a lawyer. God, that was years ago."

"What's he like?"

"He's a bulldog. Pleasant guy, unless his clients are threatened. If he's your lawyer, he's yours. He'd sit on a bomb for you."

"Does he win?" Lydia asked.

"Used to, when I knew him. Wore everyone else out, if he had to. I remember some late nights and long days, working for him."

"Do you want me to check him out? Or do you know him well enough already?"

"Do him, but save him for the second round. Let's get in some preliminary stuff first."

"What are you thinking?"

"Damned if I know. I'm thinking we should follow any path we can find, since we don't know where we're going." I put my cigarette out. "And there's something else. There's a street gang over there called the Cobras. A guy named Anthony LeMoyne, who calls himself Snake, and a fat guy called Skeletor. See what you can dig up on them, okay?"

"Sure, boss. Anything else?"

"Yeah. Thumbnail backgrounds on everyone who works at the Bronx Home."

"Everyone?"

"Start with the professional staff. But before that, start with Mrs. Wyckoff."

"The—" Lydia shuffled her papers. "The Executive Director?"

"Right. Bobby, do you know her first name?"

"I didn't know she had one."

"I'll bet no one calls her by it," I agreed.

"Francine," Lydia said, from her list.

"Okay. Francine. And who did the backgrounds on your own guys, Bobby?"

"My guys?" Bobby frowned, but he didn't argue with me. "I did."

"Get them to Lydia too, okay? For the guys who work out there now, and guys who used to."

Lydia finished her soda. "It sounds like I'll have enough to do tomorrow. And what'll you be doing while I'm buried in paperwork?"

"Pining away because you don't love me."

She grinned, threw a look at Bobby, shook her head. As always, she thought I was kidding around.

ELEVEN

I drove Lydia home. The streets of lower Manhattan were as empty as they get, a few trucks rumbling, some late-model sports cars zipping home to New Jersey. The buildings stood square and black against the clear night sky.

"Mr. Moran calls you 'kid,' the way Shorty does." Lydia's face was eerie in the sodium streetlight. "Why do they do that?"

"You mean when I'm so obviously not one?"

"Well, unless you count adolescent behavior."

I ignored that. "I was a kid when I met them. There was a tight group of guys who were friends of my uncle Dave's. Cops, mostly. Dave called me 'kid,' so they all picked it up."

"Your uncle Dave was the one you lived with?"

"For a few years. I moved in with him when I was fifteen. When I was seventeen I joined the Navy."

"Why did you do that?" She waited, then added, "Unless it's none of my business?"

"No, no, it's okay." The moon, bright and almost full, slipped for a moment from behind the old Western Union building, then hid again behind something else. "I joined the Navy because I was trouble for Dave." I wasn't sure that was the question she was asking, but I didn't want to answer the other one.

We stopped at a light. From a black custom Camaro next to us came the pounding boom of heavy metal and the sweet smell of marijuana.

Lydia said, "Trouble?"

I lit a cigarette. "Those were bad years for me. If it hadn't been for Dave I'd have a rap sheet a mile long, but all the cops in the neighborhood knew I was Captain Maguire's kid."

The light changed; the Camaro smoked out and was gone.

Lydia was looking at me curiously. "I didn't know that about you."

"No. Most people don't."

She was quiet; then she said, "And the Navy?"

I swung the car left onto Canal.

"The night I got arrested for maybe the twentieth time, the cops who picked me up knew Dave, so they didn't even book me. They called him to come down." I studied the empty road ahead as though driving it took great concentration. "I still remember the room where they put me, at the precinct. Bright lights, no windows. Hot and smelly. They left me there for a long time. When Dave finally came, he told me he'd had it. I could stay where I was, or I could join the service."

Lydia was silent beside me.

"There was something in his eyes when he said that that was never there before. The next day I enlisted. My father was Army; nothing would have gotten me into the Army. Dave had been in the Navy."

Lydia's eyes searched my face, but she didn't ask the other question.

I worked my way into Chinatown, pulled over in front of the old brick walk-up on Mosco Street.

"I'll call you in the middle of the day," I told her. "And we'll have dinner tomorrow?"

"Okay." She made no move to get out of the car, but sat for a minute, looking over the street. "Bill? Nobody said anything tonight about Mike Downey's enemies."

I nodded. "And you're thinking that's where we really ought to start."

"Well, shouldn't we?"

"Uh-huh. And I'm going to work on that end. But I don't want to bring Bobby into that, yet."

"I thought maybe that was it. That's why I didn't say anything at the bar."

I kissed her lightly. "Thanks." As she started out of the car, I said, "Lydia?"

She closed the door, leaned in the window.

"Bobby may be wrong about all of this," I said. "The cops may be right. There may be nothing to find."

Her eyes were gentle. "Then we'll find that," she said. "Then we'll know." She smiled, turned to go.

"Hey, Lydia?" She turned back to me. "Give your mother my love."

Her smile became a grin. "If I gave her your love, she'd take something for it. She thinks it's a disease." She straightened, walked away. I waited until she was inside her building, then drove home in an empty car.

The sharp ringing of the phone cut through the darkness, brought me groggily out of someplace where dark shapes slid through glistening black water. I groped for the receiver, rasped, "Smith." I coughed. The clock next to the bed read three.

"Kid? Kid, wake up. It's Bobby."

"Yeah. I'm up. What?" I rubbed my face, cursed as my hand pressed the bruise I'd forgotten.

A second's silence; then, "Henry Howe. My night super out at the Home. He's dead."

The black water vanished in the electric charge that flew up my spine. "What happened?"

"Like Mike." Bobby's voice was tight. "Beat to shit. In the back, in the parking lot."

"When?"

"I don't know. He comes on at midnight. Sometime between then and now."

"Where are you?"

"Home. They just called me."

"When'd they find him?"

"Just now."

"Okay. I'll meet you out there. Half an hour."

"It may take me longer." Which meant: get out there, take care of things.

"It'll take me less, Bobby."

I pulled on some clothes, the .38, the windbreaker over it. I sprinted the two blocks to the parking lot where I kept my car. Fifteen minutes later I swung off the Deegan where the round hulk of Yankee Stadium loomed over the neighborhood like a brooding UFO. I cut up to the Concourse, and then it was six empty blocks to the Home. Empty; but when I got there, it was as if all the activity from the deserted streets had been drawn to the Home like filings to a magnet.

Three patrol cars with circling red and yellow lights were parked near the entrance to the lot, and an unmarked one slanted onto the sidewalk. Their radios squawked and hissed. A Samaritan Hospital ambulance was pulling away; an EMS one stood in the street, paramedics leaning on it, waiting. The Crime Scene wagon was across the street.

People milled around outside the gate, the crowd you can count on whenever there's anything to see. A cop was waving them on, telling them go home, there's nothing to see. Inside the lot were cops in uniform and cops in suits. In a corner, above some parked cars, floodlights had been strung. They threw bright, flat light and sharp shadows. There were technicians, a photographer, a guy moving along the ground picking up things and bagging them.

And at the eye of this crime-scene storm was a motionless man-shaped lump on the pavement.

I parked on the sidewalk to keep out of the way. At the gate the cop told me go home, there's nothing to see.

"I want to talk to the detective in charge."

"Yeah? Who does that make you?" He was young and tough and doing something official.

"I'm Smith. I work for Moran."

"Oh, yeah?" He looked me over with a spark of interest, then hollered over his shoulder. "Hey, Lieutenant! Got something for you."

A black man in a gray suit was standing in the glaring lights next to Henry Howe's body. He looked up and found the young cop, who lifted a thumb in my direction. The black man walked around the body, toward me.

"I'm Lieutenant Robinson." He was about my age, with a mustache like Lindfors's and pale blue eyes. His gold shield hung on his jacket pocket.

"Bill Smith. I'm with Moran." I took out my wallet, showed him what he wanted to see.

"Where's Mr. Moran?"

"On his way." I pocketed my wallet. "Can I see him?"

"Who? The stiff?" He looked at me for a few beats. "Can you do the I.D.?"

"I don't know."

We walked through the gate into the lot. "Why're you here?" Robinson asked.

"Mr. Moran asked me to come down to see what I could do."

Robinson snorted. "Not a damn thing, that's what you can do."

We stopped; I looked down at Henry Howe.

He lay on his back, one leg bent impossibly under him. His uniform shirt had pulled up out of his trousers; in the harsh lights his exposed belly was purple and black. Blood crusted in his red hair, blotched his shirtfront, streaked the hand twisted over his chest. His face was a mass of darkened, pulpy flesh. One eye stared blind. The other was gone. There was blood underneath him, too, on the unforgiving asphalt.

The stench was overpowering; Howe had lost control before he died. My stomach turned over, but I felt Robinson's eyes on me, and I didn't look away.

"You all right?" Robinson asked, less solicitous than information-gathering.

"Yeah."

"That him? Henry Howe?"

"I think so. I only met him yesterday." I made myself look closely at what was in front of me. Robinson looked closely at me. "Yes, that's him."

"Sure? Otherwise I'll have Moran I.D. him, or one of the other guards. Because I don't know if Howe had family, but if he did I don't want to have to ask them."

"No, it's him." I was hoping they'd get Howe covered and out before Bobby got there. "Was he shot?"

"Shot?" Robinson repeated carefully. "Why should he have been shot? He was beaten to death."

"If this was a Cobra hit, he'll have been shot too."

"Why should it have been a Cobra hit?"

"Isn't that how the Cobras operate?"

"How do you know?"

"Hank Lindfors told me. Is he here?"

"Lindfors." Robinson looked at me in a new way. "I sent for Lindfors. He's on his way. You a friend of Lindfors's?"

"I had a drink with him this afternoon." I sidestepped the question. "He told me about the Cobras."

Robinson had another question ready, but he didn't get to ask it. A wailing siren pulled to the mouth of the lot, a car door slammed, and a few seconds later Lindfors lurched into the lights. His raincoat was open. His shirt had been buttoned wrong and it pulled across his chest. Breathing noisily, he came on a few steps, stopped still when he reached the body. He stared at it, swaying a little; then he swore heavily under his breath.

"Hank," said Robinson.

Lindfors jerked his head up, spotted Robinson. He started to say something. Then he saw me. "Ah, shit! What's this asshole doing here? Get rid of him! Fucking civilians—"

"Hey, Hank, back off," Robinson said. "He's with Moran. He I.D.'d the vic. Besides, I thought he was a friend of yours."

Lindfors looked at me, then barked a bitter laugh. "Oh, yeah. A butt-hole buddy." He turned back to Robinson. "What do you have?"

"Not much yet. He's been dead under an hour. That checks out with what the other guard, Turner, told us." Robinson gestured across the lot to the open door of a patrol car. For the first time I saw the young man in the Moran uniform who sat in the back seat, pale and staring.

"One of our guys?" I asked, stretching the pronoun. "Can I talk to him?"

"No."

"Yes," said Robinson, with a sharp look at Lindfors. "He's already given us a statement. I'm not ready for him to leave yet, though."

"Okay. Thanks. See you, Lindfors." Lindfors stared after me, then turned back to Robinson. If he said something, I didn't catch it.

TWELVE

The kid in the car looked at me through puffy eyes as I got in beside him. He'd been chewing on one knuckle; as I sat and shifted to face him, he pulled that hand down into his lap and covered it with the other, as though he'd have to force it to stay there.

"Turner?" I said gently. "I'm Bill Smith. Bobby Moran asked me to come down." I showed him my Moran I.D.

"I guess he's pissed." Turner's voice snagged in his

throat. "I guess he's pissed, Mr. Moran."

"Why should he be?"

"Because I wasn't—because Mr. Howe went—he said I—" The knuckle flew back to his mouth, got pulled away again.

I shook my head. "I don't think he's pissed, Turner. Not at you. But he's upset and he wants to know what happened here. Can you tell me?"

"I—I didn't—"

The patrol car smelled of coffee and greasy fries. A Mac-Donald's bag was crumpled on the dash. I took my Kents from my pocket, offered the pack to Turner. His hand trembled. I lit one for him, and one for myself.

"What was Howe doing out here, Turner? Supervisor does the front door, isn't that the way it is? It was late for break and early for mealtime. Why was he out here?"

I made the question long to give Turner a chance to get used to me. It seemed to work. "We were shooting the shit, you know, just for a minute, when I was coming through. 'Cause it was quiet, and . . . and . . ." He took a deep drag on the cigarette held stiffly between his fingers.

"Okay, Turner. That's okay. What happened?"

"He—Mr. Howe—his beeper went off, and he said, shit, he had to make a call, and I should watch the desk, it might take a few minutes, but that was okay, he was the supervisor and he, he was telling me to do it. . . ." Turner looked at me earnestly.

"It's okay, Turner. You did the right thing. What happened then?"

Turner swallowed, pulled on the cigarette. He coughed on the smoke. "Well, nothing happened. Nothing happened. He didn't come back. I thought he was just going downstairs, to make his call, but it got to be half an hour. Christ, it was quiet in there! So he didn't come back. I didn't know what to do. Christ, what was I supposed to do? It was quiet and I—"

"Turner!" I said sharply. His eyes widened and his knuckle jumped into his mouth again. My voice was much gentler as I said, "Turner, I know it's been tough. But you've got to stay with me. Take me through it once, Turner. Just what happened, what you did. Can you do that?"

His eyes looked into mine. He took the hand slowly from his mouth, nodded at me. I waited.

Deliberately, slowly, he said, "I came down and talked to the back-door guy, Morales. He said Mr. Howe had gone out the back. So I . . . I came out here to look for him." His knuckle hand started to move up; he pulled it down, took a drag on the cigarette instead. "I was thinking about Mike when I came out. When I found Mr. Howe I got sick, when I saw him, but it was like I wasn't surprised. Like I expected it, you know?" His voice caught again.

"Turner, tell me exactly what you saw when you came out here."

"I saw him—Mr. Howe. I didn't touch him. I—like I said, I got sick. In the bushes, over there. Then I ran back and—" he stopped, rubbed the sweat from his upper lip— "and I told Morales to call the police."

"Did you see anything else out here? Any movement, shadows, anything? Did you hear anything?"

Turner shook his head emphatically. "It was real quiet. Just my footsteps—they were loud." He paused. "I came back out. While Morales was calling. Because . . . I sort of thought that's what I was supposed to do. But I stayed over there. I couldn't get close to him."

"Okay, Turner." I finished my cigarette, stubbed it out in the patrol car ashtray. "The cops want to talk to you again; they'll tell you when you can leave. I'm going to find Morales."

"He's inside," Turner said helpfully. "He's still at the door."

"Okay. Thanks. Listen, Turner? You didn't do anything wrong, okay? You did what your supervisor told you to do; that was right. And coming back out here to wait for the police, that was right, too."

He looked at me, looked away, put the knuckle in his mouth. He took it out to whisper, "It was my shift, Mr. Smith. It was supposed to be me."

Morales was indeed at the door, at the desk where I'd sat talking with Fuentes half a day earlier. He was a heavyset Latino with thick black sideburns and a pitted face. I identified myself to him.

"Oh, good," he said with what seemed like relief. "Good. You gonna be in charge now?"

"Until Mr. Moran gets here."

"Good," he repeated. "Gotta have somebody in charge. Gotta have that."

"Morales, tell me what happened." I didn't quote Turner's story at all; I wanted to see if their stories matched.

"Well, I already told the cops . . ." He seemed a little uncertain what to do, what proper procedure was.

"Good. Now tell me."

Once was a request; twice was an order. Morales laid his pudgy forearms along the desk, leaned forward. "See, Mr. Howe, he went out, I guess about three. I didn't think about it till Turner, he came down lookin' for him. He said Mr. Howe said he was goin' to make a phone call. But, see, you can't make no phone call from outside round here. They're always tearin' up the phones, you know? The kids."

"Where did you think Howe was going, when he went out?"

"What he told me, he was goin' to get a sandwich."

"You didn't think that was strange in the middle of the night?"

"Well, sure, I thought it was strange. I wouldn't go out around here at three in the mornin'. But he did it all the time."

"Did what?"

"Went out at meal break. He took his break at four, an' maybe once a week he'd go to the all-night bodega down there an' get a sandwich an' a coupla beers. He was in charge, so I never said nothin'."

"How did he seem to you? Tonight."

Morales shrugged. "Like he always seemed. Friendly an' a little full a shit."

"Okay. What happened next?"

"Well, so Turner, he went out, an' a couple minutes later he comes runnin' back in, lookin' terrible, and he tell me, call the cops, cause Mr. Howe, he's out there an' he's dead."

"What did you do?"

"I call the ambulance, like it says here on the card, an' then I call the cops." He tapped the telephone on the desk. On it was a typed card with a list of emergency numbers.

Samaritan Hospital was at the top; it was their ambulance I had seen leaving. They must have decided that there wasn't much for them to do, so they left it for the EMS crew, who knew the way to the morgue.

"Then I call Mrs. Wyckoff."

"She's coming down here?" I hadn't thought of that, but of course it made sense.

"I guess. It says on the card, you gotta do that, in a emergency."

"Moráles, did you hear anything from outside in the time Howe was gone?"

"Uh-uh. Nothin'. I'd a gone out if I'd heard somethin'. To check it out, you know. That's my job."

"And you didn't go out with Turner, after you called the cops? You didn't go see the body?"

Morales looked at me blankly. "Why do I wanna do that? Turner says he's dead, Turner says he's all covered with blood. Why do I wanna see that?"

I couldn't answer that question, so I asked another. "You were on duty three nights ago, weren't you? When Mike Downey was killed?" I knew he had been. Bobby had told me about Morales, who had been down here in the back, doing his job, and hadn't heard a thing.

"*Sí,* I was here."

"And you didn't hear anything then, either?"

"Well, see, that was in the front. Can't hear nothin' in the front from down here." He scratched his head with a hairy hand. "Mr. Moran, he offer to change my shift after that. Me and Mr. Howe both, if we want. But I tell him no, I stay here, workin' nights. 'Cause, you know, that's my job."

I left Morales doing his job. There was another question that had occurred to me to ask Turner, but there was something I wanted to do first.

Pete Portelli's small office off the boiler room was locked. I had expected that. I took what I needed from my wallet and got to work. It was an old, simple lock; it took me under two minutes.

I groped for the light switch. The fluorescent tubes revealed the room in its paper-strewn glory. The overflowing ashtray and the dregs of a bottle of Schlitz perfumed the air.

It didn't look like much to me, but a pig like Portelli sometimes has a photographic memory for his sty, so I was careful to touch nothing except what I'd come for. I slid open the desk drawer, pulled out the manila folder, read down the scrawled names on the locker list until I came to "Howe." Number six; that was all I wanted to know.

I slipped the folder back in the drawer and the drawer back in the desk, turned out the light, closed the door behind me. I moved soundlessly down the hall to the other side of the boiler room. In the dim light from the high windows the old, dented lockers stood like tired soldiers far from battle and far from home.

Number six had a combination lock on it. I gave it three minutes and then gave up, picked the lock on the workshop down the hall, came back with a pair of bolt cutters. I snipped the lock and put it in my pocket.

I worked Howe's locker from the top down, so that anything I knocked down or dropped I'd eventually find. There was no door on this room, so I didn't dare turn the light on; Morales might see it, though he wasn't close. As my eyes got used to the dimness I felt my way through Howe's things: two magazines and a pair of canvas gloves on the shelf, blue jeans and a shirt hanging on the hooks, an old leather belt threaded through the jeans. Nothing in the pockets. On the floor, a pair of big rubber boots.

And in the right boot, wrapped with a rubber band, six thousand dollars in cash. My eyes had adjusted to the darkness by then; I was able to count it.

THIRTEEN

I got back outside in time to see Mrs. Wyckoff drive up in a late-model Lincoln. Bobby was already there, watching as the paramedics loaded Howe's draped body through the ambulance doors.

Bobby looked terrible. His face was gray and drawn, his eyes sunken. He leaned on a cane. I hadn't seen him use the cane in over a year.

"Hey, kid," he said quietly as I came up next to him.

"Hi," I said. "You okay?"

"Feel like shit." He nodded toward the ambulance. "You get a look at him?"

"Yes."

"That's what Mike looked like, too."

I lit a cigarette. The ambulance backed out of the gate with insistent beeps.

"I talked to Turner," I told Bobby. "He's over there in the patrol car. And Morales; he's still at his post."

"And they didn't see a damn thing. Right?"

"That's what they say."

"What was Howe doing outside? Either of them got any idea?"

"Turner says he went to make a phone call. Morales says he went out for a sandwich."

"A sandwich? Around here in the middle of the night?"

"A phone call? In the parking lot?"

Bobby scowled. "I guess I better talk to them."

"Bobby, tell me something first. Do your guys wear beepers?"

"Beepers? No. Sometimes radios, if there's no phone around, but mostly not. Why?"

"Maybe nothing. But Howe was wearing one."

I wanted to tell him Turner's whole story, but that would have to wait. Homing in on us, wrapped in a beige trench-coat, wearing a beige-and-green silk scarf to hold her piled hair against the wind, was Mrs. Wyckoff.

Her eyes were small slits in her stark-white face, her jaw clenched so tight I could see the white line of her jawbone running up to her ear. She came on with her head down and shoulders forward, like a fighter looking for an opening. I pitched my cigarette away.

"Mr. Moran!" Mrs. Wyckoff's bark was thrown at us by the wind. "What's going on here? How could this possibly happen?"

"I wish I knew," Bobby said, in flat tones.

She jammed to a halt, her body quivering as though she were trying to keep herself from plowing right through us. "What sort of security firm are you? My God! You expect me to tell people they're safe here when you can't even keep your guards safe? You're useless! Worse than useless! I should have let you go when—'' She stopped suddenly. She swallowed, with effort; maybe she was swallowing words she really wanted to say.

The corner of the parking lot went black like a closed film set as the technicians turned off the lights, began packing up.

Mrs. Wyckoff breathed in deeply. Her body straightened and her head tilted back. She resumed the posture I'd seen that afternoon, the one where she looked down her nose.

"Well, that's as may be," she said. "I'm letting you go now. I'll be calling another firm in the morning. As soon as they're ready to start, I want your guards off this property."

Since he'd first seen her coming, Bobby's eyes hadn't left her face. He didn't answer her now, but he didn't look away either.

She flushed, as though silence was the one answer she hadn't been prepared for. "Really, Mr. Moran, this situation is unacceptable!" she sputtered.

"Mrs. Wyckoff, I don't think much of it either." Bobby held her eyes a moment longer. Then he turned, and, leaning on the cane, walked slowly toward the patrol car where Turner still sat.

The Crime Scene wagon rolled into the lot. Lights clanked and electrical cords thudded as the technicians loaded it. Mrs. Wyckoff slipped a sidelong look at me. In a defensive tone she said, "I suppose you're thinking I shouldn't have spoken so harshly to an old man."

"He's sixty-one," I answered. "And you have no idea what I'm thinking."

She flushed again, a deep crimson. Narrowing her eyes, she asked me, "Just who are you?"

"Smith. I work for Mr. Moran."

"I know that," she snapped. "Why are you here?"

"Mr. Moran asked me to come help handle this."

"There are men who've worked here a good deal longer than you. I would have thought one of them would have been a more appropriate choice."

"Since you just fired this firm, what difference does it make to you how Mr. Moran runs it?" *Oh, shut up,* I told myself angrily. You're just what Bobby needs now, a big-mouthed idiot to completely alienate the client.

Mrs. Wyckoff seemed to agree with that thought. She

stared at me a moment longer, then dug her hands into her
coat pockets, spun and stalked away.

It didn't seem to be my night for making friends, so I thought
I might as well have another shot at Lindfors.

He was leaning on a car drinking coffee from a cardboard
cup. Two other full cups and two half-full sat in a box on the
hood; a dozen or so empties were being pushed around the
parking lot by the wind.

Lindfors's hard eyes followed my approach. He said nothing as I leaned next to him on the car, but he nodded his head
in the direction of the coffee box.

"Sure?" I asked.

He shrugged. "Taxpayers won't mind."

"Thanks." I peeled the plastic lid off a cup. The coffee
was only lukewarm, smelled and tasted burnt, but it was coffee.

Lindfors's eyes, from close up, were bloodshot, and he
squinted as though even the four a.m. darkness hurt. He kept
his gaze on Robinson, whose shoulders sagged as he stood
across the parking lot talking to Mrs. Wyckoff. Sipping coffee, Lindfors said, "You're gonna ask me if he was shot."

I watched Mrs. Wyckoff wave her arms like a bird threatening to peck out Robinson's eyes. "Was he?"

Lindfors drained his cup, crumpled it in his fist. He tossed
it in a high arc over the fence. I heard it bounce on the sidewalk on the other side.

"Maybe."

"Oh, Christ, Lindfors, give it a rest. We're after the same
thing, you and I."

Lindfors pressed his thumb and forefinger against his
eyes. "Ah, shit. I got a headache the size of New Jersey, and
a fucking P.I. preaching to me. The problem I got is, which
is worse?"

I straightened up from the car. "Thanks for the coffee." I
started to walk away.

"Smith!"

I turned.

"In the foot. But not with his own gun."

"I didn't know he was wearing one."

"In his back." Lindfors pressed his hand to the small of his own back. "They missed it."

Behind Lindfors, on the street, one of the patrol cars pulled away. The excitement here was winding down.

"So what do you think?" I asked.

"What do I think? I think they were so fucked up and stupid they forgot the rules."

"That means it wasn't LeMoyne personally?"

Lindfors grinned nastily. He held up an invisible something between thumb and forefinger. "This is LeMoyne." He mimed cracking an egg, dropping it in a pan. He made a sizzling noise in his teeth. "This is LeMoyne on drugs. Any questions?"

I looked at the hard glint in his eye, at his scornful grin. "If I have any," I said, "I'll know where to call."

Bobby was working his way out of the patrol car when I walked over. Turner still sat pressed against the door on the other side. I put a hand under Bobby's arm; he let me help him stand.

We walked a few paces from the car. The wind was bullying the paper birches, not letting them rest, though their branches drooped wearily. I asked, "How is he?"

"He's a twenty-two-year-old kid who's thinking he could've been dead two hours already."

I looked over at Turner, back to Bobby. "How are you?"

Lips pressed tight, he shook his head impatiently, waved away the question without giving it an answer.

All right, then. "What do you think of Turner's story?"

Bobby glanced over his shoulder into the car. "I think it's true."

"So do I. Can I ask him something else?"

"It's your investigation, kid. Ask him whatever you want."

"Bobby . . ." I paused, thinking of Howe, who he might have been; Mike, what he might have been doing. "Bobby, are you still sure you want an investigation?"

"Why the hell not? Because we've been fired? So what?"

"Lindfors thinks there's nothing to investigate. He thinks it's the Cobras, doing what they do."

"You believe that?"

"It could be true."

"Do you believe it, kid?"

"I don't know."

Bobby looked down at the ground, whacked at a stone with his cane. "Shit, kid. Maybe that bitch is right. Maybe I'm fucking useless. But Mike didn't know that and Howe didn't know that. I let those guys down, kid. I can't live with that."

"Jesus, Bobby!"

Turner, in the car, looked up; Lindfors swiveled his head in our direction. I lowered my voice. "What the hell do you think would be different if you could walk right? You've had guys working night shifts for years, and God knows you've had guys in trouble before. Whatever happened to Mike and Howe didn't happen because you had a stroke."

His eyes flared. He seemed about to say something, but he didn't. With a jerky motion he turned his back on me, started across the lot. I stood for a moment, then loped after him, grabbed his arm.

"Bobby, wait."

He stopped, but he didn't look at me.

"I don't know what happened out here," I said. "My brain says Lindfors may be right and my gut says he's wrong. But whatever it was, it wasn't your fault."

Bobby's voice was harsh and low. "I owe those guys, kid. I owe them and I can't pay by myself."

"You don't have to."

He turned to face me. "You're still with me?"

"Oh, Christ, Bobby, of course I'm with you. But I'm not going to start watching what I say to you because of that goddamn shillelagh you're leaning on."

Bobby looked down at the cane, then up at me again. "That's good. Because if you ever did, I'd brain you with it."

We grinned at each other in the wind, in the parking lot, in the middle of the night.

And about the cash in Howe's locker and the gun in his belt, I said nothing.

FOURTEEN

In the Home's dim corridors the silence was as thick as a blanket, but not as comforting. Behind the security desk I zipped my jacket against the chill that comes from exhaustion, not weather. I shifted in my chair, looking for a position uncomfortable enough to help me stay awake. I couldn't find one.

There was a cop out front and a cop out back, Robinson's way of placating Mrs. Wyckoff and getting out of here. Bobby had intended to finish Howe's shift himself, but I'd talked him into letting me do it. I'd told him the three hours' sleep I'd get if I went home now and came back at eight would be worse than none at all. That would have been true when I was younger; but I'd been in this hushed, dim hall for half an hour now and the idea of any sleep, even ten minutes' worth, was beginning to have the appeal of a watery mirage in Death Valley.

As I thought about mirages one formed at the limit of my vision, in the shadows down the hall. I squinted, blinked. Human-shaped, draped in pale cloth, it crept toward me with halting, soundless steps. Just beyond the small circle of light cast by the desk lamp it stopped, peered at me with its chin thrust forward.

"It's you," it whispered.

"Mrs. Goldstein?" My voice was surprisingly loud.

Ida Goldstein, in a light-blue robe and crocheted slippers, put her finger to her mouth. "Shh!"

I stood, asked softly, "Mrs. Goldstein, what are you doing down here?"

"That's a stupid question," she snapped in a stage whisper. "Who could sleep with all this commotion?"

"The commotion's over," I said. "It's been quiet for half an hour."

"Well, of course. I had to wait until it was quiet or some snooty nurse would have sent me back to my room like a bad little girl. What are you doing here?"

"I work here."

"You work here during the day. Don't patronize me."

"I didn't mean to." I thought about what to say to her. "I've had to take over this shift, just tonight."

"Something else terrible has happened, hasn't it?" Her sharp blue eyes drilled into mine. "Someone else is dead."

I didn't answer right away. I saw her jaw tighten and thrust upward again, and I saw fear behind her eyes.

"Yes," I said. "The night supervisor. Henry Howe."

Her chin quavered, but otherwise she didn't move. "Was it—was it like the other time? In the garden?"

"It was like the other time. But not in the garden. Out back, in the parking lot."

"Did the police wake the people on that side? Did anyone hear the argument?"

"The police will be back in the morning to talk to the residents. There probably wasn't an argument."

"Why wouldn't there have been?"

"I—" I wasn't sure how to tell her what I wanted to. "Mrs. Goldstein, this wasn't the kind of thing where people who know each other argue and one loses control and attacks the other. It was a different kind of crime. I know it seems more frightening, but—"

"You said it was like the other time."

"It was."

"The other time there was an argument."

I stopped, my clumsy reassurances unfinished. "What are you saying?"

"I'm saying there was an argument," she answered impatiently. "It woke me up. When I came down for my cocoa I asked Mr. Howe—" Her already pale face paled further. "Oh, dear. Poor Mr. Howe . . ." She pulled her bathrobe closer, turned away from me.

I went around the desk, touched her bony shoulders. "Mrs. Goldstein—"

"Oh, call me Ida, if you're going to put your hands all over me."

"Ida. Sit down." I pulled the chair close. She clung to my arm as she lowered herself. I perched on the edge of the desk. "Ida, tell me about the argument."

"You said there wasn't one."

"The other time."

She gave me a sly sideways look. "Maybe there wasn't one the other time either."

"Ida, please. This may be important."

"That's what I thought, but everyone else thought it was just Ida being a busybody."

"Who's everyone?"

"Mr. Howe," she said. "The Boss Lady. And that crude police detective, the one who drinks."

"Hank Lindfors?" I described him.

"Yes, that's him."

"And the Boss Lady, that's Mrs. Wyckoff?"

"Of course."

"Tell me what you told them."

"I told them I heard an argument outside in the garden. It woke me. Well, everything wakes me. That's why they moved my room, because it was so noisy on the street side of the building."

"Yes, you told me about that." I tried to curb my impatience. "Tell me about the argument. When was it?"

"I *was* telling you, if you'd stop interrupting. It was just after three."

Mike Downey had died sometime between three and four.

"How do you know?"

"I can still read a . . . a . . . I can tell time!" She blew out an exasperated sigh. "I tried to get back to sleep, but I couldn't, so I came down for a cup of cocoa. I always check the time first, because when there are people around it's risky. Closer to morning, I wouldn't have come."

"Risky?"

"If they think you're wandering—" she raised and fluttered her hands when she said this, in a minstrel-show evocation of fright— "they lock your room at night."

"They lock you in?"

She looked at me, her jaw set, the fear in her eyes almost hidden but not gone. "I have some advice for you," she said. "Don't get old."

I had no answer to that. I watched the pattern on the carpet as it disappeared beyond the light.

She cleared her throat. "I didn't hear the words."

"Sorry?" I pulled my eyes back to meet hers.

"The argument. It was two men, I think, but I couldn't hear the words."

"Did you recognize the voices?"

"Not really. I thought one of them was . . . the boy who was killed. . . ."

"Mike?"

She nodded. "I thought that when I heard them, but maybe that's only because I expected him to be in the garden."

"And the other?"

"It wasn't very loud. It could have been anybody."

"And you told the police about this?"

"I said I did."

I rubbed my chin, thinking. I reached for a cigarette, to help; then, remembering where I was, I started to put it back.

"Oh, smoke the stupid thing," Ida ordered. "It won't bother me. I gave it up before you were born. Besides, I'm going to get my cocoa." With an ungraceful motion she hoisted herself out of the chair.

I watched her move off slowly down the hall. I realized she wasn't so much lifting her feet as sliding them along the carpet. I wondered if a cane or a walker would help her; but as I wondered I also knew that, until the last possible moment, Ida Goldstein wouldn't use one.

I did smoke the cigarette, fashioning an ashtray out of a sheet of paper from the desk. I drank in the smoke, thinking about Mike Downey, and Henry Howe, and whether the brutal sounds of bravado and fear could be classified as an argument.

A few minutes after the cigarette was gone Ida Goldstein came shuffling out of the kitchen door at the far end of the hall. Very carefully, in both hands, she gripped a tray, and on it two cups rattled in their saucers. I hurried down the hall and took the tray from her.

"Well, that's good," she said with relief. "I didn't make you cocoa. I made you coffee."

"I didn't expect you to make me anything."

"Don't you want it?"

"Desperately. But I don't think you're supposed to be making me coffee at four in the morning."

"Actually I'm not supposed to be in the kitchen at all and you were very bad to let me go there."

"I didn't know that."

"Ignorance of the law is no excuse." She sat herself on the chair again, sipped at her cocoa. She didn't look at me.

I picked up the coffee cup. Coffee had slopped out over the side; the bottom of the cup was wet. I said, "Ida, are you all right? There are police outside, and the doors are locked. You don't have to be afraid."

"I'm afraid," she said, in a voice so low I had trouble hearing her. "But that's not why." She cradled her cup in her lap, looked into the darkness that led to the glass entrance doors. Outside, in the garden, the black forms of branches swayed with the wind, obscuring, revealing, obscuring the streetlights that glowed beyond the garden wall.

"Why then?"

"Because," she said, with an angry quaver to her voice, "because I've been talking to you for half an hour and I still can't remember your name."

Into the endless, empty silence I said, "Bill. Bill Smith. It's an easy name to forget."

"No, it's not! Damn you—!" She clinked her cup onto the tray, struggled to her feet. "I'm going back to bed." Without another word, she started jerkily down the corridor she had come from.

"Mrs. Goldstein?" I called. "Ida?"

She stopped, half turned. "What do you want?"

"Thank you. For the coffee."

She didn't look at me, but after a moment she said gruffly, "You're welcome. Good night." I watched as she shuffled down the corridor, past the elevator, to the stairwell door at the far end. It must be a long climb, I thought, up two flights, at four in the morning. The elevator would have been easier, though risky: someone might hear it.

But I would have bet that wasn't why Ida didn't use it.

FIFTEEN

It was a long, long three hours until morning. I smoked some more cigarettes, paced up and down the halls. I played over the Schubert sonata in my head, felt my fingers twitch at the difficult passages. I stood at the front door, where the cool air carried the scent of autumn: dry leaves mixed with the perfume of the last roses. Beyond the wall a bus whined by. I couldn't see it.

As the sky began to pale in the hour before dawn I stood on the porch with the young cop who'd drawn garden duty. He was tall, with heavy-rimmed glasses, and so buck-toothed that he seemed to be grinning even when he wasn't. I asked him about the Cobras.

"Bad," he said. "The worst."

"What are they into? Drugs? Guns?"

"Some, probably." He took his glasses off, rubbed the bridge of his nose. "Shit, I gotta get contacts. You wear contacts?"

"No. Tell me about the Cobras."

"Never thought about contacts till yesterday. Basketball game, some asshole jammed me. Almost broke my nose." He resettled his glasses gingerly. "Mostly what they do is protection."

"Glasses?"

He laughed. "Glasses. Yeah, them too. I meant the Cobras."

The first sparrow of the morning twittered in the branches above us.

"Protection? How do you mean?"

"Well, protection's all the same, isn't it? The Cobras don't give a shit who does what, long as they get their cut." He took off his glasses again, examined them. "They got this new kind now. You never have to clean 'em. You just wear 'em and throw 'em away."

That must be contacts. I declined the new conversational gambit, went back to the Cobras. "You mean other people run rackets in the Cobras' territory?"

"Sure. Lots of little entrepreneurs. The more the merrier. Makes the take bigger."

"What if they don't get their cut?"

He twirled his glasses by an earpiece. "You heard about that trucker a couple weeks ago? They didn't kill him, just broke him up. That's how they send a bill."

"And if you don't pay it?"

"You gotta be kidding."

"Why?"

"You saw that guy. The stiff they pulled outta here tonight."

"You think the Cobras did that?"

He looked at me a little blankly. "Well, sure they did. Why else was Hank Lindfors here? Lieutenant Robinson wouldn't't've called him if it wasn't the Cobras."

"Lindfors is the Cobra specialist at the four-one?"

"He's the Cobra specialist in the whole world. You're so interested in the Cobras, why don't you ask him?" He looked at the glasses in his hand, rubbed his nose. "Wish I could see without these goddamn things. Wanna know what I think?"

I wasn't sure what subject he was thinking about, but I said, "Sure."

"I think the Cobras like it when they get their cut. I think they like it even better when they don't."

The soft gray sky was beginning to glow a clear red. From somewhere over my left shoulder came the call of a mourning dove; it was answered by another.

Dayton came on at seven, half an hour earlier than usual for him. Sharp rods of yellow light streaked through the trees as he came in the front door.

"How are you doing?" he asked me.

I stood. "I'm okay," I said. "You're a little early."

"I thought you might want to get some breakfast before you come on again." His dark eyes looked me over. His face didn't register anything he saw. "Mr. Moran called me this morning."

"I'm sorry, Dayton. I'm sorry about the job. I'm sorry about Howe."

"The job . . ." He paused. "Mr. Moran will find me another place. He always has. Though I will miss it here.'' He came around behind me, punched the time clock. ''Henry Howe . . .'' He didn't finish.

''You didn't like him much, did you?''

''I didn't care for him, no.'' Dayton settled in the chair I'd vacated. His back remained straight, his bearing military, as he lifted the clipboard off the desk, glanced over it. ''But that's no way for a man to end.''

''No, it's not,'' I said. ''What was he like?''

Dayton's eyes measured me before he answered. ''He was generous with unwanted advice. He thought most men fools.''

''He doesn't sound like Bobby Moran's kind of guy.''

''He was smart, and he wasn't a coward. Mr. Moran doesn't ask much more than that, from most men.''

I took Dayton up on his offer, headed out to get some breakfast before the day shift started. The deli down by the Courthouse, he told me, opened early.

I parked in Lou Gehrig Plaza, the glorified lot at the end of the park. To my right, beyond the el, Yankee Stadium shouldered one-story bars and shops aside to get itself some breathing room. I could see the upper rows of ballpark seats, empty, waiting until next year. The Yanks had trailed their division, this year.

The deli smelled like grease and toast and coffee, coffee, coffee. Plates clanked and people shouted to-go orders at the counterman. I found a table; a waiter appeared at my elbow instantly. I ordered scrambled eggs and bacon, and took my first cup of coffee to the phone by the door to call Lydia.

''God, it's early,'' she said when she answered. ''What's up?''

''There's trouble.'' I ran through what had happened— Howe's death, his gun, his cash.

She was silent for a moment. ''Why didn't you call me?''

''When? At four in the morning?''

''I'm working this case with you. I should have come up.''

''To do what?''

''Just to be there. Like you.''

''Lydia, what's wrong?''

"I—nothing. It's okay. Sometimes . . ." She paused again, then said, "Let's go into it later. I'm sorry. You must have had a horrible night and here I am giving you a hard time. What do you want me to do? Does this change things?"

She'd thrown me off balance. I recovered my thoughts, said, "From the police point of view, no. They're calling it just a repeat performance. But it does change things for us, in one way: after today I won't be on the inside anymore. I'm not sure what my next move is, but see what you can find out about Howe. And—" I stopped, watched a tall man with glasses, thinning hair, and a good blue suit walk past me into the deli. He worked his way to a table by the window, where he joined a younger man in an equally good suit who looked as though he'd been waiting.

"Bill? What is it?"

"Guess who's here?"

"I'm not good at that in the morning."

"Arthur Chaiken. And I'll bet there are lots of things you're good at in the morning."

"Bill, don't, okay?"

"Lydia—"

"Call me later?"

"Yeah," I said. "Yeah, okay. Sure."

We hung up. I went back to my table, where my eggs and bacon and buttered toast waited. I ate, watched Chaiken drink coffee while his companion ate a half-grapefruit and then a bagel, toasted but dry. Chaiken's shoulders were broad, his waist narrow, and though it was close to ten years since I'd seen him and he was close to twenty years older than I, his long, friendly face hadn't aged.

The younger man, who looked in his late thirties, had the square build and aggressive set of the shoulders college athletes develop. He had light eyes, rounded cheeks, fleshy lips: not handsome, but his movements were quick with energy and he had a ready smile. Chaiken, I remembered, was a squash player; that would account for his physique. I wondered what the other man did for sport.

I had a second cup of coffee; then, picking up my check, I stopped by Chaiken's table on my way to the cash register.

"Excuse me," I said. "Mr. Chaiken?"

Both men looked up. The younger man had been in the middle of a sentence, of which I caught the words, "don't have to worry about that."

I said, "You probably don't remember me. Bill Smith. I'm a private investigator. I used to work for you occasion-ally."

Chaiken's face melted into a smile. "Of course. How are you?" We shook hands. "God, that was years ago. That was another life."

The younger man was smiling too, waiting. Chaiken's hand stirred the air between us as he said, "This is Andy Hill. Andy's with the Bronx Borough President's office. Andy, Bill Smith. Damn good investigator, if you ever need one."

I shook hands with Andy Hill.

"It's not something the B.P. has much use for, but you never can tell," Hill said. His light eyes, looking directly into mine, had the very slight squint of the contact-lens wearer. Maybe I should ask him how he liked them, for the buck-toothed cop.

"Well, Smith, how are you?" Chaiken asked. "What have you been up to? Have you eaten, by the way? Want to join us?"

I thought I saw a flash of annoyance in Hill's eyes, but if it was there it was extinguished immediately.

"No, thanks," I said. "I have to get to work. As a matter of fact, starting yesterday and until the end of the day today I'm working for you."

He looked at me in confusion. "For me? I don't get it."

"As a guard, at the Bronx Home."

His face clouded. "Oh. The Home. Have you . . . do you know about last night?"

"I was there right after it happened."

He nodded; he didn't seem to know what to say after that. Hill also remained silent. Either he already knew about last night too, or he had no curiosity whatsoever.

Chaiken thought of something to say. "I understand Mrs. Wyckoff's dismissed that firm. Is that what you meant by 'until the end of the day?' "

I nodded. "She blames us. The guards, I mean."

"Well, you can see her point, can't you? That's why you

hire a security firm. To prevent exactly this sort of thing."

"If it's what it looks like."

He pursed his lips. The sunlight glinting in the window flashed off his horn-rimmed glasses, hid his eyes for a moment as he shifted in his chair to face me more directly. "What do you mean?"

"I'm not sure. The police say these are gang killings. Maybe so. But maybe they're something else."

"What else could it be?" Andy Hill wanted to know.

"I don't know. Something directed at the Home, maybe. To intimidate. Or for some other reason."

"What makes you say that?" Chaiken asked.

"Instinct." And the bullet in Mike's foot. And the gun in Howe's belt. And six thousand dollars in cash. The real question, I thought to myself, is what makes me say it to you.

Chaiken frowned, and Andy Hill frowned, and I looked at my watch. "I'd better go. It was good seeing you again, Mr. Chaiken."

"Good seeing you," he echoed. We shook hands again. Chaiken's hand was large, callused; Andy Hill's, which he wiped on a napkin before offering to me, was smaller and softer; but it was Chaiken's that was manicured.

I paid my bill, ordered a large black coffee to go. Outside, I stopped to light a cigarette in the bright Bronx sun. I felt a hand on my arm.

"Smith, wait." It was Arthur Chaiken. He seemed a little ill at ease. "Look, Smith, this may be none of my business, but are things all right with you?"

"With me?" I was surprised. "I'm fine. Why?"

He grinned. "Because you look like hell."

It came to me suddenly that besides the black eye and the sleepless night, I hadn't shaved since this time yesterday. I grinned too. "No, I'm fine. This is a tough neighborhood. I'm wearing my tough-guy disguise."

He smiled in answer to that, but then grew serious. "No, it's not just that. This security-guard thing—it's not what you used to do, is it?"

"I don't do it much. Bobby Moran is a friend of mine. I'm helping him out."

"Oh. That's good. I mean, it really is none of my business, but I heard about your uncle—what was it, four years ago . . . ?''

"Five."

He nodded. ''. . . and I heard you were badly hurt then. And when I saw you, just now . . . well, listen, Smith, if you need anything, a recommendation, contacts . . .''

"Thanks. I'll keep that in mind. But I'm really fine."

"Okay." He seemed to relax. "Well, I'm glad to hear that. Listen, call me, we'll get together for a drink. You still eat Chinese food with your clients at three in the morning?''

"If the client's buying."

I promised to call and he returned to the deli, rejoined Andy Hill. The thoughtful frown that Hill was wearing as he'd watched us through the glass turned to the easy smile again as Chaiken sat down.

SIXTEEN

I drove north of the Home to a hardware store near Fordham Road. Hardware stores always open early. Then I went back, put the car in the lot. The cop in the back, who'd let me out, let me in.

Morales was still at the back door, doing his job, just as I had been at the front, even though there were cops in the garden and cops in the lot. Overkill; but maybe that wasn't the right word.

Before I went to clock in I made a quick stop, in the dingy alcove where the lockers stood. I opened Howe's, felt in the boot. The hundred-dollar bill I'd put back, clipped to a note that said, "See me—Smith," was still there. I broke the blister packaging around the lock I'd just bought, memorized the combination, scuffed the lock around the concrete floor to kill the newness and snapped it onto the locker door.

As I was heading back down the corridor to the stairs Fuentes came in the back door.

''Buenos días,'' he greeted me and Morales. He didn't smile.

''Buenos días,'' Morales replied, although he didn't look convinced.

"Hi, Pablo," I said. "You heard?"

"*Sí.* Bad thing, man. Real bad."

We started up the stairs together. I asked, "Did you know him well? Henry Howe?"

He shook his head. "The evenin' guys and night guys, we don't never see them. If he didn't come down to talk to Pete sometimes before he goes, probably I wouldn't even know what he looks like. But I'm tellin' you, he was a funny guy."

"Funny?"

"Yeah." Fuentes rubbed a finger along his thin mustache. "He don't know me and I don't know him, you know? But one day he's comin' past me and I got this bandage like wrapped around my hand, 'cause I been fixin' the plumbin' at home and I got all the wrong tools. You know how it is, man, the kid needs shoes so you buy shoes, you don't buy no wrenches."

He stopped; I nodded, to confirm I knew how it was.

"So Howe, he ask what happen and I tell him. Couple days later, he come in, he got this damn set of wrenches, plumber's tools, you know? In the box, man. He tell me, take this, gotta keep the toilets flushin'. I say, man, I can't afford this. He say it's already paid for, don't worry about it. Someday, he say, maybe I can do somethin' for him. Then he just walk away, grinnin' and scratchin' his head."

"What did you do?"

He shrugged. "Gotta keep the toilets flushin'."

"Did he ever ask you to do anything for him?"

"No, man. He never got the chance."

I walked through the garden in the sunlight and wind, and I thought. I wondered where Snake LeMoyne had been last night, and why Henry Howe had been in the parking lot, and what there would have been to argue about. I wondered how Bobby was feeling, and whether I really should have called Lydia last night, and when I should call her again.

On my next trip downstairs I spotted Martin Carter in muddy coveralls coming through the propped-open exit door at the end of the hall.

"Yo, cuz," I called.

He grinned, shook his head. "Yo, my man. What's up?"

"Same old thing," I shrugged as we neared each other. "Murder."

His grin faded. "You strange."

"Yeah. Listen, I want to talk to Snake LeMoyne."

"You left strange behind. You crazy."

"Can you set it up?"

"Snake don't like strangers. Snake don't even like his friends. And he sure as hell don't like you."

"The cops think he killed Mike Downey and Henry Howe."

"That not gonna be news to Snake."

"Did he?"

He shook his head in disbelief. "Man, what the hell you care?"

"I knew Mike Downey. I know his uncle, and his wife and baby girl."

Carter looked away. "He have a baby girl?"

"Sixteen months."

He looked down at the vinyl tile, then back at me. "What you want with Snake?"

"I want to ask him what he knows."

"He gonna say he don't know nothin'."

"I want him to say it to me."

Carter said, "What difference it gonna make?"

"To Mike and Howe, none."

"Or to Snake neither. What he done, he done. What he finally go down for, that be that."

"I'm not trying to do Snake any favors. If the cops pin this on him, even just in their own minds, they'll stop looking for the real killers. And those are the guys I want."

"Could be Snake, still."

"Could be."

Into the uncertainty between us came an echoing yell: "Carter! What the fuck's going on?" Pete Portelli stood in the boiler-room door, an angry set to his shoulders. "You get them damn drains cleaned out?"

"Wasn't nothing wrong with them," Carter told him.

"Did I fucking ask you that?" Portelli strode toward us. "You ever heard of preventive maintenance? Nah, you wouldn't've." As he came up next to me I heard him mutter, ". . . the way you people live." If Carter heard it too, he didn't show it. "Listen, if you're through with your little kaffeeklatsch here, I got work for you to do. All them damn exit lights on the third floor—"

"I done them already."

That stopped Portelli long enough for me to step in. "My fault, Pete. I should know better than to bother a guy who's working."

"Yeah, if you happen to catch him working." He gave Carter the look you give the stuff on the bottom of your shoe. Then he turned to walk away.

I gave Carter a quick look myself, then followed after Portelli. "Listen, I wanted to talk to you anyway."

"You did? Ain't that nice. I hear you been fired."

"That's true." I added, "I'm sorry about Howe."

"Yeah? Lot of good it's gonna do you."

"I understand he was a friend of yours."

He threw me a mean-eyed glance. "Friend of mine? He was a jerk."

Could be the same thing, I found myself thinking. "Did you know him well?"

"Why the hell would I know him? He worked nights. I work days. And speaking of work, don't you got any to do?"

"I hear he used to drop around to see you sometimes in the morning."

Portelli stopped walking, whirled to face me. "Yeah? Where'd you hear that?"

"Fuentes, at the back door. He told me."

"Little spic with a big mouth, Fuentes. Yeah, Howe used to come around. So what?"

"What for?"

I expected to be told it was none of my goddamn business, but instead Portelli looked directly at me. "Howe liked to unwind before he went home, but he didn't like drinking alone. He brought goddamn Johnny Walker Black. So I drank with him sometimes in the morning."

I was silent, considering this.

Portelli added: "You didn't hear that."

"Why?" I asked. "Afraid Wyckoff might getcha?"

"Ah, fuck you. Have a nice life, in case I never see you again." He spun on his heel, headed back into the boiler room. At the door he turned back. "Hey, Smith?"

"Yeah?"

"He was still a jerk."

On each pass through the building I checked Howe's locker. The first two times everything was just the way I'd left it.

The third time, the lock was gone.

I took a quick look into the corridor to make sure I was alone; then I opened the locker. The clothes, gloves, magazines were all still there, and the boots were still planted on the floor. I stuck my hand in the right boot, felt around.

The hundred-dollar bill, with my note clipped to it, was gone, too.

SEVENTEEN

After that for a while I stuck to patrolling—just my job, in and out. The atmosphere in the Home was subdued, tension just below the calm surface like jagged rocks in still water. I rounded a corner, startled a stooped old man who was laboring his walker along the hall. I stopped, smiled; he snarled, "Be more careful!" though I'd come nowhere near him. The anger that fear creates is the most difficult to control.

I didn't see Carter again that morning, but I let that be. If he was willing to do what I'd asked, he'd find me. I did the front door, then the back, at break time, and then, on my own break, I called Lydia.

"Hi!" she said. "I didn't expect you to call so soon. Is everything all right?"

"It's fine," I said. I started to say more, but she cut me off.

"I'm sorry about before," she told me.

"So am I," I said. "You're probably right. I probably should have called you."

"And I shouldn't have made a big deal out of it."

"Why did you?"

"Later, Bill. We're still having dinner?"

"Sure." For a moment I didn't know what to say, and the

silence was heavy in the carpeted hall. Then I asked her, "Are you finding anything?"

"It depends what you mean by 'anything.' According to Mr. Moran's files, Henry Howe was an ex-cop. Took his pension as soon as he could and got out. For a while after that, he was an investigator for the Health Department. He had no family, lived by himself in a place called Norwood. It's in the Bronx. Your Mrs. Wyckoff lives by herself too, by the way, in a sort of semiprivate planned condo community in Eastchester. One of those new places with redwood siding and curving walks and its own golf course."

"What's the 'Mrs.' for, and how do you know what the place looks like?"

"The 'Mrs.' is for the husband she divorced twenty years ago, and my brother Ted has a friend who's a realtor in Westchester. Did you know Eastchester was in Westchester?"

"Uh-huh. Did you know you're beautiful and I love you?"

"Bill, come on, knock it off."

"Okay, sorry. Thought I'd sneak it in and you wouldn't notice."

"Hang up. I have work to do."

"In a minute. Go back to Mrs. Wyckoff. 'Semiprivate planned condo community' sounds fancy to me. Do executive directors of nonprofit organizations make enough to afford semiprivate planned condo communities?"

"Funny you should ask. I wondered the same thing. I'm checking into her some more."

"I hope you're not doing anything illegal," I admonished.

"No, you just hope you don't find out about it."

"That too. Listen, when I saw Arthur Chaiken this morning, he was having breakfast with a guy named Andy Hill. He works at the Bronx Borough President's office. Put him on your list, too, okay?"

"Okay. Any reason?"

"He didn't put any butter on his bagel."

"My kind of guy."

"Pervert. Shorty's at seven?" Lydia liked to eat early.

"Eight. I have something to do before that."

Something to do. "Okay. See you then." I replaced the receiver gently in its cradle, stood by the phone a moment looking out into the autumn garden, thinking over the beginning of the conversation, thinking that I'd never before not known what to say to Lydia.

I had another call to make, to Bobby. I dialed the office number and he answered on the third ring, but that didn't tell me anything: the office phone rang through to Bobby's apartment.

"Moran." His voice seemed a little weak to me, but I could have been wrong.

"It's Bill. You okay?"

"You call to check up on me?"

"If I swear I didn't, will you tell me if you're okay?"

"I'm fine. Why'd you call?"

"To check up on you."

"Oh, Christ, kid—!"

"I'm lying. I called because I have an idea and I wanted to clear it with you."

"Yeah? What?"

"If we don't work here anymore, I don't see much point in my being undercover. I want to let it out why I'm really here, just to see which trees it shakes, and what falls out of them."

A brief silence. "You think that's good, kid, do it."

"If it's all right with you."

"Your case."

"You're the client, Bobby."

"You always check with your clients on your moves?"

"When they're smarter than I am."

"So what are you asking me for?"

"Sorry, my mistake. I thought I was talking to Bobby Moran."

"Kid—" I didn't get the anger I expected, half hoped for. "Kid, I told you, I don't know. I don't have that . . . that thing anymore, whatever it is. I can't smell it anymore, what's going on. Nothing makes sense to me."

I said, "It was never 'that thing.' It was never magic. It was years of experience, and guts and brains. That's all it ever was, and you haven't lost any of that."

"Yeah," he said wearily. "Yeah, maybe."

The phone was silent against my ear.

"Another thing," I finally said.

"Which is?"

"I want to go talk to Sheila. You want to be there?"

"Why would I want to be there?"

"You're the closest thing she has to a father-in-law, or a father. If I were a stranger you'd want to be there."

"If you were a stranger I wouldn't let you near her."

"Sure?"

"What the hell's on your mind, kid? You afraid she'll tell you something about Mike I don't want to hear?"

"Bobby—"

"Don't give me that bullshit. You want to talk to her, talk to her. There was something weird about Mike at the end, I told you that already. And I asked Sheila about it, the day after—" Bobby stopped. Then he went on — "the day after Mike died. She said she didn't know what I was talking about. Maybe that's true. And if it's not, she already lied to me once, so you're better off without me."

"Okay. Just thought I'd ask."

"Ah, shit," Bobby sighed into the phone. "Listen, kid . . ." He didn't go on.

"Yeah, me too. Okay, Bobby. You want to meet me and Lydia at Shorty's later?"

"Maybe," Bobby said, sounding tired already, as tired as I suddenly felt. "Maybe."

"Well, if you don't make it, I'll call you, okay?"

"Yeah, okay. Thanks, kid."

So that was Bobby, and that was Lydia. I hung up, crossed the sunny porch, strolled into the garden, and wondered which metaphoric tree to shake first.

Fate made a suggestion, in the well-groomed form of Mrs. Wyckoff. I had completed a circuit of the garden, the wall, the ground-floor windows, all tight and shipshape. The night's hard wind had pretty much wiped out the last roses, and dry leaves were huddled at the feet of the trees, as if afraid to leave home. Their days were numbered, though: a man in coveralls like Carter's was scritching them into mounds with a rake.

As I climbed the seven steps back up to the porch, where the residents were starting to spot themselves around to catch the morning sun, a tall brown-clad figure appeared on the top step, arms folded as if to bar my way. I stopped, because that seemed to be what she wanted, although as a power play it wasn't very good: it was still morning, and the porch faced east, so she was the one who had to squint.

"Good morning," I said, smiled pleasantly.

"Good morning," said Mrs. Wyckoff, and didn't. She was wearing a suit of café-au-lait wool, not a color blondes wear easily, though it was a well-made suit. Her cream silk blouse had cuffs that stuck out below the jacket sleeves and one of those big floppy bows at the neck that men executives like because they make women executives look silly.

"I've just spoken to Mr. Moran," Mrs. Wyckoff said icily, "and I've told Mr. Dayton. Wells Fargo has been engaged to provide security services here starting this afternoon. They will be sending a supervisor and crew for an orientation as early as they can manage, and they will be taking over immediately after that. As soon as they tell Mr. Dayton they're ready, I expect you out of here."

"All right," I said. "But you can also expect me back."

"What," she asked through her teeth, "does that mean?"

I mounted the rest of the steps, stood next to her. "You asked me last night who I was," I said. "We both know my answer was a dodge. I'm a private investigator and I'm looking into Mike Downey's death."

"You're *what?*" she choked. Her high cheeks filled with color. "What nerve! Whose idea was this?"

"Is it a problem?"

"It certainly is! What do you mean, coming here and upsetting the residents, the routine, lying—"

"I haven't done any of that, Mrs. Wyckoff. I've been working as a guard and I've been doing my job. I didn't tell you I was here as an investigator but you didn't ask. Now you know."

She sucked air between her teeth. "If anything you do reflects badly on the Home in any way, Mr. Smith, you can be sure that you yourself, Mr. Moran, and his entire firm will answer for it. This is a police matter. The police will resolve it."

"They're doing well so far, aren't they? They're doing so well you had them back last night for an encore."

She gave me a hint of a superior smile. "And just how well are you doing, Mr. Smith?"

"Actually," I said, "I'm doing fine. Just fine." I smiled, turned, walked back across the porch into the building, leaving Mrs. Wyckoff staring narrow-eyed after me.

I went into the building, across the corridor and down the stairs looking for another tree to shake. At the bottom an inspiration hit me and I headed down the hall to try Dr. Madsen's, but when I got there he wasn't in his tree.

"Dr. Madsen doesn't come in on Tuesdays," said Elena, the nurse with the crimson lips. "I can let you see Dr. Reynolds."

"Okay. That sounds like fun."

"If it does," she smiled, "you must be feeling better."

It was near lunchtime. I called upstairs from her desk phone, cleared it with Dayton to take my break now. Elena took my chart into the other room. It came out again almost immediately in the hands of a large, genial man with gold-rimmed glasses. Curly white hair, like foam left by a receding surf, circled the back of his skull; age spots and a few diehard hairs speckled his bald head.

"Smith?" He stuck out his hand for me to shake. I did, and I was almost sorry. He had quite a grip. "I'm Dr. Reynolds. Come on in."

We went on in together, to the examining room. Dr. Reynolds leaned back against a stainless-steel counter covered with boxes of tongue depressors, disposable syringes, plastic bottles of eyedrops and eardrops and nose drops. He folded his arms across his round belly. "Well, you look pretty good on paper. What seems to be the trouble?"

"No trouble. Dr. Madsen said to come back and get myself checked out. I don't think he meant this soon, but this is my last day working here. I didn't know he wouldn't be in."

"No, Tuesdays he's over at Montefiore, at some clinic. I'll be glad to take a look, if you want. Take off your shirt."

He turned to wash his hands and I took my jacket, gun, and shirt off. Reynolds's eyes followed the gun as I hung it on the hook.

"What do you mean, your last day?" he asked. "I thought you were the new guy, just started."

"I am. Was. Moran Security's being replaced."

"Ah." He gave me a sympathetic smile. "Well, I can't say I'm surprised."

"No, me either." I deposited myself on the paper-covered table. "I just hope it helps."

"What do you mean?" he inquired pleasantly. Show an interest, put the patient at ease. His soft, rounded fingers probed my bruises very gently. I wondered if the residents here got to choose which doctor they wanted to see.

"I'm looking at this from a little different angle," I said. "The police think it's a local gang targeting the guards, but I'm not so sure."

"No?" His voice was friendly. He cupped the business end of his stethoscope in his hand, then moved around behind me, placed it on my back. When it landed it was warm. "What else could it be? Cough."

"I'm not sure." I coughed, and again, as instructed. The stethoscope wandered my back. Reynolds came around front, smiled reassuringly, and we repeated the procedure on my chest.

"Dr. Madsen didn't send you for X rays, did he?" Reynolds pulled the earpieces down around his neck, opened my file.

"He didn't think I needed any."

"Oh, probably he's right," he said casually. Never knock another doctor, the patient might lose his faith in medicine. "I'd just like to make sure those ribs aren't cracked." He pointed with his pen at the black-and-blue streaks on my right side, where Snake LeMoyne had kicked me. "I'm sure it's nothing to worry about, but why don't you go ahead and get an X ray anyway?" He scribbled something on his prescription pad. "Take this over to Samaritan Hospital, to the Diagnostic Clinic. Your insurance should cover it. Leave me your doctor's name, since you won't be back here, and I'll forward the results."

"I will be back," I said. "I'll pick them up."

He looked up from his writing. "You said this was your last day . . . ?"

"Last official day. As a guard. As an investigator, I'm just beginning."

"You've lost me." He smiled, to show he wasn't mad that I'd lost him.

"There are people who think the killings here aren't what they look like." I stood, shrugged into my uniform shirt. "I'm working for them."

"Doing what?" He tore the prescription off the pad.

"Damned if I know. Shaking trees."

"But what else could the killings be?"

"People get killed for a lot of reasons, Doctor. They know something, or someone, or someone knows something about them." I tied my tie. "They owe money, or someone owes them money. They're in the way. Or they're just in the wrong place at the wrong time."

"Are you saying you think—the people who hired you think—that these deaths are somehow related to someone here?"

"I have no idea. It could be Martians. I'm just paid to poke around." Disingenuous, but there you are.

"Well." Dr. Reynolds waited for me to pull on my shoulder rig, handed me the prescription. "That's an unpleasant thought. I hope you're wrong. Or they're wrong, whoever hired you."

"We'll see," I said.

"Listen, if you need any help . . . I don't know exactly what kind of help I could be, but if you need anything . . ."

"Thanks. I'll let you know." I covered the gun with the Moran Security jacket. Dr. Reynolds opened the exam-room door, stood aside to let me pass.

"Good-bye," He smiled, offered his hand again. Prepared this time, I met his grip, winked at Elena, and went out.

Upstairs, Dayton was standing behind his desk, speaking to four large men in Wells Fargo jackets. I watched from the stairwell door as he gestured to the time clock, ran his finger down the log sheet on the clipboard. When he pointed to the front door they all turned their heads, followed his gesture; then they turned back, listened to his measured words.

A door opened and Mrs. Wyckoff came into the hall, followed by Bobby, who had held the door for her. Mrs. Wyck-off's eyes landed on me; then, nose in the air, she stalked past. I joined Bobby, who was leaning on the cane again.

"You okay?"

"Will you stop asking me that?" Bobby growled.

"Glad to hear it."

Mrs. Wyckoff spoke to the largest of the Wells Fargo guys, the one with "Supervisor" above the stripes on his sleeves. "Mr. Bruno, may I see you in my office, please?"

Bruno had the large jowls and mournful expression of a basset hound. "Sure," he said. "Hey, Bobby. Long time." Bobby slipped his hand through the crook of the cane, shook with Bruno, then planted the cane again.

Mrs. Wyckoff looked suspiciously from one to the other. "Do you two know each other?"

"Ours is a small world," Bruno said soothingly. Mrs. Wyckoff didn't look soothed.

Bobby introduced me to Bruno, Bruno introduced his men around, and then it was over. Bobby, Dayton and I headed downstairs with the Wells Fargo man who was replacing Fuentes. We cleaned out our lockers, then went out to the parking lot, where Bobby told Fuentes and Dayton he'd call them each in a day or two with a new assignment.

"Hey, man, you watch yourself, okay?" Fuentes said to me.

I said something similar back, shook hands with Dayton. They walked together up the hill toward the subway.

Bobby and I both had cars in the lot. Bobby, still looking after Dayton and Fuentes, said to me, "You can come in and out whenever you want. I fixed it with Bruno."

"Already?" I was impressed. "When?"

"This morning. When Wyckoff told me it was going to be Wells Fargo, I called. I know a lot of guys over there." He turned, started for his car. I walked with him. "Of course, if Wyckoff tells them to keep you out, they'll have to."

"Why would she do that? A nice guy like me?"

"Tell it to the judge," Bobby grunted. He climbed into his car, pulled his left leg after him. The car was a Buick Skylark, modified some to make it easier for Bobby to use.

"I'm going to see Sheila," I said. "Changed your mind? Want to come?"

"I'm going home to bed. One of the advantages to being an old man is you can go home to bed and let the young guys do the work."

"Or guys like me, if you can't find any young guys. I'll call you later."

"You ought to get some sleep, too. Why don't you go call your girlfriend? Maybe she'll sing you a Chinese lullaby."

"She doesn't know any lullabyes. Only rock 'n' roll."

Bobby drove off. I took my car and headed north again and west, wondering whether Lydia did, in fact, know any lullabies.

EIGHTEEN

Mike and Sheila Downey had lived on the first floor of a wood-framed three-family near the Yonkers line. Gold and russet leaves carpeted the uneven slate sidewalk, and the asphalt-shingled houses crowded each other close. Short concrete paths flanked by small rectangular patches of grass led to each front door.

The air was sharp, but the sun was warm. Sheila was waiting for me on the porch. I picked up a child's alphabet block with a "C" and a picture of a cat on it from the path, put it on the table next to Sheila after I kissed her.

She smiled a tired smile. "We'll have to talk low. Peggy's asleep." She wore a forest-green sweater that ordinarily would have set off her auburn hair; today it only emphasized the pallor of her plump cheeks.

In a playpen, Peg lay facedown, little diapered rear in the air, one baby hand resting on a tawny stuffed tiger. Her brown curls clung damply around her face.

Brushing back her own curls, Sheila asked me, "What happened to your eye? Did you get hurt?" I could hear, even in her low tones, the rolling rhythms of Ireland.

"I had an accident. I'm okay. How are you doing?"

She settled into a steel porch chair that bounced a little on its frame. I sat in one like it, waited for an answer.

"Okay, I guess. I don't know." She spoke softly, staring at the floor. Suddenly she lifted her head. "Oh, look at me, forgetting my manners. Is there something I can get you? Coffee? A beer? There's plenty to eat—people have been bringing things over, the way they do . . .''

"No, thanks. Sheila, is there anything you need? Money? Someone to help with Peg?"

She shook her head. "The neighbors have been wonderful, just rallying round. They've had us over to supper in turns, and the women come help me mind the baby. The first two nights we stopped with the Abrams, next door. Now we've come home, and it's all right, I suppose . . ." She paused. "It's only, it's so empty here." She gestured toward the apartment, as though toward huge echoing corridors and vast desolate rooms.

"I know," I said softly.

After a moment, Sheila looked up. "You wanted to ask me questions. We'd better talk or I'll start to cry." She smiled raggedly.

"Okay. But you can cry anyhow, if you want."

"I don't, specially. But I seem to, no matter what."

I lit a cigarette. Afternoon sunlight glowed on the white-painted porch rails.

"Bobby says Mike was acting strangely, the last few weeks," I said.

Sheila picked up the alphabet block, turned it in her hands. "You're working for Bobby."

"Yes, of course."

"Does that mean you'll tell him anything I tell you?"

Peg, still asleep, whimpered, slid her hand around the playpen until her thumb found her mouth. I said to Sheila, "No."

"Because Bobby asked me the same, and I said I didn't know. I don't; but whatever it was, it was to do with him. With Bobby."

"What do you mean?"

Her eyes were large, pale, troubled. "I truly don't know, Bill. But something was bothering Mike, something at work."

"How do you know that?"

She looked away from me. "You know how close they were. When Mike wouldn't talk to me about it, I said he should talk to Bobby. That's what he always would have done. But he said no, Bobby had too many troubles now. He said it was for him to take care of.'' Still without looking at me, she whispered, ''He said I mustn't worry.''

I watched the fallen leaves, a soft wind behind them, wander over asphalt and slate. After a time I asked, ''Was Mike happy at work?''

''Oh, very happy. Though what he truly wanted was to be an investigator. He loved to know things, Mike did. But Bobby said he had to start off slow, to learn from the ground up, so to say. He would have done anything Bobby wanted. Bobby was his hero.'' She raised her eyes to me. ''He used to say that was what he liked about you, how good you were to Bobby. Because of that he liked you, even when you . . .'' She blushed, trailed off.

''Even when I gave him a hard time. Even when I lost my temper with him. I'm sorry about those times, Sheila.''

She shook her head. ''He thought you were—well, difficult. But he liked you.''

''I liked him. I really did.''

Though she smiled, her eyes gleamed with new tears.

''And you have no idea what it was that was troubling him?''

''No. But one night he asked me something . . . strange. Maybe it's to do with . . . with whatever it was.''

''Strange?''

''Out of nowhere, one night—we were looking at TV— he asked which I thought was worse, a snitch or a liar. He made it sound as if he didn't care, he was just wondering, like; but I knew him better than that.''

''What did you tell him?''

''I said I guessed it would depend.''

''On what?''

''Who got snitched on, and what for, and who got lied to, and what about.''

''What did Mike say?''

''Nothing right away. Then he asked if you saw someone steal something and didn't stop him, if that made you a thief too.''

''What did you say?''

Her eyes glistened again, and she looked away. ''I said I thought he knew the answer to that.''

A breeze ruffled the trees, and a yellow leaf drifted into the playpen, settled on the hem of Peg's blanket. Peg fretted. Sheila leaned over, straightened the blanket, rubbed Peg's back. She grew still, and Sheila sat back again.

"Sheila, did Mike ever mention his supervisor on the night shift? A man named Henry Howe?"

"Not really. I know the name, but Mike didn't talk about him specially. Why?"

I ground out my cigarette. "You'll hear about it anyway. You might as well hear it from me. There was another killing at the Bronx Home last night. Henry Howe was killed the same way Mike was."

Sheila Downey stared at me, unmoving. Then, dropping the alphabet block, her curls blowing unnoticed around her face in the October wind, she started to cry. Tears brimmed in her eyes, slid down her cheeks; otherwise she was completely still and silent.

I rose, went and sat on the arm of her chair, hugged her to me. At first she was wooden, unresponding. Then she melted against me and began to sob, her shoulders shaking. I held her, smoothed her hair. I said nothing, because there were no words.

After a time, her sobs became gentle, then finally stopped. She straightened up, wiped her eyes. "Oh, God," she said, with a small hiccup. "Did I wake Peggy?"

"No."

She wiped her eyes again, tried to smile. "Look at me." Her voice was hoarse. "I didn't even know the man."

I leaned against the porch rail, facing her.

"Bill?" she whispered, then nothing more.

"I don't know," I said.

Sheila bit her lower lip, reached down to pick up the alphabet block. "What about Bobby?" she asked. "Poor Bobby."

"I don't know," I said to that, too. "He bites my head off every time I ask how he's doing. But he looks tired, Sheila."

A gust of wind showered leaves from the trees, tinkled a wind chime in a neighboring yard. "We wanted him to move in with us, Mike and I. Did you know that?"

"No, I didn't."

"Well, he wouldn't. He said we didn't need two babies to look after."

I smiled. "That sounds like Bobby."

She turned her eyes to me. "Do you suppose he would now? Come live with me and Peg? It's only, it's so empty . . ."

"Have you asked him?"

"Not since . . ." She looked down, didn't finish.

"Ask him, Sheila. He'll say no. Then ask him again."

The wind swept the trees again, and the wind chime rang. "I used to hate that thing." Sheila smiled softly. "That chime. But Mike liked it. He said it made him know other people were close. He liked to know that." She pushed the curls from her forehead. "Now," she said, "now I like to hear it. It makes me think . . . well, it makes me think Mike's close. Do you know?"

"Yes. I know."

"Do you think that could be? That people we lose . . . they could still be close?"

"I think," I said, "that you'll always have Mike close."

She nodded, wrapped her arms around herself as the wind grew colder. "I hope so," she whispered. "I hope that's so."

NINETEEN

Before I left Sheila's I called my service. While Sheila moved around the kitchen, setting cups on saucers, slicing an apple cake, I held Peg on one hip. Peg seemed unsure of me, groggy from sleep.

"You know Bill." Sheila touched the tip of Peg's nose. "He gave you that tiger, when you were just a wee thing."

Peg regarded me gravely, her right arm wrapped around the tiger as mine was wrapped around her.

"That's right," I told her, dialing the phone with my free hand. "Tony the Tiger. He's grrrreat!"

Peg stared, then suddenly flapped the tiger in the air. "Gyyyyate!" She clutched the tiger to herself again, looked at me.

"Uh-huh," I said. "Just like you."

Sheila took Peg from me, set her in her high chair. I turned away from the sudden empty feeling, switched the receiver to my other hand as though I'd needed that arm free anyway.

There was an eager puppy friendliness in the voice of the young man at the answering service. "Didn't you just call? No? Well, that would be me, confused as usual. Maybe it was that someone called *you*. Oh, my. Don't you think it's a good thing this is just my day job? I'm really a waiter. Yes, here. A Martin Carter. I quote: 'It's set up. The parking-lot gate, five-thirty.' Ooh, how mysterious! Are you sure I didn't just give this to you?"

"Yes."

"Well, I don't know. I could swear I just gave it to *somebody*," he said dubiously. "Anyhow, I hope it's as thrilling as it sounds."

"I don't see how it could be. But thanks." I hung up thinking, three's a crowd.

"Everything okay?" Sheila poured milk into my cup, and then tea.

"I think so. Sheila, let me ask you something else, and then I'll go, I promise."

"You don't have to go. If I can help you do . . . do what Bobby hired you for, I want to. I want to very much."

The tea was thick, smoky-tasting. "Is there anyone," I watched Sheila's face, "anyone at all, no matter how far-fetched, who might have wanted Mike out of the way?"

She settled her teacup in her saucer, looked into its depths. "I've been thinking about that every minute since it happened. Who, and why. No. I don't think so. No one hated Mike. He was always everywhere, popping up all over the neighborhood, offering a hand. No one hated Mike. Why would they?"

Soon after, a neighbor came over, a smiling woman with two small children who made a fuss over Peg the way children will over a baby who's not theirs. I left then, promising Sheila I'd come see her soon.

It was a quarter to four. I had almost two hours before I had to meet Carter, and I had an idea how to spend that time.

Samaritan Hospital was an ugly pile of tan brick buildings on the Concourse south of the courthouse. Each of the three main buildings had been built in a different decade. No effort had been made, it seemed, to match or even harmonize their heights, windows, detailing; but the tan brick was the same, and it was used again in the covered connections and links and annexes that tied the complex together. All the ground-level brick was graffiti-layered, names covering names, cartoon pictures obliterating other cartoons.

Inside Samaritan's main doors was an information desk, and next to it, as a portal, a walk-through metal detector. On the wall hung a sign: "Notice: No Weapons of Any Kind Permitted in Any Samaritan Hospital Facility."

"The Diagnostic Clinic?" I asked at the desk.

"Left. Follow the green line. Walk through there." The woman at the desk pointed her chin at the metal detector.

"I'm carrying a gun." I opened my jacket just enough for her and the guard who sat on a stool by the detector to look inside. The guard, his uniform shirt rolled up on his massive forearms, started to come forward.

"I have a license for it. I'm a private investigator." I took out my wallet, showed him my P.I. license and my carry permit.

He scowled as he fingered them. "Leave it here."

"I think it's safer with me."

"Suit yourself. But you can't take it in."

"Permit doesn't do me any good?"

"Not inside."

"You have a place to lock it up?"

"No, I'm gonna take it outside and pot junkies." He settled back on his stool.

"Give it here," the woman said from behind the desk. "You got a permit, you get it back." She was holding a steel strongbox with a number painted on the side.

"What if I didn't have a permit?" I placed my revolver in the box. She locked it, gave me a numbered key, put the box in a drawer, locked the drawer.

"The police come for it." She wrote me out a receipt, without my asking.

"When did you start doing this?" I asked, curious. "Checking for weapons at the door?"

Her look was impassive. "Same time the high schools did."

* * *

I went through the detector, turned left, followed the green line. It ran with the red and blue ones until they dropped away, then twisted alone down the scuffed corridor. I passed an orderly pushing a cart piled with dirty linens; two tired-looking nurses passed me. The place smelled sharply of rubbing alcohol and disinfectant, and I wanted a cigarette.

Finally the green line ran under a door labeled "Diagnostic Clinic." I pushed the door open, went in. The green line stopped; maybe it knew better than I did.

An elderly man sat next to an elderly woman on plastic chairs by the wall. The only other person in the room was the nurse behind the reception counter.

I gave her the prescription Dr. Reynolds had written me. "I need to be out of here by five. What are my chances?"

"Fair." She read the prescription, handed me a clipboard with two forms. One was questions about my medical history, the other about my insurance. I filled them out, gave them back. "I'm not sure my insurance will pay for this—"

"It will," she interrupted, sounding bored.

"Isn't this a private hospital?"

"Don't matter."

"On my Blue Cross," I persisted, "I'm supposed to call them and get it approved before—"

" 'Managed Care'." She glanced through my forms, only half listening. "That's procedures, not diagnostics."

"But how do I know they'll pay the full amount? What if they don't approve your charges?"

She looked up at me over half-glasses. "Honey, what you trying to do, talk your way outta this? It's only X ray, it ain't gonna hurt. Big fella like you. You oughta be shamed."

"It's not that, it's the cost," I said stubbornly. "I'm just worried they'll only pay part. You know, what they think it's worth, not what you charge."

She smiled. "Well, don't you worry, honey. We gonna charge you exactly what Blue Cross like to pay."

After that, it was half an hour of nothing, just staring at the old man and woman staring at the wall. Sometimes I stared at the wall myself. A tattered poster suggested I learn about the four basic food groups. A newer one exhorted me to Just Say No.

Eventually a door opened, a technician called my name, and then it was shirt off, sit, lie, sit again, while the technician stepped in and out from his lead shield and the X-ray machine buzzed briefly. Then back through the waiting room, where the elderly couple still sat, still stared; and back along the green line to retrieve my gun at the desk. I broke it open, checked the bullets. The guard scowled at me when I did that.

"The silver ones are hard to come by," I explained. Then out the double doors and onto the sidewalk, where I lit up a cigarette immediately. The late-afternoon sunlight made the tan brick glow warmly, but it didn't make the buildings any more inviting. I didn't realize how much I disliked the smell of disinfectant until it was gone.

TWENTY

Martin Carter was waiting for me at the gate to the Bronx Home parking lot. He'd changed the blue coveralls for a sweatshirt and jeans. I pulled up across the street, leaned over to open the door while he dodged traffic.

"Man, you a hard dude to find," he grumbled, climbing in the car.

"I am?"

"You didn't leave me no number, nothin'."

"I couldn't find you before I left. I'd've called you if you hadn't called me."

He was still unsatisfied. "Well, I had to ask the new guy. He call your boss. Boss don't answer. So he call your super. Dayton? Dayton got to hunt around, find your answering service number. Shit. I be 'bout ready to forget it. Plus, standing here like a damn fool and you don't show up."

"Am I late? I'm sorry."

He shrugged. "Just, I like to get away from here soon's my shift's over. Stay outta trouble that way."

"What kind of trouble?" I glanced at him.

"Any kind at all."

"Well," I said, "where to?"

He didn't answer right away. Looking out the window, he

said, "Man, you being straight with me?"

"Straight how?"

"You tell me you just crazy, just wanna talk to Snake. Snake, he got his reasons to talk to you. I don't know, maybe he crazy too. But I gotta wonder, man. You setting me up?"

"Setting you up? For what?"

He seemed about to say something; then he shook his head. "Nah, forget it."

"I wouldn't set you up, even if I knew what the hell you were talking about," I said. "But it's true I haven't told you the whole thing." I turned the car off, shifted to face him. "I said I knew Mike Downey, and I did. And his family. But this security-guard business, this isn't what I usually do. I'm a private investigator. I've been hired to find out who killed Mike."

He stared. "Private cop? Oh, shit!" He threw the car door open, started to get out.

I grabbed his arm. "Wait, goddammit!"

He sat back down, but he didn't close the door. "Man, what you tryin' to do, get me fuckin' killed? If Snake find out—"

"Snake's going to find out, because I'm going to tell him. I'm going to be straight with Snake, too. If he killed Mike— or any of his crew did—I'm going to want his ass on a platter, and I'm going to get it. But if he didn't, then I want the guys who did, and I want Snake to help me get them."

"Help," Carter snorted. "Yeah, Snake know all about help."

I took out my Kents, offered the pack to him. He shook his head. "How come you didn't tell me this before?" he said. "Why you come fronting this security guard shit?"

"When I started here I didn't know who anyone was, who I could trust."

"You still don't." He looked directly at me.

"No. No, I don't. But I'll take my chances."

For a moment, no reaction. Then he grinned. He closed the door, settled in the seat. "Okay. You crazy, Snake crazy. Might as well be crazy too."

I grinned back, started the car. "So, crazy man. Where to?"

"First we gotta make a stop," he said. "Snake expecting

us at six. I figured you had a car, we could make it.''

"Make what?''

"Errand.''

I pulled out into the street, circled back to the Concourse, went north as Carter directed me until he had me stop.

"Be right back.'' He disappeared into a brick building with heavy mesh grilles on the ground-floor windows. In a minute he came out, but he wasn't alone. One arm cradled a toddler, who rested his head on Carter's shoulder. By the hand he held a tall, long-limbed girl of maybe five, who was looking up at him, talking and giggling. He smiled as he answered; I didn't hear what he said.

I got out of the car and opened the passenger door. The girl stopped talking when she saw me, leaned a little closer to Carter.

"Who's him, Martin?''

"This my friend Bill. Bill, this Vanessa, and this Rashid.''

"Hi, Vanessa. Neat lunchbox.'' She looked down at the Bart Simpson: Rasta Dude lunchbox she was carrying. "Hi, Rashid.'' The baby shifted his eyes to me when he heard his name.

"He don't know how to talk much,'' Vanessa offered. "He just a baby.''

"I know,'' I said. "But when he grows up he'll be big and smart like you. Well, if he's lucky, maybe.''

She giggled. Carter said, "Get in the car, Nessie.''

"We gonna ride in his car?''

"Uh-huh. Bill gonna take us home.''

She climbed into the back seat. Carter sat in the front, the baby in his lap. I switched on the tape deck, clicked on the rear speakers.

"Hey!'' Vanessa said, as we were surrounded by the Brahms piano quintet. "Hey, it play ballerina music!''

"You like it?'' I asked her.

"Yeah! Decent!''

"Press the black button. It makes the window go up and down.''

She did, and giggled again. "Martin! Look!''

"Yeah.'' Carter grinned back at her. "Ain't that something?''

We went north until I found a legal U-turn, then headed back the way we'd come.

As Vanessa chased the window up and down in short bursts I manuevered the car through traffic. Pulling out around a double-parked jeep, I asked Carter quietly, "You know anybody with a tan Dodge?"

"Uh-uh. Should I?"

"I don't know. But he's been about half a block behind since we left the Home."

"No shit." Carter twisted in his seat, craned through my back window. "I see him. Can't make him out, though. Yo, here's my street. What you want to do?"

"I want to lose him."

I went on past Carter's street, waited for my chance. A few blocks later it came: an intersection where the light was changing. The Dodge was stuck two cars behind me as I sped up, ran the yellow as it turned to red. I swung left, up the quick hill away from the Concourse; then, over the crest and out of sight, I swung left again.

"Where we going, Martin?" came Vanessa's interested voice from behind me.

"Shortcut," Carter said.

I worked my way half a mile north of Carter's street, then turned and came back, using parallel avenues instead of the Concourse. I half expected the tan Dodge, which had not reappeared since I left him at the stoplight, to be waiting for us in front of Carter's building, but it wasn't there.

"Looks like that worked," I said. "But I'd sure like to know who he was."

"Maybe we be lucky. Maybe he be back."

Carter's apartment building, like so many others on the side streets, was a tired red-brick affair, never as elegant as the Concourse buildings themselves, and now, like them, shabby and neglected. Two women, one middle-aged and stout, the other elderly and tiny, conversed on the sidewalk. "There's Granny!" Vanessa bounced in her seat as I turned the car off. "Look, Granny!" she called out the window. "We riding in Martin's friend car!"

Carter and I got out. Almost before Carter had the door open for her, Vanessa squeezed out and was on the sidewalk, tugging on the tiny woman's hand.

"Look, Granny! You can run the windows up and down, and it play ballerina music from all around you—"

"That's lovely, child. Now hush so I can meet Martin's friend good and proper."

"Oh—!" The child yanked on the old lady's hand in frustration as Carter kissed her upturned cheek. He said, "Bill, this my grandmother, Miz Enna Carter. And this Miz Green, live underneath us. She studying on sainthood, don't never complain how noisy these children is."

"We ain't!" protested Vanessa. "Least, *I* ain't."

"Oh. Must be Rashid wear his roller skates inside. Ladies, this Bill Smith, used to work with me."

"Pleased to meet you." I shook hands with them both. Mrs. Green was powerfully built, with big, callused hands. Carter's grandmother's hands were callused too, but the woman herself, not large to begin with, was stooped and gnarled like a piece of driftwood. Her grip was firm, though, and her eyes sparkled.

"Pleasure be mine, Mr. Smith. It's good of you give Martin and the children a ride."

"Granny, we got to do something, Bill and me. I be back in about a hour. You want me to take Rashid inside?"

"I take him, Mother Carter," Mrs. Green offered. Carter passed the sleepy Rashid to Mrs. Green as Enna Carter peered at him suspiciously. "What you mean, you got to do something? What thing you got to do?"

"Bill got a errand, need my help."

"Bill got? Or you got?"

"I have, Mrs. Carter," I said. "Martin's doing me a favor. It won't take long."

The old woman seemed not entirely convinced. Carter kissed her again, and we got back in the car. As we drove away I could see in the rearview mirror Rashid resting on Mrs. Green's wide bosom, and gangly Vanessa still explaining to her great-grandmother the wonders of my car.

"Your grandmother seems worried about you," I said to Carter as we drove south on the Concourse. It was dusk now, the clear sky purply-blue, the lighted apartment-house windows glowing a gentle yellow.

"She know me." He directed me to turn just north of the

Bronx Home, and I did, heading first down the hill away from the Concourse, then turning left. There was no tan Dodge before or behind us.

"You didn't tell me you had a family," I said.

He looked at me with amazement. "And you didn't tell me you was fuckin' Magnum, P.I.! What you want, my rap sheet?"

"You have one?"

"You know anyone round here don't?"

I downshifted at a grafitti-covered stop sign. "They're good-looking kids."

"Uh-huh."

I took a chance. "Both yours?"

"They is now."

"Vanessa calls you 'Martin'."

Carter fixed his eyes on me. "What about it?"

"Nothing. Just making conversation."

"Save it for Snake."

"Listen, Carter, you don't have to do this."

"Do what?"

"Come with me. Just tell me where to go."

"Park here. This where you go. They waiting for you in that playground there. And you think you gonna get outta here without me?"

I parked, turned off the car. Shadowy forms played a game of half-court on the other side of the schoolyard fence. As I watched, a very tall shadow burst away from the others, slammed the ball one-handed through the netless hoop. *Good, but nothing special,* I could hear Lindfors's rough voice in my head. *An average kid.*

I said to Carter, "I couldn't have gotten in here without you. I know that. But you're edgy as a turkey the day before Thanksgiving. If you don't want to see Snake, you don't owe me anything."

"You think I'm afraid of Snake? Man, you dumb even for a white guy."

"What, then?"

He let his breath out between his teeth. "You strapped?"

"Armed? Yes."

"Leave it here."

Nobody wanted my gun around today. Maybe it had bad

breath. Muzzle breath. You're nervous too, Smith, I pointed out.

"I don't want anyone breaking in the car, putting this gun on the street."

"We fix that." He got out of the car.

I took off the .38, shoved it under the seat. It seemed a better idea than the glove compartment. On the sidewalk, Carter surveyed the neighborhood. Down the block a group of kids tossed a football around. Carter stared that way for a few moments, then yelled, "Yo! Speedo!"

One of the kids, a slight boy of about ten, swiveled his head in our direction. He called something to the others, threw the football in a high, curving arc. Without looking to see if it had been caught he trotted over to where we stood.

"Yo, Rev," he greeted Carter. " 'S up?"

" 'S up, Speedo?" Carter and the kid gave each other a handshake. "I got business with Snake," Carter told the kid. "You think you could watch my man's car for me, see it don't have no accidents?"

"No problem." The kid looked at my car with interest. "What kinda car's this?"

"Acura," I told him. "Two years old."

"Ride good?"

"Uh-huh."

"Why you don't get a new one?"

"Don't need one. It rides good."

"Yeah, but why you don't get one? Get them dope spokes on your rims, get dark windows so no one can't see your business. Like Snake got, in the Benz."

"When you rich, you buy my man one," Carter suggested. "Meanwhile, this the only one he got, so I don't want nothing to happen to this one."

"Yeah, okay, Rev, okay," the kid grumbled.

Carter turned and I followed him toward the playground gate.

"Rev?" I said.

"Drop it."

I dropped it, for now.

Carter walked lightly. His shoulders were relaxed, but his eyes roved the terrain. They covered the line of lighted windows in the school, where crayoned oak leaves were silhouetted behind heavy mesh screens; they took in the glistening shards of glass on the playground asphalt. Under a street-light, three girls giggled. One of them, light-skinned, with blond in her hair, waved at Carter, then whispered some-thing to her friends. They giggled some more.

In the corner of my eye I caught a dark figure a block up the hill, standing, watching. A sentry, an outrigger. The smell of someone's dinner deep-frying drifted from the apartment house across the street, mingled with the autumn leaves you could smell even here, on this cracked-asphalt desert. I wondered if there was any other time in this place when you could smell the season. In the spring maybe, after the rain.

The half-court game had stopped when Carter and I en-tered the playground. Six figures stood waiting, motionless in the dusk. Snake was there, shirtless, gleaming with sweat. I recognized Skeletor, a fat figure in a baseball cap. There were two other baseball caps, worn sideways by guys whose tension you could read in the tendons in their necks, the set of their shoulders. One of them couldn't have been over fourteen. Heavy gold chains and four-finger rings glinted dully in the half-light.

Carter stopped and I stopped next to him, a few feet from the silent group.

"Yo, Snake," Carter said evenly.

Snake grinned, showed a gleam of gold tooth. "Yo, my man Rev. Whassup?" He glanced at me; suddenly he snapped the basketball hard at my chest. I caught the move-ment just before he threw; so I caught the ball, too, held it where I caught it, against me. By that time, with swift, smooth motions, three of the kids had pulled guns from under their loose jackets. They held them on me, one-handed, shoulder-high. Right here on the playground, I thought. A fourteen-year-old and two kids not much older are ready to blow my head off and don't even care why, and I'm not even surprised.

Snake, who hadn't stopped grinning, gestured at Skeletor. Skeletor waited what must have been a second or two too long for Snake; to me it was an hour. Snake cut him a sharp look. Skeletor ambled forward, took the basketball away, flipped it to one of the other guys. He patted me down. I lifted my arms to help him; otherwise I didn't move. When he was through with me, Skeletor did Carter. I heard Carter hiss, "Shit!" but he didn't protest.

When Skeletor moved back, though, Carter said angrily, "Wha's up with that shit, Snake? You think I be coming at you with a joint?"

Snake's face grew hard. "Rev, nothing you do gonna surprise me. Yesterday this white boy be porking out at me, today you call me, say, can he talk. You not who you was. Can't trust 'em, bust 'em."

A cold wind swept the playground, scraping leaves before it. Snake picked up the eight-ball jacket from the asphalt, dusted it off and put it on. He pulled a gold neck chain from the pocket, slipped it over his head. A three-inch gold cobra dangled against his chest.

He stepped close to me, leaned in my face. I stayed still. "So I be asking myself, Snake, how come a limp-dick white fool be ready to buck you one day, next day want to talk to you?" He looked around at his crew, spread his hands. "And I don't hear no answer. So only thing to do, ask the fool hisself. So, fool. How 'bout it? What up with that shit?"

I could smell his sweat, and the new leather of his coat. I wanted a few more inches between us, but that was the game. I didn't move, spoke calmly. "Did you kill Mike Downey?"

" 'Did you kill Mike Downey?' " Snake whined, broadly sarcastic. He laughed. A few of his crew laughed with him. Snake stopped abruptly. "No, I ain't smoked the fuckin' dude! Wish I did, so sick of hearing his name!"

"You know who did?" My voice was as level and low as the one I would have used in a church.

"Man, why you coming like this? What you care? He your homeboy?"

"White folks ain't got no homeboys," Skeletor said.

The crew snickered; one guy slapped another's palm.

"Word," Snake agreed. His grin spread. "Hey, I got it. They faggots. Ain't that right, fool? He used to suck your ol' shriveled dick, and now you lonely? We take care of that for you, bitch!"

Carter's low voice came from beside me. "Yo, no call for that, Snake. My man ain't dissin' you. I ask you can he talk to you, you say yes. You don't want to talk, we go.''

"What the fuck he care?" Snake faced Carter. "What do he care who killed that fucking white boy? He five-o? Why?''

"Five-o?" I looked to Carter.

"A cop," Carter said, his eyes on Snake.

"Am I a cop? No," I said to Snake. "Not a cop. A private detective.''

"Say what?''

"A private eye," I said wearily. Suddenly I was bone tired, tired of posturing, tired of parrying, tired of these vicious, ruined children and their brutal world.

"Listen," I said. "I don't give a shit about you, Snake. If you didn't kill Mike, if you didn't kill Henry Howe, then you don't mean shit to me.''

"Bullshit, man." Snake poked me in the chest. "You want my ass, bitch, same as the rest of the heat. You want my ass 'cause me and my homeboys, we too fine for you. We gettin', and niggers not suppose to get.''

"I'm not the heat. I wouldn't mind seeing you go down, but it's not what I'm here for.''

"So why the fuck you here? Why you here, white meat?''

"Tell them to lower the guns, Snake.''

The three guys with the automatics trained on me hadn't moved. Snake beamed at them, pleased and proud, like a father whose children were behaving perfectly in front of ill-mannered strangers.

"Yeah," he said. "Yeah, okay, homies. Slack off, don't back off.''

The arms holding the guns lowered slowly. Two of the guys stood motionless, the guns loose in their hands, pointing at the pavement. The third, the young one, started to tuck his into his belt. Then he glanced at the others. He stopped and straightened, glared at me, let his gun hang loose in his hand, too.

The playground was silent. The sky was dark now, and starless; in the cold wind I suppressed a shiver. I wanted to zip my jacket, but I knew better than to move.

"I want to know who killed those men," I said. "And why. If you didn't I want to know why it's being made to look as though you did.''

"Well, don't that make you large. Yo, you a detective, go find out."

"How much does the Home pay you?"

"What shit is that?"

"For protection. How much?"

Snake looked from me to Carter, hesitated. Then he grinned and shrugged. "Thou."

"A month?"

"Yeah."

"Steep."

"They got it."

"Why'd you hit the trucker?"

"Say what?"

"A few weeks ago, you hit a trucker making a delivery there. Don't bullshit me, it was you." I almost said, "you punks," but I bit off the word. "If the Home makes their payments, why'd you do that?"

"Oh, that." He spoke as an executive who'd had to be reminded of an unimportant decision. Spreading his hands, he explained the obvious: "Night's extra."

"Extra?"

"Dangerous 'round here at night. Take more work keep people safe."

"They wouldn't pay the extra?"

"Guess not."

"Who wouldn't?"

"Fuckin' truckers, man! What the hell is this? I'm sick of you, fool!" Snake suddenly erupted, threw his hands in the air, brought them down on his hips. "You makin' me mad, I be makin' you sad. Don't want to talk to you no more, my brother."

Before I could answer, Carter spoke from beside me. "Okay, Snake. Chill. We going now. My man got no more questions."

"That true, fool?" Snake's eyes were bright and hard, glittering like glass. Something nagged at my memory, but on that cold, wide playground I wasn't sure what.

"For now," I said.

"Hey, Snake, man! Let me smoke the motherfucker!" The fourteen-year-old whipped his gun up, held it level. "Lemme smoke 'em both! You say it, Snake, I do it! Gettin' in our business. We the Cobras, dogshit! Who the fuck you?''

I looked at him evenly, at Snake again. "Smith," I said. "If you want me, Carter knows where to find me." I turned, at the same time Carter did. We started together across the asphalt.

Snake's voice, loud, came from behind us. "Was a time the Rev wouldn't turn his back on no Cobra."

Carter stopped walking, but didn't turn around. I stopped when he did, half-turned, just because I had to see, though I knew it would do no good. Carter, facing away from Snake, said in a voice that carried as Snake's had, "Was a time a Cobra wouldn't shoot no man in the back."

He started forward again. Together we walked toward the open gate, a hundred miles away. Cold sweat inched down my back. Adrenaline burned my veins; I could feel the fast, hard pounding of my heart. I forced my hands to hang loosely, my legs to step slowly.

"Don't say nothing, don't look back." Carter's voice was cold and low.

I kept my eyes fixed on the gate hanging twisted on its hinges, kept walking. The cold wind brought only city sounds, sharp and clear: a horn honking, a steady bass radio beat, the hiss of traffic. I strained beyond them to hear a rustle, a click, a sound I'd never hear from this distance. I heard only the leaves blowing on the pavement and, from somewhere, the slamming of a door.

Then we were outside the gate. I tried to swallow, but my mouth was too dry. We moved up the sidewalk, Carter and I, crossed the street to where the smell of dinner frying lingered in the cold air. The Cobras' sentry was still a shadowy form at the top of the block.

Something moved at the edge of my vision and I jerked around to have a look, but it was only an alley cat, skinny and furtive, scuttling across the street. A woman walked a dog past us on the sidewalk, and a ten-year-old called Speedo sat reading comic books on the hood of my car.

TWENTY-ONE

I gave Speedo a ten-dollar bill, watched him bad-walk down the now empty street. Carter stared wordlessly after him.

I climbed in the car and lit a Kent the minute I was behind the wheel. I leaned my head back, filled my lungs with the comfort of nicotine. Carter lifted the pack from the dash, took one for himself. We smoked together in silence while I dug the car keys out of my pocket.

When we were moving through traffic I spoke. "Thanks," I said.

Carter smiled, inspected the burning tip of his cigarette. "Oh, my pleasure. Any time at all."

I grinned, felt the adrenaline rush begin to subside.

Carter shook his head. "On the serious tip: stay out their way, you dig?"

"Yeah," I said, turning onto the Concourse. "I dig."

"Snake down at the cop house all day behind this," he went on. "He don't feel kindly disposed toward The Man right at the moment."

"I'm not The Man."

He looked at me. "No, you wrong," he said. "You not the law. But you The Man."

We stopped for a light. I heard a grinding noise as a merchant rolled a steel shutter down, locked it across the front of his store. "Tell me about the Rev."

Carter didn't answer right away. "Nothing to tell," he finally said, in a more distant voice.

"You and Snake used to be pretty tight, I hear."

"We used to hang."

"And now?"

"Now we don't." He took a last draw, put out his cigarette.

Traffic in the express lanes of the wide Concourse was flowing easily, commuters on their way to the highway, to the northern suburbs. In the local lanes, where we were, double-parked cars outside fast-food restaurants narrowed the street to one lane in places, and traffic backed up behind gypsy cabs disgorging customers. Our progress, though we didn't have far to go, was slow.

I said, "I heard the Rev went to jail."

"Everybody done time." Carter gestured toward the next stoplight. "This my street."

"I know." I pulled over to the curb. "I'm sorry. I don't mean to put you on the spot. But there's a lot going on here I don't understand. I'm trying to put it together."

"Who tell you you got to understand everything?"

"Christ, it's my business. It's what I do."

He looked out of the window, into the city night. When he turned back to me, there was a wariness and, I thought, a warning in his eyes. "Look. You want to find out who done your friend, I try to help you. But the 'hood, it ain't like your world. Rules is all different here. You lose, you lose big. And you can't win."

"Because I'm white?"

He shook his head. "Because you here. Ain't no winners here."

He left my car, walked down the street into the tired brick building. I watched the door close behind him, and watched a little while after that, though the sidewalk was empty.

Then I started the car, swung around into the express lanes. I headed downtown, for dinner with Lydia.

I got to my place with half an hour to spare, enough to shave, change my shirt, and give myself a few minutes to try to sort out the day. Because of the night before, and because I was so tired, things were beginning to run together. I was afraid there were things I was losing, maybe things I'd already lost.

I stood at the big front windows, smoking. The streetlights made deep shadows in the silent loading docks, shadows in which anything—people, or fears, or memories—could move unseen. The difficult, antagonistic sounds of Elliot Carter's piano concerto flooded the room, the piano and the orchestra straining futilely toward each other, unable to find common ground.

I thought about Bobby, his helpless anger over what someone had done to Mike, over what his own disloyal body had done to him; about Sheila, who through the days to come would be betrayed, over and over, by small, surprising things that would bring the stab of loss again, each time as numbing and hopeless as the first time; and about Ida Goldstein, facing now a different loss, a darkness with no guide.

I wondered about Carter, and about Howe, and Snake; and I wondered what truth would really be served when I finally found out what had happened on the night Mike died.

The cigarette was gone, and so was the inch of bourbon I'd poured. It was time to go downstairs, and I felt a little lighter when I thought of Lydia, her dark eyes, her freesia-scented hair, the solid warmth of her athlete's body. She saw so many things differently from the way I did. Together maybe we could separate what meant something from what didn't, decide where to move next. Talking to Lydia would help; it always did.

In the street below a car pulled up, idled. The streetlights gave me a clear view through the windshield. The driver was a young Asian man I didn't know. The passenger was Lydia.

They talked, he with his hands still on the wheel; she tossed her head, ran a hand through her hair in a gesture I knew well. She leaned toward him. He slid his arms around her.

They kissed for a long time; then she got out of the car, closed the door, leaned into the window and spoke. Standing back, she watched him drive off.

She turned to cross the street, and I stepped quickly away from the window in case, on her way into Shorty's she should glance up. She usually did.

The bar was close to empty when I walked in, just a few regulars scattered around, and Lydia in a booth facing the door. Dark wood drank up the light from low bulbs under green glass shades. I nodded to Shorty. The air smelled companionably of beer and burgers. Shorty's was as familiar to me as the apartment upstairs where I'd lived for sixteen years, and to a point, as always, it comforted me.

Lydia smiled when she saw me come in. I slid onto the bench opposite; I grinned but I didn't kiss her.

"Hi," she said. She examined my face. "You look awful."

"Thanks. You look gorgeous, as usual."

Kay appeared with a glass of orange juice for Lydia.

"Hi," she greeted me. "How you doing? Get you a Maker's Mark?"

"No, thanks. Just a beer. Harp."

She went to get it. Lydia asked, "Does that mean you're as tired as you look?"

"Tired doesn't begin to describe it. Jesus." I rubbed my hand across my face. "I'm too old to do this."

"To do what?"

"Work all night. Get beat up on by punks. Ask questions I don't know the reasons for, get answers I don't understand."

"Poor Bill." Lydia smiled, covered my hand with her own. Hers was soft and warm and I let mine linger under it for a few moments before I squeezed her fingers lightly and pulled away to light a cigarette.

Kay brought my beer. Lydia ordered a spinach salad and I got a burger, though I wasn't sure I wasn't too tired to eat.

Lydia sipped at her orange juice. "Do you want to talk about the case first, or do you want to talk about what happened this morning?"

I thought back to this morning, to our phone conversation, so long ago.

"I want to explain why I reacted like that," she said.

"You don't have to explain anything to me," I said. "Ever."

"That's not true." Her eyes, steady and clear, found mine. "And I want to."

I drank some beer. "All right."

"It's this," she said. "We're working together, but when trouble came, you didn't call me. When you called me, you came on to me, the way you always do. The thing is, Bill, sometimes I think that's why you work with me. That if you didn't lust after me," she half smiled, but her eyes were serious, "you wouldn't bring me in on your cases the way you do. And if we . . . stopped playing that game, you wouldn't work with me at all."

I smoked silently for a while. "I didn't know you felt that way."

She didn't answer.

"Lydia," I finally said, stubbing my cigarette out, "what I do could get me killed. When I call someone in, I want brains and balls and the ability to go from zero to ninety in ten seconds. I'm crazy, but not crazy enough to sell that out for a chance to get in your pants.'' In the dim light in Shorty's she seemed to blush. I added, ''Even those great leather ones. You know, with the red stitching on them, and the little zippers on the ankles—''

She laughed, shook her head. ''Okay,'' she said. ''Okay.'' Her eyes got serious again. ''Because I want us to keep working together, Bill. As a team.''

''The way we've always worked, since the day three years ago when I found you in the gutter—oh, wait, now I remember, that was your office. Why wouldn't we, Lydia? What's wrong?''

She ran her hand through her hair. ''I don't know. Lately I've been wondering if I really belong in this business. It's a little crazy, isn't it? Doing what we do? And then I thought, maybe Bill doesn't even really think I'm any good . . .''

''I call you,'' I said, ''because you're good.'' I wanted to add, and because I love you, and I love you because you're good. Instead, I went on, ''And I can't believe you don't think you belong in this business. You're perfect for it. For one thing, you're unbelievably nosy. For another, you have billions of Chinese relations who among them work in every profession in America and they all owe you. And for another, your mother hates what you do.''

''Those are the prerequisites?''

''Uh-huh.'' I drank some beer.

''Did your mother hate it when you started?'' she asked suddenly.

My eyes avoided hers, wandered the room, the paneled walls, the L-shaped bar with the bottles behind, the tin ceiling I'd put in for Shorty before I'd even moved in upstairs. There had been times over the last three years when I'd thought I might tell Lydia about my family, about all of it; but tonight, at the end of this long, long day, all I said was, ''I don't know.''

We were silent with each other for a while, just a short time while the regulars murmured their soft conversations and Shorty mixed up drinks behind the bar.

Lydia suddenly said, ''I'm seeing someone.''

I put my beer down, looked from it to her. ''I know.''

She frowned. Before she could speak I said, "Well, I am a detective."

Her frown lasted a second longer; then she smiled, relaxed. "His name is Paul Kao. He's a friend of my brother Andrew's. A photographer." She added, in a tone whose meaning I couldn't quite decipher, "He's Chinese."

I lit another cigarette, smoked a little of it before I spoke again. "You never promised me anything," I said. "You've always told me I was wasting my time. That's been my choice. This doesn't change anything, unless you want it to."

"No." She leaned forward. "That's what I'm saying. I don't want it to."

"Then it won't."

She smiled, that glowing smile. I smiled too, the best smile I had, and looked away.

We didn't speak again until Kay came over carrying dinner. I poured ketchup on my burger, ordered another beer.

Lydia stuck her fork into her salad, pulled out a spinach leaf, did something elegant with her fork and knife that left the leaf folded small. "Well," she said, "should we talk about the case?"

"What case is that?" I asked, working my way around my burger.

"It's a homicide case. Up in the Bronx."

"Did you find out who did it?"

"Uh-uh."

"Damn."

"But I found out something that might be interesting. That is, I'm sure it's interesting. I just don't know what it means."

"Right now I'll take meaningless, as long as it's interesting."

She grinned. "I was hoping you'd feel that way." Our eyes met, just for a second. I pulled mine away to look around for Kay, or anything.

Lydia's look may have become a little unsure, or maybe I was just wishing it would. She went on in a normal voice. "Well, it's a real estate thing. I'm only just beginning to dig into it, and I don't really understand this stuff. I had to call my brother Ted's friend the realtor and have him explain it to me, what it could mean. And of course it could mean nothing.''

"Uh-huh.'' I poured more ketchup onto my plate, dipped the edge of the burger in it. "Except your hunches rarely mean nothing.''

"I just never tell you about the ones that don't work out.'' She chased some chick peas around her bowl. "Well, anyway. Remember I told you Helping Hands owns nine properties in the Bronx? There seems to be a pattern to what happens when they buy one.''

"You mean to how they build, or renovate?''

"No, to what happens before that. First of all, they've never bought a property from an individual. It's always a holding corporation. And the thing is, these corporations are all owned by other corporations. I've found fourteen of them so far. Nine of them own one property each, and the other five own those.''

"Which makes it really hard to trace who's behind them.''

"Well, yes.'' She grinned. "But not impossible.''

"Oh, goody.''

"There were some names I didn't recognize on the ones I've been able to trace, which isn't all of them yet,'' she said. "And one I did. That guy you told me to add to the list. Andy Hill.''

"Oh,'' I said slowly. I finished my beer, waited for everything to fall into place. Nothing did.

"Okay,'' I said. "Andy Hill sets up corporations, buys properties, and sells them to Helping Hands. Does he sell them for huge inflated prices or something?''

"No. They're sold for more than he paid for them, but not more than you might expect as a normal profit.''

"That doesn't sound illegal. It also doesn't sound like something you can get rich from.''

"I said I didn't understand it. But there's a little more. The corporations—never the same ones as sold a particular property, but others of them—in seven of the nine cases they own properties in the immediate vicinity of the one that was sold to Helping Hands.''

"Andy Hill is buying up the Bronx?''

"That's what it looks like.''

"God. Why would you do that?"

"To make a fortune?"

"How?"

She didn't answer. I didn't expect her to.

Kay brought my second beer. I knew it wouldn't help the soft confusion in my mind, but probably nothing would. I took a sip.

"How about you?" Lydia said. "Did you find out anything interesting today?"

"I did. I found out all sorts of interesting things, and I don't know what they mean either."

"Tell me," she said. So I did.

I worked my way through last night, Howe's body, Robinson, Lindfors. I told her what Ida Goldstein had told me, what Sheila Downey had said as we sat on her porch with the wind chimes tinkling in the October breeze. I told her about the money and my note that came and went in Howe's locker. I bit an onion ring, crisp and salty, and told Lydia about getting X-rayed at Samaritan Hospital. At that part concern clouded her face.

"I didn't realize you were that badly hurt."

"I wasn't. I've had broken ribs. These aren't even close."

"Then why did the doctor send you? Are you sure you're okay?"

"I don't know. And yes. And another thing. Have you ever been to an emergency room?"

"No. Why? Do you think it's an experience I shouldn't miss?"

"Definitely right up your alley. The standard thing is to wait four or five hours, unless you're actually bleeding, sometimes even then. Where I was was the Diagnostic Clinic, not the emergency room, but it's the same X-ray department. I was in and out in under an hour. There was an old couple waiting when I came in; they were still waiting when I left."

"Maybe they're not real busy at that hospital."

"Maybe not. They're not all that close to the Bronx Home, either. There are two bigger hospitals closer."

"Hmmm."

"Right." I went on with my report, gave her a quick account of my meeting with the Cobras.

"God," she said, when I was through. "It sounds like you're lucky you came out in one piece."

"In one piece," I said, "and not a damn bit smarter than when I went in."

"Well." She pulled a set of files from the leather bag beside her. "I can fill you in on some of those guys, anyway. Maybe that will help." She sorted through the folders. "We owe Mary a big one for this, by the way."

Mary Kee was a childhood friend of Lydia's, now a Fifth Precinct detective. I had my own sources, people I'd have gone to in the NYPD to ask a favor like this, but when Lydia and I are working different ends of a case we keep out of each other's way.

"Tell her I appreciate it."

"Actually, I think she did it mostly for Mr. Moran. Because he used to be a cop. They get like that, cops. Like family."

I finished off my second beer. Lydia opened a file.

"This Anthony LeMoyne, a.k.a. Snake. He's quite a guy." She scanned a striped computer printout. "A sealed youth record, then robbery, robbery, assault, burglary, assault, controlled substance, grant theft auto—you get the idea. Lots of arrests, but not a lot of convictions. A few months here and there, no serious time. His friend Skeletor's pretty much the same. I have some others here, people the Youth Gang Task Force identifies as Cobras."

"You have a sheet on Martin Carter?"

"Your friend? The one you were with?" Her tone was surprised.

"They call him the Rev."

"Who does?"

"The Cobras. And the cops."

She searched my face briefly, then glanced down at her printout. "He's here, but not current."

"Retired?"

"Uh-huh. Former member. Someone to keep an eye on, but not active with the crew. In his case, with good reason."

"What does that mean?"

"He's on parole. Two years more. Being seen with some of these guys is enough to get him sent back to finish his time upstate."

My mind went back to Carter's jumpiness at meeting Snake in the schoolyard. He'd broken parole because I'd asked him to.

"What'd he do?"

"The conviction is second-degree manslaughter. He served eighteen months, and he's been out a little over a year. You want me to look into it?"

"Yes."

"Bill, he's a friend of yours."

"I know." I lit a cigarette, leaned back in the booth. A sudden exhaustion overcame me, as though a plug had been pulled and all my substance drained out, leaving me empty, and cold.

Lydia gestured at the files. "Do you want to go over the rest of this now?"

"I don't think I can. I'm falling asleep. Leave them with me, okay?"

"Okay. You want me to just keep on with this tomorrow?"

I thought. It got me nowhere. "I'll call you in the morning. I have a feeling I had a good idea, something for you to do, but I'll be damned if I know what it was. Come on, I'll take you home."

She laughed. "You have to be kidding. You expect me to get into a car with you? I've been thinking *I'd* have to take *you* upstairs."

A wise-guy come-on sprang to mind, the kind of thing I'd have said to Lydia any other time, had said many other times. I waved Kay over, told her to put our meal on my tab. Lydia handed me the gathered-up files and we went out together through Shorty's etched-glass doors.

The night air was crisp, not really cold, but I shivered a little in it as Lydia and I walked silently to Hudson Street. I waited while she got a cab, kissed her before she got in, and turned away, back toward my place, before the cab drove off. The night air, I thought, smelled gently of freesia, but I knew that wasn't true.

TWENTY-TWO

I slept until ten, awoke groggy and disoriented. Coffee helped, and so did a shower and a shave and clean clothes that were mine, not a uniform. I read through Lydia's files, learned not much I saw any use for, but you never know. I made a call from a number Information gave me; then I called Lydia.

"Hi," she said. "Feeling better?"

"Much. How about you?"

"I wasn't feeling bad."

"Be grateful."

"You sound like my mother."

"Don't tell your mother that. She'll have a fit."

"She wouldn't believe me. What are you going to do?"

"About your mother not believing you? That's your problem."

"About the case. The homicide? Up in the Bronx?"

"Oh," I said. "That. Don't you think the day will come when your mother might need a nursing home?"

"Not as long as my brothers have wives. And Chinese don't— Oh," she said. "Oh, oh, oh. Well, I suppose it wouldn't hurt to look into it. She doesn't like Elliot's wife anyway."

"Good. I'll call you later."

"What are you going to do?" she asked again.

"I'm going to see a man about a truck."

Triple-A Trucking—"Anything, Anywhere, Anytime"—was packed in behind lots of chain-link fence in the part of the Bronx where Gun Hill Road passes under the IRT. Graffiti glowed from every surface in the neighborhood: the bars, the auto-parts store, the cuchifritos place, and the steel columns holding up the subway tracks. And from Triple-A's concrete-block garage, the razor wire topping the chain-link notwithstanding.

The gate in the fence was open wide. A yellow truck with its logo obliterated by spray paint had to stop backing out for me to drive in. Its red-faced driver leaned out his window, cursed me as I passed. He rumbled out, and so did his truck.

There was nothing organized about the Triple-A yard, cars and trucks and cargo sprawled in cramped disarray inside the chain-link borders. I settled for a place alongside the garage, about as far out of the way as I was likely to get.

Hunched next to the garage, as though it were trying to get out of the way too, was a trailer. A couple of guys in the yard watched me head toward it, but no one stopped work or showed a lot of interest. Maybe I was boring, now that I was shaved and clean. Maybe I was always boring.

I climbed three concrete steps, pulled open the trailer door. Right inside, a thin, rouged, blond woman sat at a desk piled high with a mess of phone messages and ledger books. Behind her a jowly, balding man sat at a bigger desk piled just as high with bulging manila envelopes and yellow pads and five-part multicolor bills of lading. Every remaining inch of the trailer was stuffed with mismatched file cabinets, some with their drawers half open. Files and phone books and a brown philodendron littered the cabinets' tops.

The clack of the woman's typewriter, which I'd heard from the yard, stopped as I walked in. The air was scented with cigars living and dead, and with the lethally sweet output of a pink air-freshener that clung desperately to a window waiting for a chance to escape.

"Yeah?" The heavy man pushed the word out around a thick green cigar. Oh, yeah. The woman smiled a slightly mischievous smile. I liked that, so I smiled back.

"I'm Smith," I said to the man. "I called. You're Burcynski?"

He grunted, "Yeah." That must have been all he could say around the cigar, because he took it out then, rolled it between fingers that looked amazingly like it. "Two-day rental, right?"

"That's what I said," I told him. "I lied."

"Huh?" He stuck the cigar in his mouth again, tongued it around. The woman's eyes twinkled. Maybe I wasn't boring after all.

"I wanted to make sure you'd talk to me. I didn't want to risk your being suddenly called out of town when I got here."

He took the cigar out again, looked at me. "I got my suit-cases packed."

"You won't need them." I leaned against a file cabinet. "Mind if I smoke?"

The woman laughed out loud.

I lit a cigarette, dropped the match in an ashtray where it had lots of company. "I'm a private investigator. A friend of mine got himself killed and I'm working the case. I have some questions for you. Outside the answers to them I don't care what you do, with which or to whom. I'm blind, I'm stupid, and I have a short memory."

Burcynski poked the cigar in my direction. He and the cigar considered me. "How do I know that's true?"

"Just look at me."

He snorted through thick lips. "Okay. We'll do this. You ask. Maybe I'll answer."

"What happened to Leon Vega?"

Burcynski picked something off his tongue. "Some punks beat the shit out of him over by the Concourse a few weeks ago. I bet you knew that."

"Uh-huh. I hear it was because you weren't paying the road-use tax."

"Listen," he said. "In the first place, it wasn't me. Leon's an independent operator with a long-term lease. Second, no one ever sent a bill."

"No one told you about the Cobras?"

"No one told me it was my fucking job. 'Scuse me, Leon's fucking job. I pay protection over here to some other bunch of limp-dicks. Leon must've figured the receiver was paying over there. Matter of fact, when I called up that liaison guy, that's what he told me."

"What liaison guy? He told you what?"

Burcynski's cigar, sulking at the lack of attention, had gone out. He coaxed it back to life. "The Borough President's guy. Hill, his name is."

"What do you mean, liaison?"

"Borough President's Community Liaison. What the hell do you think that means?"

"I don't know."

"He helps you do business in the Bronx."

"Including paying off the Cobras?"

"Including whatever."

"And he told you the receiver was already paying? The Bronx Home?"

"Nah." The word came out around the cigar again and the cigar puffed happily. "I told him that's how I thought it was, and he said what did he know but it sounded right to him."

"Then what?"

"I told him the message on the bill was, 'Night's extra.' He said he didn't know they got night deliveries over there, but he'd look into it."

"Did he?"

Shrug from Burcynski, nothing from the cigar.

"What is it they deliver over there at night?"

Burcynski contemplated the cigar as though asking its advice. "Damned if I know. Ask Leon."

"He's still in a coma. I can't talk to him."

"That's too bad."

"So what happened?"

"So I started paying."

"With Vega out of commission? Business must be profitable."

"Leon's business. His cousin's driving for him now. I'm floating them the money. As a favor. I got absolutely no idea what business they're in. Now," he knocked the ash off the cigar into a wastebasket boiling over with papers, "beat it. I got a train to catch. I been called out of town."

"One more thing. How are the payments made?"

He looked at me in disbelief. "You write a check, with your name all over it."

"No, I mean where? How? Directly to the Cobras?"

"Are you shitting me? I wouldn't go near those guys. Some guy, I meet him at a greasy spoon."

"How'd you know how to do it?"

"He called me. Said he heard I needed protection."

"What's his name?"

"Don't know."

"What's he look like?"

Burcynski shrugged again.

Our eyes met, held each other steadily.

"Okay." I moved a mountain of cigar butts around in the

ashtray to make a place to stub out my cigarette. "Thanks."

"Yeah," Burcynski grunted. His cigar glowed a superior, contented red.

The woman behind the desk smiled conspiratorially and winked. I smiled back and left, ignoring the heartbreaking pleas from the air-freshener I was abandoning.

TWENTY-THREE

I went to see Andy Hill.

The Courthouse building held the Bronx County offices. I'd been there a few times over the years, in the old paneled courtrooms, the dim and dusty records rooms in the basement. Once I'd been hauled in and chewed out by a baby-faced A.D.A. in a government-green office, but nothing came of that.

I climbed the long ceremonial steps to the bronze doors figured with eagles and hourglasses. Inside, the lobby's marble shone and the ceiling arched high.

The upper floors, though, had been renovated, in line with a new, diminished concept of public service that saw civic grandeur as a lower virtue than serviceability. Vinyl tile covered terrazzo floors; plastic lighting grids hid high coffered ceilings. Openings had been punched in limestone walls and wheezy air conditioners stuck through them. Formica replaced teak in elevator cabs. Looming over the neighborhood, the Bronx County Courthouse represented government to the governed with limestone columns and copper friezes, marble statues and vast granite staircases. Inside it looked like any cheaply made public building in any tired city in America.

At the Borough President's suite—a formerly high-ceilinged, marble-paved area on the third floor—the receptionist asked my name and business. She was a black woman of my own age with a beauty-parlor hairdo and no smile at all.

"Is Mr. Hill expecting you?"

Interesting question, I thought. "I just took a chance that he'd be free."

"Mr. Hill is rarely free." She seemed to be controlling

her temper with an effort, as though she'd explained all this to me before. "He keeps a very busy schedule."

"I'm sure that's true. But maybe you could ask him if he'll see me, since I came all the way here?"

She didn't ask me all the way from where, which was just as well. She waved me to a seat beneath photographs of former Borough Presidents and watched, stone-faced, until I sat. She spoke into her multigadget telephone; then, covering the mouthpiece, she said, "Mr. Hill is asking if he knows you."

"Tell him we met yesterday morning. I used to work for Arthur Chaiken."

She told him. And he, apparently, told her to show me in. She pointed down a corridor beyond the heavy-traffic carpet, to the private offices. "Third door on the right."

Behind the third door on the right were high windows and a nice cream-and-tan paint job. There were plaques lauding Andy Hill's sense of civic duty, photos of him deploying it in the company of public and community figures, including, I noticed, one with Arthur Chaiken at a ribbon-cutting. A laminated Bronx map hung above a glass-fronted bookcase full of law books and phone books. As befits a Community Liaison, a massive Rolodex squatted on the corner of Andy Hill's desk and Andy Hill, when I walked in, was on the phone.

Smiling, he motioned me to a chair, made a deprecating face at the receiver. He mouthed "Be right with you" silently and with perfect clarity. Maybe he practiced in front of a mirror.

As I sat, he spoke into the phone. "No, I don't think so. Well, I haven't heard that, Mr. Molina. But I'll look into it, just to make sure. No, that's what I'm here for."

His voice, contradicting the face he'd made, exuded concern over a constituent's problems, and the dauntless ability to solve them. Don't worry, things are under control, the BP's man is on the case. I found myself wondering whether this was a real phone conversation or page 168 of *Power: How to Get It, How to Use It.* Probably the real thing; if it were for my benefit, it wouldn't be "Mr. Molina" but "Mr. Mayor."

Hill said, "Good-bye, Mr. Molina," grinned at me,

punched the intercom button. "Betty, wait a couple of days, then send Molina a we've-investigated-your-complaint-and—no, wait, that's what we sent him last time. Send the one about we're looking into it, appreciate your concern, citizens like you, blah blah blah. Thanks."

He hung up, came energetically around the desk, as though he'd been hoping for a break in his routine and here I was. "Mr. Smith! How are you? I'm sorry I went blank on your name before."

"That's okay." I stood to shake his hand. "People go blank on me all the time."

His navy suit was as fine as the charcoal one he'd worn yesterday, and his red-silk tie picked up the discreet red monogram on his shirt cuff. His pale eyes were frank and smiling as he said, "Look, I don't have much time. It's crazy around here today. But a friend of Arthur's . . ." He left the sentence unfinished. Guys like us, we know what it means to be a friend of Arthur's. "Did he send you?"

"Mr. Chaiken? No, this was my idea." I could have gone on, but I thought I'd toss the ball back to him and see how he played it.

He nodded, as though that was one of the standard serves. "Well, of course I'm glad you came by, but I really have nothing for you. I'm sorry."

Bad play, Smith, I told myself. Now you're confused. "Nothing for me?"

"Well, I told Arthur, I use investigators around here once in a blue moon, but I don't need anyone right at the moment. I could get you an intro at the Bronx D.A.'s office, if that would help." He looked pleased with the thought and reached for his Rolodex.

"Oh." And probably to that nice baby-faced A.D.A., too. "Thanks, but I didn't come here looking for a job, Mr. Hill."

"Andy. Everybody calls me Andy. Then I don't understand. Arthur said you'd been laid off and might need work—"

"My firm's been taken off the Bronx Home job. But that's not why I'm here. I've actually just come to ask you a few questions."

"To ask me questions? What kind of questions?" Glancing at his watch, he went back around and sat at his desk. He leaned forward, threaded his fingers, his eyes still guileless and eager. If he had had to throw me out just when the questions got interesting, his posture said, it would be with regret, and it would only be his hectic schedule that was to blame.

"Well, I'm not sure," I began. "Your name keeps popping up in the strangest places."

He laughed. "So do I. It's part of my job." He could have gone on then, too, but he tossed the ball back to me. It seemed we had the same instincts.

"Do you play handball?" I asked.

"Handball? As a matter of fact I do. Why?"

"Just wondered. It's my game."

"I do play. I play squash, too, with Arthur sometimes. But I prefer handball. I like as little as possible between the game and myself."

We did have the same instincts.

"Maybe we could get together for a game sometime," he said. "But that's not why you came?"

"No. Is it all right if I smoke?" Time out.

"Oh, sure." He grinned, pushed a heavy marble ashtray my way. "As long as you're not insulted if I open a window." No score. He opened the window. Crisp autumn air ruffled the papers on his desk.

"I was over by Gun Hill Road today," I said, shaking out the match. "To talk to Abe Burcynski."

"Burcynski?" His brow furrowed, but it was a feint. "Triple-A Trucking?"

"Yes."

"How's his driver doing? Vega?" One–nothing, Hill.

"Still in a coma. He's why I went. What happened to him?"

"If you went to talk about him, you must know." Two–nothing.

I took in smoke, nodded. "He was making a night delivery to the Bronx Home. The Cobras said night wasn't in the contract and wanted to renegotiate. That's what I heard, anyway."

"That's what I heard, too."

"Burcynski says he called you and you said you'd look into it."

He gave me a shamefaced smile, gestured at the phone. "I say that to a lot of people."

"Well, someone got in touch with Burcynski and straightened him out. He makes his payments now and everyone's happy."

"Really? You know," he mused, "sometimes I think it's too bad we can't focus the energy and enterprise of some of these go-getters into more productive channels."

Three–zip.

Change your strategy, Smith. Try a straight-on offense. "What do you get out of it?"

"What do you mean?"

"The Cobras must appreciate the reference."

"The Cobras? What, you think I—" Hill's fair skin flushed crimson. "You can't be serious. If the BP ever smelled a hint of a suggestion of an idea that I might be associated with someone who could even *spell* 'Cobras,' I'd be out on my ear. And I resent the insinuation, by the way. You're trying—" He stopped. The color faded from his face. He leaned back in his chair, smiling. "Well. Arthur told me you could be abrasive."

I smiled too. "Yeah. I can. Sorry." Three–one, and we were smiling at each other.

"Listen," I said. "There's something else, and probably the implications are even more insulting."

"Go ahead," he grinned. "I'll try to control myself. But first you have to tell me what this is about. Is someone investigating me? Is this politics?"

"No, not politics." I told him what I was working on, but not whom I was working for. I wasn't sure why; but something in my gut was telling me to keep Bobby out of this.

Hill frowned thoughtfully when I was through. "That's what you said yesterday morning: that these killings might be something else, not what they looked like. You didn't say you were investigating."

"No."

He waited a beat or two, but I didn't add anything. No score, again.

"And why come to me? You still haven't explained that.

Unless—'' his face lit up ''—you think I did it? God, I've been called a lot of things, but this is a new one.''

I'd played opponents like this before. Sometimes they really had no strategy, just a straightforward game, all power and speed and punch. They were surprisingly effective, if they knew their own weaknesses, their vulnerable spots.

But sometimes the openness and lack of guile was the strategy: let your opponent think you have no game to dope out, while you watch his. Then come at him suddenly, tripping him into all the mistakes of temperament, false expectation, and bad habit you've discovered him capable of.

Usually—but not always—I could beat guys like that.

I answered Hill. ''Can you tell me why you own property all over the Bronx, and why Helping Hands always buys its properties from you?''

His eyes widened, just a little. Three–two. Then he gave me a rueful smile. ''Arthur was right. You are good.'' Time out. He stood, walked to the window, where the tar roofs of smaller buildings soaked up the October sun, as though they could store it against the cold, dark time to come. ''How did you find out about that? And why did you even look?''

''I looked because I'm looking at everything and everybody connected with the Bronx Home. I found out because I looked.'' And because I have a very, very clever partner, whose name is going to stay out of this conversation too, I thought.

Hill continued to stare out the window; then, abruptly, he turned, came back to his desk and sat. Play resumes.

''I don't suppose there's any point in throwing you out of my office?''

''You could do that. Of course, I might wonder why. I might get so curious I'd have to ask Arthur why you'd do a thing like that. Or I could ask the BP what he knows about real estate.'' Three–all, and I had two balls in play.

He went after the foul one. ''You haven't talked to Arthur yet?''

''Is there a reason why I should?''

''Oh, I don't think so,'' Hill said easily. ''He'd just tell you the same things I will.''

Uh-huh, I thought. ''What things are those?''

He tapped his fingers on the desk a time or two, then

spoke. "It's important for you to know that nothing I've done is illegal."

Important to you, maybe. I didn't answer.

He sighed. "Arthur and I have an arrangement. It works for both of us."

"He's making money on the side too?" I frowned.

"Just listen, will you?" Out-of-bounds. No score. "We consult on sites for his programs. It's part of my job, helping businesses locate in the Bronx. You know, the Bronx Renaissance?"

"What's that?"

"Government facilities are located in the borough as seeds to attract other development. I help smooth the way for the other development."

"Like Helping Hands?"

Hill pursed his fleshy lips. "Arthur identifies a need, a program the foundation will sponsor. Together we look at likely sites. In fact, that's how I got started. There can be community opposition, as you might imagine. Misguided, but it's there."

"How you got started buying properties?"

"Yes. While he's getting his financing together, I buy the property he's going to want. Nobody worries about anything being sold to something called R&G Properties—all my holding companies have meaningless names like that. Then when Helping Hands is ready, I sell to them. They don't have to approach local property owners, which is usually what sets off the brouhaha. We have a system down by now, Arthur and I. We can go to closing in a matter of days."

"So this is community service? Philanthropy?"

"I'm not pretending that. I make a profit on each sale. Usually small, under five figures. Why shouldn't I? It's real estate. It's legal."

"It's money Helping Hands could use for something else."

"No." He shook his head. "The foundation doesn't supply its own capital budget, only about half its annual operating costs. The rest, and the capital funds, come from grants."

"Oh. So it's money New York State could use for something else."

"Right. To pay all the lawyers and public relations people it would take to help Arthur acquire the sites he buys from me." Four–three, but a cheap point.

"And the sites nearby?"

"Which sites?"

"In a lot of cases you own property very near the Helping Hands buildings."

"Oh," he said. "Sometimes it isn't clear to Arthur at the beginning which of a number of properties he wants. I buy the likely ones."

"And you just sit on the ones he doesn't buy from you?"

Hill grinned. "You know someone who wants them?"

"No."

"Neither do I. I'm hoping someday someone might. Bronx real estate is an investment that can only appreciate. Meanwhile, most of them are occupied. Rents just about offset expenses."

"And the profit you make on the ones Helping Hands buys takes the sting out?"

"That too. Listen, Smith, this is actually kind of fun, but I've got a lot on my plate today. Did you get what you came for?"

"I don't know what I came for, and I don't know what I got. Can I ask you one more thing?"

"If it's quick."

"What is it Triple-A delivers over there at night?"

"I don't know what it was, but I believe they've stopped."

"Not according to Burcynski."

Aha. A slight movement of the eyebrows, a brief hesitation. Four–all. "No? Well, I'm not sure about that. But I'll look into it."

I laughed. For a moment he seemed uncertain why. Then he grinned. "No, I really will. Look, I'm sorry, but I really have to get back to work. Come back any time you want to accuse me of something. It's been a pleasure."

Hill rose with a smile, shook my hand, showed me to the door.

Game called on account of darkness.

TWENTY-FOUR

I couldn't think of a thing to do next except have lunch. So I headed for that, crossing the street to the deli where I'd run into Arthur Chaiken and Andy Hill the morning before.

The sky over the Bronx was startlingly blue. The afternoon sun glowed the honey color you see on groomed lawns and stately homes in calendar photographs. Here, it picked out elaborate details of brickwork and stone, glazed terracotta, ornate cornice lines; but it shone equally upon peeling paint, vacant windows, doors twisted on their hinges, and the graffiti that lapped at street walls like breakers from a rising sea.

It was after two, and the deli was half empty. Up front, a rumpled attorney waved his fork at a thin black woman. An untouched cup of coffee sat before her; he was demolishing a corned-beef platter. Other lawyers were scattered around, most of them tired-looking middle-aged men. The few younger men and women wore the suits and power ties of people on the move. A.D.A.'s, they were, with ambitions: maybe to rise in politics; or maybe to pick up a prosecutor's mental habits, then open criminal defense practices, where, after a number of years, they would get to be tired-looking and middle-aged.

I ordered a cup of coffee and a pastrami sandwich. The coffee was to help me think. What I really wanted was a beer, to help me not think, to spread that optimistic warmth through my brain that said everything would work out one way or another.

What the hell to do now? Talk to more people, hear more half-truths. Wait for that moment, that break: the lie you catch someone in, the story that doesn't match, the offhand word that couldn't possibly be true. That's how cases are broken; but you don't get that unless you do the dogging, the footwork, the going over and over and over the same barren ground.

I ate, trying to silence the buzzing in my mind. Outside, yellow leaves rustled on the plane trees in the park, drifted carelessly to the sidewalk. I thought of the hills above my cabin, brown and orange, splashed with fiery maples, shadowed by stands of blue-green fir. If I left now I could get there in time to see the light fade, soft lavender to gray to silent black night. The air would be sharp this time of year, the icy wind from Canada cold and cleansing. I could walk in the woods, where the only smell of decay comes from last year's leaves, where rot nurtures next year's growth.

I watched the street, drank more coffee, smoked a cigarette. Finished, I made a phone call. Then I walked through the sunshine to my car and drove across the Bronx.

The sunlight seemed at home in Riverdale, bathing great trees and old stone walls, slate roofs and clipped hedges. There were new, huge apartment buildings along the highway, and older ones in modest brick clusters in half a dozen other areas; but where I was, on winding streets heading up from Broadway, the homes were big and the lawns were generous. These were old, substantial houses, of stone, brick, gleamingly painted clapboard; and occasionally a modern gem, glass-and-cedar boxes piled artfully together.

I rode, as usual, with the window down; I could smell woodsmoke. The quiet seemed less disturbed than underlined by the steady growl of an unseen leaf blower. Brown leaves lay mounded, raked into neat piles by brown men who didn't live here.

The streets, besides being clean, curving, and tree-arched, were empty. So when a green Chevy Nova that had been a few cars behind me off the Deegan stayed in my mirror as I curled my way uphill, I had a feeling there might be meaning here.

He was careful, lagging back, too far for me to read his plate or see his face. Once or twice he almost lost me as I made a turn, but I was careful too, careful to keep him with me while I decided what to do.

I gave up temporarily on my destination, meandered a little, thinking. Huge horse chestnut trees rose from a grassy center island, paused for a traffic circle, continued uphill. When I was a kid in Kentucky we'd collected chestnuts every fall. They were magical when you first cracked the green globe to reveal the brown-black nut, glossy and perfect.

In a few days, though, the chestnut would start to dry and dull. One year I kept the biggest, greenest globe unopened, hoping that way to keep the chestnut inside perfect too, though I'd never see it. But within a week the globe began to shrink. The spines turned brown and fragile, lost their ability to protect. Finally it split. The chestnut, exposed, dulled and withered like the others.

I had two choices: I could lose the Chevy, or I could confront him.

The hill flattened out before the chestnuts ended. The Chevy was far enough behind, downhill, that he couldn't see me. I swung hard around the island, sped back the way I'd come, the way he was still coming.

He was in the middle of a long block with no cross streets on his side. I expected that when he saw me, he'd speed up too, try to race past too fast for me to see his face. If that worked for him—if I didn't get a look—then I'd swing back around and chase him. That was my plan. But he had one other option, and he took it.

A short street angled sharply from my right into the boulevard we were on, and the chestnut island broke there. When the Chevy saw me coming he stomped on his gas, cut hard to his left. He whipped across me and flew up that street.

It took guts. I was coming pretty fast. I hit the brakes and my tires squealed; I missed broadsiding him by maybe three inches.

It was a good move, though. He got what he wanted. He swung left at the next corner, was out of sight before I was moving again.

I shifted, gave it gas, cut right; almost a U-turn, the angle was so sharp. At the top of the block I cornered left as he had, sped two more blocks to a twisted three-way fork. Down, down, up, and you couldn't see twenty yards along any of them, narrow streets close with turns, grand houses, hedges. I chose up: it seemed like the straighter, faster road, and he was in a hurry. But up turned down within half a block. It curved and suddenly with no warning it thrust me from the tree-lined fantasy land into the wide brightness of a bridge over the highway.

I slammed on my brakes at the stop sign, just missed a car in the intersection. He cursed me and I didn't blame him. I looked around; so many roads, so many choices. And then to my right I saw the Chevy in the distance disappearing east on the highway, in the direction that could take him upstate, or back into the heart of the Bronx.

Adrenaline raced through me and I almost threw the car into gear to charge after him. I could catch him; I knew I could. But it would be risky for everyone else on the road if I tried.

I sat gripping the wheel, breathing deep and controlled the way I do at the piano, until I was calm. I lit a cigarette; it helped. My original destination lay across this bridge. I shifted into gear, headed for it.

A grin slowly spread itself across my face. I'd caught a look at his plate. Something with L's and 3's in it. I could get that checked out. Besides, the guy had been following me for a reason. I didn't know what it was, but it didn't seem to me he'd gotten much out of our little game.

If I was lucky, he'd be back.

TWENTY-FIVE

I could hear the doorbell from where I stood, on the square entry porch of the square white house. Four deep tones, a dominant seventh chord yearning for resolution. The house was stucco, vaguely Italianate but not showy, not as large as many in this corner of Riverdale, along the Hudson. A small grove of spruces separated this yard from the yard next door. Looking down the hill through their green-blue branches I could see the river shining in the sun. The front garden, like the house, was small, modest; but it was beautifully planted and cared for. It bloomed with fall flowers, tall gold chrysanthemums and shorter, buttery ones, glowing orange marigolds and, against the whitewashed front wall, sunflowers drenched in light. I wondered if fall flowers were colored like the sun as a consolation for the approaching darkness and cold.

The beveled glass beside the front door filled with the stringy-haired face of a yapping dog. The door opened and the dog rushed out, a large traveling mop that planted its front paws on my knees and tried to lick my face from there. Probably that was because it had so much hair in its eyes it had no idea where my face was. I leaned down and scratched its head. It writhed in ecstasy.

"Scotty, get down! Smith, I'm glad to see you. Come in, come in." Arthur Chaiken, dressed in open-necked shirt, gray trousers and cardigan, wrestled the dog to a draw. He held its collar with one hand, shook my hand with the other, stepped aside for me to enter his house.

"Thanks," I said. "For letting me come on such short notice."

"It's no problem. And besides, I have to admit I'm intrigued."

The dog flopped around us, sniffing at my shoes. I followed Chaiken through the small entryway into a house flooded with light. The floors were pale wood and the walls were white, the doorways large and the windows wide and numerous.

"I hope I'm not interrupting anything," I said. "The lawyers I know mostly work at home when they absolutely have to get something done."

A high-ceilinged living room with a stone fireplace lay directly ahead, but we turned left down a short hall into a sunroom with a slate floor. The sun streamed onto the darkness of the stone, which collected its warmth and radiated it back, enfolding us.

"No, no," Chaiken said. "The fact is I don't go in every day. So much of what I do is paperwork, and sometimes it's easier to do it from here."

The dog's toenails clicked on the slate as it stretched out in a patch of sunlight, thought better of it, chose a different patch. I asked, "Who minds the store?"

Chaiken grinned. "Is this part of your investigation?"

"I don't know."

"Oh. Sit down." He gestured to a pair of tan leather chairs by a coffee table heaped with paperwork. A small desk equally heaped stood a few feet away. On both table and desk, magazines lay folded open to underlined articles above and beneath stuffed file folders. Yellow legal pads were scrawled with words in three colors of ink. Pens were sprinkled around like fallen leaves and a half-empty coffee cup sat making brown rings on a pink official form.

"Gad." Chaiken seemed suddenly to see the room through my eyes. "It's not as bad as it looks, you know. There's a system."

"I believe you."

"Would you like a drink? It's a little early, but I'm flexible." He grinned again. "Bourbon, right?" He opened a cabinet, took out a bottle of Jim Beam, the right bourbon for a non-bourbon drinker to stock, if you ask me. He clinked ice from a bar fridge into two generous glasses, poured more bourbon in one than I would have, and more scotch in the other. He handed me mine, settled in the other chair.

"Well," he said. "You've certainly got my attention. And by the way, I was glad when you called and said you were working on a case. That security-guard thing just didn't make sense to me. Skoal." He lifted his glass. I did the same, sipped the ceremonial first sip.

"You didn't believe me?"

"I didn't know any reason why you'd lie to me, but no, I didn't believe you. And look, I was right." He seemed pleased with that, like a guy who gets an off-the-wall tip on a horse, puts two bucks on it, and hits. "So. What are you working on, and how can I help you?"

The sun, pouring in behind me, warmed my shoulders. The bourbon warmed me, too. I told him what I was working on.

"Hmm." He frowned in a lawyerly way. "I wondered about that, when you said yesterday that those killings might not be what they seem. I suppose it's possible. Anything is possible. But I'm not sure what makes you think that."

"When I started this investigation I didn't really believe it either. Now I'm a lot more willing to buy it."

"Why is that?"

"Do you know anyone who drives a green Chevy Nova?"

Chaiken looked blank. "I can't think of anyone. Why?"

"He tried to follow me here. I lost him on the other side of the highway."

"You were followed?"

"Yesterday, too, I think. Different car."

"Oh," he said slowly. "I see."

"There's more. I keep running into strange things and getting explanations that don't explain them."

"Such as?"

"Such as I just came from Andy Hill's office." I related my conversation with Andy Hill.

"Andy," Chaiken mused when I was through. "Andy's a strange bird. You didn't buy what he told you?"

"I think what he told me was true. But I don't think a guy like Hill gives away anything for free. He told me how good I was for finding stuff that wasn't hard to find, and he filled in the blanks for me pretty fast. I think the point was to make me think I had the whole story, so I'd stop looking. But what it really does is make me think there's something more to find."

He crossed one leg over the other. "I haven't seen any evidence of that."

"Could that be because you haven't wanted to see?"

Chaiken looked at me over his scotch. "Ah, yes, the famous Smith tact. I remember that."

I didn't respond.

He regarded me silently for a space. Then he went on. "Andy's made it possible for me—for us, the foundation—to do our work. It's work that needs doing, even though it seems hopeless sometimes." He smiled ruefully. "A lot of the time. Our work is a Band-Aid on a hemorrhage. It's the wrong cure and there's not enough of it. But if you've got it, and it's all you've got, you have to try it, don't you?"

"I don't know," I said. "Maybe it just hides the real danger of the patient's condition. Maybe it just makes the doctor feel better."

Chaiken's eyes were unblinking behind his thick glasses. "I've heard that argument before. Try using it when the patient is bleeding to death in front of you."

We were silent for a few moments, while the gently moving shadows of tree branches striped the sunlight. A flock of finches, seven or eight, flashed by the window and settled at a bird feeder in the yard.

Chaiken followed my gaze. "I'm not supposed to be feeding them this late in the season."

"Why not?"

"They won't fly south while there's food here."

''I didn't know finches flew south. I thought they always wintered over.''

He shook his head. ''Only since there've been bird feeders. And patsies like me to fill them.''

''Will they survive the winter, if they stay?''

''Most of them. The weak ones would have a better chance somewhere warmer. I'll stop at the end of the month. I hate to stop. They seem so disappointed the first few times they come. Then they stop coming.''

I sipped some bourbon, said, ''Andy Hill.''

He turned back from the window. ''Maybe Andy's up to something, beyond what he described to you. If he is, I don't know what. And frankly, to me it doesn't matter. I have five hundred clients over there leading better lives than they would have without Helping Hands, and Helping Hands couldn't do what we do without Andy. Not just the real estate shenanigans,'' he added. ''He's an organizer. He's been there whenever we needed help. He brings political support from the Borough President's office, which I'm sure has helped get us accepted in some neighborhoods. After our first executive director left, Andy found Francine Wyckoff for us. She's been a godsend.'' He grinned. ''Though I can see from your expression you've met her. Well, take my word for it. She's a terrific administrator. A genius at paperwork. Of which, believe me, there's plenty. She takes things off my hands, things I'd have to be doing otherwise. And she's totally dedicated to the organization. Identifies with it, if you know what I mean. Helping Hands' good name is her good name, that sort of thing.''

The dog was hit with a sudden inspiration. It leaped up from its sunlit stretch of floor, burrowed under the desk and came up with a big squeaky toy. It bounded over, dropped the toy in Chaiken's lap.

''No, no, Scotty.'' Chaiken slipped the toy under the cushion of his chair. ''Later.'' The dog tipped his head to one side, wagged his tail tentatively. Chaiken rubbed the dog's head. ''Go lie down.''

The dog sighed and chose a new square of sunlight to flop into with a symphony of jingling tags.

''When my older son went off to college,'' Chaiken said, ''my younger one was fifteen. I got Scotty to keep him company. He left a few years later, and now it's just Scotty and me getting old together. Isn't it, Scotty?''

The dog raised his head, but must have decided there was nothing in this for him. He settled again, stretched out on his side.

''Tell me about Helping Hands,'' I said.

Chaiken sat back in his chair. ''A few months after my younger son left for college, I woke one morning thinking that if I came across my own obit in the *Times*, I wouldn't bother with it. The only people who needed me were people who didn't need anybody, and the only things I did well were things those people could pay someone else to do.

''I made a lot of money practicing law, and I didn't start out a poor man. My sons are doing well; one's in Denver, the other's in LA. I gave them cash gifts, retired, and put the rest of my money into the foundation. I spend my time now writing grant proposals to make up the difference between what I had and what we need to operate.'' He waved his hand at the pile on the coffee table. ''Is that what you want to know?''

''How do you choose your projects?''

''The needs are endless. But fads change. One year there'll be lots of government money for the elderly; the next year that dries up, but they'll fund group homes for runaways. The projects we start are whatever's popular that year. Then we blackmail the government and private philanthropy into supporting ongoing unfashionable ones.''

''Blackmail?''

''Not your kind. Emotional blackmail. Guilt trips. I'm a master at it.'' Chaiken grinned again.

''What happens if the blackmail doesn't work?''

''Well, that hasn't happened yet. If it did I suppose we'd have to close the unfunded programs.''

''If you closed a program, what would happen to the building it was in?''

He looked at me thoughtfully. ''We'd use it for another program if we could. Otherwise I suppose we'd have to convey it back to the state. Unless its cycle was up. Then we'd see if we could turn a profit on it.''

''Its cycle?''

''When the state buys a building for an organization like ours, it's on a twenty-year cycle. For the first twenty years we have to guarantee to run a not-for-profit program in it, or convey it back to the state for what they paid. After that we can end the program and the property belongs to us. We can do whatever we want with it.''

''Including sell it for a profit?''

''If we can.''

''I don't get that. How can a nonprofit make a profit?''

''Nobody can take money out of an organization like ours except what we pay out in expenses like salaries and fees. That is, no *individual* can make a profit. But there's no reason why we couldn't, for example, keep expanding our real estate empire forever. Or invest and grow a large endowment. Churches and universities do it all the time.''

''Do you pay taxes on property?''

''Not for those first twenty years. That's part of the arrangement with the state.''

I had a thought. ''What's your arrangement with Andy Hill?''

''How do you mean?''

''When you buy from him. Do you pay him outright, in cash?''

''Oh, God, no. The lawyer in me shudders when you say that. No, it's a complicated setup, but basically it amounts to Andy holding a mortgage.''

''Standard term? Thirty years?''

''That's right.'' He nodded, but didn't meet my eyes.

''So when you eventually sell these buildings, Andy Hill will make his money back. In the meantime he makes a profit on the interest.''

Chaiken said nothing, sipped his drink.

''It seems to me,'' I said, ''that that's perfectly legal. It might not look right, but Hill seemed less worried that I'd go to his boss than that I'd come to you. He got suddenly talkative when I implied that if I got what I wanted from him, I might forget about you.''

He watched a patch of sunlight creep across the slate. I watched with him.

''He wasn't afraid that I'd tell you something,'' I thought out loud, ''because you already know more than I do about how this thing works. He was afraid you'd tell me something.''

Chaiken still didn't speak.

"Look," I said. "I can do this the hard way. I can dig around until I come up with something that doesn't smell right. It'll be a pain, but real estate leaves a paper trail and I'll find it eventually. When I do, if that's how I do it, you won't be there to explain it to me."

Chaiken moved his eyes to me. "And you think I ought to?"

"I think you might want to."

We were both silent. Then Chaiken spoke to the patch of sunlight. "What Andy's doing—buying this real estate, cutting in half the time it would take us to open programs otherwise—it's terrifically helpful to us. People who'd be on the street, panhandling or worse, can get their lives together—" He broke off, looked up at me. "Oh, for Pete's sake, I don't have to give you the spiel, do I? But I want to make it clear that that's my priority. The clients."

Chaiken paused. I kept my eyes on him and my mouth shut. "Those kids they say did the killings," he said. "The Cobras, right?"

I nodded.

"Those kids have nothing," he said. "No families, no future. Think about that. The world—our world—tells them they're garbage. That gang is all they have. They'll do anything they have to do to be part of a group that wants them and tells them they're worth something."

In the warmth of the late-afternoon sun in Riverdale I thought of the chill dusk on a cracked-asphalt playground, and a fourteen-year-old ready to blow me away.

"If they'd had someone reaching out to them," Chaiken went on, "maybe they'd have turned out differently. Maybe just one of them would have. Just one. But that would be worth the whole thing, don't you think? And that's what I'm trying to do."

I drank, to soften the memory. "What would it be worth?" I asked.

"Andy . . ." Chaiken murmured, stopped. Then, as though coming to a private decision, he finished his scotch, put the glass down on the table, looked at me squarely. "Andy's not a philanthropist, though he is a patient man. He has ambitions and he's a natural-born planner. We have a private arrangement.''

''Which is?''

''As each property hits the end of its cycle, we will either sell it for its fair market value, with the profit going to Andy, or we will ourselves effectively buy it from him for the same amount.''

''How will that work?''

''What do you mean?''

''You can't just hand over a large chunk of cash to him. Doesn't anyone examine your books?''

''Oh, I see. No, that's not a problem. You're right, our books are audited constantly, but there are a million ways around it. We could, for example, pay Andy as a consultant—maybe a real estate consultant. There's an irony to that that I rather like.''

''That would work? It's that simple?''

''This sort of thing is done in the not-for-profit world all the time, Smith. There's a lot of money floating around, and it's not terribly well tracked. For everyone in this business for my naive, bleeding-heart reasons, there are half a dozen people here because they make a good living.''

Dr. Madsen's sardonic smile flashed into my mind. I heard his voice, bitter with irony: *It's a growth industry.*

''So Helping Hands is an investment for Hill? His private real estate trust?''

Chaiken nodded. ''That's correct.''

''How does he know it's worthwhile?''

''I don't understand.''

''What if those buildings don't appreciate?''

''They're almost bound to. Real estate tends to, in the long run.''

''There are a lot of abandoned buildings in that area. They were bad investments for someone.''

''That's true. But the neighborhood seems to be coming up a little now. There's building going on. The Bronx Renaissance is investing there heavily.''

''Jesus,'' I sighed. ''I'm out of my depth.'' Maybe, I thought, I should get Lydia's brother Ted to introduce me to his realtor friend. But Ted was one of the Chins who didn't speak to me if he could avoid it.

The air in Chaiken's study, warm and welcoming when we'd come in, now seemed a little close, a little stifling. With regret I put my unfinished bourbon on the coffee table. Chaiken had poured one damn big drink, and I had some plans yet for today.

"Well, thanks for your time," I said. "I'd better go and see if I can find something easy to do."

"Wait," said Chaiken. "You said you were investigating murder, but all you've asked me about is real estate. This arrangement I have with Andy—it's improper, I know, but it would be difficult to prove it's exactly illegal. And how would it connect to the deaths of those two men—two security guards? What would anyone gain?"

"So far," I answered him, "I haven't found anyone who'd gain by those deaths. All I've found is loss."

I stood. The dog lifted his hairy head, waited to see whether this was going to develop into something of interest to him.

"But someone is gaining something," I said. "When I find out what, I'll know who."

Chaiken stood too. That decided the dog, who scrabbled to his feet, slipping on the smooth stone. He barked, then shook himself vigorously, but he was as hairy as ever when he was through.

Chaiken walked with me to his front yard, where the long shadows of the spruces lay heavily on the golden-orange light.

"If I can do anything else," he said, "be sure to ask. And keep me informed, all right?"

"Sure," I said. "Thanks again."

I drove away in the opposite direction from the sun, which was preparing to slip behind the Palisades, turning the river crimson as a parting gift.

TWENTY-SIX

By the time I got to Norwood it was dark, dark enough to be driving with lights. I checked out the lights as they came and went in my mirror, detoured out of my way once or twice to see what would happen, but nothing happened. The guy had stayed lost, it seemed. Well, fine. For now, fine.

Norwood was an old neighborhood of dark-brick apartment buildings, solid and substantial. Mature trees grew on the verges of wide sidewalks, corner stores sold newspapers and milk, and the lit rectangles of apartment-house windows glowed softly.

I found Henry Howe's street and I found his building. I parked around the block, strolled back and watched the lobby from a distance until I caught the rhythm of comings and goings. There was no doorman, but this was the hour people came home from work, did the shopping, walked the dog. It was a large building; the lobby wasn't empty for any long enough stretch to make me confident I could get in unnoticed.

I was considering two fallbacks—coming back later, or finding a service entrance with a lock I could pick in private—when a bicycle with a big aluminum carrier on the front bounced onto the sidewalk. I was across the street before the guy piloting it had gotten it locked to the tree in front of the building.

"Hey, my friend," I said as I came up next to him, "that going in there?"

He looked at the square white pizza box he was removing from the carrier, back at me, and shrugged.

I took a guess and repeated the question in Spanish.

"*Sí*," he nodded. "*Anchovies y pimentos verdes.* Yecch." He made a face.

I told him in Spanish I'd take it in for him. He laughed, suggested I come on down to the pizza parlor and get whatever I wanted.

"*No, no*," I said. "*Esa pisa. ¿Cuanto es?*" This pizza. How much?

"*Cuesta diez dollares, pero va al apartamento 6D.*"

I pulled a ten out of my wallet, added a pair of twenties to it.

"*No te apures.*" Don't worry about it. "*Yo te lo llevo a 6D.*"

The pizza smelled great as I carried it into the building. You're interested in an anchovy pizza, Smith, I thought, you must be hungry. 6D was happy to hear his pizza had arrived, and I was happy to get buzzed into Henry Howe's building.

I made ten of my bucks back, plus a dollar-and-a-half tip, and then took the stairs down to the fourth floor, where Howe had lived.

The hallway, gray-blue patterned carpet against gray-blue textured walls, was empty. Howe's apartment door was close to the stairs, looked as peaceful and domestic as any of its neighbors. Well, I thought, it probably was peaceful. Probably nothing much had happened in there these last few days.

As it turned out, I was wrong.

I took my tension bar and a likely rake from the set I'd brought. Apartment doors tend to be tougher than the type of locks I'd whizzed through at the Bronx Home, so I was prepared.

This one, though, wasn't tough at all. It opened as soon as I touched the knob.

I stepped back quickly, flattened myself against the wall, waited. Nothing.

Okay. This was no place to hang around. I slipped my gun loose, pushed the door open, went in low with it.

Inside was darkness, tense and silent. Evening sounds came from beyond the windows: a car horn honking, heels clicking on the walk.

I stood, shut the door, strained, listening. The place felt empty, but I've been wrong before. I surveyed the room. The drapes weren't drawn and the streetlight's pale glow eased in through the windows. I didn't need to turn on a lamp to see what had happened here.

Someone else with the same idea, but, I liked to think, less finesse, had been here first.

Another step inside the door and I risked drowning in a sea of paper, of books and glass and sofa stuffing. Upturned chairs had been disemboweled, shelves swept clean of highball glasses. From the living room, where I stood, I could see the kitchen to my right and the bedroom down a short hall to the left. They didn't look much better. The kitchen drawers had been yanked out and emptied, knives and forks and spoons mounded on the floor like floating piles of seaweed. I could see open cabinets, cereal spilled from boxes. Cans and jars and bottles lay stranded on counters, on the floor, in the sink.

In the living room, pictures were down, their backs ripped off. The sofa and stuffed chairs had been gutted, and most of the rest of the furniture was capsized, open, or fractured somehow. Next to the sofa lay the kitchen knife that had been used to dispatch it to the next world.

What the hell, I could walk on water. I strode through the mess, first in here, then the kitchen, the bedroom. The scene was eerily calm and colorless, pale gray where the streetlight reached, darker gray in the shadows.

Henry Howe's bathroom had no window; here, for the first time, I risked a light.

I'd have known the bottle of aftershave was broken by the scratching of glass on the tile under my feet and the reek in the air. I'd already guessed the contents of the medicine cabinet would be strewn around the room. The surprise, sudden and sickening, was in the bathtub: Dr. Reynolds, bloody, staring, and dead.

TWENTY-SEVEN

I looked at him. I think it was for a long time. He didn't care. He was looking at something else, something the rest of us don't know anything about.

Eventually, without moving, I started looking other places, working my way out, slowly, from the doctor's blind eyes. The doctor's chest had a hole in it, a small, wet, dark one in the center of a saucer-sized red stain. He was jack-knifed in the tub, in the position of a man who'd fallen backward. Well, that could happen, if somebody shot you. I found myself zipping my jacket. I wanted a cigarette badly, the comfort of that, but I just stood there, looking.

Why were you here, I wondered. What had you been looking for? And were you killed because you found it, or because you didn't?

Two things were sure: the search had been thorough, and it had been amateur. No pro would make this kind of wild mess; it makes it hard to work, to tell where you've been.

But someone desperate might, tearing things apart, trying to bully and beat a place into giving up its secrets.

But what secrets? The person who had done this knew. I didn't. I had come here out of instinct, on the chance that if Henry Howe had been killed not randomly but for a reason then I might find the reason here.

I looked back at Dr. Reynolds. His round, soft face was expressionless, as though he had bad news to deliver but wanted to choose his moment carefully. Blood splattered his slacks and his well-polished, comfortable shoes. One arm angled stiffly out of the tub, fingertips brushing the toilet tank. Fuentes's voice, quoting Howe, echoed in my head. *Got to keep the toilets flushin'.* A wild impulse to laugh grabbed hold of me. I forced myself calm. Dead bodies throw you, Smith? Too bad, isn't it. Let's get out of here, go have a drink. Toilets flushing.

Toilets flushing.

I looked at the doctor again. Then I scanned the bathroom floor, stepped carefully. At the toilet I lifted the top from the tank. The overhead light cast a shadow; I saw nothing but black water. I pushed up my sleeve, stuck my right arm in, felt around. Slime, cold and wet. What the hell did you expect? I felt around some more. More slime.

Then, different slime. Plastic, and tape. What did people do before duct tape? They didn't hide things in toilet tanks. I peeled back the tape, lifted out the flat plastic-wrapped square. It dripped loud drops back into the tank, and cold water ran up my arm into my pushed-up sleeve. I stared at the dripping thing. It was an envelope, very carefully wrapped in heavy-gauge plastic, taped around, wrapped again.

I was willing to bet there were some important things in it.

I dried my hands and the plastic-wrapped envelope on my pants. It occurred to me I might be happier doing this with my back to Dr. Reynolds, but then it occurred to me that I wouldn't. I tore some toilet paper, because I had no gloves, and used it to handle the tape and the plastic.

The thing inside was a nice, normal, white envelope. It was sealed; that was too bad, but I'd have to risk it. I tore it open.

It held an index card, neatly lettered, and photographs.

On the index card was a name—Margaret O'Connor—
and an eight-digit number with the letters "ES" after it in
parentheses.

I didn't understand that. I couldn't even concentrate on
trying.

I turned to the photographs.

Those, I understood.

Some were fuzzier than others; all had the distortion, the
flattening of perspective, that you get when you use a very
long lens. I get it all the time when I do a surveillance. But
even distorted, photos like this are readable enough. You can
understand activities, make out faces.

Especially if you know them. I had no trouble picking out
Snake LeMoyne in some photos, Skeletor in others, in the
doorway of a building down the street from the Bronx
Home. And going in the doorway, or sometimes coming out,
was a figure I could easily identify as Dr. Madsen, clutching
his black medical bag.

I listened at Howe's door, heard nothing in the hall. But
it's carpeted, Smith. Probably the entire Major Case Squad
is out there waiting for you.

On the other hand, the NYPD didn't seem to consider the
deaths of Mike Downey and Henry Howe major cases.

I slipped out the door into the empty hall, the single photograph I had taken from the plastic-wrapped envelope feeling cold in my shirt pocket. The envelope was in another
pocket, crumpled to garbage. The rest of the photos, and the
card, were rewrapped in plastic and sunk to the bottom of the
toilet tank.

I took the stairs down, strolled casually through the lobby
trying to be unmemorable to dog-walkers. Back in the car I
drove a few blocks along the main drag until I found a Dunkin' Donuts with a phone booth in its parking lot. I called
911, reported a prowler in Henry Howe's apartment.

Then I ambled into the Dunkin' Donuts and got myself a
cup of coffee. The place was very bright, full of a greasy,
sugary deep-frying smell. The big cheery brown-and-pink
clock on the wall told me it was almost six. Thank you, I
thought, and so what?

In the car I lit a cigarette—my third since I left Howe's
building—and drank my coffee. I stared at the photo. Then I

went back to the phone and called Lydia.

The machine answered. I started to leave a message, but Lydia cut me off. "Hi," she said. "Hold it. I'm slicing scallions. Let me wash my hands." The phone clattered down, there was silence, and then she came back. "I'm here."

"Sounds domestic," I said to her.

"I decided it was time I learned to cook. Where are you? What have you been doing?"

"Talking. Sneaking around. Do any of the bad guys in this case drive green Chevys?"

"How can I tell who the bad guys are?"

"Good point. What about the Chevy?"

"I'll have to go back to the files and look. Do you have a plate? Why do you want this car?"

"It wants me. It followed me, from the courthouse to Arthur Chaiken's. The plate has L's and threes in it."

"I thought you taught me when someone tails you, always let him get close enough so you can see his plate."

"He must have read that chapter too."

"Was he a pro?"

"I'm not sure. Maybe just a gifted amateur. Lydia, listen, there's a problem. I'm going to tell you what happened, but you don't know this, okay?"

"Are you in trouble?" Her voice quickened. "Do you need help?"

"I always need help, but right now the thing for you to do is to go on with what you're doing. I'm just buying time, though I don't know for whom and I don't know why." I told her where I'd been, what I'd found.

"Oh, my God, Bill," she said softly. "Are you okay?"

"If I had a drink I'd be better. But I'm all right."

"Dr. Reynolds." Her voice was low. "He was the one who showed me around this morning."

"At the Home?"

"Uh-huh. I wanted to tell you about it. I was waiting for you to call."

"You found something?"

"I don't know. Do you really want to talk about that now?"

I want you to keep talking to me, I thought. I want you to

talk about anything, just stay with me. "Tell me. It might help."

I think she knew what I meant. Her voice took on a very normal tone, just a report, one investigator to another. "It was all pretty standard," she said. "It seemed like a good place, as those places go, but God, how awful to be stuck there the rest of your life. I can't believe that's good for anybody."

"I don't think it is. It's a bad answer to a bad problem."

"Ummm," she said, agreeing. "Anyway, the only peculiar thing was after the tour, when we were talking in Reynolds's office for a few minutes."

I heard her voice quaver slightly at the doctor's name.

"What happened?"

"He asked how soon my mother would need to be accommodated at the Home. It seems they have a long waiting list. I said I hoped it could be soon, and was there anything that could be done about shortening her wait."

"And?"

"Then he asked if my mother had any assets."

"What did you say?"

"I said she had about seventy-five thousand dollars in the bank."

"You're kidding. Your mother does?"

"Chinese people are big savers."

"Maybe I'll marry you for your money." I was sorry as soon as I said it. I'd forgotten I wasn't supposed to talk that way to Lydia anymore. I expected anger; but she laughed.

"That would be a motive she'd understand from you."

"Would she respect me for it?"

"She'd hate you. So: then I said that of course my brothers and I would expect to be paying for my mother's care, and he didn't have to worry about that."

"Had he been worried about that?"

"No. This is the part that's peculiar. He smiled and said that wasn't the way it works. 'Medicaid,' he said. 'Medicaid pays most medical costs directly related to a resident's needs. Once your mother moves in that won't be a problem. Of course, sometimes relatives give gifts, out of gratitude or whatever—' he smiled again then—'and we *never* turn them down. That's how we got our piano, for example. But,' he told me, 'the system is peculiar. Medicaid doesn't kick in until the patient's assets are exhausted. Then the patient is considered medically indigent.' He was apologetic about that—he didn't want me to think he *really* thought the Chin family was indigent.''

"Considerate of him."

"Very delicate. Anyway, then he got a little gloomy. 'Well, Miss Chin, I'd love to tell you we could take your mother right away, because I know what a burden this must be to you and your brothers—' ''

"Good thing your mother didn't hear that."

"No kidding! Anyway, he said, 'But there is the waiting list. Now, unfortunately, we have an entire wing of empty rooms on the third floor that need to be renovated. We could accommodate a good number of new residents up there; but we haven't got the funds to do the work.' ''

"Let me guess," I said. "Oh, let me guess. They estimate the cost of the renovation at seventy-five thousand dollars."

"Uh-huh," Lydia said. "Yes."

We were both silent for a few moments. Then she said, "Bill? What was Dr. Reynolds doing in Howe's apartment? Do you think he was looking for what you found?"

"If he was, it was altruistic of him. Unless he's mixed up in whatever Madsen's doing."

"Which is what? Selling drugs to the Cobras?"

"That's what it looks like," I agreed.

"Have you told Mr. Moran?"

"No."

She said nothing, waited.

"I want to sit on it for a little," I told her. "I don't know why."

"A hunch? Like you tell me to play?"

"Not even. But I want to sort some things out. I want to find out what the card means. I want to go over with you what else I did today, see if we can put some things together."

"I . . . I have people coming over," she said. "To eat my scallions. Should I cancel that?"

"No." A gust of wind raced across the parking lot, chasing leaves and trash. "The cops are on their way over to Howe's now, but it's way out of the Home's precinct. It'll take them until morning to make the connection. I'll call you later. Do you think you can look into the card in the morning?''

''You mean, try to find out who Margaret O'Connor is?''

''Yes.''

''Are you sure you're okay?''

''I'm fine. Go on back to your scallions. I'll call you.''

Maybe it was a bad idea. Maybe we should have gotten together, tried to make something out of the pieces we had. I would have liked that. I was tired, cold, alone in a street-lit parking lot in a place I didn't know. I would have liked to be with Lydia.

But Lydia was young, in a bright, crowded kitchen. She was cooking for other young people, who would bring wine and laugh and talk about their careers, their friends, their plans. I thought of Paul Kao, the photographer, the friend of her brother Andrew's. I wondered if he was coming to dinner.

I would have liked to be with Lydia, but Lydia had another life in which I had no part.

And even now I think it wouldn't have mattered. It would have made me feel better, talking with Lydia that night; but it wouldn't have helped us find our way out of the swamp this case had become. The paths were too dark, too shadowed, not blind but serpentine, twisting back on themselves, always leading to where you'd been. Finding the answer at the center would not have been enough, any longer, to lead us to the way out.

TWENTY-EIGHT

When the telephone rang the next morning I was at the piano. It was just past seven. In the loading dock across the street, trucks idled, revved, pulled in or out, beginning their day's business. It was too early for me to begin mine—the questioning, the following, the breaking or bluffing or bullying my way into lives and places where I didn't belong.

The night before, exhausted, I'd had a drink and a burger at Shorty's, trudged upstairs and fallen into bed. Toward morning I had a dream. I was fighting my way uphill on a twisting street shaded by huge chestnut trees. I was late, maybe too late; my heart raced but my legs were leaden, my steps agonizingly slow. On either side were grand villas, mansions, their twilight gates locked. I was looking for the white frame house with the black walnut tree in the front yard, but I was lost; I couldn't find it.

The unease from the dream stayed with me at the piano, got in my way at the beginning, until the focused ray of my concentration burned it off like mist. Total attention on each moment, every touch. No thinking about next, only now: where to pedal, how long to hold a phrase, how to move through it, when to end it. No distractions, no logic, and no words. Just the music.

I worked on the Schubert, on the places that were still rough, trying changes of color, tempo, stress. Mostly I knew what I wanted and was trying to make it happen; in some places, though, I wasn't yet ready to try for an answer, because I wasn't sure of the question. I worked them through, patient, probing, trying to understand.

The ringing phone jarred me, shattered my work. I grabbed for it, more to shut it up than because I wanted to talk to whomever it was.

"Kid? Did I wake you?" Bobby's voice was strange, unsure.

I wiped my sweaty face. "No, I'm up. Something wrong?"

Bobby hesitated. "I just got a call from Bruno. The cops called him as a courtesy, now he's in charge over there. They picked up a guy for Howe's murder. Bruno thinks they're looking at him for Mike, too."

"Who?" He didn't answer. "Come on, Bobby, who?"

"Your friend, kid. Martin Carter."

The station house was a new brick building with arched windows, a sawtooth overhang to walk under in bad weather, and a plaza planted with callery pears. Callery pears are always first to flower in the spring, last to lose their leaves in fall. They don't grow too big and they put up with a lot. A good value-for-money tree, a good tree for the city.

Inside, the building still looked new, tile and terrazzo and a high, coffered ceiling; but behind the rail of the raised-plat-form desk the duty sergeant's eyes had that old, weary look that even young cops get.

"Help you?" he asked, sizing me up automatically, cal-culating whether he could take me or if he'd need help, and if so, how much.

"Lieutenant Robinson," I said. "Or Detective Lindfors."

"You are?" He spoke from the side of his mouth, as though around a toothpick or a cigarette, though he had nei-ther.

"Bill Smith."

"Gianetti!" He barely raised his voice, but its tone changed completely. His eyes had never left me; but a pa-trolman who'd been lounging against a wall out of the ser-geant's sight straightened up and came over.

"Sarge?"

"Go find Robinson. Tell him his guy is here."

The patrolman headed upstairs, and the desk sergeant went back to his paperwork. He ignored me; but I knew that if I took a step he'd give you the length of my stride and if I reached for a cigarette he could tell you what brand.

For a while I watched cops come and go; then I heard my name, turned, and saw Robinson heading my way. His well-cut gray suit and striped tie said he was a cop to whom ap-pearances mattered, a cop with ambitions; but the dullness in his black skin and the bags under his eyes told me he was also a cop who'd been up most of the night, a cop who did his job.

Robinson took me upstairs to an interrogation room, by a route that didn't pass the lockup. Every police station has two routes like that: one for the perps, one for the citizens. Usually it's so the accused doesn't get a look at the wit-nesses; this time it seemed clear that they didn't want Carter to know I was here until some deal was cut.

As Robinson opened the interrogation-room door, mo-tioned me in, I asked, "Why is he still here?"

"You're lucky he is." Robinson flipped on the light. "If we'd sent him downtown already you'd've missed your chance." Then he went out, next door, and turned on the light in the viewing room too. When that room was dark and this one was lighted, the window between was one-way glass, and cops stood around in there watching other cops question you in here. With its light on I could see that that room was empty; Robinson and I were alone.

He came back, sat across the table from me, laced his fingers. "What's your relationship with Martin Carter?"

"I told you on the phone. He's a friend of mine."

Bobby had been pretty sure Carter hadn't made it as far as Central Booking, which meant he was still being held at the precinct where he'd been arrested. I'd called, asked to see him. Surprisingly, Robinson had agreed.

Now he looked at me with guarded disbelief. "I don't often hear of Cobras having white friends."

"Maybe he didn't notice. Besides, he's not a Cobra anymore."

"Don't go naive on me, Smith. You don't leave a gang like that. First of all, why? Second, you don't get the chance. Like a family. You don't like your father, you don't get to say, 'You're not my old man anymore.' You don't say it to Snake LeMoyne, either."

"You can walk out," I said. "He's still your father, but you don't have to stay. Carter's got a family of his own. Two little kids. He doesn't hang with the Cobras now."

"If that's true it's because Snake ditched him."

My mind went back to the chilly playground, leaves scraping on the asphalt, Carter answering Snake without turning to face him.

"No," I said. Then, "What's the difference? Can I see him, or are you just jerking me around?"

Robinson leaned back in his chair, slipped his hands in his pockets. "Why do you want to see him?"

"I want to tell him his kids are okay. I want to see if you guys beat the shit out of him. I want to find out what the hell is going on around here!"

"Nothing's going on. We arrested a guy on a homicide charge."

"Nine hours ago, and you haven't sent him downtown yet."

"Bus was crowded."

I didn't bother with that.

"What is it you want from him, Robinson?"

Robinson's pale blue eyes met mine. "Snake LeMoyne."

"Uh-huh." I took out a cigarette. Robinson didn't stop me, so I lit it. There was no place for the match. I shook it out, dropped it. From the scorch marks on the vinyl tile, I wasn't the first.

"And what makes you think," I said, "that Carter can give him to you?"

"The Rev and Snake used to be real tight. Cold chillin' homeboys. Watched each other's backs, laid the same girls."

"That was before."

"Before the Rev went upstate. You know what that was for?"

"Manslaughter. That's all I know."

"That was a plea bargain. An Arab shopkeeper over there thought he could get away without making his protection payments. He had a gun, see, that made him somebody. So he pulled it on the Cobras when they came to collect. They laughed at him. One of them got the gun. The guy turned and ran. The Cobras were laughing when they shot him in the back."

"How do you know?" I asked. "That that's how it went?"

"Oh, he lived two days. Long enough to talk to us and for his family to say good-bye."

"And he identified Carter as the shooter?"

"No. No, he didn't do that. He identified the Rev as being there, but he didn't know who shot him."

"So why'd Carter get stuck with it?"

"The Rev was there. The Rev was a Cobra. He got elected."

"Meaning what?"

"Meaning he did the time, but Snake did the crime."

I pulled on my cigarette. "Says who?"

"Lindfors."

"How come he knows?"

Robinson shrugged. "It's the Cobras. He knows."

"Okay," I said. "What if it's true?"

"Word is Snake did this one too. The Rev might be getting sick of this by now."

"Did you ask him?"

"He *tol'* me he don't *be* 'roun' dere no more." Robinson's parodied street talk startled me with its vicious edge. I wondered whether I'd have been surprised to hear it that way from a white cop.

"So you want me to persuade him to roll over?"

"Can you?"

"I don't know."

"Will you try?"

"What's the offer?"

"We get Snake, we forget about Carter."

"Carter says Snake says he didn't do it."

"I can sweeten the deal."

"How?"

"Get me Snake for anything. Anything the D.A. can prove. What Carter went up for, Downey, anything. It doesn't have to be this one. If the grand jury indicts Snake, Carter walks."

"Christ. I thought Lindfors was the one with the Snake fixation."

Robinson stood abruptly, paced the room. He spoke from behind me. "Lindfors was a damn fine cop, Smith. He gave the job a hundred and ten percent, but it wasn't enough. Those bastards burned him out. Now he drinks, now I've got to watch him. If I can't get LeMoyne, I'm going to get each damn Cobra one by one for whatever I can."

I finished my cigarette, ground it under my heel. "Let me see him."

They brought Carter to me in the interrogation room. They must not have told him it was me he was going to see; when the door opened, his eyes widened a little, in surprise. Then a tight, wary suspicion covered his face like a mask.

"Ten minutes," Robinson said, and left.

We looked at each other for a few moments, across the formica-topped table.

"Man," Carter said, "what the fuck you doing here?"

"I like it here," I said. "I come here whenever I can. What happened?"

"What you mean, what happen? Cocksuckers come 'round my house, middle of the night, right with Granny and the kids—shit!" He broke off, shook his head. I could see his rage in the corded tendons of his neck.

I gave him a cigarette, took one for myself. He leaned back against his chair, rubbed his eyes. He gestured with the cigarette at the one-way window, now a mirror showing us only ourselves.

"How many them fuckers in there?"

"I don't know," I said. "How many fit?"

He snorted. "Why you here?"

"To help."

"Help me? Or help them?"

"You."

"Yeah? What you proposin' to do?"

"They made you an offer."

"Fuck the damn offer!" He slammed his fist on the table. The sound boomed against the hard surfaces of the room.

"Relax," I said. "I broke my hand that way once. Hurt like hell. You have a lawyer?"

Carter glared. "Do I look like a guy got a fucking lawyer?"

"I have a good one. Nathan Cohen. I'll send him down."

"Forget it."

"Carter, let me help."

"Fuck that shit! You wouldn't be here, you wasn't with them." His eyes sent a wave of hate at the unresponding mirror.

"I called them. I asked to see you."

"They letting you."

"They want me to point out that if you don't take their offer they'll throw your ass in prison."

"They done that before."

"You like it?"

He dragged on his cigarette. "No, I ain't liked it. It sucks, baby. But I ain't about to roll on Snake. I ain't living like that."

"You did this once, Carter. You sure you want to do it again?"

"Did what?"

"Went up for something Snake did."

His eyes, fixed on me, were opaque. "That shooting?" He shook his head slowly. "I done that. I shot that A-rab mother."

"Why?"

He was silent for a long moment. "Wondered that myself, lot of times, watching the rain in the Yard," he finally said. "Don't 'spose I'll ever know." He smiled faintly. I didn't know why.

"Okay," I said. "Maybe that's true. I don't think so, but I don't care. Did you kill Henry Howe?"

He stared at me, then shook his head.

"Did Snake?"

"Snake say no."

I was silent for a few moments. "Robinson tells me if he can get a grand jury to indict Snake for anything at all, you'll walk."

"Fuck him, man!" Carter's reaction was what I'd expected. "Snake one fucked-up mother, but him and me go back. Cops want Snake, they got to do it themselves."

"All right," I said. "Let's try this: how come they picked you up?"

He looked at me blankly. "Get at Snake, man."

"Yeah. Why you? Cops can't just grab you because they want to. They need probable cause. They must have something they think a judge will buy."

He shook his head, a disgusted, hopeless gesture. "They got a witness."

"A witness?"

"Some lying mother I s'pose to've threatened. 'I do you like I done those other suckers.' "

The door opened suddenly, letting in Robinson, jacket off and tie loosened. Must be stuffy in the viewing room, I thought.

"That's it," he said. "Interview's over."

A uniform came in behind him, gripped Carter's arm, hauled him from his chair.

I stood, ignored them both. "Who?" I asked Carter.

"That's it!" Robinson said again.

"I don't know, man. I ain't never said no shit like that!"

"All right," I called past Robinson, who seemed to grow, standing in the doorway, as his anger grew. "Nathan Cohen. Don't say anything anymore unless he's standing next to you."

"Who the fuck gonna pay Nathan fucking Cohen?" Carter yelled back.

I heard the cell door clank shut behind him before I could answer that.

TWENTY-NINE

Robinson moved into the interrogation room, and then came Lindfors. They left the door open. I sat again. They stood.

Lindfors, looking at me, spoke to Robinson. "Fat lot of good he did us."

"Might've worked." Robinson's voice had no tone. "Didn't hurt."

"Fuck it didn't! The Rev's got a fancy-ass lawyer now. Thanks, Smith." His rough voice was heavy with sarcasm.

"He didn't kill Henry Howe," I said.

"Do I look like I give a shit?" Lindfors asked. He was more presentable than the last time I'd seen him, under the harsh lights by Henry Howe's body, but his eyes were smudged and his voice hoarse, as though he'd had too much to drink, or too little. "Those Cobra bastards, if they didn't do what you got them for, they did something worse you don't even know about. So any reason you can lock them up is a good reason."

"Carter's not a Cobra anymore."

Lindfors and Robinson exchanged looks, Lindfors's bitter and superior, Robinson's impatient. Lindfors made a move to speak, but Robinson was faster.

"Smith, you can shove the sanctimonious bullshit, all right? If Carter's all we can get, you better believe we'll hold onto him like a winning Lotto ticket. The only reason I let you in here was I thought you might help us. Now get out."

The telephone rang. In the squad room beyond the door a black woman in plainclothes was working a typewriter with two fingers. She grabbed the receiver without looking up from her keyboard, wedged it onto her shoulder, spoke and typed. Then she dropped it onto her desk, called, "Robinson! For you, baby.'' She never took her eyes from her work.

Robinson, with an impatient sound, strode into the room, picked up the receiver. Then he turned his back, finished the conversation in a lower tone. He hung up with a quick curse, turned, pointed at me. ''Stay where you are.''

''You told me to get out.''

''Now I'm telling you not to move. *Comprendo?*''

''Uh-huh. Why?''

He gestured with his head at Lindfors, who closed the door behind him as he left.

''The isolation booth,'' I said aloud, alone. ''With the Cone of Silence.'' No one laughed. It wasn't funny.

When Robinson and Lindfors came back I was halfway through a cigarette. This time they sat.

Robinson said, ''You're a p.i.''

''You're kidding.''

''What's your interest in any of this?''

''Any of what?''

''Oh, Christ, Smith—''

''Sorry,'' I said. ''It's instinct.'' Lindfors, his jaw set tight, didn't look at me. ''I work for Bobby Moran. I'm an old friend of his. With all due respect, he thought you guys had your heads up your asses about the Mike Downey killing, so he came to me.''

''What do you think?''

''I think so too.''

Lindfors growled. A glance from Robinson stopped whatever was starting.

''Why?''

''Because I haven't seen a motive. Because there've been two killings now, and neither of them has been quite right if you're looking for the Cobra's M.O. Have you identified the gun Howe was shot with, by the way? Or Downey?''

''We ask the questions!'' Lindfors barked. His hard eyes glittered and his hand was curled into a professional-looking fist, barely restrained.

''What is this, a Cagney movie?'' I looked from one to the other. Neither of them spoke. ''The hell with you guys. I have things to do.'' I stood, headed for the door.

''Smith,'' Robinson said, ''sit down.''

"Why?"

"Because I want you to."

"Are we going to converse?" I asked. "Educate each other, mutually assist? Or is Lindfors going to sit here mourning the loss of his rubber hose?"

"Sit down."

That sounded like the closest thing to a compromise I was going to get. I sat.

"We don't have the guns," Robinson said. "We don't have either gun." Lindfors looked away, pounded the table with his fist. A lot of that going around today. Robinson went on, "But they weren't the same."

There was silence in the room; I didn't think it was necessarily my job to break it.

Robinson spoke again. "Now," he said, "I told you those things because you wanted to know. Now you talk to me."

"You know," I said, "either you guys have a pretty subtle routine going here, or you're actually a human being, Robinson."

"Don't count on it. I want to know what you've been doing for the last few days and what you've found."

"I've been going around in circles, and I'm not sure I've found anything. Why do you suddenly care?"

"What's your theory on who killed Howe and Downey?"

"I don't have one. But I don't think it was the Cobras."

"You think it's connected with the Bronx Home?"

"I think it's likely."

"But you have no idea who?"

I shook my head.

"And you have no idea why?"

I kept the headshake going.

"And you have no idea why anyone would want to kill Dr. Milt Reynolds, the guy who ran the place?"

That stopped me. "No," I said. "No. Why would anyone want to do that?"

"Someone did. Someone blew him away last night in Henry Howe's apartment, where someone tore the place apart looking for something. It took them all frigging night to figure out they ought to call me, just now. You know anything about that?"

"Jesus." Trying not to, I saw the staring, expressionless

face of Dr. Reynolds, surrounded by white tile and the reek of aftershave.

"You seem to be taking this kind of hard, Smith." Robinson's voice made the picture vanish. I almost liked him for that, but there was no warmth in the voice at all. "You a particular friend of Reynolds's?"

"Looking for what?" I said. "What were they looking for?"

"You have any idea?"

"What was Reynolds doing there? Was he looking for something too?"

"He don't know shit," Lindfors growled. "Let's go, Lou. Forget about him. Let's go find Snake."

"No, I don't think so," Robinson said. "Smith, let me tell you something. This case is of particular interest at levels where I get nosebleed. We picked up Martin Carter this morning because it was suggested to us. The pols want this over before things get out of hand."

"It seems to me three murders is already 'out of hand.' "

"No. No, 'out of hand' is when the private security forces start carrying guns, and instead of two armies in this war you have dozens: mercenaries, soldiers of fortune only interested in their firepower, everybody wandering the streets blowing each other's heads off. That's what the Borough President would consider 'out of hand.' "

"He told you that? The Borough President?"

"Yeah, he called me at home. Somehow, Smith, the message got to my Commissioner, and somehow it managed to reach me."

"And the message said, 'Pick up Martin Carter'?"

"Maybe if we can lock someone up for this we can stop what's going to happen next."

I thought of Vanessa, swinging her lunchbox, holding onto Carter's hand. She'd be fifteen, when he got out.

"He didn't do it."

"Then bring me the man who did."

"Fucking Snake," Lindfors muttered, almost to himself.

"Usually," I said, "usually the cops tell me to stay the hell out of their business."

"Play it however you want," Robinson shrugged. "You know people I don't know. You can go places I can't. Maybe there are things in those places I want.''

"Maybe," I said. "Maybe. I don't know."

"Well," said Robinson, "I suggest you look."

THIRTY

I called Nathan Cohen's office from the pay phone in the station-house lobby, left instructions. Then I called Lydia.

The machine picked up. I left a message that she should meet me at the Bronx Home whenever she could. That was where I intended to be, and I had a feeling I'd be there a while.

As I hung up I saw Lindfors stride through the lobby and out the rear door, to where the cops park their cars. I crossed the lobby, called after him.

He turned. "Shit," he said, but he stood still and waited.

"I need to talk to you," I said, coming up to him.

"Robinson gave you a job to do. Why don't you just be a good little Boy Scout and go do it?"

"Who's your witness?"

Lindfors ground his teeth together. "Go to hell."

"Who?"

"I don't know."

"I don't believe you."

"You think I give a rat's ass what you believe?" He turned, pushed his way out the double glass doors.

I followed. He turned again, to face me. The sun was bright on the harsh surfaces of concrete, asphalt, the glass and steel of cops' cars. I squinted against it.

"You're so smart," he said through the tightness of his jaw. "You find a way to bring Snake in, you can take your buddy home."

"What is it, Lindfors?" I asked. "Between you and Snake?"

"Snake?" Lindfors was squinting too, in the sunlight, but his eyes had the hardness back in them, I could see that. "He's garbage. Fucking scum. You'd be happier if I liked him?"

"There are lots of guys like that, in a cop's life," I answered. "This one seems to have gotten under your skin. I think it's keeping you from seeing what's really going on."

"I don't want to see," he said. "I don't want to see a damn thing except Snake LeMoyne where he belongs, behind fucking bars for the rest of his life."

I looked at him, his glittering eyes and bitter mouth. "You know," I said, as a thought struck me, "I'll bet no one ever cared about that kid more in his life than you do right now. I'll bet no one ever wanted anything good for him as much as you want to tear his heart out."

I was just talking, really, just thinking out loud, and I didn't expect an answer; but I got one.

"Oh, great!" Lindfors sneered. "I got here a genius p.i., a p.i. knows everything! Fucking everything, right, Smith? Well, so happens you're wrong. There was a cop once, cared about that kid. Asshole cop, taught karate at the community center. Used to take Snake to the ballpark, back when his name was Anthony. Sometimes to the beach. Helped him with his fucking homework. You believe this asshole?"

I waited a little. A car pulled into the lot, doors slammed, three cops walked past us into the building. Lindfors didn't say anything else, he didn't move.

"What happened?" I asked.

Lindfors went on, as though he didn't want to but couldn't stop. "Even after they moved the center and Snake stopped coming around, this jerk would go out looking for him. To take him to the ballpark." Lindfors looked up. In the west, soft, country-looking clouds moved across the sky. "Took him for nuggets at Burger King. Kid used to like that. Cop didn't notice the kid was looking over his shoulder a lot now, wasn't going to school much. Cop was too dumb to see that."

"Or didn't want to," I said. "And?"

"And. And one day the cop went to take a leak at Burger King, came back and the kid was gone. So was two hundred and forty bucks from the cop's wallet. See, he was such an asshole, he hung his jacket on the chair."

"And?" I said again.

"And what?" Lindfors barked. "And when the cop found Snake later, he was hanging with the Cobras. 'You ain't got a warrant,' the kid said, 'you ain't got a witness, you can't touch me.' Skinny bastard, grinning.

"Then Snake started killing people, or just crippling them
if that's what he felt like. And then when the cop went looking for him, it was to bring him in. Fucking asshole! Served
him right."

"What happened to him?" I asked. "The cop?"

"Who gives a shit?"

"I do."

"Oh?" Lindfors said. "Yeah? Well, just for your information, motherfucker. Just so you know. He died. He didn't
have it anymore, to be a cop, so he curled up and died."

"Was he a friend of yours?"

"Yeah." Lindfors looked at me directly now. The hardness of his eyes kept him far away. "Yeah. He was a friend
of mine."

"I'm sorry," I said.

A pause; then, "Fuck you," and he turned and stalked
away.

I wasn't sure what sort of reception to expect at the Bronx
Home. On the porch, I paused. No one was there. The hour
was too early, the sun too weak to warm the residents; and
the maintenance staff, now short a man, must have had more
urgent duties than tending the garden. A movement caught
my eye. It was the tiger kitten, scuttling from behind one
stone baluster to another. I saw him peering out at me from
the shadow. I didn't see the other kitten, or the mother cat.

The big iron-and-glass door opened and a square-shoul-
dered man in a Wells Fargo uniform crossed the porch. The
Wells Fargo jackets fit well, but if you're looking for it you
can see the bulge a gun makes under them.

I thought of Robinson's words. *Dozens of armies. That's
what the Borough President considers 'out of control.'*

"Can I help you?" the guard asked, his manner not entirely friendly.

"I'm Smith," I said. "I work for Bobby Moran. Frank
Bruno said—"

"Yeah, he told me. You got I.D.?"

I showed him that I was Smith, that I worked for Bobby
Moran.

"Okay." He watched me. "Lotta real nervous people in

there. You heard what happened last night?''

"What happened last night?'' I waited. I wanted to hear what they were giving out.

"Another guy got killed. Doctor who ran the place. Someone shot him, but not here.''

"Where?''

He shrugged. "Somewhere else.''

"Do they know who?''

"Nope.''

"Do they think it's connected?''

He gave me a strange look. "They don't tell me what they think. But you gotta to be some kind of idiot not to think it's connected.''

"That's true.''

"You going inside?''

I nodded.

So did he. "Watch yourself. That crazy lady is on the war-path.''

We parted, he going down into the garden, I across the porch and into the Home.

I identified myself to the man on the desk and he nodded me past. I paused, indecisive. I'd come here to talk to a couple of people, to look at a couple of things. I wasn't sure where to start.

From down the hall I heard a piano, the patient repetition of a passage being practiced. I headed there.

In the curtained, carpeted room, Ida Goldstein was at the piano. Eddie Shawn, knitted sweater buttoned to his chin, sat in his wheelchair by the window in the angled morning sun. I watched as Ida played the same phrase a few more times; then, suddenly, without pause, she took off from it into a crashing passage of demonic, unstoppable rhythm. The music built, soared; pounding, dissonant chords shot through with glittering arpeggios, fortissimi cut precipitously to near silence, then howling again, roaring, but always a sense of contemptuous control, of ill-spirited laughter.

As I listened, swept along by the music, Ida hit a false note, then another. Her rhythm faltered, resumed, failed again. She returned to the beginning of a long crescendo passage twice. Then her bony shoulders sank. Her hands stopped their movement, her foot lifted from the pedal. She sat motionless. The silence was louder than the music had been.

I would have left then, not let her know I'd been there, but her head snapped up and her eyes locked onto mine. At first she said nothing. Then, into the silence: "Do you know that piece?"

"Liszt?" I asked, fairly sure I was wrong.

But Ida said, "That's right. The Second Mephisto Waltz. Everyone plays the First. No one plays this. Do you know why?"

"No."

"It's about old age. Schubert wrote about dying young. Everyone can understand that, it's a great tragedy. Liszt wrote about old age. It's only nasty. Do you play this?"

"No," I said.

"Can you sight-read?"

"I . . ." I didn't know how to answer her, wasn't sure what she wanted. "No."

"Yes you can. The way you follow the music, the way you listen. I can tell. But you don't want to play for me."

Something in her eyes when she said that needed an answer. "I don't play for anyone, Ida. I don't ever do that."

"Why not?" she challenged.

A mumbled sound came from Eddie Shawn's spot in the sun. His bony fingers played the controls of his wheelchair and he headed determinedly toward us.

Ida looked at him. "He thinks I'm being a busybody. He thinks it's none of my business."

I said nothing.

In my silence Ida found another question. "Why didn't you tell me you weren't coming back?"

"I'm back," I said.

"You were fired. You didn't say good-bye."

"I've come back," I said again. "To see you."

"Don't be ridiculous."

"I'm serious. I want to talk to you. You and Eddie."

The old man arrived at her side smiling, as though he'd known all along that this would work out.

She closed the cover on the keyboard, turned around on the bench. "I can't play that piece anymore," she said.

"You have to be young and strong to play it. Young and strong to play a piece about being old and feeble. What do you think about that?"

"Not much."

"I'll bet you're strong. I'll bet you can play Liszt, and Beethoven. Do you play the Symphonic Etudes of . . . of . . ."

"Schumann?" I said. "Yes. I do."

"Damn," she whispered, low and fierce. Eddie Shawn reached out a skeletal arm, patted Ida's hand.

"Oh, never mind," she said, looked at me crossly. "Do you really have anything to talk about?"

"Yes." I picked up a side chair, moved it near the piano bench. Eddie leaned forward as I sat. We made a tight circle, Eddie and Ida and I.

I searched for words, not to make it too hard, but also not to patronize. "There's more bad news," I said. "Do you know about Dr. Reynolds?"

Ida frowned, gave Eddie a glance. "They didn't tell us, but we know because I listened. Someone murdered him."

I let out a breath, realized how much I hadn't wanted to be the one to tell her. "That's right. And that's why I'm here. To investigate the killings. To find out what's really going on, and to stop it."

She said sarcastically, "You mean there's something going on?"

Eddie slapped his hand on the arm of his chair. Ida gave him a resentful look. "Oh, lay off," she said. To me: "What do you mean, investigate? Who made you Sherlock Holmes?"

I told her who I was, what I did.

She thawed just a little. "Well, what do you know? A real private eye?" She chortled, leaned forward conspiratorially. "Do you carry a gat?"

"The slang word now is 'piece'." I told her.

"Piece, schmiece. Let me see it."

I opened my jacket partway, let Ida and Eddie get a view of my .38 resting in its rig. I felt like a flasher in the park.

"Okay," Ida groused, but by now it was an act. Eddie's eyes were shining. "All right, Sam Spade. Whaddaya wanna know?"

"Dr. Reynolds," I said. "Why would anybody kill him?"

"The sixty-four-thousand-dollar question, and he starts right off with it!" Ida Goldstein peered at me. "Aren't you supposed to build up to that?"

"It was worth a try."

"Maybe Eddie killed him," she suggested. "To stay out of the hospital."

Through his thick glasses the old man focused his eyes on the ceiling, a thoughtful expression on his cadaverous face: the very picture of a man trying to remember. Then he shook his head apologetically.

"Thanks, you guys," I said.

"Try another," Ida offered.

"What about the argument the night Mike Downey was killed? Is there anything else you can remember about that that might help?"

"I told you all about that. There isn't anything else."

"Did you hear it?" I asked Eddie.

Eddie shook his head.

"He lives on the other side," said Ida. "The west side."

"The parking-lot side?"

"That's right."

"Two nights ago, when the other guard was killed," I said to Eddie. "Did you hear anything then?"

Eddie's face changed, lost its playfulness. He didn't respond, gave me a look so long I wasn't sure he'd understood. Then, slowly, he nodded.

"You did?" I said.

"You did?" Ida said. "Why didn't you tell me?"

"Why didn't you tell the police?" I asked. "What did you hear?"

Sunlight streamed silently into the room. Eddie turned angry eyes to Ida in a way that excluded me completely. "The police didn't ask him," Ida said. "They know he can't talk or write or see very well anymore, so I guess they thought he can't think, either. And how would he have told them? They're not very patient men."

I felt awkward and very stupid. "I'm sorry."

Eddie blew a short exasperated breath.

"But," I said to him, "I'd like you to try to tell me now."

The old man looked away, didn't respond. I thought his eyes were still angry, but I wasn't sure. I started to speak again. A quick, small movement of Ida's hand shushed me.

"He's thinking about it," she said. "Be quiet."

Nothing happened for few moments. Then Eddie raised his bony left hand, pointed at me.

"Me?" I said. "You heard me?"

He shook his head angrily.

"Someone like you," Ida said. "The other guard?"

Eddie nodded.

"Howe?" I asked. "The one who was killed?"

He shrugged.

"I don't think he knew Mr. Howe," Ida said. "Eddie doesn't come down here at night. You didn't know him, did you?"

Eddie shook his head.

"Then what makes you think it was him?" I asked.

"He," corrected Ida.

Eddie, eyes wide, made a demanding movement with his good hand, palm up.

" 'What are you doing?' " Ida said, still watching Eddie. "He does that when he wants to know what I'm doing."

The old man pointed a thin finger at the ground.

"Here?" I said. "What are you doing here?"

Eddie's look held a certain amount of satisfaction, as though he was gratified that I might not be as stupid as he'd feared.

"You heard someone ask 'What are you doing here?' The way a guard would if he found someone unauthorized in his area. That's why you think it was the guard. Howe."

Eddie nodded. I was about to ask another question but he held up his hand, then gestured impatiently, as though inviting me closer. I wasn't sure what he wanted, but I took a stab, repeated the sentence again: "What are you—" Eddie stopped me. He jabbed a finger emphatically.

"*You,*" I said. " 'What are *you* doing here?' He recognized someone? He knew the person he was talking to?"

This time Eddie almost grinned.

"Did he sound frightened?" I asked. "A man confronting a street gang?"

Eddie shook his head.

"Was there an answer? Did you hear the other voice?"

He nodded.

"Did you recognize it?"

Shake, no.

"Man or woman?"

His hand moved from me to himself.

"A man. What did he say?"

Eddie jerked his thumb over his shoulder.

"You're out?"

He rolled his eyes, looked to Ida.

"What is this, the World Series?" she said. "Not you're out. You're through, done, finished, over, kaput. Right?"

Eddie nodded, gave me the look the teacher gives the dumb pupil when the smart one's through reciting.

"All right," I said. "I'm trying. Did he say anything else?"

Eddie pointed to his own ear, lifted his hand apologetically.

"There was more, but he didn't hear it very well," Ida said.

"Then that's it?"

Eddie lifted a finger: one more thing. His fist came down with a clump on the arm of his chair.

"A blow? You heard the sound of that?"

His hand rocked side to side.

"Maybe," Ida said. "He's not sure."

I looked from one of them to the other.

"Well?" said Ida. "What about it, flatfoot? Did we help?"

"I think so. I'll let you know." I stood.

"Where are you going?"

"There are some more people I want to talk to, downstairs. Can you do me a favor?"

"Name it, shamus."

I grinned. "You're really getting into this, aren't you?"

"How about you call me Dollface?"

"Okay, Dollface. Run interference for me. Check the hallway to see if Mrs. Wyckoff is there. I don't want to risk being thrown out of here before I'm ready to go."

"I can do better than that," Ida said, with a hint of smugness. "Eddie, you wait here. Follow me, gumshoe."

"Wait. Eddie, thanks a lot. Can you do me another favor too?"

He nodded.

"I'm supposed to meet someone here. A Chinese woman. She's small and she'll probably be wearing black."

"She was here yesterday," Ida interrupted.

"That's right." I was impressed. "She was undercover."

"Undercover!" Ida snorted. "If people weren't getting killed around here this thing would be a riot."

"Anyway," I said to Eddie, "if you see her, head her off, okay? Get her to wait for me in some out-of-the-way corner. I don't want her to get thrown out of here either."

Eddie nodded, smiling. Ida said, "Aren't you going to give him your signet ring or something so she knows it's really you?"

I looked at my hands. Maybe I'd sprouted a signet ring.

I took a business card out of my pocket, gave Eddie that. "Good idea, Dollface. Okay, let's go."

We left Eddie driving his wheelchair into the hallway, presumably to find a sunny spot to lie in wait for Lydia.

Ida and I crossed the carpeted room to a door discreetly hidden in the paneling of the south wall. Ida pointed to the knob. "I can open it, but it takes a while."

"Stand back, ma'am." The door wasn't locked, but it was heavy, and it stuck in its painted frame. I'd thought it was a closet, but when I yanked it open a narrow passage was revealed behind it.

Ida put her finger to her lips, led me along the dim passage. It was lined with doors, and it jogged twice and seemed to branch once before it reached a set of narrow stairs.

"Where are we?" I asked.

"Shhh!" she scolded. She went on in a whisper, "The Helping Hands offices are along there."

I lowered my voice. "What's this passage for?"

"In the old days," Ida hissed pointedly, "when this was a retirement home for ladies and gentlemen and not a warehouse for the feeble, it was considered only decent for the maids and cleaners to be able to get around without crossing the paths of the retired ladies and gentlemen. Those—" pointing at the stairs— "go to the basement. It's three landings down. Don't go any farther, because there's nothing down there but storage.''

"There's storage below the basement?''

"Of course. In the old carriage house. Piles of useless old rusted-up junk.'' She grinned wickedly. ''Just like in the bedrooms upstairs.''

"Don't talk like that, Dollface. Listen, thanks a lot. I'll be back up soon. Why don't you go on back and help Eddie ambush Lydia?''

"My pleasure, hawkshaw.'' She turned and shuffled off.

I started down the stairs, circled down three landings. At the third there was a door. It would open at a point more or less opposite the staff room, if my internal compass was right. I stood for a moment, my hand on the knob, listening. No sound came from beyond it, no footsteps on the concrete floor; probably I could step out into the corridor, and none the wiser.

Right then, though, I did hear sounds: quiet scraping sounds, and footsteps. Not from beyond the door, but from below, the dimness where the stairs continued down and disappeared.

I strained to hear. On the stairs? No; the footsteps got fainter, faded away.

Well, I told myself, it's their old rusted-up junk. Still, it interested me, to know who might be walking around in it.

I continued noiselessly down the stairs. Three more landings; these servants' stairs were steeper, twisted more than the main flights, above. At the bottom there was no door. I flattened myself cautiously against the wall, inched forward into a cavernous space lit only by a row of dim bulbs hanging in wire cages from the ceiling.

I looked around, saw no one, heard nothing. The air smelled musty and damp; the floor was hard-packed dirt. About fifty feet away I could make out the outline of wide double doors, stable doors. These must be the ones that I'd seen my first day here, the doors that opened onto Chester Avenue behind the Home. As my eyes adjusted to the faintness of the light I saw the junk, in piles down the center and against the walls of the room. Well-organized junk, with rows to walk between it, the way a warehouse is set up.

And, as in a warehouse, a forklift sat in one of the aisles, off to my left.

I examined the pile closest to me. Then, moving into the room, I inspected the next.

Ida was wrong. It wasn't useless, it wasn't junk; in most cases, it wasn't particularly old. A commercial-size air-conditioning compressor, some hot-water heaters, a group of mushroom roof fans. Some equipment I couldn't identify. Something that looked like the burner for a large boiler. Lengths of copper tubing, neatly bundled; copper leaders also, green with age but in good shape, stacked in a long, low pile. And, in a row on the floor, architectural ornaments: stone balusters; pieces of an elaborate copper cornice; colored terra-cotta tile gleaming dully in the half-light. A leering gargoyle half as tall as I was.

They steal the faces right off the buildins, Fuentes had said, grinning. *They steal the faces right from under you nose.*

THIRTY-ONE

I stood in the shadows, watched the gargoyle sneer at me. He was right. Talk about dim bulbs, Smith. Right under you nose, also you feet. A warehouse. Hot building parts, half-price equipment. Landlords' specials. No manufacturers' warranties, but never you mind: at these prices, if what you bought gives out, you can always come back for another. And our little sideline, a no-questions-asked source of supply for those trendy Soho shops specializing in architectural detail and ornament. Real Pieces from Real Buildings. The perfect gargoyle for that hard-to-fill corner of the loft. Or this cast-stone cornice, just one piece of glass and voila! a coffee table.

Well. So someone was cleaning up. Who?

I was asking myself that when the lights went out.

I pushed my back against the nearest pile of boxes. My hand wormed into my jacket, came out with my .38. I listened, heard nothing; then, faintly, footsteps, and from above, the closing of a door. Not from the staircase I'd come down, but from farther north, the other end of the room.

A second stair. That made sense.

I forced myself to stay still, listen longer, until nothing had sounded in my ears except my own heartbeat for a long time. My eyes strained through the darkness. The only light came from a sharp line that forced itself in around the stable doors; but once inside it faltered in the vastness and age of the space, lost its purpose, dissipated and disappeared.

Finally, feeling my slow way along the aisle, I began to move in the direction of the sounds. When I found the opening to the second staircase it was by that skin-sense that tells you things have suddenly changed. Positive becomes negative, solid becomes void; you can't see it, but you know.

I went as silently up this stair as I'd come down the other. Three twisting flights, a mirror image. I tried to picture where I was in the building, and by the top I'd just about figured it out. I stood at the door a minute, listening to rumbles and hisses. Then I opened it. I was right. This was one end of the equipment-jammed, oil-smelling boiler room.

And facing me across it, with confusion and anger all over his unshaven face, was Pete Portelli.

I stepped into the room. Portelli and I stared at each other in silence for a few long moments. I pushed the door shut behind me, not turning around.

"Where the fuck did you come from?" Portelli growled, but he knew the answer.

"I've been downstairs." My words were almost lost in the roar of the boiler. "Examining your operation. Very nice. Neat, clean. I'm surprised."

Portelli licked his lips, glanced warily at the door behind me. "I thought you don't work here anymore."

It was hot where I was standing, near the boiler. Hot and noisy. I moved closer to him. "I'm moonlighting, Pete. Sort of like you. Portelli's Moonlight Supply. You need it, we steal it. I bet every crooked contractor in the Bronx knows your number, right?"

My approach brought me out of the shadows. Portelli caught sight of my right hand, where my gun dangled. One side of his mouth twitched; I saw fear begin to spread itself across his face.

It pleased me, to see that.

"What the fuck are you talking about?" His voice was shakier than his words.

I stopped with six feet still between us. "Your storeroom, Pete. Pretty building parts all in a row."

"Gotta keep parts around. Old fucking building like this, things break down all the time." He licked his lips.

"Three hot-water heaters? Five miles of copper leader? Terra-cotta tile, in case you decide to redecorate? Come off it, Pete. That equipment has serial numbers. And somebody must have noticed he's missing his gargoyle."

Portelli was silent, watched the gun. Then a light came into his eyes. "Ahhh, shit," he said, his voice stronger. "Awright, what do you want?"

"What do you mean?"

"You gave a shit, you'd'a went to the cops, or at least that bitch Wyckoff. Not that that'd do you any good. So what is it, you wanna be cut in?"

"Is that an offer?"

"You want it in writing?"

"Is it the offer you made Mike Downey?"

His mouth twitched again at Mike's name. "I never offered that snot-nose mick bastard nothing."

"But he knew what you were doing, didn't he?"

Portelli spat into the corner.

Something exploded in me when he did that. I had him slammed to the wall before he saw me coming. My fist pounded his stomach. He doubled over, making choking noises; then he was sick on the concrete floor.

I waited. When he was through I hauled him up by his shirt collar, shoved the gun barrel into his neck. "I knew Mike," I said. "He was a friend of mine."

A thin strand of vomit glistened on the stubble of Portelli's chin. His breath was hot and it stank. "I didn't know that," he rasped. His eyes were wide with fear. "How the fuck did I know that?"

"Would it have mattered when you killed him?"

"I didn't kill him."

"Bullshit." I felt my finger on the trigger.

"I didn't! Hey!" There was terror in Portelli's eyes now.

I suddenly wondered what was in my own.

I released him, stepped slowly away, lowered the gun. "Tell me about it."

He breathed heavily. The rumble of the boiler hadn't stopped. The air was hot and close; the reek of diesel fumes almost covered the smell of vomit.

Portelli narrowed his eyes, got stupid-crafty. "I don't know nothing about it."

"Pete," I said, "if I shoot you now no one will hear it. I'll go back the way I came and no one will know I've been here. I want to, Pete. I really want to kill you. I may anyway, if I don't like what you tell me. Now, try again."

Some piece of equipment switched on, maybe a pump. I could feel the change rumbling in the room.

"It wasn't me," Portelli said bitterly, in the voice of a man who has tried his best but been betrayed by the stupidity of others. "I told that fucking idiot he was gonna screw everything up."

Screw everything up. That's what a man's death comes to. "What fucking idiot?"

"Howe."

THIRTY-TWO

I took a beat, digesting Portelli's words. "Henry Howe killed Mike?" I asked.

Portelli's eyes flicked to the gun in my hand. "He said he didn't mean to, but I didn't believe him."

Uh-huh. Put as much distance between Howe and yourself as you can, now.

"I don't care what you believe. What happened?"

For a minute he looked as though he were deciding whether to talk. Then he glanced at the gun. He spoke to it. "Part of it you got right. The kid found out about the operation."

"How?"

"Just nosing around. Couldn't mind his own goddamn business." Portelli's mouth twitched again; maybe he'd suddenly remembered Mike was a friend of mine.

"And?" I said.

"He checked it out a few nights, until he had it figured out. Then he reported to Howe. His boss, you know." The words held a nasty sarcasm.

"He hadn't figured out Howe was working with you?"

"Working, my ass. That fat fucker never did shit. Me, I busted my goddamn hump on this thing."

"Something to be proud of, Pete. So what was Howe's piece?"

"What was his piece of anything? I paid him to keep his goddamn mouth shut."

"How'd he find out in the first place?"

"Oh, give me a fucking break! He was the night super, how was he not gonna know?" He shifted his eyes quickly back to the gun, as though it might strike without warning if he didn't watch it.

"So that's what comes and goes from here at night." I was catching on.

"No, I'm gonna unload someone else's fucking furnace at noon in Macy's window."

I thought of Leon Vega, in a coma for six weeks after delivering here at night. "But the Home's protection money doesn't cover it?"

"Used to, till the moulies caught on. Now I got to pay my own."

"That's too bad, Pete." I thought for a minute; he watched the gun. "Does the Home take a cut?"

"Are you kidding? No way. I don't know what you think, but this ain't a goddamn gold mine."

"So Mrs. Wyckoff doesn't know about this?"

He laughed nastily. "Sure she does. She found out after that greaseball got stomped."

"Vega?"

"No, my fucking uncle Luigi."

"She didn't do anything about it?"

"She tried. Called me on the carpet, told me I better shut down or else."

"What was the 'or else'?"

"Oh, screw her. She could've fired me, but she's so fucking scared this'll come out and smear shit on her precious reputation, she's got no 'or else.' Helping Hands and its reputation, that's all she gives a shit about. Makes her a wimp."

"So you didn't shut down."

"What does it look like?"

I thought about the well-ordered supply room down below, about trucks coming and going from it in the middle of the night. That kind of traffic could wake you up, if your room was on that side of the building.

Something else occurred to me. "That's why Howe wore a beeper. So he could let the trucks in."

"I hadda pay him extra for that," said Portelli in aggrieved tones. "But at least that way I could get some goddamn sleep sometimes. 'Course *I* have to be here when orders are going out. You don't watch these spics, they'll shake your hand and steal your fingers." He tried the brown-toothed grin on me.

I stared at him. "Christ, you're unbelievable."

The grin faded. He checked to make sure the gun wasn't coiling to strike.

"And the money in Howe's locker?" I asked. "That was to pay for deliveries?"

"Right. My goddamn money. He wouldn't lay out his own, the cheap bastard."

That was so ridiculous I almost laughed.

"Hey," Portelli said suddenly, "how come you know about that?"

"The money? How come you didn't know that I knew?"

"Huh?"

No, he hadn't known. That meant the hundred dollars, and my note, had vanished with somebody else.

"Did the cops know Howe had a locker here?"

"They asked me in the morning. I told them which one. I figured, so they find the cash, money's money, right? It don't tell where it came from. But it wasn't there. Maybe he took it home. Hah! Maybe he took it with him."

He grinned. I didn't want him that comfortable. I looked at the gun in a thoughtful sort of way, turned it over in my hand. "So. Mike told Howe what he knew, and Howe killed him?"

"Not like that," Portelli brownnosed quickly. "First he tried to cut him in. The kid said he'd think about it."

"But he decided no?"

"Fucking Boy Scout," he said sourly. "He wasn't about

to go on the pad. He was just buying time to figure a way out.''

"Out of what?''

"Howe worked for his fucking uncle. The kid didn't want his uncle to know one of his guys was dirty.''

I suddenly felt cold in that overheated room. "That's why Mike didn't go to the police, or to Mrs. Wyckoff? He was protecting Bobby?''

Portelli nodded. "He told Howe he'd blow the whistle if we didn't shut down. But that asshole Howe said *no-o-o*. He said we had the kid over a fucking barrel. The kid was afraid the uncle would have another stroke if he found out. Howe said the kid would come around.''

"What happened?''

Portelli seemed about to spit again, but he changed his mind. "That one night, Downey told Howe that was the end. He was gonna go to Moran the next day if we didn't shut down. No more screwing around.''

"So Howe killed him?''

"What Howe said, he tried to talk to him for a while, then hauled off and socked him because he was pissed off. The kid fell, hit his head. He died.''

The argument in the garden. What Ida had heard.

"Then Howe figured, better make it look good.''

"Good?'' I said incredulously.

"Come on, the kid was dead. Howe was covering his ass.''

"And yours. So he made it look like the Cobras?''

"Well, everybody knows about those moulies, how they do it. So that's how Howe did it.''

"And then he found the body. So if he had Mike's blood on him it wasn't a surprise.''

"I told him,'' Portelli said. "I told him it was gonna screw things up.''

"And you killed him to prove it.''

"No,'' he said quickly. "Uh-uh, no. I didn't do that, either.''

"Who did?''

He looked at me as if he wasn't sure I was all there. "The moulies. Must've been the moulies. Who else?''

"Why?''

"Because they were apeshit someone else was doing their thing. They wanted to show they were still the best. That's what I figured."

"But it was convenient for you."

"Well, yeah, it turned out great," he agreed, as though we were talking about catching a train. "At least till you come along. But that don't mean I did it."

"Pete," I said, "the Cobras didn't kill Howe. He was killed by someone he knew."

For a moment, nothing but the pounding of the boiler and the stench of diesel fumes.

"How the fuck do you know that?" Portelli finally asked.

"And the police don't think the Cobras killed Mike anymore, either." That was stretching it, but I didn't care.

Portelli didn't answer.

"Whoever killed Howe," I said, "had a reason. You're the only guy I see, Pete."

"Bullshit. To kill that jerk? Everybody had a reason."

"Who's everybody?"

"Everybody he ever met."

"Meaning what?"

"Like I said, I paid him to keep his mouth shut. That's what he did for a living, kept his mouth shut."

"Blackmail?"

Portelli shrugged.

"Who else did he have things on?"

"Don't ask me."

"I'm asking you, Pete."

"Jesus Christ! Who the fuck do you—"

I raised the gun again. "Don't get stupid, Pete. You were doing so well."

"Everybody," he said quickly, flinching a little. "I don't know. But he once said, any skeleton you got in your closet, Pete, I already counted the bones."

My gun and I escorted Portelli back to his office, where I called Robinson. Portelli had promised, nodding his head cooperatively, that he would tell the police everything he'd just told me. I knew he wouldn't. To the cops, he'd deny it all. Unless they could get Leon Vega's cousin—or Leon Vega, if he came out of his coma—or Burcynski and his cigar to tie Portelli in, there was a good chance he could make the whole hot-parts operation look like Howe's game. Who, me? I'm just the building super. How the fuck do I know what's going on?

When Robinson came he left the cop he'd come with watching Portelli while I took him down into the old carriage house below the basement, showed him around. I told him what Eddie Shawn had told me and what Portelli had said.

"What was it?" Robinson asked. "Portelli had a sudden urge to confess?"

"I was persuasive. Do you have enough to hold him?"

Robinson looked around. Stacks of equipment threw sharp shadows under the hanging bulbs. "I have enough to take him in and question him. But I'll have to look for a way to hang this on him that'll stick. Do you think he killed Howe?"

I shook my head. "He hasn't got the balls to do it the way it was done."

"Yeah, that's what I was thinking. Do you believe Howe killed Downey?"

"Yes," I said. "I believe that."

"So where does that leave us?"

"Us? I got what I came for."

"What does that mean?"

"I was hired to find out who killed Mike Downey. I found out."

Impatience glittered in his blue eyes. "This is Robinson you're talking to, Smith. Don't even try to tell me you're quitting now."

"My guy's dead. I'm done."

"No," he said. "First, we still have two unsolved murders. I don't read you as a guy who'd walk away from that. Second, your buddy's still in jail."

"You can't be serious."

"Somebody killed Howe. The Rev is still my best suspect."

"That's crap."

"Your quitting is crap, too. You just want me off your tail."

"That too."

That didn't faze him. "It's okay," he said. "I can pretend

I believe you, if it makes you happy. Just remember, I like to be happy too.''

I couldn't quite conjure up an image of Robinson, happy. ''What would do that?''

''Anything you pick up that you tell me about, that makes me happy. Anything you keep to yourself, I get unhappy. For example, the stuff you got out of that old man. That makes me happy.''

''You could have gotten that stuff, if you'd asked him.''

Robinson could have made an excuse then, tried to explain to me why he hadn't even attempted to interview Eddie Shawn; but he didn't. He didn't look away, either.

''Are you going to arrest Portelli?'' I asked.

''Not now. We'll take him in for questioning.'' He looked around thoughtfully. ''Anybody else here involved in this?''

It was a good question, and one I had had certain thoughts on myself. I gave Robinson the answer he expected. ''I don't know.''

He gave me the answer I deserved. ''If you find out,'' he said, ''I'd better be the first to hear about it.''

''Okay, boss. Is there anything in particular you want me to do?'' My voice held sarcasm, but surprisingly little.

''You know what I want you to do.''

''Uh-huh. Well, in that case, I don't have a lot of time to hang around chatting with you, Lieutenant. See you later.''

I went back up the stairs to the boiler room, through the hall and into the parking lot. I needed a cigarette, needed to think.

I wasn't sure Robinson would make good on his threat against Carter, but I wasn't sure he wouldn't. He'd been right about one thing, though: I wasn't about to drop this case before I knew all the answers. Maybe I should have; maybe more could have been salvaged at the end, if I had. Probably not. Probably Robinson would have found everything I found, eventually; maybe, because cops are hamhanded, even more would have been lost.

Sometimes, now, I comfort myself with that thought.

THIRTY-THREE

When I was ready, when I'd thought and smoked and watched the wind in the paper birches for a while, I went back in and down the basement hall.

In the doctor's office, Elena was behind her desk. Her lips were red and glossy, but her smile was unconvincing. An old woman with a humpback sat in the waiting room, both hands on the head of a cane.

I asked to see Dr. Madsen.

"He's with someone." Elena's voice was subdued. "And he has appointments . . ."

"It's important."

She seemed uncertain. "Can you come back?" She began to look down the columns of the appointment book.

"Tell him I need to ask him a question. About the Cobras."

If she had any idea what I meant she didn't show it. She buzzed the doctor, gave him the message. She hung up, said, "He says if you can wait a minute, he'll be right out."

"Thank you." I added, "I'm sorry about Dr. Reynolds."

She lowered her eyes. "It's a terrible thing." She shook her head sadly, side to side.

The humpbacked old lady did the same.

The wait wasn't long. Madsen escorted a trembling, rheumy-eyed old man into the waiting room, gave Elena rapid orders about him. He glanced at the humpbacked woman, then said to me, "Come on." He turned back down the hall to his office without waiting to see whether I was with him.

The office was small, cramped, crowded with papers and books. Both Madsen's and Reynolds's medical-school degrees and licenses were on the wall. Reynolds's were framed in teak, Madsen's in cheap chrome.

"I don't have much time." Madsen plopped himself into the chair behind the cluttered desk. "It's a zoo around here today, because of Reynolds."

"A lot of tranquilizer prescriptions?"

"Tranquilizers, sedatives, high-blood-pressure medication, heart medication. What did you want to see me about?"

"I'm in a strange position, Doctor." I settled into the visitor's chair. "I've seen something I don't understand. I want you to help me make it make sense."

"I'm not a psychiatrist. Or a psychic." He leaned forward impatiently.

"I've seen photographs," I said. "They all look like this." I took the single photo from my pocket, dropped it on his desk.

His eyes went to it; he didn't move to touch it. After a moment he breathed, "Damn!" He stood, looking like he wanted to pace; but the room was too small. He stuck one hand in his pants pocket, rubbed the back of his neck with the other, shifted his weight, sat again.

He picked up the photo, flicked it with a fingernail. His eyes met mine; in them I saw anger and, I thought, disappointment. "All right. What do you want? Same deal?"

"Same as what?"

"What the hell do you think?"

"The deal you had with Howe?"

Madsen's mouth was set tight; he didn't answer.

I asked, "What was the deal?"

"Two fifty a month. That's all I've got."

"What does it buy you?"

"Silence. What else?"

"What about?"

He tapped the photo. "That."

"What is that?"

"Christ, what does it look like?"

"It looks like you and Skeletor in a doorway. As far as I know it's not illegal for a doctor to come out of a building in the company of a gang member."

He looked at me as though I'd said something in a foreign language that he was shaky in. "Okay," he finally said. "It's not illegal. So get out and leave me alone."

"If it's not illegal why are you willing to pay blackmail?"

To my surprise he laughed, although I didn't hear much joy in his laughter.

"At least you call it what it is," he said. "Howe had other

names for it. My 'contribution to his retirement plan' was my favorite.''

"Tell me about the Cobras."

"Hey," he said, "what the hell do you want?"

"I want to know what's going on in this picture."

"Why?"

"Curiosity."

"That killed the cat."

"I'll take my chances."

"What if I don't tell you?"

"There were eight other photos similar to this. I left them where I found them."

Madsen paled a little. "You don't have them?"

"No."

"Where is that, where you left them?"

I skipped over that. "They'll be found, eventually. I may lead the cops to them or I may keep my mouth shut—I haven't decided—but they're not stupid. They'll find them. When they do I may be able to help, if I know the truth."

He abruptly stood again, walked behind his chair, clamped his hands on its wooden back. "I don't see how," he said. "Or why."

"For Christ's sake, Madsen, I don't either. But what have you got to lose?" He didn't answer. I said, "I'll tell you what it looks like. It looks like a doctor making a house call. But it isn't. It smells like a doctor writing prescriptions and otherwise supplying drugs to a street gang. But if it is, there's more proof than this, because you can't blackmail anyone over a photo that looks like a doctor making a house call."

He still said nothing. "I don't know where that proof is," I said. "But the cops will find that too. They're good at finding things if they know what they're looking for. The only way they won't find it is if they don't look."

"And why wouldn't they look?" Madsen asked.

"I'll tell you why they *would* look: if they're looking for Howe's killer's motive. They'll stop looking when they get Howe's killer and don't need to look anymore."

Madsen sat again. "So if I cooperate with you, I may get out of this without losing my license?"

"Or going to jail. I can't guarantee that, Doctor. I'm not a cop or a D.A.; this isn't a plea bargain. But I'm a private investigator working on these killings and if I can find out something that helps, I don't see how it could do you anything but good. Unless you're the killer.''

He flushed but didn't answer that. His look was wary. "I thought you were a security guard.''

"That was a story.''

"But you were here before Reynolds and Howe—''

"I came here about Mike Downey. Since I've been on this case two more men have been killed. That sort of thing puts a big chip on my shoulder.''

"I can see that.'' He stared into the photo again, as if trying to change its images. "All right,'' he said suddenly. "What *do* I have to lose?'' He punched the intercom button on the phone. "Elena, I'll be another little while.'' He didn't wait for her answer.

Madsen and I looked at each other in silence for a short time. I noticed the disinfectant smell from the examining rooms had crept in here, too. It made me want a cigarette.

"Okay,'' Madsen said. "You're right. There's more proof. There are records going back years here of drugs ordered for which no prescriptions were written. But if you check the storeroom you won't find the drugs, either.''

"What sorts of drugs? Speed? Downers?''

"No,'' he said.

"What, then?''

His eyes were on the photo. "Antibiotics. Gamma globulin. Insulin. Occasionally Demerol or morphine, but not often.'' He looked up at me again. "And one-use disposable syringes. Hundreds of them.''

The early afternoon sun was beginning to spot the ivy leaves outside Madsen's window. "I don't get it,'' I said.

Madsen sighed an impatient sigh. "About five years ago I'd just left this dump one night when a kid came charging out of a building down the street. Fourteen, hysterical. Later I found out she knew I was a doctor because doctors on TV carry black bags.'' He jerked his thumb at his medical bag, on the floor by his chair. "She dragged me into a first-floor apartment. There were half a dozen kids there, teenagers, including one who was having a baby in the middle of the living-room floor.''

A gentle wind ruffled the ivy. I wished the window were open.

"She was actually doing fine," Madsen went on, "but there was the pain and the blood and the other kids, who were scared and useless and frightening her more. I sent one of them to call an ambulance, got rid of the others and delivered the baby." He added, "It was a girl."

He paused for a moment. "The ambulance came and took them to the hospital. Later I went to see them, to see how they were doing."

"Did you know her?"

He shook his head. "But when you deliver a baby, it makes you proprietary, if you know what I mean."

I thought I did. "What happened?"

"They were all right. I asked her—her name was Charlene—I asked Charlene why she hadn't gone to the hospital when she'd gone into labor. She told me she wasn't sure it was her time, because she didn't know what it was supposed to feel like and she wasn't sure when the baby was due."

"How can that be?"

"That can be," he said, "if you don't see a doctor the whole time you're pregnant."

"She didn't?"

"No, she didn't. Know why?"

"Why?"

"She was on drugs. Crack, sometimes heroin. She thought if you were on drugs and you went to the doctor they made you have an abortion. One of the other kids told her that."

"Jesus."

"She'd been trying to kick the drugs. She was going to go to a doctor when she did."

"How was the baby? If she was on drugs—"

"She was fine. Sometimes they're lucky."

I waited while Madsen's thoughts seemed to drift somewhere else.

"Charlene was convinced it was me, though," he continued. "That I was why the baby was all right. She thought I was a hero."

"It's nice when people think that."

His eyes told me he had no use for grandstanding. "A few

weeks later that same fourteen-year-old showed up at the door here, hysterical again, but controlling it better. She asked me to come with her." He shook his head slowly. "I went."

"Another baby?"

"No. Diabetic coma. A kid who'd never been diagnosed. I got him stabilized and to a hospital. He lived."

"Wait," I said. "What am I hearing here? Eric Madsen, personal physician to the Cobras?"

"Look, I don't give a shit what you think. Those kids are throwaways. No education, no jobs, no family. No chance."

"Those kids are killers."

"Some of them. Some are the brothers and sisters and friends and girlfriends of killers. Is that a capital crime in this state?"

"Aren't you being a little melodramatic?"

Madsen's smile was small and bitter. "In Nazi Germany they didn't start using gas chambers until near the end of the war. Mostly prisoners were just overworked, underfed, underclothed, their medical needs ignored. You can kill millions of people that way."

"You think there's an analogy?"

"You don't?"

I had no answer.

"Anyway," he said, "they trust me. I do what I can."

"A clinic?"

He shrugged. "I go over there a couple times a week and deal with whoever comes. I give them needles so the ones who shoot up won't give each other AIDS. I try to get them into legitimate programs: prenatal care, drug abuse, AIDS testing. But the ones who won't go are better off with me than no one."

"So you steal from here?"

"All these millions spent on people who think they're already dead, or wish they were, but not a nickel on fourteen-, sixteen-, eighteen-year-old kids? Damn right I steal from here!" His face was suddenly livid. I was silent; he calmed a little.

"The only thing," he said, "and I made this clear to Snake, I won't have anything to do with gang activities. They get themselves shot or stabbed taking care of business, they get themselves to a hospital and leave me out of it.''

''Do they stick to that?''

''Pretty much. Every couple of months I get some kid bleeding, dish towel wrapped around the cut, and I'll hear, 'My man jes' walkin' down the street, mindin' his own bidnez, these dudes jump on him.' '' Madsen's street accent was almost as good as Robinson's. ''But Snake makes them play it pretty close to the rules. He doesn't want to lose me.''

''Snake cares?''

''Is that a big surprise to you, Smith? Snake's vicious. But he's organized himself a little family over there, and he takes a lot of pride in providing for them.''

I thought of Snake on the playground in the dusk, beaming at the other guys, the ones holding the guns.

''What do you get out of it?'' I asked.

''Funny,'' he said. ''I almost thought you were one guy who'd know the answer to that.'' That was all he said.

We regarded each other across the desk in the cramped office. It occurred to me that the sharp smell of disinfectant, which I disliked so much, was part of Madsen's daily life.

''Reynolds was killed in Howe's apartment,'' I said.

''I know that.''

''Did you know the place had been searched thoroughly—so thoroughly that you might think the searcher never found what he was looking for, otherwise he might have stopped?''

He frowned. ''No,'' he said. ''What does that mean?''

''I thought the searcher might have been looking for these.''

He looked at the photo again without touching it, then abruptly looked up. ''Me, you mean? And then I killed Reynolds because he came in and found me at it?''

''It's believable.''

''It's crazy.''

''No, it isn't. It may be wrong but it's not crazy.''

He held a breath, let it out slowly. ''All right. It's not crazy, but it's wrong.''

''Were you there?''

He shook his head.

''At any time, were you there? To look for these?''

''No. I was hoping with Howe dead no one would know

what they were. Besides, how the hell would I know where to look?'' His expression changed as he considered me. ''How did *you* know where to look?''

''Forget it. You break the law your way, I'll break it mine.''

It seemed to me then that he wanted to smile, but he didn't smile.

''Now what?'' he said. ''You want money, or what?''

''I want to know how Howe found out about you. About this.''

''He said he got curious when he saw me with Skeletor. Then he rooted around until he found the discrepancies in the records, then came to me. God, he had a smirk on him . . .''

''Did you kill him?''

He stopped, startled; but his eyes and his voice were clear as he said, ''No.'' Then he asked, ''Do you believe me?''

''What's the difference whether I believe you?''

''Partly it's practical. If you believe me maybe you won't go to the police.''

''What's the other part?''

''For some goddamn reason I'd like you to believe me.''

''For some goddamn reason I'd like to.'' That wasn't enough, but it was the best I could do for him. ''What about Reynolds?'' I asked.

''What about him?''

''Suppose he was killed by someone who'd gone to Howe's to get back something like this. It isn't hard to believe you weren't the only person being blackmailed. That still leaves me wondering what Reynolds went to Howe's to do.''

''Maybe,'' he said, ''to get back something like this.''

''What would that have been?''

''I don't know.''

''Care to guess?''

''No. We didn't know each other well. We'd consult on patients and that was about it.''

''What kind of guy was he? Would you be surprised to find out he was involved in something illegal, something blackmailable?''

''Smith, I wouldn't be surprised to find out Mother Teresa

was involved in something illegal. Reynolds was a friendly, warm, insincere son of a bitch. I didn't like him and I didn't trust him, but if he was up to something he never told me about it. Listen, I have patients to see. I'm going to be here late into the night calming these people down. Can we end this?''

"All right." I stood, pocketed the photo. He didn't move to stop me. "Tell me one more thing. You were in trouble in Wisconsin before you came here. What was that about?''

For a moment he didn't answer. Then he said, "I killed someone.''

I waited. He said, "An old woman. She had liver cancer. Horrendous pain. It was what they call assisted suicide.''

"How'd you get in trouble? Don't doctors do that sort of thing all the time, and everyone just looks the other way?''

His grin was wry. "Seemed she'd sent a letter to the papers about how assisted suicide should be legal and how she'd only found one doctor brave enough to help her. Her son had a fit. He hadn't known. She didn't name me but it wasn't hard to track me down. The state was backed into a corner. They had to arrest me.''

"But you didn't do time? Or lose your license?''

"The grand jury wouldn't indict me. But the AMA took a tight-ass moral position. My license was suspended for a year and it was clear I'd never work in Wisconsin again.''

"So you came here?''

Madsen shrugged. "I figured," he said, "that it's easy to hide shit in a sewer.''

THIRTY-FOUR

Upstairs was quiet, residents napping in the dayroom, soft Muzak on the PA system. I wondered how Ida stood that. The Wells Fargo man at the desk nodded to me when I came up the stairs, but said nothing.

The piano parlor was empty, less bright now that the sun had moved around the building. The piano was closed.

Now what?

I'd given Robinson time to do whatever he was going to

do and clear out, if clearing out was on his agenda. If it wasn't, he was still here, fishing, stirring up the waters. Part of me wanted to stand back and let him do it. Maybe this hot-parts business was it, was enough to explain everything that had happened, and maybe Robinson, a lieutenant of New York's Finest, could wrap the whole thing up without me.

But another part of me said no. That part said that Robinson was after something else. It said Carter was in jail. And it said Howe, who was dead, who was a blackmailer, who had killed Mike Downey, was one of Bobby's guys.

I should have called Bobby. He was the client. His case was solved, now I should report. But I wasn't ready. I wanted to have more to give him, more than just bad news. The truth was I didn't ever want to have to tell him about Howe, about that kind of betrayal. I could see his face as he heard, gray, tight; could see where the blame and the anger would go. Probably nothing I could do would stop that. But it would help if I knew all the answers, if there were no more questions to ask.

I turned to leave the parlor. Maybe Lydia was here, spirited away somewhere by Ida Goldstein and Eddie Shawn. I'd find her, we'd talk, maybe we'd find a way to make things come out all right.

I opened the door into the hall and ran straight into Mrs. Wyckoff.

Her eyes narrowed and her back straightened. ''What are you doing here?'' she demanded.

''Visiting,'' I said.

''Get out.''

''Mrs. Wyckoff—''

''Remove yourself from these premises immediately or I'll have you arrested. You were told not to come back here.''

''No, I wasn't.'' And I hadn't been, though I couldn't have honestly said I'd expected to be welcomed.

''You're trespassing. Get out.''

''Why, it's Bill!'' came a voice from behind her. ''You've come for a visit! How nice.'' Mrs. Wyckoff's head spun around. Ida Goldstein, her face a bland, smiling mask of pleased surprise, was shuffling toward us. She was fol-

lowed by Lydia, pushing Eddie Shawn's chair. They were
smiling too. Mrs. Wyckoff's cheeks crimsoned and I
laughed before I could stop myself. I tried to cover it with a
cough, but it didn't fool anybody.

"Get out!" Mrs. Wyckoff sputtered at me again.

"He's my guest," Ida objected, as the little rescue party
approached. "He's come to visit me."

"He's a troublemaker and a trespasser. I won't have him
here. It's your fault I've had to deal with the police all day,"
she accused me.

"My fault? I'm just the messenger. The bad news has
been going on around here for a while. Right under you
nose," I added, quoting Fuentes.

"Police?" Ida said. "Your ladyship may remember there
have been police around here for days, investigating murder.
Unless this is—"

"Oh, Ida, please!" Mrs. Wyckoff dismissed her. Ida's
hands clenched, opened, clenched at her sides. She stopped
talking. "I hold you responsible, Mr. Smith, for any damage
done to the Home's reputation," Mrs. Wyckoff went on.
"This could have been handled in a far more sensitive way.
And just how did you get in?" She shifted her suspicious
glance to the guard at the desk.

"I'm visiting Ida. My name wasn't on any persona-non-
grata list."

"It is now," Mrs. Wyckoff said. "Guard!"

The Wells Fargo guy snapped his head up, stood toughly.

"You can't do that," Ida said. "Bill's my guest."

Mrs. Wyckoff crimped her lips, glared at Ida. To the
guard she said, "Throw this man out."

"No, I'm leaving," I said. "I'm starving. I have to get
some lunch anyway."

"You should have eaten with us," Ida said. "It was
awful."

I smiled, kissed her dry cheek. "I'll see you later, Dollface." I shook Eddie Shawn's left hand, the one he held out
to me. *"Hasta la vista,"* I said.

"Geronimo," said Ida. She shuffled determinedly past
Mrs. Wyckoff and into the parlor. Mrs. Wyckoff had to step
back as Lydia wheeled Eddie into the parlor right behind.

The Wells Fargo guard seemed relieved as I walked past

him, out the front door and into the garden, leaving Mrs.
Wyckoff fuming in the hall.

Lydia caught up with me on the sidewalk outside the walls.
The shadow of the building fell on the wide stone porch, and
the trees I'd walked under were barer now than three days
ago, when I'd first come here.

"She doesn't like you much, does she?" Lydia asked.

"I don't see why she should."

"Besides you're obnoxious, aggressive, and abrasive,
what's not to like?"

"Aren't those three of the seven dwarfs?"

"Except 'aggressive.' He's one of Santa's reindeer."

"How come you know about Santa's reindeer?"

"It's incumbent upon a member of the model minority to
study the social customs, political organization, and reli-
gious mythology of the ruling class."

"Oh," I said. "How about lunch?"

"It was terrible."

"I was offering to buy you some. You ate with them?"

"You can still buy me some. Ida said Mrs. Wyckoff rarely
comes into the dining room so it was a safe place to hide. If
she came in we were going to pretend I was checking out the
food for my mother."

"She's a natural, Ida is."

"She likes you."

"Well, so maybe she's not so smart. Of course, she likes
you too."

"What's wrong with her?"

"That she likes us?"

"That she has to be here."

"I asked Dayton about her," I said. "She's had a series of
small strokes, and she's likely to have more. She's on medication but there's no real way to prevent them."

"But have they really affected her?"

"So far the effects are only minor, but they're permanent.
She has trouble with nouns, especially people's names, for
example. But mostly what's wrong with her is that she's old
and frail and has no relatives."

"And that's a crime," Lydia said. She turned back and
looked at the Home, wrapped in its tall garden walls. "It gets

you a life sentence, and you serve it here.''

I said, ''Or someplace worse.''

Lydia was very quiet. I wanted to put my arm around her, just as a friend, just to reassure; but I didn't.

The light changed, traffic started up. Across the Concourse a bus stopped, picked up some citizens who went in the front door and paid their fares and some teenagers who went in the back door and didn't.

I lit a cigarette, held it in my left hand, the side away from Lydia. ''Do you mind walking?'' I asked.

''No, I'd like to. I don't know this neighborhood.''

We walked the long blocks to the deli, past six-story apartment buildings with little entrance courtyards. One courtyard had a fountain in its center, long dry, chips in its concrete sides and trash in its bowl. Beyond the buildings, leading up to the courthouse, was the park. On a boulder in the center of a circle of trees a young couple sat, he murmuring in her ear, she looking down at the ground as she smiled and answered. The wind came up, blew leaves around them.

''Why does Mrs. Wyckoff blame you for the police coming around today?'' Lydia asked.

''Because I called them.'' I told her about the storeroom below the basement, with the carriage doors on Chester Avenue, and about Pete Portelli, who had busted his hump on the operation.

''Wow,'' she said. ''I may be in the wrong business after all. I don't think I have enough of a criminal mind. In a million years I wouldn't have thought of that.''

''I didn't think of it either.''

''What are you saying? That even the best criminal minds sometimes slip?''

''There's more.'' I told her what Portelli had said about Howe, and Mike.

She stopped walking, faced me. The wind lifted her short glossy hair. ''Oh, my God,'' she said. ''Is it true? Do you believe it?''

''It makes sense to me. I hardly knew Howe, but the picture I've gotten of him makes it plausible. And what Sheila Downey said about Mike being upset about something at work and refusing to talk to Bobby about it, that fits too. But mostly what convinces me is Portelli was terrified. He thought I was going to shoot him.'' I paused, looked across the street as though there were something I wanted to see there. ''I thought so too.''

Lydia's fingertips brushed the back of my hand. ''You didn't.''

''No.'' I dropped the cigarette butt, crushed it underfoot. ''Anyway, I don't see him coming up with a story like that on the spot.''

We started forward again. ''Could he have had it invented in advance, in case he needed it?'' Lydia asked. ''With Howe dead, it's convenient to point to him.''

''If he had, why not invent a story that let himself out completely? He's up to his ass in alligators now. He may squeeze out from under this stolen-goods rap but it'll take some doing. Why not set the story up better from the beginning, if it was a story?''

''All right,'' she said. ''But if Howe killed Mike Downey, who killed Howe?''

''Portelli says it was the Cobras, reestablishing their ownership of that particular method of operation.''

''And they picked a man doing the same job in the same place, to make their point?''

''That's the theory.''

''Then why would they deny it when you talked to them? Wouldn't they have bragged about it if that's why they did it?''

''I think they would have. I don't think they did it. But let me tell you the rest.'' I told her what I'd gotten from Eddie Shawn, and I told her what had happened in the police station that morning, and in the parking lot behind it.

By the time I was through we'd reached the deli. It was half empty, the last of the lunch crowd dividing up their checks and gulping down their coffee. As we sat Lydia said, ''So Howe was killed by someone he knew. And the police think it was Carter.''

''No, they don't. They think they can convince a jury it was Carter. They think they can use that to get either Carter or me to give them Snake.''

''Do they think it was Snake?''

''Lindfors does, but he can't see past Snake and he doesn't want to look. Robinson thinks getting Snake off the street is a more urgent priority than finding out who actually killed Howe." I added, "He may be right."

"What do you mean?"

"If Howe was killed for a reason, his killer may never kill again. Snake kills for fun."

The waiter brought menus. I didn't need one, but Lydia is always interested in people's dining customs. I ordered chopped liver and a cup of coffee while she studied it. She asked for tea and a toasted corn muffin.

"Is that all you're having? I thought lunch was terrible," I said.

"It was. But I was undercover, so I ate it."

It was the kind of deli where they have pickles in stainless-steel bowls on the table. I bit into one, tasted garlic and brine.

"Well," Lydia said. "So that's what you know. Do you want to know what I know?"

"Yes, I do. But there's something I didn't get to yet." I told her about Dr. Madsen while the waiter brought lunch.

"You had a feeling about him, didn't you?" she said after a pause, when I was through.

"What do you mean?"

"That's why you didn't tell the police about the pictures in the envelope."

"Maybe."

"You liked him."

"That first day? No, not really. But I didn't think he was bullshitting me, and I can't say that about many people in this case."

"Do you think what he told you today was true?"

"It would be easy enough to check. But even if it's true and even if you think it's admirable, it doesn't mean he couldn't have killed Howe. Or Reynolds."

"Do you think it's admirable?"

"It's illegal."

"That's not what I asked you."

I finished off the sandwich half I was holding. "Jesus, Lydia, I don't know. If you're asking if I think Robin Hood was anything more than a thug with style, no, I don't. If you're asking if I think the world would be a better place with more Dr. Madsens and fewer Mrs. Wyckoffs, yes, I do.''

Her black eyes caught mine. ''I like him for it,'' she said.

''I knew you would. Now, tell me what you know.''

''What I know.'' She sipped her tea. ''Oh—the first thing I know is that Mr. Moran called. He wanted to know if you know where Mr. Dayton is.''

''Should I?''

''Mr. Moran's been trying to reach him. He's got a new job for him.''

''I have no idea.''

''Mr. Moran says it's strange that Mr. Dayton hasn't returned his calls.''

''I think it's strange that you call everybody 'Mister.' ''

''Only those who deserve respect, Bill,'' she said pointedly. ''Anyway, I think Mr. Moran is worried that Mr. Dayton is avoiding him.''

''Did he say that?''

''No . . .''

''I think they've been working together too long for that. If Dayton doesn't want to work for Bobby anymore, he'll tell him.''

''Even if the reason is . . . the one Mr. Moran is afraid of?''

''That Bobby's old and sick and he's lost it?''

She nodded.

''He might not tell him the reason,'' I said, ''but he wouldn't just duck Bobby's calls.''

Lydia sipped her tea in silence. I thought about Bobby, wondered whether his fear was in Lydia's mind, or his own, or whether Dayton, in fact, really did want nothing more to do with Moran Security.

''Lydia?'' I said. ''What else do you know?''

Her eyes came back to me from where they'd been, far away. She smiled. ''The name on the card in Henry Howe's toilet tank?'' she said. ''Margaret O'Connor is the Administrator at Samaritan Hospital. 'ES' stands for Emigrant Savings. Bank. The number you gave me is a checking account there.''

''Margaret O'Connor's checking account?''

Lydia had just bitten into a piece of corn muffin. She

shook her head while she swallowed. "As a matter of fact, no. Did you know that?"

"I don't know anything. I guessed. Whose is it?"

"You'll have to guess that too, because I haven't been able to find out yet."

"How do you know it isn't Margaret O'Connor's?"

"Because I called and said I was Citibank and she'd given Emigrant as a reference for a loan. They said there was such an account, but that wasn't the name on it. They wouldn't tell me the name, though, and I didn't want to make them suspicious by calling back with some other gag right away. I'll have to think of something else."

"Well, I'm sure you will." I signaled the waiter for more coffee. "So. Where the hell are we? Howe was killed by someone he knew. Reynolds was killed by someone. Someone put the cops onto Carter, with faked evidence, for some reason."

"Assuming," Lydia said, gently but precisely, "that Carter's really innocent."

"Yes. Assuming that." I went on, listing what I thought we knew as though, like practicing a new piece, I could consolidate ground and move on to another level. "Portelli was running a stolen-goods racket out of the Home, Madsen was stealing drugs and needles, Howe was blackmailing them both." I looked at Lydia. "Well? What do we have?"

"What is it you people say? A nest of worms?"

"A can of worms. Or a nest of vipers." I sighed. "Okay. Let's get back to work."

"What do you have in mind?"

I checked my watch; three-thirty. "Samaritan's right down the Concourse from here. I think I should go see Margaret O'Connor, before she quits for the day."

"Do you want me to come with you?"

"My first choice is always for you to come with me. But I think maybe you should go back to the Home. As the daughter of a prospective resident. Talk to Mrs. Wyckoff, and whomever else will talk to you. Just get a feel. I'll meet you back there later."

"You'll just get thrown out again."

"Maybe. Or maybe Mrs. Wyckoff will go home without remembering to tell the guards about me."

"Uh-huh."

"Uh-huh. Well, my car's there. They have to let me back in to get my car."

"Is that why we walked here?"

"We walked here because you wanted to see the neighborhood."

She said, "Uh-huh."

THIRTY-FIVE

I paid the check, walked out with Lydia into the fading day. The sun hung low in the haze over the ranks of brick buildings, and the light it gave was gold shot through with red glints. I looked around, long and carefully. I didn't see either the tan Dodge or the green Chevy. I didn't see anything that looked like it was following me.

"I talked to Nathan, by the way," Lydia said as she zipped her leather jacket. "He went over to the precinct and worked things out with Carter. The arraignment will be this afternoon—maybe it's been already. Nathan thinks bail will be high."

"I think he's right. Maybe I should go see Carter's grandmother and the kids."

"Nathan called them. Carter asked him to."

"Good."

We scanned the street for cabs. "Nathan had trouble finding the police station," Lydia said. "He says it's a good-looking building if you like police stations but it's nowhere near the old one. Why do you suppose they did that?"

"Moved it? To shore up the neighborhood, I guess."

"What do you mean?"

"The neighborhood around the old forty-first was pretty much burned out. The new building is in a neighborhood that could go either way. I guess the City wants to stabilize it."

"Does the City really think like that?"

I nodded. "Dave and Bobby and their cop friends used to gripe about it, every time a new station house was planned."

"Because the City was messing with police buildings for non-police reasons?"

"It's not just police buildings; the City does it all the time, sort of maximizing resources. No, I think they were just cynical."

"Were they right, or does it work?"

"Sometimes, I guess. As a seed sort of thing. A City building opens, there's more investment, property values go up, which brings more investment, stuff like that."

"How come they don't do it in Chinatown?"

"Because you people are doing fine all by yourselves."

"Only the big-money interests."

"Okay," I said. "Call the Mayor. Tell him what you want. I'm right behind you. There's your cab."

Lydia and I caught separate gypsy cabs—regular yellow cabs don't cruise the Bronx—and she headed north. I went south down the Concourse, checking the traffic out the rear window periodically. I knew Lydia was doing the same, watching her back.

Cars came and went, but nobody stayed with me long enough to be tailing me. Unless the guy had a relay team, he wasn't here. Whatever he was up to, it would have to keep.

Margaret O'Connor was fiftyish, athletic-looking, with short gray-streaked black hair and beautiful gray eyes. She put me in an upholstered chair on one side of her desk, seated herself in a leather chair on the other. I told her who I was and what I was working on. She told me she would like to help.

"Though I don't know how." Her voice was deep and slightly hoarse. I didn't see any ashtrays but I wondered if she smoked. "I don't really know why you've come to me."

I looked around the office: pale pink walls—pink makes everyone look healthier—and strong, simple furniture, good but not new. It could have been any office, anywhere, except for the disinfectant smell faintly tingeing the air. "You're a private investigator," she said, fingering my card. "Might I ask for whom you're working?"

"I knew the first victim."

"The young man?"

I nodded.

"It's a terrible tragedy, dying that young," she said.

"So is murder, at any age. You knew Dr. Reynolds?" I asked.

She gave me a strange look; maybe I was being obnoxious, aggressive, and abrasive. "Of course. He had privileges here. We have a contract with Helping Hands, which includes the Bronx Home."

Warm it up a little, Smith. I tried to change the tone of my voice. "What sort of contract?"

"They send us patients in need of hospital care. We provide it."

"Why does that need a contract?"

"They're assured of a bed for any patient at any time; we guarantee that. We're assured a steady stream of patients. It helps keep us above the eighty-percent mark."

"The eighty-percent mark?"

She smiled. Her smile was both efficient and comforting. Comforting, maybe, because it was efficient. No sentimentality, no illusions; we'll do what we can, and then we'll move on to the next thing. Enough time in a hospital in the Bronx might give you that smile. "You're not in the health-care field, are you, Mr. Smith?"

Hardly, I thought. The question was rhetorical but I answered it. "No, I'm not."

"In this field, there are many government regulations. One of them holds that in order to receive certain funding, our beds must be maintained above eighty-percent full. The thinking is if we can't do that, we're not needed in the community. Clearly we are, but percentages are tricky for a crisis-oriented institution to achieve. There are epidemics, or just bad flu seasons. Or Saturday night." She smiled again. "The capacity we have to handle those times can make us appear underutilized at other times. Helping Hands' patients, because they tend to be hospitalized on a nonemergency basis—though not always, of course—help us even out those peaks and dips."

From her office window I could see nothing but more tan brick buildings, the rest of the Samaritan complex. Something was ringing a small, tentative bell in the back of my mind; I wanted time to listen to it. "I've learned more in the last few days about nonprofit institutions than I ever wanted to know," I said.

"And you're disillusioned."

"I suppose I am."

"Everyone is, at the beginning. But the rules are what they are. I'm sure there are regulations in your field that you find arbitrary and counterproductive. But your choices are few: live with them, find a way to change them, or find a new profession. Most of us do the first. Many of us do the last."

"And few of us ever change anything," I finished for her. "Your contract with Helping Hands—does it involve money?"

"No. Who would pay whom? It's just a mutual guarantee of performance."

"Do you have an account at Emigrant Savings Bank?"

She frowned. "I beg your pardon?"

"Emigrant Savings." I rattled off the account number from the card in Henry Howe's toilet tank.

"Are you asking whether that's my account? I do my banking at Chase. Why do you want to know?"

"How about the hospital?"

"Our checking accounts are with Chemical and our pension fund is with a private insurer. I really don't understand why you're asking this."

"I don't either. Your name was mentioned in association with that bank-account number."

"By whom?"

"I'm not sure of that either."

"Mr. Smith," she smiled, "don't you think it's odd that you should come asking questions that you don't know the reason for, or even the meaning of?"

"Yes, but I do it all the time. What if I were to tell you that checks with your signature, drawn on Samaritan Hospital accounts, were regularly deposited in that account at Emigrant?" Or what if I were to tell you the moon was made of green cheese?

She tapped the corner of my card on the desktop. "I wouldn't be a bit surprised," she said, "but we write a lot of checks. One rarely knows where one's checks are deposited."

"This is a big hospital."

"I don't follow you."

"You must have an entire financial department. Accounts Receivable, Accounts Payable, Payroll, the whole thing. Why is your signature on any checks at all?" Jesus, Smith, I thought. First you make up a story and then you ask someone to explain it to you.

She explained it. "I have a discretionary account. To buy birthday presents for the staff, put on cocktail receptions for potential donors, things of that sort. Why is this your business, Mr. Smith?"

"Because someone was blackmailing a number of people connected with the Bronx Home over a number of different things. I think this Emigrant account was part of that."

"You think that I was making blackmail payments?" Her voice held amusement. "Well, it's a more interesting class of crime than we usually see at Samaritan. Generally it's limited to gunshots, stab wounds, and drug overdoses."

"No," I said slowly. I was working this out as I went along. "I don't think you were paying blackmail. I think you were paying for something else, and someone else was being blackmailed."

Margaret O'Connor's smile flickered. She stopped tapping my card. The little bell in my mind was playing a tune, a theme from the Second Mephisto Waltz.

"You'll have to explain that," she said.

And you'd better get it right the first time, I told myself.

"What happens," I asked her, "if you fall below the eighty-percent mark?"

"I told you. We risk the loss of certain funding."

"No. I mean what happens if you see that happening?"

She frowned as if she didn't understand, but she didn't say she didn't.

"Here's what I think happens," I said. "I think when you see your beds emptying you call the Bronx Home and they send you patients. For tests, or for elective surgery, or for no goddamn reason at all. What's the big deal, everyone figures. Most of those people are ga-ga anyway, and all of them have something wrong with them. No surprise to anyone if they pop up in the hospital a couple of times a year. Am I right so far?"

Margaret O'Connor said nothing.

"You need a doctor to admit them here. That was Dr.

Reynolds. 'Go ahead, Margaret, keep 'em as long as you need 'em.' He had that reputation around the Home, always sending people to the hospital. He even sent me for X rays I didn't need.'' I stopped to think some more; she didn't interrupt me.

"I was in and out fast, too. I would guess policy is to treat people from the Home with special care, so they don't start demanding another hospital. I had a feeling something was wrong, and I made a big deal about making sure my insurance would pay, but that was only because I couldn't think of any other scam, and I wasn't even sure how that one would work. But I've got it now, don't I?''

Silence.

"Isn't that how it goes?'' I pushed. "And Samaritan's funding stays solid, and Dr. Reynolds receives little tokens of gratitude out of the Administrator's discretionary fund.''

Margaret O'Connor still said nothing. Maybe I'd have done better telling her about the green cheese.

"It can't be that hard,'' I said, "for the police to subpoena that bank account. They may have done it already.'' If they've stuck their hands in the toilet tank.

Her face grew hard. She snapped my card down on the desk. "You're one of those righteous people.'' Her voice was sharp. "One of those people who thinks there are no excuses. I'll bet you despise people weaker than yourself, and I'll bet you see a lot of those.''

"Tell me about the excuses.'' My face flashed hot but I kept my voice level.

"Do you know whom we service here?'' Her eyes glowed with anger. "There's a sixteen-year-old boy brought in yesterday, shot for winking at a girl from a different high school. He'll live, but he won't walk again. We have an entire ward of children dying from AIDS. Some of their families don't even visit anymore. We see malnutrition on a level unknown since the Depression. TB is a new epidemic, but mostly it's run-of-the-mill rape, child abuse, shootings and stabbings and beatings. This is a war zone, Mr. Smith. We're a field hospital. Our mission is to provide care to whoever can make it to our door.''

I said, "And to do that, if a couple of old men and old ladies get scared half to death, spend a few days disoriented and uncomfortable, have minor surgery they don't need, well, what's the difference, right?''

"If those old men and old ladies expect to have a hospital to come to when they really need one, maybe they should consider this their contribution to the war effort.''

I looked at her, erect in her chair, her jaw held tight. "I know a cop you'd like,'' I said.

"Is that a threat?''

"No. No, not at all. I think it might have been a compliment.'' I scanned the room again. The disinfectant smell was really getting to me. "Can I smoke?''

After a brief moment she yanked open a desk drawer, pulled out an ashtray and a pack of Gauloises. I struck a match before she did, lit hers for her. I wasn't sure she was happy about it but she wasn't rude enough to stop me. She nudged the ashtray between us on the desk.

"Ms. O'Connor,'' I said, lighting a Kent, "I don't know if what you're doing is right, or can be justified. I don't even know how to think about it. Right now I'm going to deal with it by not dealing with it, except for this: three men are dead. Their deaths seem related to various illegal operations involving the Bronx Home, and this was one of those operations. I want to know how it ties in to those deaths.''

"This may surprise you.'' She tilted her head back to avoid exhaling directly at me. "But if that's true, I'd like to know, too.''

"Then help me.''

Her beautiful gray eyes regarded me without blinking. She wasn't a doctor; the degrees on her walls were all management degrees. Still, I felt like a specimen of something unlucky enough to be caught on a glass slide.

"I want you to understand,'' she said, "that my first priority is this hospital. If I help you, I want a guarantee that you won't go to the authorities with anything I tell you.''

"I can't give you that. Anything that will help solve these murders I won't keep to myself. But I haven't told them any of this yet.'' Because I only just figured it out, I thought to myself, and there's never a cop around when you need one.

We smoked in silence for a while, alternating using the ashtray. Finally Margaret O'Connor said, "Well, there isn't very much more in any case. Samaritan's arrangement with the Bronx Home is largely as you describe. It's part of a broader contract with Helping Hands, as I said, to provide all hospital-related care, including ambulance and outpatient services. Like your X rays. It was only a short step from Samaritan providing services because we needed the patients, to the Home providing patients. Both inpatients and people like yourself.'' She smiled. ''I hope you weren't terribly inconvenienced.''

There was a self-mocking tone to her words that kept me from an angry answer.

''And you recruited Dr. Reynolds for this?''

She glanced up quickly from tapping cigarette ash. ''Good grief, no. It was his idea.''

''The whole scheme?''

''Our contract with Helping Hands was in place when Dr. Reynolds came to the Home. After a few months he came to me and offered this increase in sensitivity to Samaritan's needs.''

''This what?''

''That's what he called it.'' The ironic tone, again.

''And in return Samaritan was responsive to Dr. Reynolds's needs?''

''He was taking a risk, though I couldn't see that it was ever a big one. After all, there was no way to prove that any particular patient he sent here didn't actually need hospitalization. The worst he could have been accused of was bad judgment. But on the other hand, the payments we made weren't big either.''

''So the account at Emigrant was his?''

''I couldn't tell you that. But the checks we wrote were to an entity called Medical Services, Inc.''

''Why not directly to him? He was a doctor. It wouldn't have necessarily looked strange for you to be making payments to him.''

''To our auditors, no. But that was Dr. Reynolds's idea.''

''A man full of ideas.''

Margaret O'Connor had smoked her unfiltered cigarette down to a half-inch butt. She jammed that into the ashtray with her thumb. ''I got the feeling,'' she said as she settled back in her chair, ''that Dr. Reynolds was not making this up as he went along.''

"What do you mean?"

"That it was all very well organized, and if you looked into that account, you would find more money than Samaritan was ever the source of. Did you know him well?"

"We met once. The time he decided I needed X rays." And then once more, when he was in no position to decide anything at all.

"Dealing with him was distasteful," she said. "He was similar to some of our donors. Outwardly quite charming, but I don't value charm. There are other qualities I value, such as perseverance and honesty." My face must have changed. She smiled again. "You have a right to disbelieve that, after what you've heard, but honesty is a complicated virtue."

"I always thought it was one of the simpler ones."

"None of the virtues is simple," Margaret O'Connor told me. "Only the sins."

THIRTY-SIX

There were no gypsy cabs outside Samaritan. The sky was a soft blue-purple, and the light it reflected improved everything, even the tan brick, as long as it lasted; but it didn't last long. Sodium streetlights built up slowly, efficient but finally harsh, draining everything of color. I caught a bus up the Concourse, watched the buildings slip by in place as they were slipping by in time, part of a past that was getting harder and harder to see.

By the time I got off it was night, a starless night of high haze and chill air. I zipped my jacket, crossed the street to the Home. My car was in the back lot; I'd put it there on purpose just after Robinson came, for the reason I'd told Lydia. I wanted to make sure, when I was ready to come back, that the Wells Fargo guys had a legitimate reason to let me in.

I reached the garden gate, lifted the latch.

"Yo." The voice came from a shadow that detached itself from the shadows around it, stepped forward. A small kid, baseball cap turned backwards. It took me a second.

"Speedo?"

"Yeah," he said. "Snake want to see you."

"To see me?"

"Yeah. I take you there."

"Where?"

"Where Snake be waitin'."

"He tell you why?"

"Naw. Just to bring you."

I looked at him, the baseball cap, the cocked head, the aggressive lean to his shoulders. No, I wanted to say, Speedo, there's no future with Snake. Find another dream, something else you can practice being that will let you grow up. But a voice in my head said, Like what, Smith? Where is he going to look for something else, and what chance does he have of getting it if he finds it?

"Okay. I have to do something first, in here. I'll be right back out."

He stepped between me and the gate. "Snake say now."

"And I say later. Ten minutes. I'll meet you back here." I stepped past him, opened the gate.

"On the corner," Speedo yelled after me as the gate clanked shut. "Meet me across there, on the fucking corner."

Yeah, I thought, okay. You got the last word, Speedo. You're still in charge.

I went in, down, out the back swiftly, greeting the guards but not stopping. They didn't seem particularly interested in me. Either Mrs. Wyckoff had forgotten about banning me, or Bruno's instructions overrode hers, at least as long as she wasn't around.

Out in the parking lot I left my gun and holster under the seat of my car. If Snake checked my gun at the door I had a feeling I'd have more trouble getting it back than I'd had at Samaritan Hospital. And I couldn't imagine him neglecting to ask.

I checked the piano parlor and the dining room for Lydia, but it was too early for dinner and the parlor was empty. If I'd found her I'd have told her where I was going, how long to give me before she called Robinson and the Marines; but I didn't find her and I didn't want to spend a lot of time looking. I didn't want to keep Speedo waiting; I had a few questions for Snake myself and this was a good time to ask them, unless Speedo got offended and split on me. I walked out, crossed to the opposite corner. Speedo sat waiting under a streetlight, with a Coke, a comic book, and a scowl.

I recognized the doorway from the photos in the toilet tank. The building was two blocks down the hill, and the apartment Speedo led me to was on the first floor. We didn't have any trouble getting in the building; the guy in the hooded sweatshirt on the stoop nodded to Speedo with no change of expression, and Speedo affected the same hard face as he returned the nod, pushed open the door.

The hallway was dark, two broken lightbulbs overhead, a working one down the other end. The air was stale and reeked of garbage. Speedo pounded a coded knock on a scarred door. It opened on darkness; we stepped inside. The door clicked shut, softly and finally.

There were shadowy figures, not much light in the room. A slight, broad-nosed guy, who might be fifteen or he might be twenty, blocked my path.

"Hands on the wall!" he snapped. "Spread 'em!"

They must hear that on these blocks as often as most people hear "Have a nice day." I turned, planted my feet wide, palms on the wall. Speedo, looking as though he hoped no one would notice him to throw him out, strutted casually across the room, dropped onto a couch. The wall was spray-painted with silver-and-gold grafitti; it glinted in the light from the streetlamps outside.

The broad-nosed guy went over me expertly, the small of my back, my ankles, my crotch. He kept a hand on my shoulder as he said, "Okay, Snake. He clean."

Lights went on behind me and footsteps came forward. I started to turn.

It was a mistake. A fist slammed above my kidney, arching me with pain and surprise. I spun, made a grab for the guy who did it, but Broad-nose and someone else locked onto my arms, yanked me around, and I was face-to-face with Snake.

Now there was light. Now I could see two guys with guns across the room. Speedo sat forward on the couch, eyes bright. A round-faced guy sat next to him, relaxed with a beer, and a guy in a baseball cap leaned on a windowsill. There were the two guys holding me, and there was Snake. That made a lot of them.

"What the hell was that for?" I asked Snake.

" 'Cause you kept my man Speedo waiting. And 'cause I don't like you."

"Okay," I said. "I got it."

"No, you ain't got it." A flash of gold-wrapped knuckles; pain burst in my jaw. The second punch was to my stomach, knocked my breath out. The guy pinning my right arm laughed. As I raised my head to look at Snake I tasted a salty trickle from my lip.

Snake stepped back, rubbed his left hand over the gold rings on his right. "Okay." Gold gleamed from his grin. "Now I b'lieve you got it."

The guys on my arms released me, but the guys with the guns didn't put them down.

I looked around. A kitchenette stood against one wall, cluttered with pizza boxes, beer cans, wadded napkins. The chairs, lamps, couch were sprung and broken down and smelled of mildew, but the stereo was new. A doorway led to a bathroom and beyond it a bedroom; I could see a bare mattress on the floor. Some of the impassive faces watching me I recognized from the other times. Some were new to me.

"Where's Skeletor?" I turned my eyes back to Snake.

"Got business. He be along later."

"All right," I said. "You got me here, you smacked me around a little—was that it? That's what you sent Speedo for?"

"Naw," Snake said. "I want to talk to you, white meat. Just first, I had to pay back what I owe. Now sit down."

One of the impassive faces picked up a hard-backed armchair, clonked it onto the floor near me.

"No, thanks. I'd rather stand."

"Ain't no fucking invitation! Sit down."

Broad-nose put a hand on my arm. I shook him off, looked at Snake. In his eyes I saw what I'd seen the first time we'd met, when I'd had to pull a gun to keep him from killing me with his fists.

I sat. "Can I smoke?"

Snake's eyebrows rose; he was a man considering a rea-

sonable request. "Yo, my brother. I got no problem with
that. Anybody got a problem with that?" he asked the room.

There were some snickers, some headshakes. The guy
who'd helped Broad-nose hold me said, "I wanna smoke
too, Snake. Only I ain't got no butts."

"Ain't no thing but a chicken wing," Snake said. "Our
white brother gonna share his with us."

I took out my Kents, pulled one for myself, handed the
pack to Snake. Still looking at me, he passed it to the other
guy. It went around the room; it never came back to me.

"Now." Snake perched on the arm of a chair. "We got a
problem."

"Oh?" I held smoke in my lungs, let it go. I could feel my
lip beginning to swell. "What's that?"

"Fact is, we got a lot of problems."

I didn't answer.

"And it seem to me," he said, "that mostly, we got them
'cause there a private dee-tective 'round here, don't know
who he working for."

"I'm here to find out who killed men you say you didn't
kill. I don't see what the problem is."

"That because you ain't looked to see what the problem
is. You ain't asked yourself, 'Do Snake got a problem? And
if he do, what I'm gonna do about it?' "

"You're right," I said. "I haven't."

"Well, you gonna start. And I'm gonna help you out." He
counted on his fingers. "One problem: my man Rev got his
ass in jail."

"Why is that a problem for you?"

" 'Cause he my homey! He be talkin' about, Snake, I
don't hang with you no more, but that bullshit. He don't
want Snake to fix him up, he wanna bust his ass for chump
change up to the Home of the Living Dead up there, that his
choice. But Cobras don't sit in no jail, white meat. Not if
Snake can do something for them."

"Ex-Cobras."

He grinned, pushed up his right sweatshirt sleeve. On the
inside of his forearm was a tattooed cobra, coiled to strike.
He flexed his tendon, made it move.

"See that? It don't never go away. Once you got that, you
always got it."

He rolled his sleeve down again, still grinning.

"Okay," I said. "So what are you going to do for him?"

"First thing, I'm gonna find out why some ass-wipe private dee-tective say he my man's friend, then he be down at the cop house for a hour, come out suckin' on Lindfors's dick."

"I was there an hour and a half," I said. "How do you know about that?"

"I got people tell me things."

"Have you had someone following me? First in a Dodge, then a green Chevy?"

"What? Man, you trippin'. I don't need no one following you. I got homies all over, tell me where you be. So," he said, "what you been doin'? You sellin' my man, collectin' a re-ward? What?"

"I got your man a lawyer," I said. "Someone set him up. I thought maybe it was you." I hadn't thought that, and it was a stupid thing to say. Snake's eyes flashed. He jumped to his feet. I tensed, forced myself to stay seated. The room crackled; from the corner of my eye I saw Speedo, half off the couch, grinning a grin he was probably unaware of.

Then Snake relaxed. The electricity in the room eased, as though the juice had been turned down, but not off.

"You one wise-ass motherfucker." Snake settled onto the arm of the chair again. "Don't seem to me you got much respect."

"He dissin' you, Snake," called the kid on the windowsill.

"Word." Snake nodded. "And I got a idea, what to do about that. But first, white meat, I'm gonna tell you the rest of my problems."

Snake lifted his fingers again. "One, we got my man Rev in jail. Two, we got that faggot Lindfors all over my ass, because some motherfucker be killing white boys, make it look like Cobras is doing it. This a problem because you got a cop on your ass, it hard to do business. How-*ever*—" Snake folded his arms across his chest—"how-*ever*, right now it hard to do business anyway. You know why, white meat?"

"No," I said. "Why?"

"Because I ain't got no . . ." Snake hesitated. "Einstein!'' He half-turned his head to the guy on the couch next to Speedo. ''What is it I ain't got?''

''Liaison,'' the round-faced guy answered over the beer can. ''You ain't got no liaison.''

Snake beamed, turned back to me. ''Liaison,'' he repeated.

''What are you talking about?'' My cigarette was almost gone. I was sorry about that. I took a last drag, crushed the butt under my foot. ''What do you mean, liaison?''

''Your liaison,'' Snake explained patiently, ''he the guy do your business for you.''

''A bagman. I've been wondering who your bagman was.''

''Liaison,'' Snake corrected. ''See, some places me and my homies take care of, we just go on in, 'cause we know we be welcome. Other places, nigger don't just walk in the front door. Right, homies?''

Murmurs of ''Word'' and ''You so right, brother'' from around the room.

''Anybody be coming like that,'' Snake went on, ''I ain't give a shit, just send 'em my honky liaison. Then I be sending my main man Skeletor, go meet my liaison. Course, that way, it cost the customers more,'' he added, grinning. The grin faded. ''But now my liaison be dead. Now what I do?''

''Honky?'' I said. ''Dead?'' The headlights of a car stared into the room momentarily as it turned the corner outside. In here, nobody moved. I thought of a motionless body in the eye of a storm. ''Oh, Jesus,'' I said, half to myself. ''Henry Howe.''

''Yo!'' Snake high-fived Broad-nose, who was standing near him. ''Maybe you ain't so stupid, white meat.''

I wasn't sure that was true.

''If you ain't,'' he continued, ''that a good thing, 'cause look what we got.'' The fingers, again. ''We got the Rev in jail. We got Lindfors on my ass. And we got no liaison. No liaison mean we losing money every day, 'cause ain't no one collecting. We losing money, and I got expenses.'' He gestured broadly at the group behind him. Their eyes were all on us, their faces blank; this was live television, without commercials.

''Plus,'' Snake expanded, ''we ain't collecting, people be

talking. That Snake, he got his homey in jail, he got a cop on his ass, plus he ain't collecting. Maybe he ain't so big as we thought.'' He stuck his hands on his hips. ''See, I got a reputation I got to protect. What I sell, people don't think they need it, they ain't gonna buy it. They be talking about, Snake getting old. Skeletor, he fat—'' grins and snorts from the Cobras—''and that motherfucking Einstein spend so much time on his butt thinking, he don't know how to get down no more.''

Einstein rose, lifted his beer, took a bow.

''See,'' Snake went on, ''long as the brothers and sisters think we cool, we cool. But long as I got my problems, maybe they thinking we ain't cool.'' He shook his head.

''Sounds bad,'' I said.

''Fucking right it bad! Now, you probably sitting there thinking, what can I do, help Snake out?''

''Yeah,'' I said. ''That's just what I'm thinking.''

''Good.'' He smiled. '' 'Cause you gonna fix it all, my brother, now that you working for me.''

''Wrong. I'm not working for you.''

''No.'' Snake stood. From my low angle, his head and shoulders eclipsed the ceiling's bare bulb. I squinted against the glare surrounding him, but his features disappeared in it. ''My brother, you is so wrong. You working for the Cobras now. You working for Snake.''

He folded his arms. The room was silent. ''You gonna find who fronting these fake Cobra jobs, so pencil-dick Lindfors get off my butt. You gonna get my man Rev out the can, any way you got to. Then things gonna settle down. Then I get me a new liaison,'' he said, savoring the word, ''and the Cobras be back in business. And it all be thanks to my own private eye!''

He laid a finger on his cheek, pulled his lower eyelid down, leaned his face very close to mine. I smelled his sweat, saw thin veins of blood in the white of his eye.

I said again, ''I'm not working for you.''

He straightened up, nodded to Broad-nose. That looked bad to me. I started to stand. Broad-nose grabbed me from behind, slammed me back onto the chair. One of the guys with the guns circled closer. The gun was a 9-mm SIG Sauer automatic; I suddenly, irrelevantly wondered if the kid holding it had ever fired anything that big before. It has a kick, I thought. It'll hurt your shoulder, if you fire it one-handed, like that.

"Snake—" I started.

"Shut up."

The barrel of the SIG Sauer nuzzled my chin.

Broad-nose reached into his pocket, came out with a roll of adhesive tape. He snapped off the cover, pocketed it. An organized guy. Maybe he kept the Cobras' books. He pulled the end of it. It made the ripping sound tape makes, coming off a roll. There might have been other sounds in the room; I only heard that.

"What—"

The gun pushed against my jaw. I shut up.

With a quick smooth motion Broad-nose taped my left wrist to the arm of the chair. Then he stepped between me and Snake and did the right; but this one he turned over, so my palm was up.

My hands, I thought. Oh, Jesus. I felt a line of sweat trickle down my ribs. "Snake—" I started again.

"I told you, shut up!" Snake's voice was ice on a griddle.

No one's interested in your hands, Smith, I tried to tell myself. No one except you gives a shit about your hands.

"Want me to do his mouth, Snake?" offered Broad-nose.

"We gonna need that?" Snake asked me.

I shook my head. I didn't know what was coming, but I was fighting to control my breathing already, to make my breathing control the crashing of my heart.

And the ability to yell might be useful, though the chances of this neighborhood responding to sounds from this apartment, I thought, were small.

Snake stuck his hand out. Someone put a switchblade in it. Snake sprang it open, stuck the tip under my right jacket cuff. With a jerk he sliced the sleeve open to the bend of my elbow. He did the shirt too, peeled them both away.

Then he stepped back, smiled. He reached under his sweatshirt, lifted the golden cobra from around his neck. Its chain made a slithering sound as he slipped it from the loop, dropped it on the kitchen counter.

He rooted around in a drawer, came up with a pair of tongs. I realized everyone in the room was moving, slowly, dreamily, positioning themselves to see. The guys with the guns both stood next to me now, one on each side; but I wasn't watching them. I couldn't take my eyes off Snake.

At the stove he twisted a knob. Blue flame sprang up. Snake held the cobra over the flame with the tongs, until he was ready; then he walked back, stood above me.

"Now, my brother," he whispered, "you working for me."

I heard the hiss before I felt anything. What I felt when it came was pain that seared down into my fingertips, up to my shoulder; and then, unable to escape, it ricocheted back and forth, building up, becoming unbearable, centered in my forearm but now, finally, everywhere.

I smelled burning flesh, my own flesh, and gagged on the smell.

It was over fast. Ten seconds maybe, maybe not even. It wasn't until Snake pulled the cobra off my arm that I heard myself start to cry out, a strangled sound. I choked it back. Breathe, dammit, I told myself, breathe, it's only pain, and I tried, pulling air in through my half-closed throat as I watched my right hand beyond the tape clench, open, clench again, rhythmically, uncontrollably, alone.

THIRTY-SEVEN

My memories after that are sketchy. I've been told that's because of what happened later. Maybe; but the images in my mind are confused and disjointed enough to make me think that the next few minutes would never have been mine in any case.

I remember Snake, and the knife. The blade glinted; so did Snake's gold tooth. "So." He hovered above me. "Who you work for, white meat?"

I didn't answer until he touched the glistening snake on my arm with the knife point. I drew air sharply, forced the words through my teeth. "You, Snake."

I remember the stink of garbage, and the guy in the hooded sweatshirt on the stoop. He hadn't moved, I marveled. All that, and this guy never moved.

Then I was alone on the sidewalk. It was cold, I remember that, much colder than before. I wanted to zip my jacket but my right hand wouldn't cooperate. Foolish, I told it, you'll feel better; but it wasn't interested. My sleeve dangled. My left arm held my right in a grip like a vise. I forced my hand not to touch the burn, because I knew that was right, though I couldn't think why.

Later, after everything was over, through all the other bruises and the mess I was, I could see the marks I'd made myself, gripping my arm.

I started up the hill, because that was right too. Back to the lot, to my car, home; I could put something on this, ice, I didn't know, something, but I knew it would hurt less, out of the Bronx.

I didn't make it out of the Bronx that night, of course, and my last clear memory is of the parking-lot gate, my own hand reaching for the bell. Then, sounds behind me, moving shadows. A thick arm coiling around my neck. I remember the first blows, though those memories are hazy, and I don't remember fighting back, though I've been told I did.

Just before the blackness, though, I do remember something: running footsteps approaching, and loud cries for help. Through the pounding pain and the darkness I felt myself curiously reassured by the shouting voice. It was, I thought, a voice I could trust. It seemed important that I see the owner of the voice, know who it was. I tried to see, reached out to find him, but it was like struggling through thick black water, and it was too hard. I gave up, slid back, and everything was muted as the sea closed over me.

THIRTY-EIGHT

Cold, and darkness, and noise and pain: pain like a sea, flowing over and around me. I hurt everywhere; I struggled for breath.

Warmer. Quiet. But still the darkness, and the pain.

Something new: a hand in my hand, warm and soft. A mooring. I clung to it, to keep from disappearing in the pain sea.

Later: a woman's voice, and a man's. His impatient, hers soft but unyielding. "Do what you have to do," she said. "It's not my problem. He's supposed to be kept quiet and I won't let you wake him."

I didn't understand, but I knew the voice: it was Lydia. I wanted to see her, to talk to her, but the darkness wouldn't lift.

The darkness wouldn't lift.

Panic ignited in my chest and sizzled through me. The jolt of it clenched my hand on the hand I was holding. I forced out a word, in a voice I could barely use: "Lydia."

It was a whisper, too soft to be heard, but she answered me. "Bill? Bill, are you awake?"

Through the fear clanging in my chest I told her, "I can't see."

"I know," she said, "I know. It's okay. It's just swelling. It'll be all right in a day or two."

Her words worked on my panic like cool water on a burn. *It'll be all right.* I let them ring inside my head. *Be all right. All right.*

"Bill?" Lydia said, bringing me back. "Are you strong enough to talk? Detective Lindfors is here. Just for a minute?"

"Smith?" Lindfors's voice, gravelly, close, urgent. "Just tell me who it was. It was Snake, those fucking Cobras, wasn't it? Just say it."

Snake. Impassive faces; glinting gold; searing pain I could feel now.

"Smith? C'mon."

Snake.

"No."

"No? No what? I have him in the fucking can, Smith, but I can't keep him without your I.D. Just finger him. Just say it."

"No."

A pause.

"What the hell is this? What's he doing?" Lindfors's voice was farther away now; Lydia answered, something I couldn't make out. Then he came back. "Is she right? You're telling me you didn't see? That's bullshit. There's a fucking cobra on your arm. You saw that."

"Before," I said. My mouth was dry as felt; words were difficult.

"Okay, before." Lindfors's voice was impatient. "And then they beat the shit out of you after. Right? The Cobra crew. Snake and the Cobras."

"No." I felt the room moving, swaying on the tide; it was hard to think. I knew what he wanted, and I knew he was wrong, but I couldn't put two words together to tell him why.

"Dammit!" Lindfors exploded. There was a thud, a fist hitting a wall. "Fucking cowboy! You don't need the fucking cops, is that it, Smith? You're gonna wait, you're gonna get him yourself, in a year or two, when you're walking again? Motherfucker!" I could feel his rage boiling through the room. Lydia's hand tightened on mine.

"If you died I could take 'em up for murder!" Lindfors snarled. "You gonna live, you gotta help me. Come on, Smith!"

His voice was hard to hear; it came from many directions, it echoed. I did what I could, working hard.

"Not them," I finally managed. Then, as I floated away on the sea, I laughed, silently, just for myself.

I had done it: put together two words.

THIRTY-NINE

By the next day I could see, a little. I didn't know it was the next day until Lydia told me. I didn't know much, until she told me.

I watched her, a fuzzy shape taking fuzzy shapes out of her fuzzy shoulder bag. I wasn't sure she'd wakened me when she came in; it seemed to me that I hadn't been sleeping, just staring at the blur of yellow walls and the moving shapes outside the soft gray rectangle of window. But it was early afternoon, she said; Bobby had been with me most of the morning, was downstairs now getting something to eat. She'd gone home when he came, for the first time since I was brought here. Now she was back.

I didn't remember any of that, so maybe I had slept some.

She moved forward without coming into focus, kissed me lightly. "How do you feel?" she asked. "Is it very bad?"

"No." My voice, weak and coarse, had a hard time getting past my lips, which seemed twice their usual size. "Doesn't hurt."

This was true. I felt no pain at all. I was floating, drifting on a gentle sea. Sometimes I got dizzy from the swells, but dizziness isn't so bad, really. It all would have been fine, except I was thirsty. Enormously thirsty. Floating on the sea, not a drop to drink.

"Water?" I tried.

Lydia moved to where I couldn't follow. I heard a soft rushing. When she came back she brought a plastic cup with a straw stuck in it. I tried to reach for it, but it was impossible.

"I'll hold it," she said, so I drank until she took it away, which was much too soon.

"More?"

"Later. Not too much at once, the doctor said." She put the cup beside the bed. "Lindfors is ready to kill you."

That, actually, was one of the few things I knew.

"Bill, can you tell me what happened? Do you know who it was?"

It seemed like a very hard question, with an answer much longer than I had the energy for. I floated for a little bit, watched her be blurry.

"There's a cop outside," Lydia said. "I'm supposed to go get him as soon as you wake up. Lindfors stuck him there last night. Lindfors was here when they brought you in, and he was here late. Do you remember that?"

"Think so."

"You wouldn't tell him who it was, but you kept saying it wasn't the Cobras. But there's that." She gestured to my right arm, thickly bandaged from elbow to wrist. I was suddenly afraid she meant to touch it. I moved it closer to my side. I thought her face changed then, softened, but I couldn't see well enough to be sure.

"Tell me about it," she said.

I closed my eyes, but I started to drift too far away from her. I opened them again.

"Snake," I began.

"Lindfors is right? It was the Cobras? Why did you tell him it wasn't?"

"No," I said. "Wait."

In a softer voice, she said, "I'm sorry. I won't interrupt. Tell me."

So in two- or three-syllable phrases, with pauses in between, I told her.

It was a short story, but it took a long time to tell. A few times the tide I was floating on seemed to turn, to take me away, and she had to bring me back with a touch or a word. It became an effort to stay with her, working against the tide. She understood that.

"Bill?" she said. "Just finish. Just tell me the end, then go back to sleep. When you got up the hill to the parking lot, who was there?"

"Don't know."

"Why do you say it wasn't the Cobras?"

"Had me." I took another breath. "If they . . . wanted this . . . why not then?"

"Okay. Tell me about the man who jumped you."

"From behind. Didn't speak."

"How big?" she asked. "Black or white? What was he wearing?"

Good, Lydia, I thought drowsily. Get the witness to tell you things he doesn't know he knows.

"Strong." I thought as hard as I could about the arm tightening around my neck. "Shorter than me. Dark fabric." I wanted to give her more, but that was all I had.

No, it wasn't. "Someone else. Maybe he saw. Called for help. Recognized the voice . . ."

As the sea rose, lifted me away from her, I heard her, dim and distant, from the shore.

"Al Dayton?" she said. "No, he didn't see. But he saved your life."

FORTY

The blurry walls were a cheerful yellow, a color I could come to hate. The air smelled, even tasted, of disinfectant. A thin shape traveled slowly across the window. The neck of a construction crane? Or a dinosaur. I couldn't tell.

I tried to turn my head, look for Lydia.

"I'm here." She touched my hand, moved into view. "How do you feel?"

"Better." I must be getting better; I hurt everywhere, dull aching pain mostly, with some sharp spots. One of those was my right arm. "Samaritan?"

"No, Montefiore. Dr. Madsen had the ambulance bring you here."

"Oh," I said intelligently. I squinted at her, to see if she was still fuzzy. The warmth of her hand on mine was reassuring and familiar. A vague memory, more like a dream, came to me. "You were here. The whole time. You were holding my hand."

"It helps," she said simply. "It keeps the spirit anchored."

"Chinese superstition."

"Tell it to my mother."

"No way." I thought about my mooring as I was lifted on the tide. "Lydia? It helped. It did help." I closed my fingers around hers, not very impressively, but as well as I could manage.

She smiled a small, smudged smile. "Tell it to my mother."

Something else was trying to push through the sludge in my brain, something Lydia had said before I'd drifted away. I fished around for it, then gave up. As soon as I quit it popped up by itself.

"Dayton."

"Yes," said Lydia. "He's here. He's down the hall. Shall I get him? He's been waiting to talk to you."

I was confused, so I said, "Yes."

She left; she was gone; then she was back, with a fuzzy

black man, his right arm in a fuzzy sling. He wore a bathrobe over a hospital gown.

A sudden wave of memory broke over me: pain, yelling, a kick to the side of my head. I closed my eyes. "Oh, Jesus."

Lydia's hand fit itself over mine. "Mr. Dayton saved your life."

"Dayton." I opened my eyes. "That was you?"

"I never saw his face." The deep, measured voice was Dayton's, was the shouting voice I'd heard through the darkness. I squinted again. The bristling mustache, the graying hair. Fuzzy, but there. Also a swollen bruise, and an adhesive patch on one cheek. "A black man. He jumped you outside the parking-lot gate."

"Dr. Madsen and I heard Mr. Dayton shouting," Lydia said. "I fired a warning shot as we ran out of the building and he ran away."

"Who?" I said.

"We don't know who he was, Bill," Lydia said gently.

I knew that; I couldn't think why I'd asked the question.

"Why?" I said; then, realizing I was about to be misunderstood, I added, to Dayton, ". . . were you there? Why were you there?"

"I was following you."

I closed my eyes again. I tried to add that up to something, but the drugs were making me stupid. Or maybe not the drugs; but the result was unquestionable.

"Following me?"

There was silence, then Dayton's voice. I could hear the frown in it. "I know you knew. You lost me on the Concourse, and I had to go some to lose you in Riverdale."

"Green Chevy? Tan Dodge?"

"The Dodge is mine. The Nova is my wife's."

"Why?" I asked.

There was more silence. I was suddenly afraid he was going to tell me why he'd bought his wife a Chevy Nova.

"I didn't know what was going on between you and Howe," Dayton finally said, "but I thought Mr. Moran deserved better than he was getting."

Forget it, part of me thought. This conversation is hopeless.

"What?" asked the other part. I opened my eyes. Might as well have fuzziness everywhere.

"The morning after Howe was killed, I broke into his locker while you were on the door. I found a hundred dollars and a note from you. I thought the note was to him."

That made sense. No, it didn't. "Why break in?"

"I didn't like Howe and I never had trusted him. I didn't trust you either. I thought something might be happening that someone should know about."

"The police?" Two or three words at a time seemed to be the most I could handle, and I was pleased with myself that I was getting the hang of it.

"I might have gone to them later," Dayton said. "I wanted to know first what was going on."

"Why?" That one was the best—an all-purpose, one-syllable question.

"For Mr. Moran." I suppressed the urge to say "Why?" again, just waited. "Mr. Moran has been good to me over the years. He'd already lost his nephew and he'd taken Howe's death hard. He'd spoken very highly of you, but you acted in strange ways once you came to the Home. I'd watched you." He paused. "I wanted to prevent Mr. Moran's being hurt again, if I was able."

Some things floated through my mind, some things I used to know.

"Ducked Bobby's phone calls," I said.

"I didn't want to speak to Mr. Moran until I was sure."

Phone calls. Phone calls. Why was I thinking about puppies? Then I heard, from somewhere long ago, a puppy-friendly voice: *Are you sure you didn't just call? I was sure I gave this message to someone.*

"My service," I said. "My messages."

"Mr. Bruno called me for the number of your answering service. He told me it was for Martin Carter. I knew who Martin Carter was and who he had been."

"How you knew . . . how to find me."

"That first evening," he agreed. "And after that, whenever I lost you, I returned to the Home. You always appeared there eventually. That's why I was there last night. I'd lost you, but your car was in the lot. I waited there. I knew you'd be back."

"Jesus," I said, more to myself than to them. "I . . ." That wasn't going to work; I started again. "Bobby . . ."

"Miss Chin has told me," Dayton said. "And I talked to Mr. Moran last night. I'm sorry, Smith. I had you wrong. I should have had more faith in Mr. Moran."

"Me, too. He wanted . . . to tell you. From the beginning."

"I wish you had. I might have helped."

That struck me as funny. "If you trusted me . . . you wouldn't . . . have followed me. Saved my life."

"True enough," Dayton said.

He started to say something more, but the door opened behind him. He stepped aside to let Bobby near the bed.

"Jesus, kid." Bobby leaned on his cane. His voice was shaky. "I'm sorry."

"No. I'm stupid."

"Maybe. But I never heard stupidity was punishable by death."

"Very stupid."

"I talked to Lydia," he said. "I want you two to turn over whatever you have to the cops, and get lost. The job is over."

I looked for Lydia, found her. "No."

"Yes." Bobby's voice was under control, the words all careful and right, but I could hear the effort that took. "Too many men down, kid. I don't want to lose any more." Abruptly, hoarsely, he said, "I don't want to lose you." He pivoted on his cane and left.

Dayton looked from me to the door. "I'll come back, Smith." He went after Bobby.

"He's serious." Lydia kept her hand lightly on my arm, as though she knew that with my eyes so bad I needed a different set of connections. "You should have seen him when he got here last night, Bill. He looked scared, and . . . old."

"No."

"Maybe we should. Maybe it would be better for him, not to have to worry about you."

"No." Howe, I was thinking. Mike. Madsen. Too much going on, too much to hide. My job, to make it all come out right. Carter. No way to stop, now.

Lydia smiled. " 'No'? Short and easy to pronounce, is that it?"

"Yes."

"Go to sleep," she said. "When you wake up I'll tell you a story."

FORTY-ONE

Yo. Yo, white meat. You sleeping?"

The words were like a shock of cold water. I was instantly awake, heart racing, skin electric.

It was dusk, the room dark and hazy. A yellow square of window showed in the closed door, but there were no lights in here. A long dark figure stood by the bed, hands in the pockets of a hooded sweatshirt. A gold blur lay against his chest. I didn't need to see it clearly to know what it was.

"Snake," I said, in as strong a voice as I had. "Get the hell out of here."

"No, no." He shook his head. "You got it wrong, white meat. I come to thank you."

"Get out."

"Yo," said Snake softly. "You and me, we connected now, my brother. You working for me, and I 'preciate what you done already. So I come to thank you, and tell you what I'm gonna do for you."

"The only thing," I tried to clear my throat and my head, "you can do for me," I stopped, breathed, "is to let me be there . . . when you step on your cock. And I sure as hell . . . haven't done anything . . . for you."

That was enough for me. I was ready to go back to sleep.

"No, you too modest, my brother. Last night I be down to the cop shop, Lindfors in my face talking about he got me now. Yo, he stink, too!" Snake interrupted himself. "You notice that?"

When he got nothing from me, he went on. "Then, next thing, I be diddy-bopping out the door. Lindfors, he cursing you out, white meat, and your momma too. So I say to myself, Snake, you got to go thank that dee-tective. And plus, I tell myself, you got to ask him why. So here I am."

"Get out."

"You ain't told Lindfors it was me mess you up. He want to hear that so bad it make his dick hard. How come you ain't?"

"Shit," I breathed. Suddenly it struck me there might be a silver lining to this cloud. "You have a cigarette?"

A reflected streetlamp flashed gold in the blur of his smile. He pulled out a pack. Maybe Camels, I wasn't sure. He lit one, put it between my lifted fingers. I impressed myself by bringing my hand all the way to my mouth.

The smoke snagged in my throat; I coughed. Pain seared my ribs, banged against the inside of my skull. I forgot Snake, forgot everything in the agonized effort to stop moving, still the cough.

Finally motionless, I let myself breathe again, slowly, shallowly.

"Man," I heard, "you ever think of quitting?"

"Someone," I rasped at Snake, "tried to kill me. I want to know who. And why." Breathe. "I want him cut into little pieces. If I say you, Lindfors locks up your ass. That's good." Breathe, very slowly. "But it doesn't get him. Him first. You later."

Snake grinned. "I get him for you."

I tried to focus on his eyes, but I couldn't. "What?"

"I be hiring you—" he nodded toward the bandage on my arm—"find out who settin' the Cobras up. Figure this some honky shit, need a honky dee-tective. But now, things be different. You was working for me. And it a brother done you."

"What's the difference?"

He shook his head. "Not on my blocks. Word get out, Snake don't protect his boys. That ain't right, white meat."

"I'm not . . . one of your boys."

"You was working for me." He leaned closer. Light from the window gleamed dully on his cheekbone. His eyes were hidden in the shadow of his hood. "Prob'ly you don't like Snake. But Snake take care of his boys. All the brothers and sisters know that. You stick with Snake, you got what you need."

"I don't need . . . anything from you, Snake."

"We find him for you, white meat," Snake whispered. "I

got the street looking. When we find him, we do him for you. We do him good.''

I wanted to answer that, but the room was swaying a little too much, and the weight on my chest was a little too heavy. I closed my eyes. I didn't want to see Snake leaning over me, didn't want to smell his sweat, hear his whisper. Maybe if he thought I was sleeping he'd go away.

Instead, a light flared, stabbed bright through my swollen eyelids. I opened my eyes, squinted. The room light was on overhead, and a blur that looked like Lydia was standing just inside the door staring at Snake.

''Who are you?'' the blur demanded.

''Yo! Pretty momma.'' Snake's eyes were as wide as his smile. ''My, baby, you fine! Yo, white meat, you holding out on Snake.''

''He's Snake,'' I said to Lydia. ''He's leaving.''

''Good.'' She elbowed past him, dropped her black bag on a chair.

''Yo, yo, momma—'' Snake protested, chuckling.

''Should I call security?'' Lydia picked up the room phone.

''Oh, no,'' Snake squeaked in a falsetto, lifting his hands. ''Oh, momma, you so mean. Okay, Snake leaving. But my brother, remember what I told you.'' He grinned, made a wet, kissing noise at Lydia, and left.

Lydia took my cigarette out of my hand. ''You were on oxygen until this morning,'' she said.

''I wanted it . . . for a weapon. In case Snake tried anything.''

''You wanted it for a cigarette.'' She went and threw it in the toilet. ''What was he doing here?''

''Telling me . . . not to worry. Snake's taking care of me.''

''Did that make you feel better?''

''I feel like shit.''

''Well, that's how you look. Are you hungry?''

''No. Thirsty.''

''The doctor said you could eat if you wanted to.'' She took a thermos out of her bag, poured something into the screw-cap cup, put a straw in it. ''Here.''

''Water?''

''This is better.''

"I'm not sure . . . I can hold it." I reached for the cup.

"You held the cigarette."

I held the cup. She took other things out of her bag.

"You're not as blurry," I told her.

"As what?"

"As before."

She turned from what she was doing, smiled. "Good," she said gently. "I'm glad."

I tasted the pale liquid she'd given me. It was salty and sweet and warm; it echoed with flavors like the tones that linger when a chord has almost died away.

"God," I said. "Great."

"It's full of minerals and Chinese herbs. It's a healing broth. It's very good for you."

"Did you make it?"

"My mother did."

"Your mother?" I felt myself smile. "She likes me." I sipped my Chinese herbs.

"She hates you. She also hates that I spent the night here with you. If you were a decent man, you'd die, she tells me. But since you won't, this will help you get better fast, and then maybe I'll come home where I belong."

"That's what I said. She likes me." I drank some more. "Where's Bobby?"

"He went home. The doctor said you're out of danger now, it's just a matter of healing. Mr. Moran needed to rest."

"How is he?"

I couldn't quite read her expression, even with the light to help. "Not well, Bill. He doesn't look good."

I finished my healing broth, settled back, closed my eyes. I hurt in a lot of places now, but my mind was clearer. Maybe they were giving me fewer drugs. Or maybe the Chinese herbs were working.

"We're close," I said. "I can feel it."

Something was working its way up from the depths, trying to break the surface of my thoughts. Floating, I tried to relax, give it room, and that almost worked; but two deep, muffled booms that I felt as well as heard scared it off, sent it diving for the bottom.

"Christ," I said. "What's that?"

"From the construction next door," Lydia told me. "It's driving everyone crazy, Dr. Horowitz says."

"Who's Dr. Horowitz?"

"Me!" a voice rang from the door. It belonged to a mustached, curly haired man with a stethoscope stuffed in his pocket. "God, what an entrance! I love that! How's he doing?" he asked Lydia.

"He's fine," I said.

"Hey, he talks, he walks—well, maybe not that." He lifted the chart from the foot of the bed. "Five minutes for some man talk?" he asked Lydia. "You could powder your nose, or have a cigarette."

"Bill already had one," Lydia ratted on me.

"Did you?" Horowitz raised bushy eyebrows. "Well, there would've been no point in powdering that nose."

Lydia smiled at him and left.

"Has she got a sister?" Horowitz asked.

"Four brothers."

"Hmmm. Listen, you shouldn't be smoking."

"You do."

"Wow. They told me you were a detective. What is it, my yellow teeth? The tobacco odor on my breath?"

"Newports . . . in your pocket."

"Oh. Well, they didn't bring *me* in here on a stretcher yesterday. Of course," he reflected, "if I don't quit, eventually I suppose they will."

"Can I . . . get out of here soon?"

"Are you kidding? You can't even get out of bed soon." He listened to my chest, lifted the blanket, poked around. I asked him some questions, he gave me answers.

He peered at my eyes. "Well, you're lucky. Ten days, maybe two weeks, everything should be clear."

"If only."

He laughed. "I meant your eyes."

The muffled booms came back, and the distant roaring of a large engine.

"God," Horowitz said. "Well, it's almost five. They knock off at five. Pain in the ass, huh? I guess you know all about that."

"Construction?"

"No, pain in the ass. You're going to be sore for a long

time, my friend, so get used to it. But it wasn't true what I said about your getting out of bed. I want you walking tomorrow.''

''Tonight?''

''Don't be greedy. Listen, this isn't an official visit. I was on my way home and I thought I'd drop by. You know, get introduced to someone I already know so intimately. But I'd like a look at this. Can I?''

By ''this,'' he meant my right arm. I wanted to say no, but that sounded stupid, even to me.

Horowitz stuck his head out the door, asked a nurse to step in. She was a tiny, tan woman; he spoke medical words to her. Then he started to unwrap my arm.

''Your wife,'' he said as he worked. ''She's a gem, isn't she?''

Maybe I hadn't heard him right. ''My wife?''

''She was here all night with you. She's a private eye too? I think you win the Most Exotic Couple of the Month award.''

''Lydia?''

''She brought in a specialist to look at your hands. I told her there was nothing wrong with them, but she said besides your eyes, that was the only thing you'd care about and she wanted to make sure.''

''She was right.'' It occurred to me this whole conversation was designed to distract me from what he was doing. It only half worked; as he lifted the gauze pad from my arm I felt my left hand dig into the sheets, felt my breathing stop.

''I know,'' Horowitz said sympathetically. ''The good news is I think it'll heal nicely.'' For all his casual air, I saw he had positioned himself to block my view. He took something from the nurse, dabbed at my arm. It tried to yank itself away, but he wouldn't let it move.

''All right,'' he said soothingly, ''all right, I'm through. I'm going to wrap it up now.''

''Let me see it.''

''You really want to?''

''Yes.''

Horowitz hesitated, then moved aside, cradled my arm differently. I tried my best to focus. Lifted in the doctor's hands, my whole forearm glistened with whatever he'd put on it. Under that, red, purple, angry, a hooded cobra seemed to shimmer, as though seen through water.

I closed my eyes.

Horowitz rebandaged my arm. "I'm going to send Sol Mayer down here tomorrow," he told me. "He's a plastic surgeon. There's a lot he can do for something like this."

"Does it need that? Skin graft? To heal right?"

"No, it doesn't need it—"

"Forget it."

"It'll be a pretty ugly scar."

"Either way."

I could see he was confused, but after a moment's pause he chose not to argue with me.

"All right. I'll be back tomorrow." He prepared a syringe. "This is for the pain."

"Wait," I told him. "Not yet. Puts me to sleep."

He grinned. "That's part of the point."

"I want to . . . talk to Lydia first."

"This takes a few minutes." Horowitz pricked my arm with the needle. "I'll send her right in." Then, smiling, he left, stepping aside with a flourish to let the nurse go first. It was a nice exit, but not as good as his entrance.

FORTY-TWO

Lydia came in soon after, just enough time between them that I knew she'd stopped to discuss me with Dr. Horowitz.

"The doctor said you wanted me," she said.

"Always. When did you . . . marry me?"

"In the ambulance on the way here. I thought they'd be more likely to tell me things and let me stay with you if they thought we were married."

"Was the . . . honeymoon good?"

"We're getting divorced as soon as you can get out of bed."

"Long time."

"Dr. Horowitz says you'll be up tomorrow."

"Blabbermouth." I asked casually, "What about Paul Kao?" Maybe I'd hallucinated the guy in my delirium.

Lydia didn't answer me.

"None of my business?" I offered.

She smiled softly but still didn't say anything.

I got it. "He was mad? Because you . . . stayed here?"

Now she said, "None of your business."

Her tone ended that discussion. "You should sleep," she said. "Look, I brought you some music." She pointed to a small boom box and a handful of tapes. "I didn't know what to bring. I just took some from your shelf. I did find the one that was open on the piano."

"The Schubert?"

"I think that's it." She flipped through the tapes. "Do you want to hear that?"

"No. Not yet. You said . . . before . . . a story?"

"Once upon a time," she said promptly, "there was a bank account at Emigrant Savings Bank. Now it's closed."

"Reynolds?" What was it Margaret O'Connor had said? "Medical Services, Inc.?"

"You know this story?"

"Closed?"

"Yesterday."

"Yesterday?" The room had started to sway gently. "Reynolds was . . . already dead."

"That's the punch line."

"Who, then?"

"I don't know."

For a minute, nothing. Then, floating on the gentle waves, I started to laugh. It hurt too much; I had to stop.

"Bill? Why is that funny?"

"Doesn't end," I said. "Always another. That place. Think you found it . . . back to the beginning. World without end. Amen."

"All right," she hushed. "Go to sleep. Don't think about it now."

Floating, I didn't have the strength to open my eyes. "Lydia?"

"I'm here." She touched my hand.

"Chopin?" Music suddenly seemed very important.

"Wait," she said. "Let me look."

Silence, then clicking. Then the room was flooded, whirling with the Chopin C-major Prelude. Half a minute, then the A-minor; then the others, G-major, E-minor, D-major, the rest, all independent, separate pieces, but all connected, interrelated. I'd never learned them all. Always meant to. Unfinished business. Maybe Ida played them, used to. Lots of unfinished business. Separate. Connected, interrelated.

"Bill?" Lydia's voice was soft. "Is that good?"

"It's good." I reached for her hand, found it. "It's good."

FORTY-THREE

The next day was different. I ate Jell-O. I drank coffee. I had all my remaining tubes and wires disconnected, and I got out of bed.

The tiny, tan nurse, whose name turned out to be Amy Isham, bustled into my room after breakfast and said, "Let's go."

"Anywhere," I told her.

She helped me maneuver onto my feet. My legs were strong as rubber bands. The room took up spinning again.

"Lean on me," Amy Isham ordered.

She couldn't have weighed half of what I did. "I don't think—"

"I used to work at Bellevue, stuffing psychotics into straitjackets." She lifted my arm onto her shoulder.

I leaned. Her bones were so sharp through her uniform I thought they were going to cut my hand.

"Let's go," she said again.

We went down the hall, a full twenty yards. At the end of this accomplishment we stood at the window, gathering strength for the hike back.

Outside, a huge dewatering apparatus sprawled in the center of a deep excavation. Gray sludge rushed away through a wide-mouthed pipe. For the most part, everything was blurry to me, but there seemed to be moments when, briefly, my vision was clear.

"Is that going to be part of the hospital?" I asked. A whole sentence without a pause for breath, and after strenuous exercise, too. Must be the Chinese herbs. Or the Jell-O.

"No," Amy Isham said. "It's part of the Bronx Renaissance."

Back in bed, I was listening to the Chopin Preludes again and trying to see if there was a way to breathe without moving my chest when a large bouquet of chrysanthemums floated through the door, followed by Arthur Chaiken.

"Hi," Chaiken said tentatively. "Are you up to visitors?"

"Sure," I answered. "Figuratively."

"That's good enough." He let the door close, then opened the cabinet by the bed. "Ah! Just what I need. Let me take care of these." He took the flowers to the bathroom, came out with them spreading from a plastic vase. He put it on the windowsill, where the yellow and white blossoms glowed fiercely in the morning light like junior suns.

"From your garden?" I asked.

"Yes." He beamed back at the chrysanthemums, then came around the bed. "I tried to come yesterday morning, but they told me only family. I didn't know you were married, by the way. Congratulations."

"No, that's my partner. She lied so she could keep an eye on me."

"Oh." He must have decided that whatever that meant wasn't his business; he went on, "How are you? Are you all right? Is there anything you need?"

"No, thanks. Just time. Unless you have a cigarette?"

He shook his head. "I gave it up. Smith, what happened? Who did this? What was the point?"

"The point was to kill me. I don't know who and I don't know why."

"I feel responsible."

"Did you order it?"

His mouth fell open. "Good God, no. You're not serious?"

"Then why would you be responsible? No, I don't think I was serious."

Chaiken shifted in his chair. "Still. You were carrying out an investigation at one of our facilities. I should have been able to offer you some kind of protection. It didn't—" A muffled boom stopped him, as it had stopped me the day before. "What was that?"

"The Bronx Renaissance. I don't know what that means, but that's what it is."

He smiled. "The Bronx Renaissance? It's sympathetic magic."

"Sorry?"

"You know. You want the courage of a lion, eat a lion's heart. You want the stealth of a panther, wear a panther's pelt. You want to stimulate the economy of the Bronx, seed its neighborhoods with publicly financed development."

"Money attracts money?"

"That's the dogma."

"You don't sound like a believer."

He shrugged. "I don't know. Each time the City does this, or talks the State into it, real estate booms in the immediate area and service establishments expand. I suppose it could work. But there's no commitment." He looked toward the window, where his flowers filled a small patch of sky. "No staying power. It's like planting a garden and not watering it. The politicians want instant success, and when they don't get it they wander off looking for something else."

"What would work?"

"Oh, any idea will work if you stick with it long enough. The Bronx Renaissance is as good as any. But they'll give it up as soon as the Mayor and the Borough President get tired of each other." He stopped abruptly, looked at me. "Oh, for Pete's sake. I'm sorry, Smith. It happens it's one of my hobbyhorses, political fickleness. I'm sure you don't need a public-policy lecture right at the moment."

"I don't know," I said. "I think I just need distraction. Or a cigarette."

The phone rang.

"Shall I?" Chaiken asked.

"Thanks."

Chaiken answered the phone, told it to hold on a minute, moved it to where I could reach it. "It's your partner," he said. "I'll wait outside."

I thanked him again, took the receiver out of his hand.

"Hi," Lydia said, after I'd grunted at her. "How are you feeling?"

"Lousy."

"Good. That's much better than yesterday. Can I go through with the divorce?"

"See if I care. I was hanging all over a cute little nurse this morning. She picked me up."

"Literally, I'll bet. I'll be up soon. Is there anything you want?"

"Cigarettes."

"Hah. Bill, who was that who answered the phone?"

"Arthur Chaiken. He brought me flowers."

"Oh." Her voice was worried. "Bill, be careful. Someone tried to kill you. It could be anyone."

"I thought of that. But if I tell them no visitors I'll die of boredom. Besides, whoever wanted me dead the other night could've just shot me, if he was going to do it himself. It's surer and easier." "Surer" was tough to pronounce. I reprimanded myself for getting cocky. "But I get the feeling this was hired out. I don't think whoever's behind it is going to stroll in here and try it himself."

As it turned out, only half of that was right.

Chaiken came back a few minutes after I'd hung up the phone. "Do you want more distraction?" he asked. "Or do you want to rest?"

"Either one."

"Spoken like a man who wants to rest. Listen, Smith, I've thought of something I can do for you, and I'd like you to let me."

I raised my eyebrows, but it was the facial equivalent of saying "surer." "What would that be?"

"This." He nodded at the room. "It gets expensive. I—" He stopped, because I was shaking my head.

"Wait," he grinned. "I wasn't offering you money. I assume you're insured."

"That's right."

"What I'm offering you is expertise. By training and long practice, I've become, if I say so myself, one of the great form-filler-outers."

I must have looked bewildered, if my expressions were readable.

"It matters." Chaiken was still grinning. "You have no idea. If the forms are correctly filled out you're much less likely to have your claims questioned. Sometimes I think they don't even care if the claim is completely bogus, as long as the paperwork is correct. You're bound to find yourself drowning under paperwork, with a thing like this. Call me if you need help with it. Let me check it before it goes in.''

"Well," I said doubtfully, "if I need to."

"I'm telling you, it's all that matters," Chaiken said. "How good your paperwork looks."

It was much too bright, but not warm enough. A snake slithered up my right arm, scraped me like a rope burn. "It has to be correct." The tight-lipped woman waved a SIG Sauer at the blindingly white piles of paper that towered above the walls of my roofless cabin. "Or they'll know." The door clicked behind her. I looked up where the roof had been, aching to see the glowing autumn hillside sloping up from the cabin; but the trees were gone, the hills bare and sandy. I heard the ocean, breakers pounding, felt the sudden hammering of my heart. I'd never have time to finish before the sea crashed over the walls, sucking the snake, the papers, me, into a whirlpool the depths of which I was afraid to even imagine.

"Bill? Bill, what is it?" Lydia's voice. "It's all right. You're dreaming. Come on, wake up. That's right. That's better."

It was still too bright. I lifted my hand to ward off the light. "Oh," I heard Lydia say. "Wait." Footsteps; a swishing noise; the brightness was gone.

I looked around the room. Lydia was resettling the vase of chrysanthemums on the windowsill, where the slatted blind was now closed. The full midday sun bled in around the edges. Lydia turned and smiled.

"You were having a nightmare. What was it about?"

"Paperwork," I muttered. Slowly, carefully, I reached for the cup by the bed, sucked lukewarm water through a straw. The Bronx Renaissance boomed outside. "Paperwork."

"The flowers are lovely." She went back to to her bag, fished out the thermos. "Here. This is different from yesterday. Stronger. For a different stage of healing—"

"Paperwork."

She stopped. "What?"

"Jesus Christ," I said. "It has to look right. That's all that matters."

Lydia put down the thermos, came over to the bed. "Bill? Tell me."

"I don't know," I said, suddenly confused. "I may be wrong."

"When did that stop you?" There was amusement in Lydia's tone, but seriousness too.

"Chaiken," I said. "He said . . . it has to look right . . ."

"Tell me what you're thinking."

I took a breath, told her what I was thinking and why I was thinking it. "I might be wrong," I said again. "And if I'm right it still might not explain everything."

"It would be another piece. A big one. Shall I call Lieutenant Robinson?"

"No. No, I want to check it out ourselves first."

"Why?"

"Leverage."

She knew what I meant.

I drank the new soup, this one richer than the other, more pungent, with bits of greens floating in it. Lydia made two phone calls: one to Emigrant, to confirm what we were thinking, and then one to get the ball rolling.

"Half an hour," Lydia said, hanging up from the second call.

"Good. That should just about give me time to get to the bathroom and back into bed."

"Want me to help?"

"I do not. I'm a big boy; I can do this by myself."

That turned out to be almost not true. I leaned on every piece of furniture in the room on my way to the bathroom, grabbed every grab bar once I was there. I managed to stand at the sink long enough to catch a look in the mirror. I saw a Neanderthal blur, purple and dark red, shadowed where I hadn't shaved, set off by white patches of bandage on forehead and nose.

Sometimes, a reluctant voice said inside my head, there are advantages to not seeing.

The hell with it. I went back to bed.

Lydia had settled in, a small brushstroke of loose green shirt and black pants against a cream-colored chair. I mountaineered into the bed as she chose a tape for the boom box. We were listening to an early Beethoven sonata when the door opened and Mrs. Wyckoff stalked in.

FORTY-FOUR

Actually, Mrs. Wyckoff only stalked in about a foot, then stopped. Even blurred as she was I could see her nose wrinkle with distaste.

"Come on in," I said. "It's not contagious."

Reluctantly she let the door close behind her, stepping only as far into the room as she had to to get out of its way.

"I . . ." She swallowed. "I had no idea . . ."

"No?" I said. "This is how it looks just before you get to the Mike Downey–Henry Howe stage."

She drew herself up. "How can you say a thing like that? You are the crudest man—"

"I know. And you're a very subtle woman. That's why it took me so long to catch on."

Lydia pressed a button on the boom box, stopping Beethoven in his tracks.

"Mrs. Wyckoff, you know my partner, I think?"

"Your—" She spun to look at Lydia. Her pale skin flushed with anger to the roots of her piled blond hair. "It was you who called me? But you were at the Home. Ida said—Dr. Reynolds showed you— Why, how dare you!"

"Pleased to meet you," Lydia murmured, smiling.

"You two deceitful—"

"Forget that part," I said. "I don't have time before my next shot. I want to ask you some questions. There's no reason you should answer them, except I might be more understanding than the cops. You may have to talk to them too; but this way you get to rehearse. Unless it was you who hired someone to beat the crap out of me. That makes me less understanding. Did you do that?"

"I?" she sputtered. "Certainly not! What are you talking about? Why on earth would I do a thing like that?"

"To protect your reputation," I said. "To protect the paperwork."

"What are you talking about?" she demanded again.

"Helping Hands' reputation. All-important, all-consuming, right? That's what everyone told me about you, and I'm an idiot, so I believed it. Except in a way it's true, isn't it?"

"Mr. Smith, I really don't—"

"Sure you do. I thought it was just your ego, but I was supposed to think that. Me and everyone else. Just don't make the place look bad and you'll stay out of trouble, Bobby told me. And it's true. Helping Hands' reputation really is of vital concern to you. Only it has nothing to do with ego. It has to do with money."

"I have no idea—" she huffed.

"It was Mr. Chaiken," I rode right over her, "who clued me in. He offered to help me with my paperwork. He said they don't care if your claims are phony if your paperwork is right. That's true, isn't it? And, besides your paperwork being right, if you run a model facility, with everybody well taken care of and all your inspections passed, I'll bet you can steal like a son of a bitch and nobody gives a damn."

"Mr. Smith!" Mrs. Wyckoff gathered herself together. "I will not have you speak to me this way! I came here because this woman—" she looked daggers at Lydia— "called and said you had information for me concerning the murders at the Home. I certainly will not stay and subject myself—"

"Yes you will, for just another little while. I'm too worn out to put up with you for long. See," I went on, "we knew about Reynolds after we found the Emigrant account, but we thought he was working alone."

The color drained from Mrs. Wyckoff's face as if someone had pulled a plug in her big toe.

"What account?" she asked, in a voice not as convincing as before.

I started to speak, but Lydia rattled off the account number, adding, "Medical Services, Inc."

"I don't—"

"Oh, knock it off," I said. "Lydia, you take it. I need a drink."

I reached for the plastic cup and straw. Lydia said, "Actually, Dr. Reynolds was sort of obvious. He tried to extort money from me to get my mother into the Home. And he was killed in Mr. Howe's apartment, which probably means he was looking for something, which probably means he was being blackmailed.''

Lydia took the cup, which had turned out to be empty, and went to fill it in the bathroom. Mrs. Wyckoff's eyes followed her warily, as if Lydia might suddenly turn and bite her.

"But we thought he was at the top of the food chain," Lydia said, bringing me back the cup. "Actually, it was you.''

"Don't start," I said as Mrs. Wyckoff opened her mouth. "I don't care. If we're right it'll be easy to prove, once the auditors and examiners start swarming. If we're wrong I'll apologize.''

"I should hope so!" she managed.

"Uh-huh. And you can explain why you didn't fire Portelli and shut down his operation, why you even moved Ida Goldstein's room to protect Portelli's privacy. Howe blackmailed you into it, right?''

She stared at me. I closed my eyes, realized my head ached and my chest was sore.

"God, I wish you weren't here," I said. "So let's finish, okay?" I looked again, tried to focus on her, but I really didn't need to. Her pale, tight face and rigid posture spoke volumes.

"The Home is a model institution," I said. "I'll bet they all are, all Helping Hands' places. They have to be. Complaints would mean investigations. You never made the mistake almost all crooks make: you never got greedy. You probably never stole from the client-care budget, or the maintenance budget. Just double-billing. A little extortion, like Reynolds tried on Lydia. The kickbacks from Samaritan we know about already—'' Mrs. Wyckoff's face hardened when I said that—''and I'll bet there are bills for consultants who never existed for services to patients they never saw. And all kinds of other scams I never even thought of. But all very low-key and high-class. It went on for years, and you made enough to buy a nice condo near a golf course. Do you play golf?''

"I—?" She squeaked. Her mouth opened and closed; she seemed startled that I'd called on her to speak. "Play golf?''

"I don't," I said. "No excitement. No risk. Of course,

that's probably why it attracts someone like you. Excitement can draw interest, and interest can be risky, especially the kind of interest a place gets where people get killed.'' I sipped some more water. I could afford the time out; I had her attention, now.

"Mike's death was bad enough. Howe's was a disaster. But me, I was a catastrophe. An investigator poking around—God knows what I might find. You couldn't let that go on.''

She frowned. ''You can't mean you think that I hired someone to do this to you in order to get rid of you?''

''Don't be silly,'' I said. ''That would have been very stupid. Another murder at the Home? No, on the contrary, I'll bet you were upset when you heard about this. Thanks for your concern. No, what you did was smarter. Mrs. Wyckoff, who do you think murdered Mike Downey and Henry Howe?''

''Those boys,'' she said stiffly. ''That gang. I don't see why that isn't obvious to everyone. I don't see what the big mystery is.''

''Even though you pay them a thousand dollars a month to leave the Home alone?''

A pause; then, unruffled, ''The Home's monthly extortion payment is fifteen hundred dollars, and I don't see any reason to expect, when dealing with people like that, that one will actually get what one pays for.''

''And do you think the ones who did it will ever get caught?''

''I understand the police have arrested one of them for Mr. Howe's murder.''

''Martin Carter,'' I said. ''He used to work for you.''

''Yes. He came out of our halfway-house program. It's one of Helping Hands' services to the community, giving our ex-felons their first job out of prison.''

''Oh.'' I sank a little into the pillows. Everything would be so much easier without the weight on my chest. ''So that's how you knew.''

''Knew what?''

''Enough about him to choose him as your sucker.''

''I—Mr. Smith!''

''If you really believe the Cobras are your killers and that they'll never get caught, then this makes sense. Get an arrest, at least the police go away. Probably I'll go away too, especially if the sucker pleads guilty. In fact, I might have, if you hadn't happened to choose a friend of mine. Tough break, Mrs. Wyckoff.''

"What can you possibly mean?" Mrs. Wyckoff wondered. "*I* had that man arrested? I suppose I just called up the police and suggested—''

"You called up your old friend Andy Hill. You suggested to him it might be a good thing if people stopped poking around the Home. You sold him a nice line of concerned bull involving your donors, bad publicity impacting negatively on your future ability to effectively intervene—'' I broke off, turned to Lydia. "I'll bet you didn't know I could talk like that.''

"I had no idea," she grinned.

"And you thought Hill bought it." I was back to Mrs. Wyckoff. "Actually, I think he may have his own reasons for wanting to avoid people like me and Lydia sniffing around Helping Hands. But anyway, he agreed with you. He liked your idea about framing Martin Carter—I mean, the guy is a killer, isn't he? He probably deserves to spend the rest of his life in prison, whether he actually did these killings or not—''

"You're absolutely right!" Mrs. Wyckoff couldn't hold it in any longer. "He *is* a killer! Filth like that, walking the streets, draining our resources—why should I spare a thought for him? The publicity was affecting our ability to operate, and whatever you think of me, Mr. Smith, Helping Hands is caring for people who otherwise—''

"Jesus!" I blew up too, within the limits of my ribs. "Spare me. I've heard that same crap from more people than you could imagine, these last few days. Everyone has one hand in the till and the other feeding the hungry. Mrs. Wyckoff, I'm going to call the *Daily News* and tell them all about you unless Martin Carter calls me by five this afternoon to say the charges against him have been dropped.''

"You are—what? How do you expect me to—''

"The same way you had him arrested. You and Andy Hill worked out this crap about his threatening you. You were the complaining witness." Her beet-red face and her silence told me I was right. "So work out something else. Andy Hill's always eager to oblige, especially if you're a friend of Arthur's. Now get the hell out of here. If I hear from Carter, I'll keep my mouth shut and let the police dig up what Lydia and I have dug up already. That may give you time to get out of town with a little hot cash—like what you cleaned out of Emigrant yesterday—instead of just the shirt on your back. That's my best offer. Now beat it."

Either I hadn't made myself clear, or desperation makes people deaf. "Mr. Smith," Mrs. Wyckoff began in a clenched-teeth tone that might have been intended to be conciliatory, "I can't just pick up and leave like that. The people in my care—people like Ida Goldstein—depend upon me and my staff to look after them. I—"

"Mrs. Wyckoff," I said, "yesterday Snake LeMoyne stood right where you are and told me the same thing. How people depend on him to take care of them. I threw him out too."

Talking about Snake reminded me that when he was here I'd closed my eyes, hoping he'd go away. I tried that again.

The room began moving, swaying in syncopated rhythm with the pounding in my head. I kept my eyes closed, calmed the room down, calmed myself down. I heard Lydia's voice, and I heard the door click, and then another woman's voice, maybe Amy Isham's. She said something to me and I said something to her. An insect stung me on the arm. The darkness settled into a velvety deep sea, and I settled into the darkness.

FORTY-FIVE

When I woke up I had it.

I was alone, except for the answer. It was different from what I'd thought, uglier in a way; it made me sad.

Under the circumstances I was surprised at myself for feeling that.

I wasn't sure what to do. Lydia wasn't here, and I was groggy, floating: Amy Isham and her trained insects. Wait until you come down, Smith. Maybe it won't even look so true, then.

I groped through the tapes by the side of the bed, realized I couldn't read the covers anyway. I fumbled one open, slipped it into the boom box. It turned out to be Liszt, the First Mephisto Waltz. The one Ida Goldstein said everybody plays. I don't, but Artur Rubinstein seemed to want to, so I let him.

I worked my way to the bathroom and back. A nurse, not Amy Isham but a solemn and sturdy Jamaican woman, brought me chicken soup with noodles in it. When the sun moved, I got out of bed just to open the blinds, a frivolous trip. I was proud of myself for making it. I listened to the wild, nasty cackling of the Mephisto Waltz again, and then Lydia came back.

"Hi," she said.

"Hi," I said. "Listen."

I told it to her as it had come to me, as I had gone over it waiting for her, looking for the mistake that would make it not true. I hadn't found one.

She didn't either. "Wow," she said. Then, "What are we going to do?"

"Robinson," I told her. "And Lindfors."

Lydia called Robinson at the station house. In twenty minutes he and Lindfors walked into my room.

Neither of them was smiling, and they didn't start with the usual pleasantries.

"I understand you want to talk to us," Robinson said. He stayed on the door side of the bed; Lindfors went around to the window side. "This better be something you've just remembered, not something you've just decided to come clean on."

"Nice to see you, too, Lieutenant. Or it might be, if I could see."

"I guarantee you it wouldn't. What do you want?"

It occurred to me I didn't often feel surrounded by only two people.

"I think I know who did me, and why. And who killed Henry Howe. And who killed Dr. Reynolds."

"You know all this very suddenly."

"It came to me in a morphine dream. It's all theory. I have no proof."

"Go ahead. Theorize."

I did.

Lindfors, hands jammed into his pockets, paced the tiny room. He was a dark blur passing back and forth in front of the window, and I couldn't watch him. I kept my eyes on Robinson, who didn't move.

"Son of a bitch!" snarled Lindfors, when I was done. "Goddamn—"

"All right," Robinson said sharply. He spoke to me, didn't look at Lindfors, but Lindfors stopped pacing, stopped snarling, when Robinson spoke. "What if it's true? How are we going to prove it?"

"Pick them up, for Chrissake," Lindfors said.

"On what? The speculation of a drugged, beat-to-shit p.i. with an ax to grind?"

"You got a better idea?"

"I do," I said.

They both looked at me, waiting. "I'll wear a wire," I said. "They'll be expecting me. They'll talk to me."

"Wear a fucking wire?" Lindfors barked. "You need a goddamn guide dog to find your way to the bathroom."

I didn't tell him that I'd gotten rather good at finding the bathroom. "I'll be out of here in a few days," I said. "It can wait that long. I can do it, but there's a deal that goes with it." I told them what it was.

"I don't like it," Robinson said.

"I don't either," said Lydia.

I looked from one to the other. "You got a better idea?"

FORTY-SIX

Martin Carter called me at a quarter to five. "What the hell happen to you?" he asked. "They tell me, you free to go, but you suppose call this dude. Then they give me a hospital number. What the hell going down?"

"Someone decided I wasn't ugly enough."

"Hard to b'lieve. How come the cops tell me call you?"

"Insurance."

"You ever make sense?"

"Not that I've noticed."

"C'mon, man. Straight up: you hurt bad?"

"I was," I said. "I'm okay now."

"What happen?"

"You at a pay phone?"

"Yeah."

"Give me the number. It's a long story."

I called him back, told him what I knew and what I thought, why he'd been arrested and why he was out.

"It was my fault," I said. "Mrs. Wyckoff thought if there was an arrest, I'd go away. You were just unlucky."

"My middle name. Now you tell me what you doing up to the hospital."

I told him about the beating I didn't remember, about Snake and the ground-floor apartment two blocks from the Home.

"Son of a bitch." Anger shook Carter's voice through the telephone wires. "Son of a motherfucking bitch, do you that way. Talking about he doing it for me. I find that mother-fucker—"

"You don't even look. Carter, go home. Your kids need you."

"That fucker. I ain't letting this go, cuz. I owe you two now. You gonna get paid."

"I'll be out of here in a few days," I said. "I'll take care of Snake. When I do I'll need your help, and I'll call you. But you feel like you owe me something, this is what I want: go home. Take Granny and the kids to Mickey D's for dinner. Eat something you have to chew."

Carter was silent; then he laughed. "Mickey D's. Shit. Awright, cuz. I ain't looking for Snake. But if I come across him anyway—"

"Vanessa," I said. "Rashid. Granny. Go home. I'll call you."

I was, in fact, out of there in a few days. My eyes were a little clearer, my legs strong enough to carry me out under my own steam, although I ran out of steam quickly.

Lydia and Bobby were both there the morning Dr. Horowitz released me on my own recognizance. "Come back in a week," he told me. "Don't drive."

"You have to be kidding."

"You'd be surprised what some people try."

Before I dressed to leave the hospital, I made some phone calls.

"Are you sure you want it to be tonight?" Robinson asked. "We've waited this long."

"Now that I'm out, maybe he'll get nervous. I know I will. I want to get it over with."

Bobby didn't like the whole plan. "I fired you," he growled.

"Uh-huh. I hired myself." I hadn't told him about Howe and Mike. There was a chance, small but worth clinging to, that if this worked out the way I wanted I might not have to.

It was a cold gray day, wind kicking up sidewalk cyclones, trees trying to shake themselves free of their last leaves. Bobby drove me home, not talking much. From behind dark glasses I watched the Bronx slide by, saw Manhattan grow, square-edged and indifferent, until it was suddenly life-sized and we plunged into it over the Second Avenue bridge.

We stopped at the deli for a few things—milk, bread, cigarettes. Bobby brought my bag up the two flights from the street, while I brought myself up.

"Want to stay a while?" I invited, reaching the summit where my sherpa waited. "Have some coffee? A drink?"

"No." Bobby shook his head, put my bag down. "Kid, I don't want you to do this thing tonight."

"It's all right, Bobby. I'm all right. See? I'm standing. I'm walking. I—"

"You needed a cripple to carry your goddamn suitcase. Kid, please. I'm asking you not to."

"I have to, Bobby."

His watery blue eyes looked me up and down. "Twenty-five years, you haven't changed."

"You, either."

We looked at each other, then at ourselves: his cane and his useless left arm; my battered body, my growing collection of scars. I grinned, he laughed, and I started to laugh

with him until, stopped by the pain in my ribs, I lowered myself onto the couch.

"Shit," Bobby said. "Okay, kid. I'll be back later to pick
you up."

"I'll get a cab."

"The hell you will." He grinned a small, ironic grin, and
then he left.

I spent the day at home. I listened to music, Scriabin and
Bartok: quick, nervous pieces. I went through the ac-
cumulated mail. With concentration and squinting I found I
could read, though not for long. I slept, not as well as I
wanted to. If I could have, I'd have paced, but that seemed
like a bad idea, so I smoked.

Toward the end of the afternoon Bobby came back. I went
downstairs when he buzzed, climbed into the car next to
him. Lydia was in the back.

"What is this, a baby-sitting service?"

"Is that what you need?" Lydia asked.

"No," I said. "I'm sorry. But there'll be cops all over the
place. I'll have backup."

"I used to be a cop," Bobby said. "I know all about cops.
Right now I'm a chauffeur and you need a ride, so I'd shut
up if I was you."

I did. Half an hour later we were back in the Bronx, in the
station house, Robinson and Lindfors trying to fit me up
with a remote microphone somewhere between my jacket
and my Kevlar vest.

"Shit!" I winced as Lindfors pressed on the adhesive
tape. "Watch it."

Robinson took over from Lindfors. When he finished, I
put my jacket back on and he said, "Are you sure you can do
this? You don't look too steady."

"I'm fine," I said. "I want this over with. I want to go
home and not come back here. Let's go."

Bobby told me to watch myself, and I said I would. Lydia
said nothing, just looked serious. I kissed her cheek; she
smiled a little.

I rode in an unmarked car with Robinson, Lindfors behind
us. We went north up the Concourse past the Bronx Home,
then east, to the tired brick building that was our first stop.

Robinson pulled to the curb, left the car running as he got out. Carter was waiting on the stoop. He slid behind the wheel.

Robinson leaned in the window. "If anything happens to this car—"

"Y'all just send me the bill," Carter said.

Robinson straightened, his face hard. He walked to the other car, got in beside Lindfors.

Carter drove around the block, turned south on the Concourse again. The car wasn't big, but the engine was powerful; I could feel how ready it was for whatever was coming. I wished I felt that way myself.

I looked over at Carter. He didn't look back.

"You don't have to do this," I said.

"Seem to me you say that the last time."

"You didn't have to do it last time either. But that wasn't a setup. This is."

"Maybe you wrong."

"I don't think so."

He was silent. We drove down the hill by the Home, parked across the street from the playground. We sat for a long minute, as though we had agreed to do that. Then we got out, walked together through the twisted gate.

The wind was cold. To me, everything was softly out of focus, haloed streetlights pulling shadows from smudged unmoving figures. There was no basketball this time, no pretense of a game. They were all there, Snake and Skeletor and Einstein, some of the others from the apartment; and Speedo was there too, with his baseball cap and his scowl. The wind turned, blew from behind us, pushed us toward them.

"Yo," Snake grinned as we neared. "You looking better, my man."

He lifted his hand. Skeletor moved forward. I stopped.

"I'm unarmed," I said. "I have five broken ribs and I don't want that bastard touching me."

Snake nodded. "I'm down with that. Ease off, homey. White meat working for us now."

Skeletor glared at me, started to protest.

"Yo!" Snake snapped. "Where you going with that shit, homey? I say ease off!" Skeletor shifted his glare to Snake. He didn't move back, but he didn't frisk me, either.

"And you ain't got to worry about the Rev." Snake looked at Carter. "I heard 'bout Lindfors's deal he offer you. I heard what you tell him. The Rev can say what he want, don't matter shit. He still a Cobra. Just like the rest of you niggers. Once you got it," he tapped his right arm, "you don't never lose it."

Carter's eyes met Snake's. He said nothing.

"Now." Snake's gold tooth glittered as he smiled at me. "My man Rev say you got a report for me. Say you got it all dee-tected, who fronting these fake Cobra jobs."

"Uh-huh," I said. "Only they're not fake."

"Say what?" Snake's smile vanished. "Jump back, Jack. I ain't pulled that shit."

"No, not you. You were too busy protecting your boys by blowing Dr. Reynolds away."

"Yo, my man." Snake shook his head in warning. The Cobras, some muttering obscenities, circled closer. "You gonna end up with trouble behind that shit."

"As soon as you found out Henry Howe was dead," I said to him, ignoring the others, trying to slow the racing of my heart, "you thought you'd better go get the photos. You'd been willing to pay Howe a little extra to keep his mouth shut about Dr. Madsen, but you didn't want those photos ending up with anybody else. Like the cops."

"Yo, Snake." That was Einstein, looking a question at Snake. "You was paying that fat motherfucker? What photos he mean?"

"Photos that could have gotten an investigation going," I said. "Something that most likely would have ended with Dr. Madsen in jail."

Snake glanced from Einstein to me. He shrugged, folded his arms across his chest. "Man, no big thing. Chump change. Two-fitty a month. Easier than smoking him. Plus, he useful to the Cobras."

"To your boys," I said. "But once he was dead, you wanted those photos back. So you went to his place. He also had something Dr. Reynolds wanted back, a name on a card. Reynolds was there first, making a hell of a mess. He saw you. You shot him. And you never found what you wanted."

"Shee-it." Snake rolled his eyes. "Now, I ain't saying that go down, ain't saying it ain't. What I'm saying, it ain't your business, white meat. Other things, they your business.''

''Did you know Madsen was paying Howe over the same photos? Same price?''

Snake cocked his head, scowled at me. It was the scowl Speedo wore. ''Fuck. That true?''

''It's true.''

''Shit.'' Snake shook his head. ''Motherfucking bastard. Well, don't matter now.''

''It does,'' I said. ''It means Howe was used to playing both sides of the street.''

''So?''

A powerful gust of wind came barreling down the playground, shouldered through the group. I staggered, almost fell. Carter grabbed my arm, steadied me; then he let go.

''So?'' Snake said again, leaning closer.

''You told me you collected a thousand a month from the Home,'' I said.

''Man, I know that shit. What you—''

''They pay fifteen hundred.''

Silence. The Cobras' eyes flicked warily from me to Snake, to each other. Snake's eyes never moved. I wished mine were clear, wished I could see what was in Snake's, but I knew it wouldn't help. I had Carter; somewhere, in dark parked cars at the edge of the playground, Lindfors and Robinson and some uniforms were listening for their moment. That would have to be enough.

''That sorry-ass white mother!'' Snake snarled. ''He wasn't dead, I'd smoke his white ass myself—''

''No,'' I said. ''You don't get it.''

''Fuck that! Man, fuck that shit! Don't get what, white meat? What I don't get?''

''Howe was greedy, but he was careful. He wouldn't have asked for fifty percent more. It would've been too risky.'' I checked around me for the other Cobras, to know where they were. ''My guess is that he was skimming an extra hundred, maybe a hundred and fifty. Skeletor took the rest.''

''Yo!'' That was Skeletor. ''Yo, motherfucker! What shit you talking, white boy? I stomp your ass, motherfucker!''

''Like you did before,'' I said.

Skeletor grabbed for me. Carter put himself between us.

So did Snake.

"You best listen to my man," Carter said quietly, eyes on Skeletor, speaking to Snake.

Carter and Snake moved slowly aside; Skeletor and I were facing each other again.

"You'd been doing this for a long time," I said to Skeletor. "Snake wouldn't have trusted Howe, but he trusted you. You were skimming from every payment he collected for the Cobras."

Snake stared at Skeletor as I spoke. A car drifted slowly by, its stereo thumping up from the pavement.

"It was fine," I went on, "until Howe found out. I don't know how that happened. Some casual word, some mistake. Maybe something you said yourself. Anyway, he didn't care, he just wanted some. Otherwise, he'd tell Snake.

"So you cut him in. But you didn't like it. And you wanted to do something about it, but you didn't know what. Then someone killed Mike Downey. It wasn't the Cobras, but it was done to look as though it was.

"And the guy who did that gave you a great idea, didn't he, Skeletor?" Because of the deal I'd insisted on with Robinson I was careful not to say who it was; Bobby might hear this tape someday. "You could kill Howe and make it look as though it was the same person, for the same reason, whatever the hell that was. Nobody except Lindfors really thought it was the Cobras. I practically told you that myself.

"And everything was fine. Snake would get another liaison and you'd be back in business, except you'd probably be a little more careful this time. Then Carter got arrested, and Snake hired me. That was a problem, but the solution was simple: fake another fake Cobra killing. Do me."

"Yo!" Skeletor burst. "This ain't nothing but bullshit, bitch. Talk about I'm stealing from my main man. Talk about it was me done you! Man, I do you now, you cocksucking faggot!"

He made a grab for me. Snake pushed him back as I said, "I saw you, Skeletor. I recognized you."

"Man!" Skeletor's arms waved wildly; he tried to push past Snake, to me. "Lemme at that motherfucker, Snake! White faggot, talking shit!"

"Yo." Snake's voice was deep and harsh. "Yo, nigger. You do me like that?"

"What?" Skeletor stopped. Everything stopped: traffic, the wind in the trees, my heart. "What? Fuck, Snake, man, he lying! I never touched the mother! Snake, man, how you think I'm gonna play you?"

Skeletor was right. I was lying, and I lied again. "I saw you."

"Yo! Yo, bitch! You seen me, why you ain't told faggot-ass Lindfors it was me? Why not, bitch?"

"All your homies would've alibied you," I said. "That's what Cobras do, isn't it? Stick together? Besides," I added, "I was working for Snake. I thought he ought to know."

Snake's eyes were slits as he stared at Skeletor. "What up with this shit, my man?"

"Oh, man!" Skeletor exploded. "Oh, man, what difference do it make?"

"Oh, it make a difference," Snake said, soft. "You stealing from me, nigger? You stealing from the Cobras?"

Snake and Skeletor faced each other. The wind tossed shadows of tree branches over them like a net.

"The Cobras." Skeletor's voice was soft as Snake's had been. "That all you ever be thinking about, Snake. The fucking Cobras. New stereo for the crib. Little bike for Speedo's sister. Man, we could'a had it *all,* but you wasn't interested. You happy just sitting on your skinny ass looking at the Cobras. You sorry-ass nigger. Well, Skeletor ain't living like that."

He jabbed himself in the chest with his thumb. "I been studying that fat white bastard. Your li-ai-son." Skeletor's face twisted with contempt. "Only way that fucker could'a made more money be if he have three hands to take it with. Everybody give him something, like it Christmas and he their favorite charity. So I be thinking, why not me too?"

Snake was taut as a piano string. He didn't move. Wind yanked a sheet of newspaper around the playground as though it were on a chain. I was cold, and weak; I knew I couldn't last much longer.

In a deep, quiet voice, Snake said to Skeletor, "You do me like that?" I thought Skeletor flinched, looking into Snake's eyes, but I wasn't sure.

Then Snake's leg snapped out, slammed into Skeletor's soft stomach. A beautiful roundhouse, a karate move. Skeletor, surprise bulging his eyes, doubled over, heaving. Snake threw another kick, to his jaw. Skeletor staggered, then lunged wildly forward.

Snake kicked again, but Skeletor shoved him off balance. They grappled. Snake, ignoring Skeletor's punches, pushed his shoulder into Skeletor's, twisted his hip, flipped the fat kid over. Skeletor went down hard and Snake followed, raining fast snapping blows on Skeletor's face.

Behind us, doors slammed. Running feet pounded pavement. Then a silver flash, something pulled from Skeletor's shirt. A voice, Speedo's, hissing, "Shit! Oh, shit!" Then an explosion. Snake lifted half into the air, staggering backwards, falling. Something warm and wet splashing my cheek.

And Lindfors, at the playground gate, roaring, "No!" into the night.

FORTY-SEVEN

Skeletor rolled to his feet as voices yelled and shots rang out. Carter shoved me; I went down, ribs screaming as I skidded onto the asphalt. Carter was on the ground too, half on top of me.

"Thanks," I choked.

More shots, more bullets filled the air. Suddenly, on a shout, they stopped. I twisted around, looked up in the silence.

Skeletor, clutching Speedo in front of him, was easing his way to the playground gate.

"Yo." Speedo writhed in Skeletor's grip. "Yo, man, it's me! Yo, lemme go, brother!"

"Shut up!" Skeletor held the gun against Speedo's head, held Speedo between himself and the cops who stood, motionless and futile, where they'd stopped. Robinson, Lindfors, Carter, three uniforms and I all watched helplessly as Skeletor, dragging Speedo with him, inched out the gate, started backing down the hill.

Snake, bleeding on the pavement, groaned.

Then, right behind Skeletor, a car door flew open. A small dark figure leaped onto the sidewalk, legs planted wide, gun held two-handed. "Drop your gun and don't turn around!" Lydia's shout carried across the asphalt, cut into my heart.

Skeletor whipped around, yanking Speedo with him. He fired, but Lydia was already on the ground, knocked there by a larger, clumsier figure who staggered back when Skeletor's shot rang out. Skeletor started to run, but he tripped, pitched forward, his feet tangled with Speedo's and with something else, something long and thin.

Lydia rolled over, smashed the butt of her gun onto Skeletor's hand. She pulled his automatic out of his loosened grip, slammed her elbow into his face so he'd know she'd been there. Then she held her own gun two inches from his nose, kept it there while she climbed to her feet and the uniforms and Robinson charged over.

Bobby stood also, shouldering the car he'd fallen against, leaning on it as his right hand gripped his left arm above the elbow.

I pulled myself up, to go to Bobby and Lydia. The other Cobras were long gone, scattering when they had the chance. The cops were all over by the car, cuffing Skeletor, trying to hold Speedo, who cursed and fought until they finally cuffed him, too.

All except one.

Lindfors stood near me, motionless. His eyes were on Snake, but his face was dark and distant and I wasn't sure he saw.

Then Snake groaned. Slowly, Lindfors knelt, peeled off his jacket as if in a trance. He balled it up, pressed it against Snake's chest, against the endless flow.

Snake's eyes opened, moved wildly. They found Lindfors. "Shit," he murmured, but he smiled. "You seen that? Cocksucker."

"Shut up," Lindfors said. Something was wrong with his voice.

"No, really, man. You seen it?" Snake's words were a whisper torn away by the wind. "I have him down. I have the cocksucker, if he ain't shot me. One, two, he be going. Just like you show me, Hank. Just like you show me."

"Yeah." Lindfors's voice was worse now, ragged and torn. "Just like I showed you."

"Hank?" Snake's eyes closed. "I'm cold, man. Fucking cold."

"All right," Lindfors said. "All right, Anthony. It'll be all right now."

"He ain't shot me, I have him," Snake muttered. "I was winning, Hank. I learned it good, what you showed me. I'd've won."

"Yeah," said Lindfors. "Yeah. You'd've won."

Sirens cut the night. Lindfors stayed kneeling beside Snake while the ambulance howled into the schoolyard. The attendants spread a sheet over Snake, and then the Crime Scene wagon was there.

Lindfors stood stiffly, looked around like a man unsure of where he was. His eyes met mine, but I didn't think he saw me.

Then, slowly, he crossed the asphalt, headed down the hill. In the blowing darkness, I lost him very soon.

FORTY-EIGHT

I slept for the next two days.

After Lindfors was gone I'd turned away from Snake's body. Lydia was by my side by then, and I leaned on both her and Carter as we left the schoolyard.

"Bobby?" I asked.

"He's fine," Lydia said. "He even laughed. He said he never uses that arm anyway."

I talked to Bobby as he lay on a stretcher in the ambulance waiting to be hauled off to Samaritan.

"Tell them you're a friend of Margaret O'Connor's," I said. "You'll get a better table."

"I did okay for an old cripple, huh?" Bobby's face was white with pain, but he was grinning. Across his lap he held the cane he'd shoved through Skeletor's legs.

"Twenty-five years," I said. "You haven't changed. What the hell were you two guys doing here?"

"We didn't think you could do it without us. Your girlfriend's a little crazy," he added.

"No kidding." I glanced at Lydia, on the sidewalk talking to Robinson. I looked back to Bobby. "Thanks."

He grinned at me again, and I thought I saw, in his eyes, what I used to see.

I sat in a cop car until the cops didn't want me anymore. I answered their questions and gave them back their microphone and somebody brought me a cup of coffee. After a while Lydia drove me home.

She helped me upstairs and I told her I'd be all right. When she left I took my shoes off, lay down on the still-made bed, pulled the quilt over me as though you could get warmth from a blanket. I called Samaritan, to ask about Bobby. Good condition, they said. Just a flesh wound. I don't remember hanging up the phone.

Toward morning I woke, washed, had a drink, and went back to bed.

Much, much later I woke again and had coffee. I lit a cigarette and called Robinson at the precinct.

"How's Lindfors?"

"When he turns up I'll know," Robinson said.

"You're a sentimental bastard."

"You want me to break my heart over every cop who couldn't draw the line? Someone has to stay behind and do the job."

I pulled on the cigarette. "We still have a deal."

"I remember."

"I mean it. I don't want Bobby to know about Howe and Mike."

Robinson paused, a long pause. "Portelli's looking at some hard time. Receiving. Accessory before and after, for Vega. Maybe racketeering. Guys in his position say just about anything. Most of it we don't even write down."

"Thanks, Robinson. I owe you."

"I don't want you to owe me. I want to never see you again, except in court when Skeletor's trial comes up."

"Yeah," I said. "Okay."

I called Shorty downstairs and asked him to send me up some chili. He sent a lot and I ate it all. I had some bourbon and went back to bed. Before I fell asleep Bobby called.

"How're you doing?"

"Fine," I said. "Just tired. You?"

"Fine," he echoed. "Just shot in the goddamn arm. Had a hell of a time getting out of the hospital. I think they were waiting for me to have another stroke."

"You planning on it?"

"I didn't like the first one. Listen, kid. I just talked to Robinson. I wanted you to know."

"Know what?"

"The bullet in Howe's foot came from the gun Skeletor shot Snake with."

"Good. They going to charge him?"

"I think so. The bullet in Mike . . ." Bobby stopped, went on, ". . . it came from some other gun. They don't have it. But it's a good bet Skeletor did Mike, too."

"How do they figure?"

"He was meeting Howe in the garden. S.O.P. with them, Robinson says, to pass the cash. Mike must have found him before Howe got there." Bobby's voice grew rough. "That bastard Howe must have known, when he found Mike. Son of a bitch, working for me—" Bobby stopped again. I said nothing; when he could, he went on. "Only good thing about that bastard is that Skeletor did him the same way."

Thanks, I said again to Robinson, in my head. For not testing Howe's gun. Whatever you say, I owe you.

Bobby and I talked a while longer. Bobby said he'd go see Sheila, tell her about Skeletor.

"Good," I said. "Get her to make you a cup of tea. She's got some great thick Irish tea."

I thought of Bobby at Sheila's kitchen table, maybe holding Peg on his lap. The trees would be bare by now, the wind chilly on the porch; but the kitchen was warm, and maybe, as long as Bobby was there, the rooms wouldn't seem so empty.

Later that evening I woke again, and called Lydia.

"Are you all right?" Her voice was gentle. "I would have called but I was afraid you'd be sleeping."

"I was," I said. "And will be soon again. I'm okay."

"Did you talk to Lieutenant Robinson?"

"Yes. And to Bobby. They have Skeletor for Howe. They'll never charge him with killing Mike, but it'll be understood.'' I rubbed my eyes. Since morning there had been stretches when my vision was clear.

"Bill?"

"Yeah," I said. "I'm here."

"It was right, what you did."

I didn't know if that was true, but for the first time in two days, I felt warm, hearing her say it.

"You want to sleep," she said. "Will you call me when you're better?"

"Yes," I said. "Lydia? Thanks."

The next day nobody called and I talked to no one. The day after that, I was ready to go out.

My eyes were clear and my legs were steady; that meant I could drive. I did, though slowly, both because I didn't quite trust myself and because I didn't really want to go back to the Bronx.

I had to, though. And the first place I had to go was to see Andy Hill.

I parked in Lou Gehrig Plaza, climbed the long granite Courthouse steps, stopping halfway up to catch my breath. I hadn't called, so I was prepared to wait, but Andy Hill didn't make me wait.

"Smith!" Hill trotted out as soon as the secretary announced me. He ushered me into his office, shut the door behind us. "God, you look like hell," he said cheerfully.

My eyes moved past him, past the plaques and photographs, to the window. It wasn't two weeks since I'd first come here, but now the day was gray, the tree branches bare and damp-looking, as though we'd entered a whole new season.

"Are you all right?" Hill asked, into my silence. "I mean, do you need anything? I heard about what happened. Anything I can do?"

"One thing," I said. "I have a friend who needs a patron. A godfather. What cops call a rabbi. That's you."

His look was quizzical, but open, interested. I wanted to punch him.

"If I can help I'd be glad to," he said. "That's why I'm here."

''No, that's not why you're here. You're here to make money.''

Hill cocked his head. ''I'm afraid I don't understand.''

''And I've been beat to shit and I don't have the energy for games. I'm talking about your little real estate gold mine.''

''I told you about that. I make a few dollars, Arthur gets what he wants—''

''Oh, sure, you told me about the few bucks you make every time you sell to Helping Hands. And Arthur told me—'' His eyes seemed to narrow slightly, so I said it again: ''Arthur told me about your private arrangement, how much you'll make over the next decade as his buildings hit the ends of their cycles. Poor Arthur, he feels pretty guilty about that. But it's worth it to him, doing business with slime like you, if it's good for his clients. Only he doesn't know the half of it, does he?''

''I'm afraid you've lost me, Smith. I've got—''

''At the time I thought that's what you'd been hiding. You were so quick to tell me about the meaning of what I'd found that I knew there was something else you didn't want me looking for. I thought your private arrangement with Arthur was it. But it wasn't.''

''No?'' Hill's tone of voice was carefully controlled to sound casual. ''Then what was?''

''The Bronx Renaissance.''

''The Bronx Renaissance is a political program—'' he began automatically.

''In which the city and the state direct money into development projects in particular places. How do they decide where?''

''How? There are studies. A lot of people get involved—''

''Including the Borough President's Community Liaison. The man who knows the neighborhoods, has his finger on the pulse. A new police station? Put it here. An open-air market? Over there. Look, this neighborhood already has an anchor—one of those Helping Hands places. We love those. Employers, good neighbors, stable. All this area needs is just one more little boost. How about right here? Right near the Helping Hands place? We can put a land deal together fast.

I'll talk to the property owners. R & G, a couple of other holding companies. No problem. All this land, for sale to the city or the state. Or to some other sucker who believes in the Bronx Renaissance enough to invest in it!''

Hill had stopped smiling, but he hadn't moved.

"And?" he said.

"And suddenly properties you bought for next to nothing are hot. You make a little on the ones you sell to Helping Hands, but you make a mint on the ones the City buys for the Bronx Renaissance. We checked on this, Hill.''

His mouth opened automatically; he shut it before any sound came out. I wondered if he'd been about to tell me to call him Andy.

"You've made a quarter-million profit already, and you have two more sales pending in the Bronx Renaissance program. You stand to pick up another hundred thousand if they go through. There's probably more. If we look, we'll find it.''

Slowly, coldly, Hill said again, "And?"

"I know. It's real estate. It's legal. You told me that before."

"It is."

"Uh-huh. It's legal, but it's lousy. The B.P. wouldn't like it. Arthur Chaiken wouldn't like it. Your career wouldn't be worth a pitcher of piss if it came out."

He gave me a level look. "I could resign. Start over somewhere else. There are a lot of places."

"Would you like that?"

Behind him, out the window, iron-gray clouds moved dispiritedly above the asphalt roofs. "No," he finally said. "I wouldn't like that. What's your offer?"

"A job for my friend. Union. Security, training program, benefits."

"A no-show." Hill nodded.

"Bullshit. I mean real work. Something worth doing. Something with a future. Construction, maybe. He's young and strong and smart, my friend."

"So why does he need someone to run interference?"

I took out my Kents. "He's from the neighborhood. He's an ex-Cobra." I struck the match, reached for the ashtray. "And an ex-con."

"Oh," he said. "Martin Carter."

"You're damn right."

"He's working now."

"That's a crappy job. Dead-end. And they may not want him back now that he's just out of jail."

Hill tried a sincere smile. "I'm sorry about that. Francine Wyckoff was very convincing. She thought he—"

"No, she didn't, and you didn't either. You both just wanted the spotlight off Helping Hands and Carter was convenient. He has two little kids at home. That didn't bother you at all, did it?"

"If he was guilty—"

"You never believed he was. Hill, you've been coasting and you've been lucky. Now it's payback time."

Hill picked up a pencil, tapped it on the desk. He frowned in thought. "That's the offer? A job for Carter, and you keep your mouth shut?"

"And the rest of the deal is, he doesn't know about it."

"How the hell am I supposed to arrange that?"

"You get it set up. I'll tell him I did it. He'll be pissed at me, but he'll take it. He won't take it from you."

"That's it?"

"As long as Carter's working I won't go to anybody with what I know. If you're really smart that'll give you time to cut yourself loose from anything that might get caught up in the Helping Hands investigation. Are you that smart?"

Like the sun breaking through clouds, Hill grinned. "Yes. Yes, I think so."

Outside, the day stayed gray.

I smashed out my cigarette, got up to go. "Just one more thing."

Hill was still smiling. "What's that?"

"Seven or eight years ago, the City closed a community center with a PAL program in it, near the Bronx Home. It was reopened about six blocks away, across the Concourse. Did you do that?"

"I think so. I think that was one of my first . . . projects. Why?"

"How much did you make?"

He shrugged. "Not much, I don't think. Maybe ten thousand."

I looked at him, his frank smile, his well-kept body, his expensive suit. "I wish I believed in an afterlife," I told him. "I wish I believed in Hell." I left his door open, left him staring after me as I stalked down a corridor that had once been marble.

FORTY-NINE

The garden at the Home was brighter because the trees were bare, but the light was colorless, the air dank. I felt as though I were walking through a black-and-white photograph.

The guard at the desk looked at me and I looked at him and he didn't stop me. I went to the left, to the piano room.

The curtains were open, the windows shut on the view of the empty porch and bleak garden beyond. There was no sound in the room, no movement. I turned to leave.

"Since neither of us is dead yet, you might as well sit down," said a sharp, familiar voice.

"Ida?" I turned. She was seated on a sofa at the end of the room. I had missed her in the featureless light.

"You look terrible," she said.

I crossed the room, took a chair next to her.

"You should have seen me last week."

"They wouldn't let me see you last week. Dr. Madsen said hospitals aren't healthy places for old people. He should have told that to Dr. Reynolds. Are you really married to that Chinese girl?"

"No."

"That's what I thought. Well, you should be."

"Tell her."

"You tell her. I'm not in the matchmaking business. Why are you here? They arrested that delinquent, the one with the foolish name, and they said the other one killed Dr. Reynolds. Your investigation must be over."

"It is. I came back to see you."

"Why?"

I did palms-up. "Why not?"

She waved her hand in disgust. "Don't start with the

Borscht Belt. On you it doesn't look good. Did you know the Boss Lady ran out on us?''

"Mrs. Wyckoff?" I took out a cigarette.

"Of course Mrs. Wyckoff. She took the money and ran. Don't you drop ashes on my carpet."

I pulled the cellophane from the pack, used it as an ashtray. "Your carpet?"

"It's the only thing I brought from home. It was a wedding present. Before this they didn't have anything under the piano. Can you imagine? It sounded terrible." She glared at the piano, as though it had sounded terrible on purpose. "I think they're closing this place." She didn't look at me. "Did you know?"

"I didn't know," I said. "Why?"

"Why? Because the Boss Lady—Wyckoff, Wyckoff, Wyckoff, her stupid name is!—was stealing and so was everybody else. Three murders, plus what happened to that truck driver. And what happened to you didn't help." Now she glared at me. "Mr. Domenico's daughter came yesterday and took him home. One of the nurses today just happened to mention how lovely it was where she used to work in New Jersey, where they have trees and grass. I told her we have that here."

She stared through the window at the gray garden.

I tapped the ash from my cigarette. "There are beautiful places in New Jersey."

"Oh, don't be reasonable with me! If I want reasonable I'll talk to a social worker. I'm an old woman and I want to be upset."

"Okay," I said.

We sat together, watched a squirrel hop along the porch railing. He looked anxious and harried. He had a lot to do in a short time.

"They don't have a piano. At the beautiful place in New Jersey. I asked the nurse."

I didn't answer, didn't know what to say.

Ida shot me a sharp look. "It doesn't matter, you know. I can hardly play anymore anyway." She surveyed me. "You haven't played since you got beaten up, have you?"

"I can't. I have trouble just opening a can of beer."

"Do you miss it?"

"The beer?"

She snorted. "I can see why Anna Mae Wong won't marry you."

"Lydia Chin," I said. "I can too."

Ida looked back to the window. The squirrel was gone. Empty branches shook in the wind.

"What will happen to the cats?" she asked the windowpane.

"The cats?"

"It was cold this morning. I couldn't go feed them. It will get colder, and then they'll move us to New Jersey, and then nobody will be here . . ." Ida's voice caught. "Damn!" she whispered angrily. "What will happen to the cats?" A tear moved tentatively down her parchment-colored cheek.

"I'll take care of them," I said.

"Don't be ridiculous! You'll come feed them, every day, all the way here? You will not."

"No. But I'll think of something. I'll take care of them."

For four days I came out to the Bronx Home early in the morning, sat on the porch next to a bowl of 9-Lives. The first day only the tiger kitten would come and eat, jerking back at every leaf scraping across the tile. The black-and-white kitten and the mother cat watched from between the stone balusters, the cat peering silently while the kitten mewed, approached, retreated. The second day both kittens came. The third day I put the bowl into a shallow cardboard box, sat still while the kittens jumped in, ate, jumped out. They chased each other around the porch; the tiger kitten, taking a shortcut in the game, ran across my lap.

On the fourth day, while the kittens were eating, I closed the top on the cardboard box. The mother cat, who had never come near me, watched from the balusters.

"You can come too," I said. "You could stay with me."

She twitched her tail. Small mews arose from the box I was carrying. I turned back at the top of the stairs. She was gone.

I took the kittens to the vet, got them baths and shots. I kept them for three days at home, until they seemed used to being held and they knew what to do in a litter box. Then, late in the afternoon, I put them back in their cardboard box and took them back to the Bronx.

The uneven slate sidewalks near the Yonkers line were the same color as the sky. I walked up the short walk to Sheila Downey's porch carrying a shopping bag, cradling a kitten inside my jacket.

Sheila answered the bell holding Peg. Sheila smiled when she saw me. Peg looked serious. Otherwise they were identical—glossy curls, round pink cheeks, deep brown eyes.

"It's so good to see you," Sheila told me.

I kissed her cheek. "You look great, Sheila."

"And you look—" She broke off when she heard a peep from the inside of my jacket. "Mother Mary, what have you got?"

I unhooked the kitten's claws from my shirt, took her out for them to see. "She needs a home."

"Oh," Sheila said. "Oh, my."

"I brought cat food. And kitty litter." I lifted the shopping bag.

Peg had been staring at the kitten, watching her mew. A smile burst onto her face. "Beew!" She reached for the kitten.

"No." Sheila pointed to me. "That's Bill. This is a baby cat. C-A-T, remember?"

Peg stared at Sheila, waited for her to stop talking nonsense. "Beew," she said firmly again, pointing a tiny finger at the black-and-white kitten.

"Well," said Sheila, "I guess we'll call her Bill. Big Bill and Little Bill. You'd better come in, you Bills, before we all freeze. Will you stay? I'll make some tea."

"Yes, thanks, but not for long. I have another delivery to make."

Sheila lit the stove under the kettle while the kitten explored the kitchen and Peg crawled, giggling, after her.

"Bobby was here." Sheila put a plate of shortbread on the table. "He told me about that gang member. He told me what happened."

The kettle started to sing. Sheila poured boiling water into the pot. The kitten scrabbled up the leg of a wooden chair, peered at Peg from over the edge of the seat. Peg clapped her hands and laughed.

Sheila smiled. "They'll be great friends." Then her smile faded. "Bill? The things Bobby told me—they don't explain it all, do they? They don't explain the way Mike was acting. The questions he asked. Do they?"

"No." I watched while she poured milk into the china cups, and then the strong, dark tea. "Bobby doesn't know the whole story."

Sheila paused. "Do you mean the police are hiding something?"

"No. I am."

I told Sheila the truth, watched her face.

Sheila sipped her tea, didn't speak for some time while Peg and the kitten chased each other around our feet.

When she finally spoke her voice was soft. "Mike was trying to protect Bobby. He wasn't . . . he wasn't doing anything wrong." She smiled softly. "Do you know, I never even let myself think that, until just now. When I knew for sure it wasn't true."

"That's why I wanted to tell you. So you'd know that."

She turned away. "Thank you."

I drank my tea, ate a buttery shortbread. The kitten galloped over my shoe.

"I don't know if I'm doing right," I said to Sheila. "Not to tell Bobby about Howe. I'm not sure what right I have to do that."

"The same right Mike had." She put her hand over mine, pressed gently.

I finished my tea. Sheila lifted Peg, and they showed me to the door.

"You know," I said, standing in the doorway, "Bobby likes cats."

Sheila smiled. "I already thought of that."

Going across the Bronx traffic was slow, but the car was warm and the music was Brahms and I was okay.

I parked across the street from the tired brick building, took the other shopping bag and the tiger kitten and went inside. Carter's voice croaked through the intercom and I croaked back. He buzzed me in. The elevator was about as shaky as I was, but we got there.

"Man," said Carter, unhooking the door chain, "what you doing here?"

"It wasn't my idea," I said. "It was his." I took the tiger kitten from the warmth of my coat.

"Yo! Yo, what the hell is that?"

"It's a cat."

"Oh, no shit! What you bring it here for?"

"For Vanessa."

"What you talking about, for Vanessa?"

"He needs a home. She needs a kitten."

"Who say?"

"Ask her."

"I ask her, she say yes. Then I got to feed it and worry about it."

"I can solve that problem too, if you let me in."

"Martin?" The tiny bent form of Carter's grandmother appeared at his elbow. "Martin! Why on earth is you keeping your friend standing out there, after all he done for you?" She bustled past him, took me by the arm, led me inside. The room was shabby but trim, full of mismatched furniture and the spicy scent of baking. The Lord's Prayer, cross-stitched, hung on one wall, a photograph of Martin Luther King on another. "You just come on in and—oh, my! My, now look at this!"

"I brought him for Vanessa," I said. "I promised a friend of mine I'd find a home for him. But Martin doesn't want him."

Rashid charged into the room, flat-footed and swivel-hipped, laughing at his own unsteadiness. Vanessa, running after him, stopped in the doorway when she saw me. She put her thumb in her mouth, pressed her lanky body into the jamb.

"Martin?" she said. "Who's him?"

"This my friend Bill, Nessie. He give us a ride home from school, remember?"

The thumb came out of Vanessa's mouth and she brightened. "Yeah. You got the car play ballerina music. It nice!" She looked more closely. "What that there?"

"It's a kitten," I said. "Want to play with him?"

She nodded, came near me.

"Here." I took a piece of string with a knotted end from my pocket. "He likes to chase things." I put the kitten down, showed Vanessa how to drag the string along the floor for him to pounce on.

"You better take that out of here when you go," Carter said to me in an undertone. He picked up Rashid, who was clinging to his leg.

"Why?"

"I tell you why. Cause she gonna start to care what happen to it, and then it gonna run away or some dog gonna snap it in two. Then what I'm gonna tell her?"

I had no answer, but I didn't have to make one.

"Martin, that ain't but foolishness," his grandmother scolded. "You ain't never gonna give her a chance to love nothing, case someday she lose it? What you thinking of? Mr. Smith, seem to me we got room in here for a thing that size. Plus, he look like a mouser to me."

"I think he will be. And please call me Bill."

"And who gonna pay to feed it? Who gonna take it to the vet?" Carter said.

"You're going to have to take it yourself, but feeding it won't be the problem you think."

"Why not?"

"Bill," Enna Carter said, "you plan on trying to talk sense into this boy, you best sit yourself down. I get you some coffee and some sweet-potato pie. Nessie, go find Rashid's bottle."

She disappeared into the kitchen. Vanessa, with a look at the tiger kitten, flew off and flew back, thrust a bottle at Carter. He gestured me to the flowered couch, sat with me. Rashid reached for the bottle. Carter helped him hold it.

"Look," he said. "You spring me from the joint. I owe you. Snake done what he done, tell you it for me, I owe you. But it ain't easy, keep together what I got here. And they tell me the Home be closing soon. Thing that size don't eat much, but whatever it eat, I can't afford to buy it."

"If you made a better living you'd keep it?"

"Sure, maybe. But food stamps don't buy no cat food."

"Well." I made a thoughtful face. "I promised Ida Goldstein I'd take care of the kittens. I guess I don't have much choice.'' I pulled a piece of paper from my shirt pocket. ''Call this guy. Tell him I sent you.''

Carter, feeding Rashid, strained to see the paper. ''What guy?''

''It's a union shop, but he can get you in the union. Masons and bricklayers. He's got a lot of renovation work right now. City contracts, part of this Bronx Renaissance thing. He needs guys.''

''What trash you talking, union gig? Ex-con, don't know no godfather, now how I'm gonna get in some union?''

''Call this guy.'' I put the paper on the battered, polished coffee table.

''Man,'' Carter said, ''I don't get it. I ain't never gonna be nobody. You ain't got nothing but pain since you met me. Why you coming like this?''

''Because when Vanessa's President of the United States, I want her to remember who gave her her first kitten.''

I stayed and had nutmeg-scented pie and strong coffee. I held Rashid, now asleep, while Carter ate his pie, and I showed Vanessa how to pick the kitten up. Then, as Vanessa yawned and the kitten fell asleep in her lap, I stood to leave.

''Thank you for your present,'' Enna Carter said. ''And for all you done for Martin.''

''You're welcome, Mrs. Carter. I hope the kitten doesn't give you too much trouble.''

''Ain't but one source of trouble in this house,'' she said, glancing at her grandson. ''You call me Mother Carter, now. And you come back to see us, you hear?''

''Yes, Mother Carter. I'd like to do that.''

Carter rode down with me in the rickety elevator. Outside the air was damp, cold with a north wind.

''I'm sorry about Snake,'' I said.

He looked down the street, at nothing I could see. ''Snake go off his own way, long time ago. By the time Skeletor smoke him, wasn't nothing left nohow.''

''Sometimes that doesn't matter.''

''No,'' he said. ''Sometime it don't.''

''Can I ask you something?''

''Do I got to answer?''

''No.''

''Then go ahead.''

"Vanessa is Snake's, isn't she?"

His eyes were hard. "I tell you already, she mine now."

"But Snake was her father?"

Carter didn't answer, and he didn't take his eyes from mine.

"I'm sorry," I said. "It's none of my business. I just want to know the whole story. Always."

"You ever do?"

"No, probably not. But I want to."

He blew air between his teeth. "Yeah, she Snake's. Her mama Rashid's mama."

"Where is she?"

Carter shrugged, pushed something off the curb with his toe. "Charlene? She O.D.'d, man. Three month after she have Rashid." He looked into the distance. "Been clean for years, too. After Vanessa born, Dr. Madsen get Charlene into a program over to Montefiore. Snake don't want nothing to do with her no more, but Charlene and me, we get a place, start to fix it up . . ." He trailed off.

"Charlene," I said. A scared fifteen-year-old, in labor on the living-room floor, in a ground-floor apartment down the hill from the Home.

My right arm twinged where the burn was healing. I didn't expect any more, but Carter went on. "She try to get me straight, but I be busy, taking care of business. Then I go to the joint. She have Rashid, don't have nobody with her, help with the kids, you know? Guess it got hard. Guess it just got hard."

Carter leaned on the car, folded his arms. "Granny, she take both kids to live with her. One visiting day, she carry the two of them all the way up to the joint. 'This your son,' she tell me, 'and this his sister. They got no momma. Her daddy ain't worth spit. All they got is you, Martin.' That what she tell me. 'All they got is you.' "

"What about Snake?" I asked quietly.

"What about Snake? He boasting, bragging about he got a kid. 'Take a life, make a life.' He a big man behind that. But don't care nothing about her. Try to give Granny money while I'm inside, still trying when I'm out. But he don't come see her, don't hardly know her name."

He gave me a strange look, almost smiled. "That first day

we met? First time you save my ass? That what we fighting
about. Snake be sending Nessie a bike. UPS man bring it.
Man, he one nervous dude.'' Carter shook his head at the
memory. ''I send it back. I tell Snake, next thing he send her,
he gonna need Dr. Madsen pull it out his butt.''

The wind was cold, scouring the air. ''Those kids are
lucky,'' I said.

I got behind the wheel of my car. Carter leaned in the window. ''Look,'' he said, ''one thing you got to know.''

''What's that?''

''Everybody think what I go up for, Snake done it. Snake
so crazy, he believe it hisself. But it ain't like that. Like I told
you: I shot that A-rab. In the back. I done that.''

I tapped a cigarette against the steering wheel. ''Okay.''

''Lot of shit I done, I can't never pay it back.''

''It's that way,'' I said. ''A lot of things can't be erased.
But you're lucky. You have Vanessa and Rashid. They're
not part of those things. They're what you have, now.''

''Yeah,'' he said. ''Word, cuz.''

''Be good.'' I started the car. ''Cuz.''

I pulled from the curb, drove around the block, headed
back downtown, back to what I knew, out of the Bronx.

FIFTY

The phone was ringing as I came in. I grabbed it up, told
it who I was. It told me it was Arthur Chaiken.

''How are you?'' he wanted to know.

''Healing,'' I said. ''How are you?''

''This hasn't been a great week for me.'' He sounded subdued, ironic. ''There's going to be a full investigation of
Helping Hands. And from what I can see, now that I'm looking, we deserve it.''

''Will the organization survive?''

''I don't know. I don't know if we should.''

''What would you do if it didn't?''

''I don't know that, either. Listen, Smith. I've talked to
Andy. What he was doing—his little development
scheme—I knew about that.''

I lit a cigarette, drew deeply on it. Closing my eyes, I fought the urge to hang up, to walk away from this.

"You were in on it?" I said.

"No. My God, no. And he never thought I knew. But I saw the Bronx Renaissance funds get funneled again and again to areas right around us, and it wasn't hard to figure out who was making money on it."

"Why didn't you tell me?"

"Andy was vital to Helping Hands. And I didn't see how what he was doing could possibly be related to what you were investigating."

"Except that to hide what he was doing Hill was willing to pull strings to help hide what everyone else was doing."

"Francine Wyckoff, you mean."

"And she was hiding what Reynolds was doing, and Howe and Portelli. And what they were doing got Mike Downey killed." And Mike's death sparked Howe's. And Howe's death caused Reynolds's. Leon Vega was still in a coma. Snake LeMoyne was dead.

"I thought . . . I thought the good we were doing outweighed the possible harm. I was wrong. Now I'll have to live with that. I'm not sure how."

Behind my eyes I saw squares of sunlight on a slate floor, and a man reluctant to stop feeding the birds so late in the season.

"Maybe you were right," I told him.

"What do you mean?"

"There's no balance sheet. A number of men died because of corruption you hid. Maybe more lives were saved because of the reasons you hid it. There's no way to know. But it may be easier to live with the question than with the answer you've come up with."

Chaiken was quiet for a moment. "I'm surprised to hear that coming from you."

"I am too."

"In a way it's why I called. I know about the deal you made with Andy. And I know that unless someone makes a point of exposing him, he'll come out of the Helping Hands investigation untouched."

"And you want to expose him?"

"I want to stop hiding things, Smith. I want to stop being

the one making the decision about what's more important than what.''

''You can't.''

''Why not?''

''Oh, you could expose Hill. But you can't stop making those decisions. This is one of them. If you break my promise to Hill, a guy with two little kids loses a chance at a new beginning. One guy. One chance. Maybe no big deal, except to him. But against what? Hill won't go to jail. He'll move and start again. And those Bronx Renaissance buildings might be doing as much good where he put them as they would have anywhere else. It might soothe your conscience to come clean now, but I don't think it'll help anybody as much as it would help you.''

In Chaiken's silence I finished my cigarette.

''Another thing,'' I said. ''Even if Helping Hands doesn't survive, you're clean. You can find another organization, or set one up. There's a lot of work left you have to do. If you connect yourself with Hill and what he did, you won't be able to do it.''

''I thought you didn't approve of our work. Of our Band-Aids.''

''I can be wrong.''

''And you're not pleased that I've come around to your point of view?''

''My point of view sees pretty dark things. I keep hoping that from somewhere else, to someone else, maybe they look brighter.''

After Chaiken and I hung up I went to my desk, took out my checkbook. I wrote a check to a man I'd gone to see the day before, a man who'd run an ad in the paper about a piano for sale.

It was a good piano, the smallest of the Baldwin grands. I didn't know how much room they had in the place Ida Goldstein was going to in New Jersey; I thought smaller was probably better than big.

The man's daughter had just started college, and there were some costs he hadn't counted on. His price on the piano was $4500. It was a good price, and I didn't bargain with him.

Buying the piano left me with $1400 from the money I'd taken from Henry Howe's locker. I wrote another check, to the PAL.

Then I stretched out on the sofa, had a bourbon. Then I had another. I smoked another cigarette, closer to the filter than I usually get. The drinks didn't help, and stretching out didn't help. I was exhausted and I ached, but I was restless, on edge.

When the phone rang again, I was grateful.

"Hi." Lydia's voice smiled. "I've been calling; you've been out."

"I've been cleaning up."

"How are you doing? I sort of want to talk. I thought you might, too."

"I—" I almost told her no, I'm all right, don't worry, see you later. "You're right. I would."

"Shall I come over?"

"I'd like that."

"About an hour?"

"That's great," I said. "Thanks."

I hung up the phone, looked around the room. I had an hour. I couldn't sleep, wasn't hungry, had had a drink.

I knew what I was putting off.

I stood in front of the piano for a minute, just standing. Then I opened the top, fingered the keys. I sat, flexed my hands. They'd be weak, I told myself, weak and clumsy. Well, that had happened before. I played some scales, easy exercises, up and down the keyboard. It felt hard and familiar; it fit my hands well.

Finally, I started the Schubert. Most of the notes were there, at first; but then I started to miss. I took out the music, spread it on the stand, began again. Now I had the notes; but I had nothing else. The watchmaker's joy was gone.

I kept at it; I don't know why. Time passed, and it didn't get better, but I kept working. The doorbell made me jump, broke the spell.

"It's Lydia," the intercom said. "Can I come up?"

"Yes," I said to her. "Yes, of course."

I buzzed her in, waited at the open door. Her face was serious as she came up the stairs, and beautiful.

"I was listening to you play," she said. I closed the door

behind her. "Outside. Before I rang. I know you don't like people to hear you. I didn't want to pretend."

I looked at the piano, at my hands. "I wasn't very good."

"You're not strong yet. You will be."

"I don't know. I almost had it, that piece. Before. Now . . ."

We stood, silent for a moment, awkward with each other.

She turned away, walked to the window. I crossed to where she stood, wrapped my arms around her from behind.

"Bill . . ."

I said nothing, breathed in the scent of freesia.

"When you were in the hospital, that first night?" she said. "I was angry. Furious."

"Why?"

Her reflection in the glass looked at mine. "That you might die. That you might leave me like that, no words, nothing. I was furious."

I turned her around, felt her solid shoulders under my hands. "I didn't," I said.

I kissed her. I ached everywhere, but there was no pain where her arms held me.

In the end, as I knew it would be, it was she who pulled away.

"I don't know," she said softly. "I don't know what I want."

"That's okay. You don't have to know. I know."

"Do you?" A question, many questions, shone in her eyes.

I kissed her forehead, held her for a moment. Then I stepped back, grinned. "You know what I want?"

Her brow furrowed slightly. "What?"

"Dinner. Pepper shrimp. Wintermelon soup. Bass in black-bean sauce. You like Chinese food? Come on, I'll take you out."

She laughed, and the tension between us broke like a wave on the shore. We locked up, headed down the stairs. She was faster than I; she waited for me at the bottom. I felt a little shaky, but that was all right. We didn't have very far to go.

THE FOLLOWING IS AN EXCERPT FROM THE NEXT
LYDIA CHIN/BILL SMITH MYSTERY,

MANDARIN PLAID

NOW AVAILABLE FROM
ST. MARTIN'S/MINOTAUR PAPERBACKS!

It's not that I don't like spring in Madison Square Park—
I'm a fan of the fat little buds on the trees and the sun spar-
kling off the puddles. It's just that I'm not usually strolling
through here with fifty thousand dollars, looking for the
right trash can to drop it in.

My footsteps crunched gravel on the curving path. The air
was chilly, but the soft March sun grazed the back of my
neck. Snowdrops and bright crocuses were up everywhere.

The sweat tickling my spine had nothing to do with the
weather.

Squirrels chased each other down trees and over spring-
soggy grass. The dogs in the early-morning run chased each
other, too, while their owners chatted by the fence. The fresh
breeze smelled sweet.

My skin prickled.

I kept my eyes jumping, trees to paths to dogs and their
owners.

On a bench up ahead, Bill Smith, my sometimes-partner,
pretended to read a book. He had a thermos of coffee beside
him, which was a good thing. His job was to watch my back,
and then, when I was out of sight, to watch the trash can until
someone came to withdraw my deposit. That could take a
while.

Madison Square Park, which spreads north and east from
Twenty-third and Fifth, is a happening place in the early
morning. Rising young executives hurrying to work maneu-

ver around dogwalkers and their dogs, while others, whose positions in their companies are either more secure or more hopeless, sit drinking coffee and chatting before they go on. Some of the benches are occupied by the homeless, who stretched out on them the night before and are in no hurry to move anywhere. At this time of year, this early in the morning, half the park is in shadow from the tall buildings on Madison, while the sun billows through the budding trees and into the other half. The line between the two halves keeps moving. If you watch, you can see it.

My instructions, which Genna had gotten over the phone, were to leave the envelope in the can and keep walking. I'd been given a time, 7:30, and a warning: no funny business. The thief had been told I was a friend of Genna's who was doing this for her because Genna was spooked. I didn't know if he believed that, but I didn't care. I was too annoyed that, although this was my case, Bill was going to have all the fun.

Once I dropped off the money I'd have to follow the instructions to make myself scarce; to the client, a successful operation meant having the exclusive rights to her own sketches again, and my first responsibility was not to jeopardize that. I'd probably head back to Chinatown and my office, where I'd call Genna, report in, and then sit and wait for Bill to call me.

Bill, meanwhile, would be waiting for, spotting, and then shadowing the bag man all over town.

I looked at him, up there ahead on his bench, probably full of adrenaline already, edgy to start the cat-and-mouse. He hides that rush better than I do—he's been in this business longer, and he's got more self-control in general—but I know he feels it.

I was feeling a little of it myself as I neared the trash can, even though I completely expected nothing at all to happen. Reaching into my pocket to pull out the envelope, dropping it casually on yesterday's *Post* and a half-eaten hot dog, I felt that jumpy sense of triumph you get when an important job's successfully done. Plus that irrational disappointment that now there's no more to do, that now it's over.

That's the part I was wrong about. It wasn't over.

I heard the bang and whine as soon as I'd turned away

from the can. Instinct took over from thought. Something caught me in the face as I dove behind a tree. I rubbed at it: a splash of mud thrown up by the impact of the bullet. The second shot sprayed gravel from the path into the air. Dogs barked and howled. Executives hit the dirt. Screeching birds wheeled into the sky. People ran and yelled and ran some more.

I crouched in the mud and forced myself to count to sixty. I gave it up at five. My heart was pounding and time took forever.

I peered out. Around me were people lying still like fallen park statues. Even the squirrels were hiding; nothing moved. Somewhere at the other end of the park a dog was barking, over and over. At that end people were running and shouting. I looked for Bill. His book was lying alone and open on the bench, its pages flipping forlornly in the wind. No third shot came. I emerged from behind my tree.

In the distance, approaching fast, I heard the wail of a police siren. People stirred and stood. I moved a little way from my tree and blended into the quickly gathering crowd. I examined the faces around me. Fear, anger, and confusion bathed them all. I glanced into the trash can.

The envelope, of course, was gone.

LOOK FOR

MANDARIN PLAID BY S. J. ROZAN

In all of New York's Chinatown, there is no one
like P.I. Lydia Chin. A nose for trouble,
a disapproving mother, and a partner
named Bill Smith who's been living above a bar
for sixteen years.

Hired to find some precious stolen porcelain,
Lydia follows a trail of clues from highbrow art
dealers into a world of Chinese gangs.
Suddenly, this case has become as complex as
her community itself—and as deadly as a killer
on the loose...

China Trade

**AVAILABLE WHEREVER BOOKS ARE SOLD
FROM ST. MARTIN'S/MINOTAUR PAPERBACKS**